JESSE

GLEN ALAN BURKE

Praise for *Jesse*

"*Jesse* is a touching and beautifully rendered evocation of an ugly time and place in America and of the enduring power of race and racism to shape lives and destinies in a country still divided along the color line."

—Charles F. Whitaker, journalism professor, Northwestern University; former senior editor, *Ebony* magazine, and former director of *Ebony's* Gertrude Johnson Williams Literary Award

"This novel takes me back to my teaching days. It captures the emotional culture of the times. It's fantastic."

—Jerry Harris, retired Alabama public school teacher

"*Jesse* is an inspiration for me to treat others fairly and to not be judgmental, but it also gives me a very detailed perspective of what life was like for African Americans during the beginning of integration."

—Taylor Rogers, Sand Rock High School Class of 2013

"*Not To Kill a Mockingbird, The Hunger Games*, the *Twilight* series—no book I have come across has made reluctant student readers this excited. This suspenseful, gut-wrenching novel will take you on twists and turns that no book has ever taken you on before. This will be a new sensation for students and teachers, with its deeply engrossing—and, because of its historical fiction nature—disturbing content that needs to be discussed."

—Shannon Hood, English teacher, Sand Rock High School, Alabama

"I would encourage anyone I come in contact with to read this jaw-dropping, action-packed novel of a mixed-race child going to an all-white school at a dangerous time in our history. Many of my classmates, me included, found ourselves straying from our teacher's agenda of reading one chapter per day simply because it is impossible to limit yourself to only reading one chapter a day of *Jesse*."

—Meghan Parker, Sand Rock High School Class of 2013

JESSE

GLEN ALAN BURKE

Jesse

by Glen Alan Burke

© Copyright 2023 by Glen Alan Burke

ISBN 979-8-9893842-3-5

All rights reserved. No part of this publication may be reproduced, stored in a retrieval system, or transmitted in any form or by any means – electronic, mechanical, photocopy, recording, or any other – except for brief quotations in printed reviews, without the prior written permission of the author.

Jesse is a work of fiction. The characters are both actual and fictitious. With the exception of verified historical events and persons, all incidents, descriptions, dialogue and opinions expressed are the products of the author's imagination and are not to be construed as real.

Published by

SpineText Publishing

Cover design by Donnie Ramsey

*To my daughter Shannon,
thanks for the suggestion that I try writing.
It could work out.*

*"I know not how to tell thee who I
am. ... Had I written it, I would tear the word."*
WILLIAM SHAKESPEARE

I don't care if I tear the word, it had to be written.
GLEN ALAN BURKE

Lord, lord, what have you for me to do
Children's spirts are asunder their future is askew
Then go below child and sway their ways
For a little tough love goes a long way these days

TABLE OF CONTENTS

CHAPTER 1 1
CHAPTER 2 6
CHAPTER 3 10
CHAPTER 4 27
CHAPTER 5 34
CHAPTER 6 42
CHAPTER 7 53
CHAPTER 8 61
CHAPTER 9 71
CHAPTER 10 81
CHAPTER 11 90
CHAPTER 12 102
CHAPTER 13 112
CHAPTER 14 123
CHAPTER 15 138
CHAPTER 16 155
CHAPTER 17 163
CHAPTER 18 173
CHAPTER 19 186
CHAPTER 20 197
CHAPTER 21 210
CHAPTER 22 221
CHAPTER 23 233
CHAPTER 24 248
CHAPTER 25 258
CHAPTER 26 269
CHAPTER 27 278
CHAPTER 28 288
CHAPTER 29 296
EPILOGUE 308
ACKNOWLEDGMENTS 316

CHAPTER 1

THE FIRST TIME I FELT pity was when I saw Jessup Christopher Savorié. Oh, I had felt the sympathy for farm animals that were hurt, birds that tumbled out of the nest and such in my brief six years, but this was different, and I didn't like it. My young brain couldn't quite process what I was supposed to do. Helping someone is what the grownups do, so I just sat in my seat and did nothing.

He could be naked, and I wouldn't have noticed or cared. I was too busy noticing a schoolhouse classroom for the first time; the commotion of people I didn't know. All these kids who were bigger and meaner looking than me. I didn't know where to sit or what to do. Where did my mama go? Did she just walk me into the room and leave? I was scared—no, terrified.

Through the watery eyes that welled up when Mama first let go of my hand and took off, I noticed Jessup. I soon forgot I was scared, and for a perverse few moments he made me feel better because I wasn't him.

I didn't know him, but at six, I could tell that something was terribly wrong.

Take a look at a class photo from a 1960s elementary school in rural Alabama—a good look. We all looked haggard. Didn't we? The same haircut, sheared; teeth too large for our mouths; necks too small for our heads; ears too large for our hair; and bodies too skinny for our clothes; and thank God, too ignorant to know the difference. But Jessup was different. He had the same Southern characteristics we all had, but to the nth degree. He stood in the middle of two rows of seats holding one hand with the other, quietly looking around at a world that was foreign to him. I was scared, but he wasn't—he was lost; he didn't belong there, and he knew it. I was too terrified to be running and playing grab-ass with the other kids in the room, so I found a desk and my eyes innately fixated on Jessup. All the clamoring and boisterous children seemed to whiz by him in slow motion, without sound or significance, while he stood perfectly still, motionless, and seemed positively enchanted with the walls, the chairs, the desks, the ceiling, all new to him.

I stared at him like he was a freak at one of those carnivals that would blow into town from time to time. He seemed to be a foot taller than everybody else, with shoulders that were wide and pointed at the ends. Thick, extra curly, jet-black, greasy hair was combed straight back and obviously cut by someone from home. His pants were three sizes too big and rolled up what looked like a foot. It seemed they hadn't been washed in a year, if ever.

There were two large grease-covered spots in the front, reflecting the florescent light. His shirt was probably white at one time. It was so big and baggy that only two of the buttons showed; the rest were tucked in his pants. The pants were pulled tight with a belt that had a full twelve inches turned down from the last loop. Brogans that had to have been size eight bore a resemblance to shoes.

We were all skinny back then—junk food hadn't been invented yet, at least not where we lived—but he was emaciated. His jaws were sunken; his eyes were sunken; deep, dark rings curved around the bottom of his eye sockets, and his cheekbones were prominent—too prominent. His hands were skinny; his elbow joints were skinny. They reminded me of universal joints on old hay rakes, way too big for his arms, that is, what you could see of his arms. His short sleeves came down nearly to his wrists.

He caught me staring at him. His eyes transfixed on mine. Perhaps it was because of the unspoken, universal acknowledgment code that floats around and eases awkward moments such as this, and only for kids—but he smiled at me. This magical universal acknowledgment code seems to elude adults.

His front teeth were too big, too much space in between and tinged brown from never being brushed, but this one deficiency was his best feature. His tender smile seemed to whisper to me *It's going to be OK, you're OK; please just think I'm OK*. And, for that frozen moment of time, just before the ugliness of the natural human pecking order ranked us, we were indeed ... OK.

I knew some of the boys in the class from the football games we played with wadded up paper cups at the high school team's home games on Friday nights. My brother just made the varsity team as a running back at good ol' Jess Rulam High School. With much nagging and pleading, we'd squirmed away from our mamas and daddies—this wasn't easy because they knew we would come back with our clothes the same color as grass—and we would meet on the practice field and play tackle football with a couple of paper cups rolled up in the shape of a football. I don't ever remember playing with a real football at one of these impromptu games.

I couldn't wait to talk to them; I needed reassurance, badly. They weren't as bashful and backward as me.

"Everybody, please find a seat," the teacher, Miss Bishop, said slowly, and then, restated slower, "Everyybodyyy, pleeease find a seeeat."

That meant we'd better sit down.

"I'm going to call your name. When you hear your name, please say 'here' and hold up your hand so I can see you."

She wanted to put a name with a face.

"Jude Adams."

"Here."

"Jonathan Beasley."

"Here."

"Please hold your hand up, high, thank you."

"James Famer."

"Here."

"Matthew Levy."

Hey, that's my name. "Here," I said sheepishly.

"Hold your hand up." I worked up the nerve and raised my hand even with my head. She finally noticed me and smiled. I was relieved.

And so it went—teacher calling names and kids answering.

"Simon Redding."

"Here."

"Jessup, uh, um." She paused to ponder. "What a name, Sa-vor-e, Sav-vo-e."

Kids laughed.

"Shhhh," she snapped. "Sav-or-ray. Is that how you say that?"

Nothing said.

"Who is Jessup Sa-vor-ay?"

He held his hand up meekly.

"OK. Am I saying that right?"

He nodded. "Yes'm," he said, barely audible.

3

She looked relieved. "We'll just call you Jesse, like the guy the school's named after." She finished calling roll and from then on he was Jesse.

* * *

Finally, fifteen hours later—actually it was more like four—recess came. Miss Bishop marched us outside to the playground. It was time to mingle with my friends.

Pete came strolling up with his hands in his pockets. "Wanna play football?" I nodded yes.

"OK. I'll pick my side." Pete was confident.

Harold came busting over also. "I'll be the other team."

Harold Spartani was the biggest, strongest, and meanest kid in the class. He made the rules. He had the right. He was the only kid that wasn't skinny. At least compared to us, he wasn't skinny. I remember he was the only kid who had biceps. He was the quarterback, and the running back, and the referee. If you were on his team, you just watched, but he would let you play defense. He didn't like to tackle, unless he could clothesline you. He was the king. They started choosing sides one by one until everybody got picked; six on one side and five on the other.

"We need one more." Pete was counting with his fingers.

"How about that big, poor guy?" By poor, Bart, who was the skinniest among us, meant skinny, not broke.

"Look how he come to school. My mama won't let me go looking like that," Andy said, with a frown toward Jesse.

"He's been in prison," Philip said with a warning, "or jail or something for bad kids."

By prison, Philip meant reform school. Actually, it wasn't reform school, but the foster care system. In some parts of the South, this was tantamount to the same thing.

"Reckon he'll kill us if we don't pick him?" Philip was serious.

"Hey, tall boy, wanna play?"

"Shut up. We don't want him. I'm not playing." Andy stormed off.

"Why, are you afraid of him?" Harold looked disgusted. "You want me to run him off?" He walked toward Jesse. "Get out of here; we don't want you playing with us. Now go on, get, go over there, or we're gonna kill you."

Jesse looked straight at Harold, never taking his hands out of his oversized pockets. He understandingly smiled, and slowly strolled toward the other kids, dragging the oversized brogans behind him the way a bear drags its paws. He meandered along, observing, studying, and completely lost in an unfamiliar world. The news about him being a killer stunned me, because he sure acted non-threatening. Still, he looked strange and he acted strange.

* * *

Getting used to school took time. Being away from Mama took time. Getting used to people took time; but time always makes things better, for most of us anyway. Time is also a perfect barometer. Who you are is ultimately, unforgivingly, exposed by time and circumstance. That's all it takes, really.

The origins of character, of personality, of destiny, can be followed backward in time. Set a snail down on the ground at any point. Hours later, no matter how short or far it's traveled, one can trace backward its point of origin; just look for the trail of slime.

Everyone has a slime trail—everyone. We are guaranteed that every life has shameful things to cloud our memories. Remember the first shameful thing you ever did? It takes a minute, but by concentration, and the temporary suspension of sanctimony, it can be done. How old were you? Three or four; five or six; two perhaps, but you can remember it.

And so the trail of slime began for us at Jess Rulam Elementary School. We were ready to learn, but lessons come hard sometimes.

CHAPTER 2

IT'S ALL ABOUT NUMBERS. ALL it takes are two; three are better; four are better still. It is in numbers that ugly is born and nurtured. We do in the safety and the protection of numbers that which the lack of conviction would otherwise thwart. We were sitting at our desks one morning, while Miss Bishop went to the office, talking and jostling and such, the way that all first graders do when the teacher is out of the room.

"I hate that kid." Harold had venom in his tone as he glared at Jesse.

"What'd he do?" Pete was curious.

"I just don't like him." Harold scowled at Pete like that should be enough.

"I'll bet he steals stuff," Jude chimed in. "I'm gonna put my stuff in my desk where he can't get it."

"He don't look right," Harold said through gnarled teeth. "What is he, a Chinaman?" Jesse was dark.

"He don't say nothin' to nobody, just smiles," I said. I didn't want to be left out of the piling on, of course.

"I'm gonna whoop his damn stinking ass." Harold was the first kid I ever heard cuss. I heard Mama and Daddy say "shit" and things like that, but I hadn't heard a kid say cuss words before. I would get used to it.

"You ain't afraid he'll kill you?" Pete warned.

"He ain't never killed nobody before. He's just a damn liar."

Jesse never opened his mouth. Harold was right about one thing. None of us took a bath more than once a week back then, but Jesse stunk. We all wondered if he had ever had a bath. Even I could figure out why Miss Bishop sprayed that can of stuff every day. She said it was for flies.

The bell rang for recess, and I confidently cantered to the spot where we all met each day to choose sides for football. I was good at football. Though I was the runt of the class, I was equalized with quickness.

When I arrived, nobody was there. There were other kids on the playground, but where was the gang? I searched for a few minutes before I spotted one or two of their backs, the rest hidden from view on the other side of the building.

A full circle of a dozen or so boys and some girls were cheering. Some of the girls, however, looked aghast and were screaming and waving for one of the teachers. Two kids were on the ground, one was pummeling the other. I asked Pete who was fighting.

"Harold is whooping that tramp kid," he said excitedly.

"Why?"

"'Cause he's a tramp and ain't got no money or nothing. He ain't even got shorts. Look!"

Jesse's pants, at least a size twelve, came off and slid down to his knees. Pete was right—no underwear. Jesse wasn't fighting back, just trying to block Harold's slaps and scratches with one hand and attempting to pull up his pants with the other. The laughs were so loud that the echo reverberated off the side of the schoolhouse. Everybody laughed; I laughed.

Miss Bishop came stomping. She swung her arms and elbows from side to side while taking long, bouncing strides. Her feet struck the ground, harder and harder. The thud of her shoe soles turned into a slapping sound. She busted through the line; everybody stopped laughing. She was furious. I knew Harold was about to get his.

She reached down, lifted Jesse up by his arms and put both hands on either side of his pants. She pulled so hard that when they lifted up, it raised his frail, bony body off the ground. In one motion she put her arm behind Jesse's head, bent him slightly over her leg, and beat his ass viciously with the palm of her hand. At least twelve licks. Jesse offered no resistance.

I looked at Pete, then Andy, then Bart, Philip, and Thomas. I wanted to see if they were as shocked as I was. Some were, some weren't, and some shook their heads and grinned at each other. I didn't know what to think.

I had only witnessed one paddling before, that being when Miss Bishop quickly returned from the office one morning and caught Jimmy pouring half the goldfish food in the fishbowl. She gave him a couple of light taps on the butt, but that was enough to make me shiver with fear the rest of the day. However, this wasn't a paddling; this was an assault.

Jesse never looked up, just kept his head bowed like he was ashamed and got what he deserved. Or, maybe he was just embarrassed about not having underwear, but I don't think so. His look telegraphed he was not at all surprised he had gotten a beating.

After Miss Bishop harshly pulled Jesse by the arm back to our room, he emerged a few minutes later, strolled over to a crosstie and sat down with an unconcerned look on his face as if it were merely part of his job description.

Meanwhile, Harold strutted along victoriously. Three or four of the gang walked slightly in front and to either side while gazing in awe at his face as if they wanted an autograph. Even though Jesse was a good two inches taller, Harold had given that tramp a good whipping. He was more of a king than ever. He had taken care of that thieving tramp, and he'd think twice before stealing any of our stuff again.

* * *

I went home that day and told Mama about the whipping that Harold gave that Japanese tramp kid. I couldn't remember what Harold had called him.

"Japanese?" Mama didn't have a clue.

"That big, poor tramp kid that looks funny, that's in my room."

"Oh, him." She knew who then. Laughing, she said, "That poor dark-skinned boy. Is that who you're talking about?"

"Yeah."

"Why did you call him Japanese? He ain't Japanese. He's some kind of mixed-up thing from Louisiana is what Miss Bishop told me."

"Harold stopped him from stealing our stuff by beating his a, uh, end." I had started to say ass, but Mama had never heard me cuss.

"Was he stealing things?" Mama was getting mad.

"I don't know. He ain't been caught yet, but he looked like it." I could tell by looking, apparently.

"Good, maybe he won't start. He's got a bad family they say. You don't hang around him, OK?" Mama was firm.

"All right, Mama." She made things right.

From then on we had the authority to do what we deemed fit to Jesse. It was our right; it was justice; the grownups thought so, and so he deserved it.

* * *

The next day at play period, we chose up sides as usual. Somebody was out that day, and we totaled up to an odd number.

"Go ask that nigger if he wants to play." Harold smirked and nodded toward Jesse, who was sitting on one of the crossties staring into space.

"He ain't no nigger," I countered. "You said he was from, uh, from, somewhere else."

"I thought he was a nigger too, Harold." Jude always was Harold's ass-kisser. "I could tell by lookin' at him," he added with a scowl.

"He can't be a nigger and be in our school. They got to go to their own school. We don't allow niggers in here. They go to school on The Hill somewhere." Pete was sure about this. This was 1964. Pete was talking about Orr Elementary and Orr High School, where the colored kids went.

"Hey, nigger, can't you hear good? Quit looking at the sky!" Harold walked toward Jesse. Jesse never heard a word. His eyes were closed, and he seemed to be pondering something.

CHAPTER 3

THE WARM BAYOU BREEZE GENTLY mingled the pleasant aroma of Spanish moss and honeysuckle. Maria's blondish hair was writhing in the Louisiana air. She stared remorsefully out the raised window of her upstairs bedroom, wondering how life could have dealt such a mysterious and yet certain reality to her young world.

What did she do to be so cursed? She reviewed everything moment by moment and came up with no answers as to why *this* should happen. All she knew was that she was not a hussy. She knew some hussies, and she would never consider herself to be one. She could hear her father's quivering voice, but she wasn't listening or comprehending, just staring at the sky and wondering.

"I knowed if we let ye start gallivantin' around wid 'em hussing galfriends tis gonna hap'n. I knowed it sure." Maria's father, Bobinôt, wasn't letting up. He reverted back to his natural Cajun dialect when he became excited—a dialect he had practiced hard to overcome when he became a businessman.

Maria recently won some independence when her paranoid father allowed her to visit a school-sponsored dance with some friends.

"You tell me, girl, you tell me true—you done slept wid dat nigger boy Jojo dat sweeps up at the shop?"

"No, Daddy, I can't be expecting, I just can't!" Maria argued.

"Dat not what da doctor say." Bobinôt was getting more agitated. "Dat's why you'd been sick ever' mornin'."

Bobinôt was gesticulating wildly, trying to get Maria to turn around, but she didn't move; her chin rested on her folded forearms, and she gazed into space. "Dat bed'n not be no nigger's child, dat's if it is."

"No, Daddy, we just friends." Maria was calm and unapologetic about Jojo. Josephus Savorié, or Jojo, was a sixteen-year-old mulatto who was given a chance to work at Bobinôt Bergeron's successful house-construction business in the central Louisiana village of Creola.

Jojo was pleasant and hard working. He took pride that a white man had taken interest in him. Soon after he started sweeping floors at the Bergeron woodshop, he boasted to his family that Mr. Bergeron had made him an apprentice carpenter. He had visions of his own house-construction company someday. He was going to be the first black builder to construct the expensive white people's houses and not be consigned to just the cheap government ghetto houses that sorrowfully lined his neighborhood.

Maria had liked Jojo instantly. He had an infectious smile and a completely nonthreatening manner. He was tall and thin with olive skin. He began to dress neater, from pride in his newly bolstered stature. Maria was entertained by Jojo's ambitions and dogged determination not to fail.

He talked for hours, full of delight and dreams about his plans. Jojo was proud of the fact that a pretty white girl would take her afternoons to visit the workshop and listen unremittingly to his damn fool dreams.

Everyone was surprised that Bobinôt had hired Jojo. Maybe he was acting out of guilt. Bobinôt nervously observed Maria's friendship with Jojo from afar, never a word said. He felt proud of himself for that. He felt progressive. He had a natural predisposition to act otherwise though.

* * *

Bobinôt Bergeron came up the hard way. His family landed in New Orleans fresh from the French city of Saint-Gaultier. They soon commingled into the Cajun neighborhood and were adopted as authentic coonasses. As a boy he worked at the docks as a longshoreman, but started an apprenticeship for a local house builder and methodically worked his way up to crew foreman. The task was arduous for an uneducated Cajun.

The Bergerons were poor, even by New Orleans standards. The remnants of the Southern caste system were still stingingly visible as demonstrated by the depredation of the poor and the lorded affluence of the wealthy. Though romanticized in novels and movies, few moments in the caste system were romantic. There was only hard, backbreaking work, and one's only reward was for the foreman of the dock not to call you a coonass that day.

Young Bergeron's world was a constant reminder of rank and file, rich and poor, the respected, and the coonass. The branding iron of discontent burned into Bobinôt's brain. *I will be respected someday.*

Through one bitter disappointment after another, Bobinôt Bergeron did earn respect. He saved at least ten percent of his meager wages every week and capitalized on his experience as crew foreman. He proudly launched his very own business, Bergeron Builders. He majestically painted the name on the door of his worn-out 1951 Chevy pickup truck. His prideful smile was hard to hold in as he nervously, but confidently, placed his first bid on a fifteen thousand dollar three-bedroom A-frame renovation. He got that bid as well as the next, and the next.

He moved to Creola, Louisiana, shortly after he saved seven thousand dollars because his new wife, Genevieve, had family there. He soon hired a new crew and built a respected business. A few years later, as a present to his expecting bride, he built a beautiful two-story colonial that was modeled after some of the plantations that he observed from afar, enviously gazing from his truck window on his way to build such houses that he himself could not afford.

But there was one curious trait that Bobinôt Bergeron did not shake from his childhood. It was as hard to shake as his Cajun dialect. Within the caste system of the lesser was a microcosm of the caste system of the greater, by which the Cajun society of French descent ranked higher than the Creole heritage of African descent. Bobinôt and most of his family were as bigoted and condescending to blacks as the rich were to them.

* * *

"Baby girl, I love you with all I have left in this world." Bobinôt was staring down at the floor pitifully. He was unconsciously twisting his hat with trembling hands, like wringing water from a washcloth, over and over.

"I've failed you, I've failed you." Tears welled up in his eyes and his voice cracked. "I thought I could do it. I promised your precious mama on her dying bed that I could raise you right. I'm just too ignorant to do things like dat. I thought I could do it by myself. I should have took another wife later on to help me show you tenderness and all dem otha things dat baby girls supposed to get when de'is little, but I was too busy being important. I didn't raise ya right, I just dina know how!"

"Daddy, you raised me right!" Maria could no longer hold back the tears. She leapt from her position at the window and enveloped her father in a deep, loving bear hug. "I am the one who has failed. I am cursed, Daddy."

"Dat Devil done his job aright. Da Devil always gonna do what he gonna do. It was just yo tun, baby girl. It floats around and lands on people. Now, it is my tun."

A sickening dread filtered through Bobinôt's soul. All of his wealth, all of his standing, all he had worked for was about to evaporate. How could he explain this to the town's people? What would they think? What would they say? Not only was his only daughter going to have a bastard child, but she was going to have a nigger bastard child.

He slowly let the girl go. Gently taking her arms in his hands, he peered comfortingly into her tear-filled eyes. He whispered, "It's gonna be awright, baby girl. We gonna get dis taken care of tamorrow. Now you git ta sleep. It be awright after tamorrow. I've heared 'bout a doctor. He'll be helpin' us. Go to sleep, baby girl."

* * *

A few days later, Bobinôt and Maria slowly pulled in the back parking lot of what used to be one of the first feed/hardware stores in town. The sign, which was painted over the faded Purina Hog Chow drawing on the side of the dingy old brick building, now said, "Doc Dressler, M.D." They had just driven through the worst slums and dilapidated houses on the West Side of New Orleans.

"Come on, Maria." Bobinôt opened the door of his truck. Maria, who fought and pleaded all morning with her father to let her keep the baby, sat staring straight ahead. Her father slammed his door and glared at her. She opened the door slowly, reluctantly capitulating to her stern father.

As they opened the heavy metal door and crept meekly inside, a disheveled man of about fifty that needed to comb his graying hair and shave two-day-old stubble gradually and unenthusiastically eased up from a chair. He carelessly threw his newspaper toward another chair, missing it completely, then he greeted them at the door.

"Good afternoon, sir. Doc Dressler. How may I help you?" he asked with an overly exaggerated Southern drawl, much slower and deliberate than necessary.

"I was told you could help us," Bobinôt said with trepidation in his voice, but no dialect.

"Why sure, sir, that's what I'm here for," he said even slower and more exaggerated, somewhat like a young Southern belle from years ago. They could tell that Doc Dressler's sarcasm was the result of a disappointing life.

"My daughter's had an accident."

"Oh my," he chuckled with snarky contempt. "You mean she tripped over her shoelaces and fell on somebody's penis." Bobinôt could smell the alcohol on the doctor's breath. "That happens a lot around here. I do declare these kids are going to have to start tying their shoes up tighter."

"I truly don't appreciate your humor, sir." Bobinôt was gritting his teeth, but kept his composure. He disciplined himself like a Southern gentleman.

"Let's not be coy here, not now, Mr. Bergeron." The doctor no longer had a Southern drawl. "*You* are the one with the knocked-up daughter. I'm the alcoholic doctor. We need each other. Do we understand one another,"—the doctor's voice returned to Southern belle—"Mr. Bergeron?"

"How did you know my name is Bergeron?"

Leaning slightly to one side and looking through the still-open door, the doctor said, "It says 'Bergeron Builders' on the side of your new truck. Now I don't suppose the owner would let one of his workers borrow his brand new truck, so I can only deduce that you are Bergeron. Follow me, you accident-prone child." The doctor made a "follow me" sign with his arm as he exaggerated a prissy motion in his walk.

"For your information, sir, she was raped." Bobinôt was angry.

Chuckling unnecessarily hard and putting one hand on his stomach and purposely leaning forward, the doctor said, "You mean she's going to have a black baby. That's what *raped* means in the South, Mr. Bergeron. She done accidently fell on a nigger penis." His snarky laughter upset Bobinôt, but he knew the doctor was right, and he was somewhat comforted to know that he wasn't the only father that had been in this mess.

Bobinôt's silence and lack of retaliation seemed to change the doctor's demeanor. "Look, I'm sorry this has happened to you, Mr. Bergeron. I'm getting mean in my old age. It costs three hundred dollars. Do you have three hundred dollars?"

"Yes." Bobinôt fumbled in his pocket and pulled out a roll of bills and counted out the money. The doctor looked more disgusted than ever as he held his hand out and watched Bobinôt count out his wages for the week. "One hundred, two hundred, two fifty, two seventy, two ninety, three hundred."

"Go into that room and put on the green smock and then get up on that table and put your feet in those stirrups please, child."

"Daddy, do we have to do this?" Maria began to cry.

"Help your daughter on the table, Mr. Bergeron, and then go and wait in the other room. This won't take long. It will be all right, Mr. Bergeron." The Southern drawl returned.

The heat was stifling. A large ceiling fan swirled hot air on Maria as she fumbled with her clothes. The stench of urine from the open toilet made her nauseous. She felt faint and dizzy; the floor would sometimes seem closer to her face.

She stripped and for several minutes tried to figure out which was the front and which was the back of the worrisome gown. She slowly opened the creaking bathroom door and shuffled her way to the table. Her father had left the room.

"Just hop on the table, young lady, and we'll make somebody's hubcaps safe in the future." The doc truly had a singular sense of humor.

"Why is it so hot in here?" Maria was pale and feeling faint.

"Well, you gots to get hot to get it in dar. You gots to get hot to get it out." The doc was doing a minstrel show Sambo impression.

"I want my dad …" Maria fainted limply to the floor.

* * *

Maria awoke in her father's truck on the back roads of New Orleans. She felt sick to her stomach. A wet washcloth was on her forehead.

"Where are we, Daddy? What happened?"

"I couldn't tun you over to dat drunk butcha. You passed out, and I told dat doctor I change my min'." Bobinôt had both hands on

15

the steering wheel, his eyes focused straight ahead, not looking at Maria as he drove.

"You gonna find a cleaner doctor, Daddy?"

"No."

"Then what?"

"I'm gonna talk to Bethel."

"You're gonna talk to Aunt Bethel in Shreveport about what?"

"I'm gonna let you visit her for a few months. They got ovah five hundred acres on dat fam. You be outa da way there."

"Am I gonna keep the baby, Daddy?"

"We take it someplace when it born." Bobinôt had relief in his voice.

"OK, Daddy." Maria didn't argue.

She wondered if maybe this wasn't the Devil's doing. She started to accept a harsh fact: She was cursed. She wondered if this baby was actually going to be born. She wondered if it should.

* * *

Time passed quickly on the Broussard farm. Aunt Bethel and Uncle Herbét were reluctant at first, but soon they accepted Maria as their own daughter and made her feel worthy of their Shreveport home. Their own daughter had passed away many years ago at the age of eleven from juvenile diabetes, and they remained childless.

Maria took many long walks around the large lake centered on the picturesque farm. The big willow trees surrounded the banks and made it cool and pretty. She often contemplated life and in particular, her life. She could not explain why this happened to her but a longing for motherhood replaced apprehension. Now well into her eighth month, she was convinced she had to keep and raise this baby. Over these months she no longer considered her unplanned pregnancy a curse, but a blessing.

The sun started its descent, leaving a sardonic orange line on the western horizon, when Maria realized the pain piercing her side was not the normal tumbling of the unborn child. She was taking her usual afternoon stroll around the lake and was a good half-mile from the house. The last time she went to the doctor he informed her that his best guess would be somewhere around the last week of January, but this was a full month before then.

She knew she needed to quicken her pace; panic pushed her forward fast. Something warm oozed down the inside of both legs. There was a familiar aroma from the time she had witnessed her first calf being born. She knew her water had just broken. Thoughts flashed brilliantly through her mind. She was amused that the one thought she momentarily held on to was how similar the smells were of embryonic fluid from a cow and a human.

She stopped for a moment and leaned over, putting her hands on her knees. She caught a glimpse of red commingling with the clear fluid. She reckoned it was normal, but feared there was not much time. She hurriedly made for the house again.

She felt weary and faint, so she put her head down determinedly to gain momentum. To her horror, she could see her blood splattering from the end of each shoe with each stride, creating a bright apple-red paint design on the dirt road. Maria was fearful. She stopped and looked in all directions. She screamed at the top of her lungs.

* * *

Josephus Savorié had been on the run for over five months. The news of a black man talking to a white girl in 1957 Louisiana was a beating offense. A black man having sex with a white girl was a killing offense. A black man that possibly raped a white girl was a mob lynching offense.

Despite all that Bobinôt could do to keep the secret, the scandalous news got out the way that all scandalous news gets out. It's inevitable really. All that a scandal needs to grow is time and conversation.

The news was that Jojo had tried to seduce Maria, and when she wouldn't reciprocate, he beat and raped her. Though Bobinôt never said so, the town assumed that the subsequent pregnancy and the sudden disappearance of his daughter to visit faraway kinfolk was merely the rational reaction of such a bereaved father.

And while Bobinôt Bergeron was too fine of a man to kill that raping nigger himself, many of the town's people would see that justice was done for him. What else could they do—Bobinôt hadn't pressed charges with the police, due most likely to his shame, they reckoned.

Jojo was running out of hiding places. Two weeks with a cousin here, three weeks with an uncle there, a friend for a month and pretty soon you run out of friends, especially when a mob of drunken Cajun rednecks find the cousin, the uncle, and the friend and go about beating the hell out them for harboring a raping nigger. Helping a fellow traveler in need is one thing, swinging from the end of a rope is another. Very soon, Jojo was friendless.

Family and friends told him to flee north where Cajun justice could not reach. Jojo took their advice and all the money they could pool and headed north by way of a friend of a friend and his car. But the friend of a friend and the car were slow in coming, and the rumors of the Cajun posse being close made Jojo decide to light out on foot. He'd crawl his way out of there if necessary.

He knew the general direction that was north and he knew the back roads that led out of town, but unfortunately, he knew nothing more. Any plans he made on the way were better than any plans he made from the end of a rope. It was time to move now.

On a dirt road north of Creola, a tired and hungry Jojo decided instead of darting behind a tree every time he heard the sound of an approaching car, he would stick his thumb out and just pray that it was not the posse. He could hear a vehicle of some sort quickly approaching behind him. Though scared, he closed his eyes and meekly held out his thumb.

Jojo knew that the odds of a white man offering a ride to a black boy were slim, and the odds of it being a white man in the car were great. And he also knew the odds of a black man giving a ride to a black boy were great, but the odds of it being a black man in the car were slim. He had to try nonetheless.

The metallic powder-puff blue 1957 Chevy whirled dust all around Jojo's head and made him cough and wipe his eyes as it sped by. The unmistakable sound of squeaking brakes startled Jojo as the Chevy came to a halt and started slowly backing up toward him. Jojo had never seen a '57 Chevy before in real life, only in pictures in magazines.

A window rolled down and a pleasant voice from a sharp-looking gentleman in a business suit asked, "Where you headed to?"

"North, sir," Jojo said meekly.

"So are we. Get in." A man in the backseat scooted over to make room.

There were two men in the front and one in the back. All were distinguished looking, in their fifties. Jojo was just happy to get off his feet. All three men were white and wearing business suits. They had the distinct aroma of class and money. They weren't from around there, obviously.

Jojo was curious as to why they had picked him up, but too tired and too dejected and too disheartened to care. For some reason, he felt safe with them.

"I'm Roland," said the driver, sticking his right hand over the seat toward Jojo.

"Jojo. Thank ya, sir, for stopping," Jojo said graciously, accepting his hand.

"I'm Cort," said the man next to the driver, also turning to offer his hand.

"And I'm Jake," said the man in the backseat, shaking Jojo's hand warmly.

"I'm sorry. Did you ever say where you were going?" asked Roland, taking his eyes off the road temporarily to glance back at Jojo.

"Naw, sir. Anywhere. Dat be fine, sir."

"Well, we're going to Shreveport on business," Roland continued.

"That's fine, sir. I can take a bus from there."

"Do you know where you're going from there, son?" Jake's voice was sympathetic and yet inquisitive.

"I'm going to wherever my money runs out." Jojo could easily go to sleep right now.

"Where your money runs out is not a place, but a time, son," said Cort.

These white men, for some reason, seemed genuinely interested in him. He had not experienced this in a long time. The men seemed happy to help Jojo, but kept turning to look at each other as if they were not exactly sure why they had stopped and not exactly sure what to do.

"Maybe you should grow where you're planted, son," said Jake. This seemed like strange talk to Jojo. He didn't quite understand.

"Grow where I'm planted?"

"Yes, make the best out of where you are, you know."

"Oh, I see. Dat's jus' not poss'ble fa me hea."

"I understand, son." Jake had an amused look on his face, like he really did understand.

An hour or so passed, and Jojo was nodding off now and again. The soothing voices of the men's conversation so relaxed Jojo, he could hardly keep his eyes open. Images flashed through his mind; small bits of movies played on an enormous screen—incomplete outtakes that quickly moved from one pleasurable scene to another.

Jojo saw vivid stills of himself holding and loving an infant son. He could not quite see his happy little face or know his name, but he could feel the warming sensation of love, the unconditional love that only a father can have for a son. "What's that fellow's name we're going to see?" asked Roland.

"Ah, Broussard, I think." Jake wasn't sure how to say the name. That name woke Jojo instantly. He had heard from friends while he was on the run that the Broussards' was the place where Maria was staying.

"I have a friend dat staying on dat farm, sir."

"Really! That's great. You can come with us to the farm and see your friend," said Cort.

Jojo nodded affirmatively, knowing this was bittersweet irony.

"We've been to a ... Mr. Bergeron's place to talk to him about being a primary chicken barn builder for the area, but he wasn't there," continued Cort. "Some kind of a family medical emergency came up, or so his employees informed us, so we didn't get to meet with him. So now we're on our way to Shreveport to meet with Mr. Bergeron's brother-in-law, Mr. Broussard, who just happens to want to put in six barns of our birds. We are the owners of Missouri Valley Foods from Illinois, but we're expanding into Louisiana."

Jojo was wondering if there was some way he could see Maria without seeing the Broussards. They might know who he was.

When they pulled up to the house, no vehicle was in sight. Jake went to the door and came back, shaking his head.

"The note on the door says they have gone to the hospital with somebody named Maria. We drove a long way and struck out at both places," said Jake with a sigh.

"Maria's my friend's name," Jojo said with sudden concern.

"Well, we'll find the hospital then; we've got nothing else to do," said Roland, shrugging with his palms up. The other men nodded in agreement.

"Where would a hospital be around here?" asked Cort.

"We'll just look for the signs," said Roland.

"Yes," agreed Jake.

So the men and Jojo drove toward town and found a tall building in the first suburb they came to in Shreveport. "That's it. See the sign?" asked Roland excitedly

"You're right. The sign says Shreveport Baptist Hospital-Manger Air Lift," said Jake, in a hurry to get the words out.

The building had a large spotlight on the roof so a helicopter could find it. It was one of the first helicopter airlift support hospitals in the state of Louisiana in fact. Jojo recognized Bobinôt's pickup truck in the parking lot. For some strange reason, he was compelled to enter the hospital and see his girlfriend. He opened the emergency room door and hypnotically started walking straight to the room where Maria was. He didn't fully understand the radar in his head directing his steps and why he wasn't scared.

* * *

Bobinôt stood over his dead daughter's body. His eyes were red, his face was contorted, and his countenance was that of the saddest man on earth. He picked up Maria's lifeless body by her shoulders and pressed her head against his chest, and then gently lay her down. He repeated this again and again.

"I didn' luv ya right, baby girl. I shoulda ben here wid ya."

"The doctor said there wasn't anything you could have done to save her life, Bobinôt," said Bethel, standing beside the sobbing father.

Jojo overheard a lady in a black dress holding a clipboard solemnly and patiently asking questions.

"What name do you want to go on the baby's birth certificate, Mr. Bergeron?" she asked, looking down at her paperwork.

"She said she like the name Jessup if it was a boy," Bethel answered and nodded at Uncle Herbét for confirmation.

"And the middle name?"

"I never heard her say," Bethel said.

"My husband's name is Christopher," the lady suggested lightly.

"That would be fine." Bethel was satisfied with the suggestion.

"OK, what is his last name?"

"Bergeron, B-E-R," Bethel was spelling when Bobinôt spoke.

"No, Bethel, I can't," he said in a soft broken voice. "Don't you understand?"

"OK, fine, it's Broussard, B-R-O-U-S ... do you mind Herb?" Bethel looked at Herbét for an answer. Herbét, who had his hands in his pockets, shrugged in that *fine with me* manner, and then she spelled out the rest of the name.

"His father's name?"

"He don't got a father," Bobinôt said before Bethel could speak.

"Yes he do." Jojo walked toward the lady, never taking his eyes off Bobinôt, who was glaring at him. Tears were streaming down his face. "You write Josephus Savorié, yes'm," he said, and then he spelled his last name. "And put that as his last name too. He's my son and that be his name."

Bobinôt said nothing. He looked down at his daughter, shaking his head and welling up inside.

"Occupation?" The lady tried not to act shocked.

"Carpenter/builder." Jojo forced a smile and glared back at Bobinôt.

"I understand. We need to contact the county as to the baby's primary care before the state puts it up for adoption," the lady said with a sigh.

"No you don't, ma'am. I'm gonna take my son wid me." Jojo's jaws were tense, determined. No one was going to stop him.

The lady looked at Bethel and then at Bobinôt for an answer. But an answer did not come.

"The doctor is almost through examining the baby, and we'll have him out in a few minutes. You can take him home tomorrow."

"Can I take him now, ma'am? I gotta go."

"Well, I guess, if he's healthy. I mean I don't ... we'll have to get a bag with some formula and things. Let me check on that." The lady left hurriedly.

Bobinôt walked up to Jojo with fire in his eyes. He reached into his pocket, grabbed one of Jojo's hands, and placed five hundred dollars in it with a slap. In a guttural voice, through clenched teeth, he said, "Take dat bastard child of Satan and don't ever let me see ya again, Jojo!"

An hour later, Jojo emerged almost zombielike from the front entrance of the hospital with an infant wrapped in a blanket and a cloth bag filled with bottles, formula, diapers, and other paraphernalia hung loosely over his shoulder. He had tried to formulate some kind of plan while he was waiting for the nurse to bring Jessup, but nothing had sprung from his weary brain.

He was surprised to see the Chevy still parked in the same spot. Two hours had passed, and the men still sat inside. He could see his breath from the cold winter's night form in large puffs in front of his face. He wondered what the men would say if he got in their vehicle with an extra passenger. He didn't have to wonder long. The window rolled down and he heard a heavenly voice say, "Get in, Jojo."

"We witnessed what happened back there, son. We followed you in and heard the whole thing. That was a hell of a thing you just did. It's not every day a man of your age, or any age, would take on that responsibility by himself for his son," said Roland, looking at the others for confirmation.

"He's not my son, sir. That would be impossible," Jojo mumbled, looking down at the infant.

"Then why did you take him?" asked Cort curiously.

"I jus' couldna leave him dar, sir." He paused and said sadly, "I know what dat feel like."

"I think that's the most impressive thing I've ever seen," said Jake, looking at the other two with a happy smile. "But not very wise," he added. "How do you plan to take care of him?"

"I'ma gonna grow were I is planted, sir."

An appreciative chuckle came from the men.

"You don't have any family nearby?" asked Roland.

"I cain't go home agin, sir," Jojo said dejectedly, raising his head and looking at Roland.

"Get out of the car for a moment, guys, we need to talk. We'll be right back, Jojo," said Cort.

The men huddled in a circle for ten minutes, gesticulating sometimes with loud voices, and sometimes in whispers. One went off to the payphone while the others talked. When they were all together again, they got back in the car.

"We have a new feed facility we're building on the backwaters near Huntsville, Alabama. You can start to work there as a carpenter, and we'll see to it you are paid well for your skill," said Roland with a bit of pride.

"I have an aunt dat lives in some place called Jess Rulam, Alabama, or something like dat. I heard my mama say once it be close to Huntsville." Jojo's spirits were lifting.

"Fantastic! You'll need a woman to help you with the baby," said Jake, nodding at the other two.

"I don't know." Jojo was hesitant. "My mama be white an' my aunt be a white woman too. I only met her once, and I didn't get no notion she liked me much."

"She'll soften up when she sees you with a cute little one in your arms, Jojo."

"Any woman's heart can be thawed by the preciousness of a little one," said Roland like he knew what he was talking about.

"I don't know. I've heard she had a rough life. And I've heard white folk up dar is as mean to black folk as da whites is down here, sir." Jojo was starting to get apprehensive again. "Dis aunt had troubles befo', so Mama say. She may drinks a bit and likes to lay wid da men."

"If things don't work out with the aunt, we will help you find a renter house," said Cort, sensing Jojo was starting to get skeptical of the plan.

"The important thing, Jo, is to grow where you're planted, right? For some reason you have this baby. He is going to depend on you to take care of him and provide nurturing that little ones need. This may be a blessing to you, Jo," said Roland, "and may be a blessing to us all."

"I'm startin' to feel blessed. Is funny. I ask da Lord to save my soul at a revival meetin' a few months ago, and I ain't got nothing but trouble since. I felt like da Lord was through wid me. But I guess I got a coupla things to do yet."

"I believe you are right," said Cort, looking at Jessup. "I think we all have a few things to do yet, including helping young ah, what was his name?"

"Jessup." Jojo was sure that was the name.

"Well, young Jessup ..." Cort took a breath. "You're off to an inauspicious start in the world," he said, nustling Jessup's chin with his finger.

"Did you ever notice it's always the ones with inauspicious starts that do things in the world—you know, the ones that make a difference." Cort looked solemnly at Jessup.

"Da's one thing I gotta to know though. Why did you fellas stop to pick up a hitchhikin' nigga on da side of da road fer?" The tiredness returned, and he was slurring words again.

"I don't know," said Roland, looking at the others and shrugging. "Something just come over us, I guess." He chuckled softly.

"This trip we started a week ago has taken two days longer than we planned. We had to visit several farmers for site locations. These farms in Louisiana are not exactly easy to find. We've come up on Christmas, and our wives are going to kill us. We've got to get home. You and the baby come with us and stay with me, in my house, until the holidays are over, and then I'll drive you to the building site in Alabama and get you set up. Is that OK with you, Jo?" asked Jake as if it were now his responsibility.

"I don't know how I can ever repay you fine gentlemens." Jojo's eyes were watering.

"You may have blessed us all, Jo," said Roland. They all seemed to agree.

* * *

Jojo was right about his white aunt—she was troubled. But it was not her drinking, or her drug addiction, or her propensity to lie with any man for a pocketful of pills. No, it was her big blabbering mouth that sealed his fate, and in turn, that of his son.

The tale of Jojo's heroic escape from would-be coonass assassins proved too irresistible to keep to herself. From her mouth to another's ears, to another, and from there, to yet another, it didn't take long for the pipeline to carry the story far and wide.

It was, of course, not all that surprising that one morning in early March 1959, Jojo parked his company loaner truck at the job site when a bullet found its mark in his temple and he hit the ground, dead. The only thing anybody could agree on was that the shooter was a marksman and that the tag on the gravel slinging, hard-to-identify speeding car was from Louisiana. Cajun justice has a long reach.

Motherless, and now fatherless, young Jesse had to accept a harsh reality: He was being reared, if that's what it could be called, by a drugged-out slut. She must have felt just guilty enough not to give him away to the State of Alabama, because in her few moments of sobriety, a tender heart showed itself. As it turned out, that decision made Jesse's life a living hell: filthy conditions, hardly any food, no healthy food for sure, and an endless parade of would-be fathers that seemed to take out their frustrations by beating poor Jesse.

Yes, Jessup Christopher Savorié seemed to be put on this earth to suffer. And as he pondered his situation, he came to the conclusion that he was doing a very fine job of it.

CHAPTER 4

HAROLD ADVANCED TOWARD JESSE SHOUTING, "Nigger!" The familiarity of that word snapped Jesse out of his reverie. I was sure I was about to witness another assault. Jesse eased up from the crosstie he sat on and looked down at the ground, never making eye contact with Harold.

"Why don't you look at somebody when they're talking to you? What's the matter with you? You're a nigger, ain'tcha? Answer me! Ain'tcha?!" Harold pushed his finger into Jesse's chest, hard. Jesse fell backward over the crosstie the way a ninety-year-old man would—in sections, ass, back, head.

"Hey, everybody, we got a nigger in class. We got a nigger in class." Harold pranced around like he had just knocked out Cassius Clay.

"Hey, Harold, leave him alone. Let's play some football." I was really more annoyed that we weren't playing football than I was concerned for Jesse.

"What are you? A nigger lover?" Now Harold was mad at me.

"No, I wanna play. Let's play."

Harold picked up the football and threw it at me. "Let's play then."

"We still need one more," Pete said quietly. He didn't want Harold mad at him too.

"I wanna play." It took a moment and a lot of self-introspection to realize those words came from Jesse, who was still lying on the ground, propped up on one elbow.

Other than saying "here" every morning to answer the roll, I never heard Jesse say a word unless the teacher asked him a question directly. If asked a question, he would either nod his head, or whisper *yes'm*, or *no, ma'am*, or say nothing at all. I could tell he wasn't dumb though. You could see intelligence in his eyes the same way you could see intelligence in a dog's eyes.

"You can't play with us, nigger, you're a nigger. Niggers can't play with white boys. What's the matter with you?"

"Let him play, Harold," said somebody, and then another said, "Yeah let him," and yet another said, "Come on." Everybody was feeling the same about this. By everybody, I mean everybody but Harold.

"OK, good," said Harold with a maniacal laugh, clapping his hands. We all figured out this was not going to be a good thing for poor Jesse.

Jesse jumped up quickly, surprisingly quick. He walked with a noticeably longer stride as he made his way to Pete's side of the team. He carried himself with a discernibly different demeanor. He was completely upright. His shoulders were no longer slouched as they usually were. His reflexes were sharper. He stuck his chest out. He looked us in the eyes. He wore confidence on his face, not smugness, but happiness, as if he were about to eat a Thanksgiving dinner. *Who is this guy?* I wondered.

"You probably don't know how to play," Pete said, trying to reassure Jesse, "but we'll teach you."

"I know how," Jesse said without hesitation. We looked at each other with stunned faces. We wondered how and why this transformation had taken place.

Harold Spartani was the biggest, strongest kid, not only from our class, but at least through the first two grades in Jess Rulam Elementary. It was rumored he once whipped a third grade boy while riding home on the school bus. He was of Italian descent, though he had light-colored hair. He had broad shoulders, a barrel chest and thick neck. To me he was like a grownup. I was as scared of him as I was of most grownups. He must have been close to four feet tall. To me that made him a giant. He was unconquerable, unchallengeable, and indisputably, our leader.

If he looked at me, I paled with fear, which always brought a smirk to his face as if he knew I was a coward. We were all cowards back then. I envied Harold. How was it that he was born with such physical prowess, and I was but a runt? I spent many an hour pondering what a wondrous existence it must be to be born king. There was nothing for him to fear, and he feared nothing, or so we all assumed.

When you are the lesser, fear becomes a way of life, and life itself is feared. When you are the greater, life fears you. We all feared him, and we all envied him. He enjoyed his kingdom at our expense, but we didn't mind. That was our station; it was merely that, and nothing more. I imagined myself as Harold Spartani almost every day, wondering what it would be like to be him.

The football lifted high off of Harold's foot and soared into Jesse's hands. A flash of apparel whizzed by me, flapping in the wind. I heard the rags make a whipping sound, like a flag in a stiff breeze, as he zipped past.

I was transfixed as I watched him approach Jude, who was hunched in the familiar football position, poised with both arms about to make a certain deadly embrace and put an end to Jesse's newfound valor. Jesse planted his foot, juking his head. He waited for Jude to shift his body weight in that direction, then cut sharply and effortlessly in the opposite way and left Jude grasping at air. Jude hit the ground with a crunch, looking exasperated. He thought victory was so close at hand, but it proved just beyond his reach.

Harold was not as easily faked. Grunting with every stride his thick legs made, he rapidly advanced toward the suddenly hard-to-catch Jesse. He quickly closed the ground between him and his prey, held out both hands and shouted, "Yeah, nigger!" He was about to clobber his adversary, an enemy he in reality feared because he was a threat to his kingship. Though he was much skinnier and lighter, Jesse was a couple of inches taller than Harold. To a discerning eye, it was obvious he'd grow and fill out a lot more, and someday, might be a formidable foe.

Jesse braced himself for the horrific impact. I knew from Harold's mass, Jesse's amazing speed, and their general trajectory, that this was not going to end well for Jesse.

When Jesse first aligned himself under that floating football and gathered it in, I was, for that split second, proud of him. I was proud of him because he was demonstrating something in this inevitable suicide mission that I lacked—intestinal fortitude. I could avoid most would-be tacklers on the playground, including Harold. He even got angry at me one day because he couldn't catch me and looked somewhat embarrassed by the fact. From that moment forward, without saying a word, and with little more than a glare, I'd simply slide to the ground whenever he got within reach. I was like an abused puppy, totally submitting to a greater master.

Jesse, in my eyes anyway, was about to take a stand for all the small people, on all the kids' playgrounds, and all the grownups' playgrounds in the entire world. Even though I wanted to *be* Harold, for the reason that it's much better to bethe hammer than the nail, I was nonetheless proud of Jesse.

I wanted him to beat Harold, and then maybe, I could beat him too someday. Jesse took my place. He was about to take this crushing blow, for me. He was where I wished to be, if only I could. *Go, Jesse, go,* I was secretly thinking—safely though, within the confines of my cowardly mind.

Jesse suddenly extended his long arm and planted the palm of his hand in the middle of Harold's barrel chest. I watched the back of Harold's head bounce off the ground with a thud like a ripe muskmelon. Jesse crossed between the two car tires we used for the end zones. With a tiny smile, he whirled around to see what had happened.

I had seen Jesse smile before, but only after somebody sneered an insult or cursed at him—but this was a different kind of smile. It wasn't his usual apologetic smile. This smile said something *fun* just happened for the first time.

Harold rubbed the back of his head, vigorously. He sat there dumbfounded on his humiliated ass. When he saw we were gaping at him like he'd just sprouted wings or grew a third arm or something, he looked at us, one by one, and began to cry, not out of pain, but out of embarrassment.

"Damn you, Jesse," he said between sobs. "I wasn't gonna hurt you. Look what you did to me. I'm bleeding."

Snickers were coming from one, then another, then another, then everybody, except me. The irony was deliciously funny, but the reality of the moment was glorious. I took it in like a dry-backed sponge. Not a laugh-out-loud moment, but a smile-quietly-and-ponder-the-magnificence-of-the-universe moment.

After Jesse scored his illustrious touchdown and turned back to see the whimpering fallen leader, the brief smile vanished from his lips and was replaced by a sadness. His shoulders slumped, his clothes appeared looser, and his head tilted downward. In a span of three heartbeats, he converted from a confident, statuesque champion of payback immortality, to a downtrodden, humble wisp of societal debris. He looked exactly like he did when he was lying on the ground, watching Harold perform his *we got a nigger in class* dirge just moments earlier.

Jesse shuffled toward Harold, as if drawn by an innate responsibility to apologize for the crime of momentarily being good at something. He approached the sobbing boy. Slowly, he held out his hand as an offering of peace, but had a regrettable look on his face as if he knew what was about to happen.

Harold quickly and viciously slapped Jesse's hand away. He jumped up wiping his nose and started pummeling Jesse savagely. His teeth clenched, he snarled, and his fist hit hard. Jesse went down with a thump, fast. Harold used every curse word he had ever heard and vaguely knew how to pronounce. I didn't recognize most of them, but some I knew very well. Jesse offered no resistance. He accepted the fist to his face willingly and only meekly exposed one hand to deflect the pummeling. I watched, not in horror, but in disgust. What had become of my new hero? He briefly appeared as a glorious champion for all the small people, in all the playgrounds in the entire world, but now disappeared just as quickly. He went back to the humble dust of the lowest rung from which he sprang. In the span of less than one minute, the thoughts in my head went from the noble, *Go, Jesse, go!* to the ignoble, *You are just a damn nigger.*

I went home that day and felt ennui for humanity.

***

Jesse appeared one morning a month or so after the football incident, as it would come to be known by the Jess Rulam community, with a terribly beaten face. Both eyes were black with a protruding knot above his eyebrow. His lips were twice the normal size. He was slightly bent over to one side and had a discernible limp. It was obvious someone had beat the hell out of him. My first thought was that it was Harold's father.

After the football incident, Mr. Spartani made an appearance at the principal's office. He wanted to know, "How is a nigger child in this school and how could you allow him to almost give my son a concussion?"

Mr. Spartani was rumored to have a violent temper, and he vowed that he would do something about this outrage.

"He better watch himself," Mr. Spartani threatened.

"I don't think he's colored," Principal Sherbet retorted.

"He had a nigger daddy that got shot dead. Everybody knows that," Mr. Spartani shouted back.

"His aunt is white. She put on the form that Jesse is white. What can we do?" Principal Sherbet said, incensed.

"You can tell by looking at him he's not white. Are you damn blind?" Mr. Spartani's voice was reverberating down the halls. He stormed out of the office, pissed.

As it turned out, somebody beat Mr. Spartani to the punch, so to speak. A part-time pulpwood cutter—Jesse's aunt's full-time shack-up—didn't *like the way that damn weird breed is always looking at me all the time*; at least that's what he told the police.

A couple of days later, the principal, accompanied by a man in a suit with a badge on his jacket and two finely dressed women with satchels in their hands, interrupted the class. They were from the State of Alabama Welfare Department, and they all looked solemn. They called Miss Bishop to the side and were whispering among themselves. Miss Bishop called out Jesse's name and asked him to come forward.

Harold had glee in his eyes and could hardly keep himself in his seat as Jesse passed by him. He actually thought the police came to arrest Jesse for hurting his head. I had the exact opposite thought, and so did the rest of the class. We thought they had come to arrest Harold and whisk him off to kid prison for beating the hell out of Jesse, or maybe for his father threatening to.

We came to find out later that Jesse's aunt called the police, not Miss Bishop, nor the principal. She told the police that Norman, the pulpwood cutter, told her that he was going to kill Jesse. The police reported Jesse's sorry living conditions when they arrested the pulpwood cutter for the assault.

At the police station, Norman's affidavit stated:

That damn nigger kid, or whatever he is, has something wrong with him. He don't ever cry any. I've kicked the shit out of him several times, but he don't cry or say a damn word. Just, 'I forgive you; have mercy, sir,' over and over. He's just plain weird. I slapped him around a little last night, and he came around and sat at the other end of the couch. Every time I'd look at him he'd be looking back at me and say, 'All I ask is mercy, all I ask is mercy,' over and over until I couldn't stand it no more. That damn stare of his. It ain't natural. It was like he could see the back of my brain or something. Right through me. Do you know what I mean? I don't know how, but he knew my thoughts. It hurt me. I had to stop him. I just had to, I just had to do it.

They said he sobbed uncontrollably as they walked him over to the cell.

Jesse was taken away that day and placed in the foster care system. This was not the first time this had happened, nor would it be the last; in fact, it would become a regular occurrence. The aunt would get the house fixed up enough to temporarily regain custody for a while, then relapse, then recover, then relapse.

Jesse never stayed more than a few months at any one place. Unfortunately for Jesse, kids that are rumored to be colored were not always easy to place in a home in 1960s Alabama. So the state would reluctantly return Jesse to his aunt, with the promise that she had straightened up. Of course, the welfare payments and the food stamps that accompanied him, thanks to the freshly launched Great Society by President Johnson, might have helped her commitment to motherhood a little.

We would become accustomed to the routine: in school for a while, then out; show up with fresh bruises, then gone. In, then out, bruises, then gone. That was his life, such as it was, and he seemed to wear it well.

CHAPTER 5

IT WAS SEPTEMBER. SOME YEARS had passed, and the ritual of the first day began for the fourth time. The apprehensiveness of being under the stern tutelage of one Miss Elsa Luck, whose reputation was legendary to fourth graders, was temporarily alleviated by the gathering of the gang.

Pete seemed to have grown taller; Jimmy had gotten thicker; Andy, Jude, Bart, and John had all changed a little over the summer. Harold was still holding his position as our king, and we were still his subjects. But his luster had faded somewhat, especially after the incident three years earlier.

"That Miss Luck is supposed to be a real bitch," Pete updated us.

I had my own news for them. "My brother and my sister both had her, and they said she was the meanest teacher in the whole elementary."

"She used to paddle my brother's ass every day when he had her," Bart chimed in.

"I wonder how many times I can get her to whoop ol' Jesse's ass this year?" said Harold, nodding his chin toward Jesse, whom we had not seen in two years.

"Dang! Look how big he's got."

"He was tall in the first grade, but look at him now."

"He looks darker."

"Yeah, he looks more like a nigger than ever," Harold said, matter-of-factly.

"He's got better clothes now."

"He's standing a little straighter or something, ain't he?"

"Yeah, he's changed a little since we saw him."

"He ain't that much bigger." Harold's voice was sarcastic.

"Harold, he's as big as you!" I was just stating a fact. Harold grabbed me with one hand around the front of my shirt and jerked me up to his face.

"You little scrawny shit. He ain't as big as me. He ain't as strong as me. I'm gonna whoop your ass at recess." Harold had rage in his eyes.

"What did I do, Harold?" I was terrified and trying to weasel out of getting my ass beat.

"Are you getting mad 'cause Jesse growed some?" Pete was trying to take up for me. Harold reluctantly let go of me with a long sigh.

"Both of y'all shut up. That damn nigger ain't nothing," said Harold, glaring at everybody.

Harold whirled around and stormed into our classroom. We looked at each other and wondered what was eating him. But of course, we *knew* what was eating Harold. Jesse was eating Harold, and he had been since the first time any of us had laid eyes on him.

* * *

It was the second day of school, but the first day of recess. We gathered at our same old spot just like we had done for the previous three years. I couldn't help but look to see where Jesse was. Ever since *the run*, I could not get that image out of my brain whenever anything about football came up. Whether watching it on TV, or playing it in the backyard, or just simply thinking about it, no matter the circumstances, Jesse's run pushed through to the center of my thoughts and always, surreally, in slow motion.

I wondered, *Did I see it, or did I think I seen it?* Each time my mind went over that slow motion image, it was a little foggier, and a little foggier; not as clear as the previous time, or the time before that.

We all talked about it from time to time, except Harold of course. Me, Pete, Bart, Andy, and even Jude—the gang—spent many an hour pondering that stupendous, yet mysterious football run of Jesse's. It slowly gained legendary status among us.

Pete gave a philosophical summation of it one day. "Aw, it probably weren't as good as we remember it being. We were just kids then."

Why, of course, that was probably it. Now that we were nine years old and damn near grown, that had to have been it.

Just as mediocre high school plays from the rather mediocre high school teams gain in stature with the passage of time, so did *the run*. Forty-yard passes invariably become sixty-yard passes; twenty-yard runs are hazily remembered as seventy-yard runs. I was beginning to think that *the run* was just that—an apparition of fruitful, wishful minds.

* * *

I was curiously scanning the playground to see what Jesse was doing. I caught sight of him by the swing sets. We shared our recess period with one of the first grades and one of the second grades. I watched him as he watched some first grade kids rambunctiously playing on the swings. He was leaning against one of the Formosa trees scattered about. He seemed happily transfixed on the children, just watching, nothing more. He wore a pleasant look on his slender face, as if he was pleased that somebody in this miserable world, which he had become accustomed to, was permitted to have fun.

It seemed odd to me at the time that somebody as big as Jesse would prefer to watch small children at play on the swings, instead of cracking heads with the boys.

"What are you looking at? That ol' nigger sissy boy?" Harold caught my attention. "He'll be over there swinging with 'em in a minute," he continued with a chuckle. "Why don't you go on over there and play with him yourself, you candy."

"Come on, Matt, we're kicking off." Bart was trying to get my attention.

"He's not going to play with us, Matt," Harold said sarcastically. "He's too scared of me."

"Yeah, like he was the last time he played against you." The words just popped out of me.

Before I had time to think about the consequences of what I had just smarmily said, Harold was on top of me, beating my face with his huge, hard fists. I never fully realized just how powerful Harold Spartani was until now. It was as though he was a grownup and I was but a child. As the fists hit me, that part of my face went numb. Each time the fists hit my face, my ears rang, then there was silence. The fists struck over and over. Thoughts were hard to hold in my head.

I turned my head slightly to the right just in time to see the powerful arm swing back into the cocked position, and then the tightly bunched knuckles—there seemed to be twenty of them on one fist—were gaining size as they approached my eyes. There was nothing I could do but brace for impact.

Suddenly, as if in a blurry dream world, I saw a shadowy dark hand, larger than Harold's, grab firmly hold of the rapidly advancing fist with a slapping sound, skin against skin.

Harold's eyes were the size of silver dollars before shrinking to mere slits. His furrowed brow and sternly set jaw framed the most hateful, seething scowl I had ever seen on a human being.

"Take your damn hands off of me, nigger."

Jesse let go of Harold's hand.

"Enough, Harold," Jesse said calmly, never breaking eye contact. I was too lightheaded to feel gratitude at the moment. All I knew was I didn't get hit again.

Harold stepped forward, bumping against Jesse's chest, staring him in the eyes with the same hateful scowl on his face. They stood there face to face, chest to chest, eye to eye, and nose to nose. From my vantage point on the ground, Jesse was at least two inches taller. Instead of his usual sunken chest and slumped shoulders, Jesse was fully inflated with no evidence of backing down.

"Not this time," said Jesse firmly.

Not this time! That's what my subconscious was shouting over and over, the words Jesse just spoke to the king. *That person* made a reappearance. *That person*, the one I had seen ever so briefly three years earlier, had returned to prove he was not a myth. I didn't imagine *the run*. I saw what I thought I saw, and so did Pete and Bart and Jimmy. *Now, old boy!* I was so excited I couldn't tell if I was thinking or speaking the words, *You're gonna get yours this time!*

I regretted the thoughts I had of Jesse three years earlier as I saw the two boys posed like statues, defiantly composed face to face in an unflinching stare down. Looking closer, there was something wrong. Harold had the vile, hate-filled scowl on his face; the same one that all who had the misfortune of being the object of his ire were accustomed to. But Jesse, well, he looked calm, too calm—almost peaceful.

"Don't think I'm scared of you."

What?! Harold was telling Jesse that he wasn't scared of him, which of course meant he was scared of him.

"I don't want you to be scared of me," Jesse said softly, still looking Harold in the eye. "I just want you to stop hitting my friend."

"Oh, he's your friend," Harold said as he turned and looked at me with a smirk. "I thought so." He nodded his head.

"I would like to be friends with all of you. You too, Harold." Jesse's voice was even slower and more deliberate.

"I don't know about that squirt-ass Matt there," Harold said, nodding toward me again, "but we ain't gonna be no friend to no nigger 'round here."

"Why?" Jesse asked, almost whispering.

"'Cause white boys don't play with niggers, see."

"Why?"

"'Cause niggers are, ah, just, ah … are niggers, damn you!"

A rush of anger and adrenaline came over Harold. He drew back his arm and clocked Jesse hard on the cheek. The thud of fist on flesh hung in the air. Jesse's head went down; his body bent at the waist and leaned to the side. He paused there for a moment and then stood upright again.

Harold had his fists cocked and moving in a circular motion. His feet were positioned in a boxer's stance, ready to fight. He had the fear of the unknown in his eyes. His chin quivered. It was clear he was scared.

Jesse's face never changed. His eyes never moved, his mouth never opened. His eyes showed a sad look of disappointment. I couldn't tell if he was disappointed in Harold or himself. Something deep down inside of me knew that this was going to happen. Jesse stood his ground with Harold and yet would not defend himself. I could tell by the look on his face he would not fight Harold.

I came to the realization that Jesse was a coward. But then again, he didn't exactly look like a coward, he just acted like a coward, and yet at the same time, he didn't. All I knew for certain was that I was through with Jesse.

"I knew you was scared of me, nigger," Harold said coldly, triumphantly.

"Niggers don't fight good, do they?" asked Pete.

"Niggers is cowardly, ain't they?" Jimmy was looking at Jude for agreement.

"Go on, nigger Jesse," said Bart, to indicate the show was over.

Jesse turned and walked away with his head down. I knew in my heart I should have run over and thanked him for saving me from a worse beating. How could I thank someone who is a bigger coward than me? It's not natural. I couldn't do it. I was through with Jesse.

Just then Miss Luck grabbed hold of Harold and Pete by the arms.

"All you boys here, come with me," she said angrily.

Apprehensively, we followed her back to our room. We knew she was mad at us for fighting at school. I was hoping somebody told on Harold for beating the hell out of me. I wanted to see her paddle Harold's ass until he cried like a baby. Maybe she knew from the bruises on my face.

"Don't ever let me hear you say the word 'nigger' again to Jesse. Not another time! Do you hear me?" She was as angry and stern as I had ever heard her.

"There will be Negro children coming to this school in the following years, and you had better get used to having them around. That word is a bad word to say. It is an insult and degrading to them, and I won't have it." She was talking faster and faster.

"We had Negro people that worked on my father's farm picking cotton, and they were good people. People used that word then. I heard my father say it a thousand times. People say it in town till this day. But I'm telling you not to use that word in my class again, or I will paddle you hard. Do you understand me?" She looked all of us in the eye one at a time, very deliberately. We all nodded yes.

"Then go on back ... and find Jesse and apologize to him," she insisted. Of course, none of us did.

* * *

Funny thing, I was seven or eight years old before I ever realized "nigger" was a bad word to black people. I think my mother told me not to say it in front of a black person because it reminded them that that was the word they used to call them when they were slaves. Until then, I never knew that word was insulting to a black person. That was simply what they were. Just like a dog is a dog, a cat is a cat, a chicken is a chicken, and a nigger is a nigger. Not an insult, just what black people were. It was merely that and nothing more. We all managed not to use *that* word again—in front of Miss Luck anyway—for a while; even Harold restrained himself.

* * *

Miss Elsa Luck was an elderly gray-haired lady of about sixty-eight. She walked slightly bent to one side to compensate for a hip displacement, consequently, her right leg dragged a little, like Igor in *Frankenstein*. Osteoporosis bent her at the shoulders, and her back showed the familiar small humpwe associate with it. She had lost her husband ten years earlier, and her only child had died at age eleven of leukemia.

Perhaps the stretch of lonely years relentlessly unwinding before her was the reason for her meticulous nature and strident disposition. Maybe she needed someone to care for, to cook for, to clean for, and to fuss after for making messes. This seems to be a natural maternal gift bestowed on all women, to the detriment of all men and all children.

Miss Luck was also a clean freak. To Miss Luck, nothing was ever clean enough, especially the floor. Our desks were never clean enough; the blackboard must never have a hint of a chalk outline; the erasers must be banged thoroughly, and especially, the floor must be speck free. I don't know this for a fact, but I heard that one year she made the entire class take their shoes off before they entered the room. Only the complaints to the principal prevented it from happening all year.

She carefully observed the janitor as he buffed the floor once a week, barking out precise instructions, and finally, becoming annoyed, she'd take hold of the machine and perform the task herself, bad leg and all. What was this strange compulsion about the floor? All of us were baffled.

I saw her tear John's ass up one day because he had moved his desk next to a classmate, raising the probability that he had slightly scuffed the forbidden floor. She busted his butt at least a dozen licks right there in front of us, instead of the usual slow walk down the hall. She screamed all the while, with each lick on John's reddening ass, about a scuff mark. There was no scuff mark. The funny thing is, John knew better than to slide the desk. He was warned, no, threatened so many times to lift the desk off the floor, never, ever slide it. He would never make that fatal mistake again.

One day, shortly after John got his ass molecules rearranged, Miss Luck left us alone to run an errand. We were cutting up and playing grab-ass as usual, you know, normal stuff. Jesse got up to put some pencil eraser filings he had gathered onto a piece of paper—so as not to get any on the forbidden floor—and then he dumped them into the wastebasket. Someone said, "Here she comes," which spurred Jesse to hustle back lest he get caught out of his seat.

For some strange reason, Jimmy got a spur of the moment brain fart and decided to stick his foot out and trip Jesse. This was very unusual for him. He later said he had no idea why he did it. Jesse had on large brogan-type boots with large black soles. As he fell, one of the boots dragged across the shiny, freshly waxed floor and left a long, wide black skid mark.

Jesse sat staring in horror at the mark. His mouth was open as he put his hands underneath himself to push up and spring to his feet. Just then, Miss Luck entered the room.

"What's this?" she said.

Jesse plopped back down on his butt and turned to look at her. She walked slowly, with hands on hips, to the aisle where Jesse sat looking like a condemned prisoner, awaiting execution. We all knew that Jesse and Jimmy were going to get a terrible tongue-lashing and a horrific ass beating.

"You damned nigger," she whispered slowly. But it was loud enough that we all heard it, including Jesse. This was the first time in my nine years I remember experiencing a pregnant pause.

The entire room went deathly silent for what seemed like evermore. If ever the word "surreal" was personified, it was then. The scene was a vivid snapshot of a 1967 Alabama grammar school: boys with crew cuts, with ears too big for their heads; girls in checked dresses and flip-flops, hair rolled up in a curl in the back. We all stared blankly at Miss Luck. And Miss Luck stared blankly at Jesse. And Jesse stared at Miss Luck with disappointment in his eyes.

CHAPTER 6

MISS LUCK NEVER RECOVERED FROM the words she spoke that fateful day. She spent much of the next few days standing in front of the windows with arms folded behind her back, one hand holding the other, gazing out into space in lonely reverie. I often wondered what she was thinking at those times. I wondered if she was contemplating her hypocrisy, or her loneliness, or maybe, she figured that age was closing the inevitable gap between time and senility, and the latter was taking her mind.

Whatever she was thinking made a change in her though. Her voice was much softer, kinder, and less strident. She never apologized to Jesse, but I would catch her sometimes looking at him while we were silently doing our classwork, with her eyes gazing off into space and then slightly shaking her head—no. It wasn't long afterward that she retired without notice. One day she was there, and the next day she wasn't.

She was replaced by a Mr. Terry Harrison, Jess Rulam's first male elementary teacher in a long time. He was slated to be a fifth grade teacher next year, but found himself filling in for Miss Luck for the rest of the year. He was young and genial, with a rather pleasing manner. He never raised his voice, instead he lowered it a few octaves when somebody was too rowdy. But, by far, his greatest attribute was that he played quarterback for both sides of our recess football teams. You see, next year he was also going to be the assistant junior high football coach and the head coach for the pee wee team. We liked him right away.

His easy disposition and constant encouragement, especially with the players at recess, made football fun again. I would literally count down the seconds by way of the large clock hanging over the door of our classroom. Though the clock was never precisely in sync with the two o'clock bell, which was recess time, I still hung on every second. When that bell finally rang, I knew, that this day, I was going to catch a long touchdown pass from Mr. Harrison and piss Harold off. It had become my favorite pastime—pissing off Harold.

Apparently, it was Jesse's too, because Harold always seemed to be pissed at Jesse.

"OK, Bart, you do a curl, about five yards. Matt, you do a post," said Mr. Harrison, making a curving gesture with his hand.

"Andy, you and Philip try to hold Harold out this time. I know he's big, but you can get leverage on him." He was bending his knees and springing forward in a bouncing motion and lifting his elbows in the familiar blocking posture for demonstration purposes.

The problem wasn't that Andy and Philip didn't know how to block a pass rusher. The problem was that Harold was twenty pounds heavier, exponentially stronger, and infinitely meaner and rougher than the rather meek Andy and Philip.

The ball was snapped. Harold put one hand in Andy's chest, the other hand in Philip's chest. He threw both aside with little effort and sprinted to Mr. Harrison and tagged him on his back as he was attempting to evade the pass-rushing locomotive. Harold wouldn't have tackled Mr. Harrison anyway; we stopped playing tackle in the third grade, principal's orders. Instead it was two-hand touch.

"I hope Harold's as tough to block when we put the pads on as he is out here," said Mr. Harrison, catching his breath a little. "We need some bigger bodies on the line for Mr. Harold." Mr. Harrison scanned the playground.

"Hey, how about Jesse? Why isn't he playing?" He was looking at us, but asking himself.

"Hey, Jesse," shouted Mr. Harrison. "Hey, Jesse!" Louder. "Somebody go get Jesse," he said, motioning to me then pointing at Jesse. "Why is he always playing with the second graders?" he asked with a chuckling "huh" sound. "Is he funny or something?"

His voice tapered at the end and he gave the same odd chuckle. I didn't know what he was talking about then. I do now. Fag jokes wouldn't get introduced to us until junior high.

Pete and I couldn't resist. "Jesse is the best football player I've ever seen," I said like the words had been trapped in my mouth and desperately needed to escape.

"Me too," Pete said with the same enthusiasm. "He can run faster than any boy in high school and is so quick you can't see him move." Pete's eyes were getting bigger and bigger.

"Is that right?" Mr. Harrison was amused by our wild-ass exaggerations.

"Yeah, we can't even touch him when he's running." I was on fire.

"He returned a kickoff one day and ran over everybody out here."

"He's like a professional." Now Pete was getting a little carried away.

"He is." I was too.

"Oh, come on, guys, y'all are sounding nuttier than a fruitcake." It was obvious that Mr. Harrison wasn't buying any of it. "First of all, he's too tall and lanky to be real quick, boys." Mr. Harrison held up one finger and hit the palm of his other hand with it like there would be more points to follow. He was teaching us a lesson in human physiology and kinesiology, the same way he taught the multiplication tables when somebody didn't know what eight times seven was, except we had no idea what the hell he was talking about—just like the multiplication tables.

"Real tall guys just can't move as quickly as short guys. It's nature's way of equaling things out." He looked around a minute to make sure we were all listening to this lesson. "If you got long bones and a lot of space in between joints," he said, moving his hand from his thigh down to his knee, "you have a longer reaction time. Now guys like him can run fast when they get going."

By guys like him, I assumed at the time he was talking about long-legged, but I know now he meant colored. I didn't know then, but I would find out later, that black boys could run fast. I was ignorant to that then.

"He can run fast, and he's quick as lightning. Nobody out here will be able to touch him," I said, as I couldn't let this go on any further. I was about to bust, really. I couldn't hold my enthusiasm back. I wanted to see the look on Mr. Harrison's face when Jesse ripped one about fifty yards. I wanted to see him tell me about that bone-length shit then.

"He can't play football," Harold piped up.

"Boy, he sure looks capable," said Mr. Harrison, looking back at Harold.

"Well, he's kinda sissy." Harold showed a smirky grin. A couple of short laughs came from others.

"Well, go get him anyway."

I ran to where the second grade was playing. I had to reach up to tap Jesse on the shoulder. He was rolling a huge orange ball on the ground so the second grade boys and girls could take turns kicking it. The second grade teacher, Miss Greer, was rather appreciative that Jesse was a de facto teacher's aide on the playground.

"Oh, hi, Matt," said Jesse, a little startled.

"Mr. Harrison wants you to play with us."

"I don't want to, Matt." He turned back to make another roll.

"I know you don't, Jesse, but Mr. Harrison told me to get you."

"That game is nothing but trouble. I wish they would do away with it." Jesse nodded toward the other side of the playground where the game was going on.

"What! Why?" I was stupefied, incredulous, and getting angry. If Jesse said they should ban Christmas, I couldn't have been more offended.

"That game causes pain." Jesse was looking me right in the eye.

"Not if it's played right, Jesse, with pads and all." I thought I made a good point.

"That's not what I mean, Matt." Jesse turned away again to roll the ball, leaving me to ponder what he had just said.

"I've always wanted to ask you something, Jesse." I actually did always want to ask him what I was about to ask him, but now that he had pissed me off, I developed a stiffer spine. "How come you like to play with little kids?" My question lingered in the air as a large girl kicked the ball over everybody's head. Kids went scrambling for it.

Jesse turned, approached me, and lay his long arm across my shoulder, sort of pulling me a little closer, then let go. It was the first time Jesse ever touched me. I felt a little squeamish at first, but when I saw a gentle smile come across his face and brightness flash across his eyes, for that moment anyway, I felt secure, comforted, and safe.

"All of my life that I can remember has been a lot of bad memories, Matt. Can you remember your life? I can't remember all of mine, but I remember some of it. It's been painful for me. Not just hurting pain on the outside, but all pain. Pain in my heart. I don't get to have fun like the rest of you. I've tried to have fun and play with kids my age, but it doesn't work right. It never works right. Why do I always have to be a nigger? I don't know what that is Matt." He was shaking his head no, like he really didn't know. "What is that? Why does anybody have to be one? All I know is that it must be a bad thing, and I must be one."

Jesse was looking down at nothing and then raised his head and caught sight of the boisterous kids and pointed toward them.

"But when I see one of these little kids playing and enjoying life, I think to myself that this is the way it should be. These little ones shouldn't be hit in the face or stomped on the head or kicked in the ribs. For those that this happens to, I want to help them. Just for these few minutes out here, I want to have a fun life with them. Here, we have a fun life, like it was supposed to be for them and me too. I pretend that I get to live when they live. Do you understand, Matt? So that's why I rather do fun things than painful things." Jesse eyes were tearing, and I hate to admit this, but mine were too.

I ran back to the game, and when I made eye contact with Mr. Harrison, I shrugged, like I didn't know why Jesse didn't come with me. But I knew. And my heart was hurting because of it.

*　*　*

The next day in class, Mr. Harrison made an announcement as the recess bell rang.

"OK, everybody has to participate in a game with the other children. *Everybody.* We have some people who are not playing anything."

We knew who he was talking about.

"All the girls are playing kickball at the spot close to the first entrance to the school, you know, behind the swing area. The place in front here, where you've been playing, is too small. The boys will *all* play football where we've been playing. Any questions? Good. Let's go."

I sprang out of my seat like a deer. I might have been prancing, I don't know. All I knew was that Jesse had to play football today, and for lunch they'd serve a huge plate of crow stew. I wanted to see Mr. Harrison eat it—just like the dish known as revenge—served cold.

*　*　*

"Huddle up," said Mr. Harrison loudly, sounding just like a football coach.

"OK, Matt, split wide right. Run a deep square in. Jimmy, you split to the left and run a post. Jesse, you get on the line and block Harold. Just watch Pete and Andy and do what they do."

This is not what I wanted to happen. "Mr. Harrison, put Jesse in the backfield and hand him the ball. They'll never touch him," I pleaded.

"No, don't argue with me, Matt, just run the pattern." Mr. Harrison was a little annoyed.

The ball was snapped and Harold busted over Jesse, who offered no resistance, and tagged Mr. Harrison. The same thing the next play, and the next.

"Jesse, you've got to put more into it than that, son!" Mr. Harrison was clearly aggravated with Jesse and could tell that he didn't want to be out there.

"He's not in his position, Coach. Is it all right if we start calling you 'Coach'?" I wanted to cover my ass.

"Yeah, that's fine, boys," said Mr. Harrison, exasperated over Jesse.

"No, he's not where he ought to be. Put him as running back and give him the ball, Coach," said Pete, who was as anxious as me to see the expression on Coach's face when Jesse finally got the damn ball.

"OK, Jesse, get where Thad is. Thad, you block Simon. Pete, you slide down and block Harold. Jesse, swing out to the right side. Sweep right on one. OK, break."

This is it, finally! About damn time, I thought. I wouldn't even try to block. There was no need. I was just going to watch. I wanted to take it all in—the quick cut, the planting of the foot, and then the explosion and a flash of saggy clothes flapping in the wind.

I wanted it all: the jaw-dropping expression, the shaking of the head in disbelief, and then the turning of Coach's head slowly toward me with that smile that a person wears only when they've just seen something they weren't supposed to see. And all this would be followed by him saying, *My God, did I see what I just saw? Yes! You did*. The ball was snapped. I didn't move a step but simply turned around because I knew it would be over in a heartbeat. Coach pivoted, underhanded the pitch to Jesse, and Jesse took a couple of steps to catch the ball.

Harold and Simon quickly defeated the attempted blocks and closed in on him. Jesse snatched the ball out of the air, placed it under his arm, and took a couple of more long, slow, and awkward strides right at Harold, who promptly smeared him into the ground with Simon falling on top. The football came tumbling out of Jesse's hand and came to rest at Coach's feet.

"OK, boys, two-hand tag, no tackling," said Coach with a deliberate sigh. He snatched the ball from the ground and underhandedly tossed it in the air with a spiral to himself all while looking at Pete and me with a rather cocky smile and a raised brow.

I could not believe what I'd just seen. In my mind I attributed it to the lack of blocking and Jesse not being ready.

"Try it again, Coach. He wasn't ready," I said with concern and an air of apprehension. Surely Jesse wasn't going to do this to me again, was he?

"He is really good, Coach. A lot better than that." Pete was with me.

"Yeah, give him another chance. You ain't seen him loose yet," said Bart.

Finally, somebody besides Pete was vouching for me. It was a relief, as *that feeling* had starting to come over me again.

Very reluctantly, Coach said, "OK, Jesse, can you catch?"

"I don't know." Jesse shrugged.

"OK, Bart, you run a buttonhook. Matt, you go long so Thad will follow. I'm going to fake like I'm going to throw to Bart, then I'll flare the ball to you, Jesse, and you can put the moves on 'em and get enough for a first down. On one, break." Coach's voice had skepticism written all over it.

The ball snapped, the fake to Bart, the flare thrown, the ball caught, and Jesse was smeared by Harold. This time though, Harold lifted Jesse in the air and replanted him in the soil. The sound was horrible. Harold jumped up quickly and made a pump with his fist and let out a, "Yeah!"

"That was a very good form tackle, Harold," Coach said as he approached Harold and swung an arm around his shoulders and tugged him in close. "But we're not playing tackle out here." His voice had sternness in it, coming through almost clenched teeth. Coach was really pissed at Harold.

"Don't do that again, or I'm going to bust your butt. You get me?"

"Yes, sir," Harold said, but was still laughing.

"You all right, Jesse?" Coach asked with sincere concern.

"I'm fine, Mr. Harrison." Jesse grimaced.

"Jesse, what's the matter with you?" I couldn't hold back my anger at him any longer.

"Play like we saw you do that time. Don't you remember that?" Pete was as pissed as I was.

"Listen to me, boys. Come in here closer. I want everybody to hear this." Coach waved his arms in that "come closer" motion. He saw this as a teachable moment.

"This is not Jesse's fault." He pulled Jesse over next to him and put his hand on top of his head, which came to Coach's shoulders.

"You see how tall Jesse is. A boy this tall is not going to be real agile, especially at this age. When boys grow this fast, their bodies can't catch up with them, so to speak. This is called your 'awkward stage.' Now, when he gets older I'll bet he will make a really good basketball player, or might even make a good tight end. Who knows? But he's just too tall and in this awkward stage right now to be a good running back. So I don't want to hear another person criticizing Jesse, OK?"

Bart couldn't restrain himself. "I'm telling you, Coach, we all saw him make like that big nigger Jim Brown one time." Coach glared at Bart and shook his head and closed his eyes like he wanted to slap him.

"I mean, ah, that really good ... ah, running back that plays for ... on TV last Sunday." Bart was embarrassed as Jesse was standing right beside him, but Jesse seemed oblivious to the slip-up.

"We got time for a couple more plays before the bell rings." Coach was gazing at his watch. "OK, I'm going to give you another chance, Jesse, at tight end this time." Coach was tired of hearing us nag.

"Line up on the left. Don't split out as far as Bart. Run ten yards and turn around, and I'll throw it to you. You got that?" Coach was nodding his head up and down, hoping Jesse would do the same, which he did.

The ball was snapped. Jesse jogged ten yards and slowly turned around. Coach spun the ball into Jesse's hands; it skipped off his hands into his chest, and off his chest into Harold's hands, who ran it in for a touchdown.

"Come on, son, you have to put out more effort than that." Coach had his hands on his hips, staring down at the ground and shaking his head.

Again! He has done it to me again. I'm through with that nigger for good. I won't have faith in Jesse. No! Not another time. If I had the backbone, and a stepladder, I would have kicked Jesse's ass right then. I was sure Pete, Bart, and the rest felt the same way.

"We got time for one more play. Let's hurry up." Coach was motioning for a huddle. "Jesse, listen. Don't get discouraged, son. Football may not be your game. You may not have the temperament for it. But you can get better at it every day we play. You'll catch on and—"

"Coach," Jesse interrupted. He looked concerned.

"Yes."

"If I try really hard on this last play, will you let me go back and help Miss Greer like I was before?" Jesse was earnest, and there was a touch of anxiety in his voice. You could tell he was worried about playing football every day.

Coach looked at Jesse and exhaled a long sigh. "OK, Jesse. You run as fast as you can straight down the field, and I will throw it up to you. If you will at least try to get close to the ball, you can help Miss Greer." Coach was aggravated and ready to get this period over and go home.

We all lined up, me and Jesse on one side, Bart on the other, just like before, except Jesse looked different. The ball was snapped. Jesse exploded down the field in a blur. Coach spun the ball as high and as far as he could. Jesse went past me so fast that out of my peripheral vision, I thought that another object was on the field from the highway, a motorcycle perhaps.

I stopped running and looked up. Jesse was thirty yards ahead of everybody. The ball lobbed down right into his hands. He caught it effortlessly, crossed the goal line, laid the ball on the ground, and jogged into the schoolhouse as if nothing had happened.

Coach's mouth was agape. He was still staring downfield at the spot where Jesse had laid the ball. He looked around at me, Pete, and Bart, and then at everyone else. Instead of the jubilant expression we all had on our faces—even Harold had a slight smile as he jogged toward the schoolhouse—Coach's face was a mask of concern. Not what I was expecting. I wanted to see him roll around on the ground and beg me and Pete for forgiveness. But he didn't. He looked troubled instead, like he'd seen something he wasn't supposed to see and didn't know what to do about it.

***

Coach wasn't himself for a few days after that play. He didn't say as much, and when he did, it was very softly spoken. While we were doing an assignment in class, I'd catch him gazing at Jesse. Then he'd look off into nothingness for minutes at a time. He had to be wondering, as the rest of us were, about the play.

I'm sure he was confused. An educated mind is not supposed to be confused. Confusion is a malady reserved for the weaker minded, or is it the reverse? None of the physical education classes, the kinesiology classes, the weight-lifting classes, the nutrition classes, the study of angles and leverage, or even the psychology classes offered a remedy to the confusion muddling his thoughts.

If a mere simpleton witnessed the play, it would be a slap on the knee and a couple of "boy oh boys!" and that would be the end of it. It would retire itself to the recesses of the brain where all the thoughts of the simpleminded go to retire. But intelligent, educated brains are different. Witnessed feats that are not supposed to happen will linger in the brain and stubbornly demand resolution. For an intelligent brain like Coach's, it was damn near maddening.

We never spoke about the play to him, or he to us. He kept his end of the bargain, though, and never asked Jesse to play touch football with our class again. And Jesse kept his word and dutifully helped Miss Greer every day with the children. Whether by pleasantly pushing a swing or rolling the oversized kickball, he seemed at total peace and happy to be allowed to share in a fun life, even if it was only for one hour.

Coach wasn't the only one affected by the play. I caught other members of the team occasionally snatching glimpses at Jesse from their desks, as I'm sure they did me. To tell you the truth, I was scared of Jesse. Not a horrified scared, but an uneasy scared. And I wasn't alone. So was Harold, the king.

***

It was recess. Coach was out that day, and the substitute let us do whatever we wanted. Harold caught Jesse on his way to the second grade playground for his usual duties and showed how scared he was of him. To hide his fear and insecurity, he overcompensated with meanness.

Harold started harassing Jesse, and there was a crescendo of bullying. Harold grabbed Jesse by the arm and whirled him 'round and 'round and flung him to the ground. Harold insisted that it was so easy that any of us could do the same thing. So, with Harold's orders, Pete, Bart, Simon, Andy, and Philip whirled Jesse by the arm and flung him to the ground. Jesse offered no resistance. When I noticed the commotion, five of the gang had already had their turn.

Next it was Thad, then Jimmy. It was easy. One revolution whirl, let go of the arm, and watch Jesse tumble to the ground. Then it was John and Thad. I was the only one left. Harold shouted, "It's your turn next, squirt-ass." From the look in his eyes, I had no choice.

Jesse was on his knees, solemnly looking me in the eyes, and faintly and gently nodded his head yes. He got up and lifted his hand so I could take hold of it. I whirled him to the ground with him more or less supplying the impetus. We left Jesse lying there. We were not as scared as before.

"He's just a fast nigger, that's all," Harold said as we headed to a different part of the grounds. "My daddy said that most niggers can run fast."

Harold was trying to sound like this was a well-known fact. That statement was a little reassuring. But the thought kept creeping back into my mind, *But that damned fast?!*

CHAPTER 7

OUR FIFTH GRADE SCHOOL YEAR began in September 1968. That same year, integration began to really take root in our area. The black elementary school on The Hill was shut down and the students were bused five miles to Jess Rulam Elementary School. The high school would close the next year. The bittersweet irony was not lost on most of the residents of the town of Jess Rulam.

Between 1850 and 1880, Jess Rulam was the largest cotton farmer in the area. In 1859, he donated all the land and most of the money to start the school that would eventually bear his name. It was recorded that Mr. Rulam was also one of only two people in the entire county to have ever owned slaves. It was also recorded, if one dug through the hidden-away archives long enough, that Mr. Rulam was a bombastic bastard.

Most of the residents heard that the founder of their town had been rich, well-respected, a man of God, and that he had had an unsuccessful run for governor. Eighth grade students could read with pride about the life of Jess Rulam in the textbook *Alabama History*.

Like most men of renown, the public expects to find out, eventually, that once the veil of history is lifted, men are just men, women are just women, and all have foibles and shortcomings.

If you thought that most of the residents of Jess Rulam knew the *real* history behind the founder of their town, you would be wrong.

* * *

Jess Rulam was about to take a stroll on his nightly "constitution" as he called it. It was a way to walk off a big supper of fried chicken, collard greens, stewed potatoes, and a double portion of peach cobbler, of course. He was usually so full that he undid the top button of his trousers to accommodate an already distended and bloated belly pressed to the limit of its tensile strength.

Strolling along on his three-thousand-acre plantation with a seven-thousand-square-foot mansion—complete with everything including granite imported from far-off Rhode Island, a billiard table specially imported from even farther-off England, and his eight barns and fifty-six cabins housing two hundred and fifty-six slaves—made a man prideful.

In addition to surveying his own great accumulation of wealth and allowing supper to settle, Mr. Rulam had another purpose for his constitutional—a rather evil one. You see, Jess Rulam enjoyed a rather distasteful, repulsive but rather common consequence of slave ownership—a devilish fringe benefit if you will. It was one that almost all masters, from large plantation owners to the forty-acre sodbusters partook of, or so he thought. It was all justified in his mind of course, but evil nonetheless. And like all evil, it had to be punished. Retribution must be paid and accounts settled, and, the hand that rises to settle the accounts can sometimes cast a long shadow.

* * *

Minnie was startled when she heard the rather forceful knocking on her cabin door.

"Whose dar?" Minnie asked almost too quietly to hear.

"Why it's Jess, Minnie," said Mr. Rulam, amused that Minnie would pretend not to know.

"Please, sir, not tis evening. Don't be studin' me tis evening. I don't feel good right now." Minnie often pleaded this way. Sometimes it worked, sometimes it didn't.

Slave women were always expected to submit to the sexual advances of their owners. It was part of the job description. They were property owned by their master, just like the land or a mule. Part of the right to ownership of property is to do whatever you like with it. This was clearly understood by all parties. Mr. Rulam merely thought of Minnie and the others as concubines, bought and paid for.

"I be sick today, Massa Rulam," she said, almost frantic.

"Servants, be obedient to them that are your masters according to the flesh, with fear and trembling, in singleness of your heart, as unto Christ," said Mr. Rulam, raising his voice slightly with a touch of aggravation. This was one of Mr. Rulam's favorite quotes from the Bible he used whenever Minnie or any of the other wenches protested servicing him. He wielded it like a sword.

"Please, Massa, pass by me tonight. I accepted the Lord Jesus at the revival meetin' last Thursday. It not be right for me, Massa. You had that 'vangelist come preach to us. I got the spirit in me, Massa. I done what I was compel by the Holy Ghost. Preacher say it not be right to lay wid menfolk until we had rightful matrimony." Minnie was crying.

Minnie wished she knew more of the Bible. She just knew that somewhere in it there had to be something to combat this bondage. Why would the Lord allow this to happen? she wondered. If only she could get the master's daughter, Miss Deborah, to give her some more Bible lessons. She wished that the Lord would hear her prayers and seek vengeance on Jess Rulam someday.

Minnie made her way to the door and let her master in. He pushed her back a little as he entered the tiny cabin.

"I hope you freshened yourself this morning, Minnie, as you were told."

"I didn't hap time to, Massa. Sorry."

"Well, that's all right, Minnie. You look fresh enough to me." A smile briefly appeared on his face then vanished as he saw the sorrowful look in Minnie's eyes.

"I don' want to give myself to you anymore, Massa!" exclaimed Minnie. "You can give me a whippin' if it be your will." Minnie turned defiant.

"It be my will all right," growled Rulam harshly, slapping her face with his hand. He grabbed her cheeks and squeezed her lips together, hard.

Minnie pulled his hand down with both of hers and said, "My man George don't like it when you comes 'round here, Massa. We gonna be in matrimony soon."

"You're not going to be in any matrimony soon or any other time, Minnie," Rulam said savagely.

He took one step back for leverage and backhanded Minnie so hard she landed on the floor. She jarred the bed so violently that her four-year-old son, Jeremiah, was startled out of his sleep and began crying, "Mama, Mama."

Rulam turned and stormed out of the cabin, slamming the door while Minnie tried to comfort the little one.

A few moments later, the cabin door was kicked in with a bang so loud that Jeremiah jumped in Minnie's arms. Two overseers dragged George, who was semiconscious and wearing chains around his wrists, into the cabin. Then Rulam followed in. Two more overseers followed in behind him.

"Bind one arm to that rafter and one arm to this one here," Rulam said, pointing. Blood and spit made a thick mixture oozing from George's bloody mouth. One eye was completely shut and swollen; the other had a large knot above the brow. Bruises peppered his face.

Fully stretched out and bound, he looked like a half-dead bird with its wings spread out. He willed his feet to support him, but they could not. He could only manage to bob his head up for a second or two.

"Take her and stretch her over this table. Now bind her hands with the rope to those two legs of the table," Rulam said, pointing again.

The overseers roughly bent Minnie at the waist and slammed her hard against the table. Her teeth cut her lips and blood gushed out. With her feet on the floor, bent at the waist, both arms stretched to their fullest and tied, her mouth bleeding profusely, she groggily slipped in and out of consciousness. Rulam ordered the men out of the room. He was ready to do what he came to do.

"What about the boy?" one of the men asked quickly.

"Leave him!" Rulam ordered. "He can watch. It will be good for him."

Minnie heard the cabin door as the men shut it behind them. The one lit lantern cast silhouetted shadows on the floor and walls of the winged George and the slavemaster as he stood menacingly over Minnie.

By now, little Jeremiah was standing in front of the table. He joined his mother in synchronized sobbing. Tears left a wet trail down his tiny cheeks and dripped silently to the floor.

Rulam undid his trouser buttons with one hand and lifted Minnie's raggedy dress with the other. As he raped her she could only turn her head toward her hysterical son and cry uncontrollably.

"Nooo, noooo, nooo!" she screamed.

She shook her head and pulled on the ropes trying to get away with each thrust. All that George could do was raise his head long enough to see his woman being raped. His head drooped down, and he whispered inaudibly, "No, Massa, noooo, Massa."

Little Jeremiah shouted at the top of his shrill voice, "Mama! Mamaaaa! Maaaaama!"

After a few agonizing minutes of what Minnie envisioned hell to be, it was over and the slavemaster left the one-room cabin.

Looking back inside, Rulam said to the men waiting there, "Take him down and dispose of him," nodding at George. "Your services are no longer required at this establishment," he laughed. "Unbind Minnie so that damn bastard child will shut up."

"Where should we dump him?" asked one of the overseers.

Rulam lit a cigar. "Take him to the ravine near the bottoms, you know the one. We'll let the varmints dispose of the carcass." He paused then said, "Wait a minute." Rulam had an epiphany. "I'll sell him to that crazy Frenchman that's coming here tomorrow. He's coming to look at some breeding Hereford stock. That's it—I'll sell him George and throw in that scowling bastard over there for free. Don't that child ever shut up?!"

"No, Massa. No, Massa," screamed Minnie, wrapping herself around her master's leg. "I'll be good, Massa. From now on I be real good to you, Massa."

Minnie pleaded, squeezing the master's leg tighter and tighter. "He be yo' son, Massa. Yo' own son, Massa. Yo' own flesh and blood."

"Get her off me! Take George out front and stake him out for the night. I'll see you tomorrow, Minnie."

Minnie was left with an inconsolable Jeremiah for a sleepless night.

*　*　*

The bright morning Alabama sun caused Minnie to hold her hand in front of her face to shield her eyes. They were tender and sensitive after the beating she took. She saw her master's horse cantering toward the cabin. He was accompanied by a distinguished looking gentleman riding in a small carriage.

They alighted and approached George, who was staked and shackled nearby. She was going to make one last intercession on his behalf. She was positive her master was not serious about sending Jeremiah away. As heartless a master as Jess Rulam was, nobody could sell his own son.

She was awake all night planning every word. She was going to offer to be his best wench. She'd bathe and perfume herself twice a week if necessary to please her master. She'd promise no back-talk, no unpleasant looks, no more pretend sick nights, just a willingness to serve him however he wanted, just the way he wanted.

"I'll have those Hereford cows and the bull shipped out of the stockyard if you would be so kind as to get them to Huntsville for me, Monsieur Rulam," said the French gentleman.

"I think we can do that," Rulam answered pleasantly.

"Now where is the buck slave you wish to make me a bargain of, Monsieur Rulam?"

"Straight ahead."

Approaching George, the French gentleman stopped and looked somewhat puzzled at the shackled and severely beaten slave.

"Is he so troublesome as to cause all this, monsieur?"

"He got out of hand a little last night, but we have adjusted his attitude."

"Adjusted it?!"

Minnie came running over to make her well-rehearsed speech, carrying Jeremiah in her arms. Rulam snatched the child from her and tossed him toward the Frenchman. The gentleman caught the toddler, looking at Rulam for an explanation.

Rulam motioned for the overseer to take Minnie away. She struggled hard but was silent. She realized she'd suffer even more later if she made a sound. She felt her heart breaking and her will giving up.

"There you are. A free gift just for taking George off my hands."

"Well, I don't know what to say, messieurs," he said, astonished.

"I will let you have George for …" Rulam hesitated, fondling his chin, then picked up, "for five hundred dollars."

"Five hundred dollars, well that is a bargain, monsieur. I'll have a bank draft for the cattle and the buck sent to your bank first thing in the morning." He was anxious to close the deal and get on his way.

He motioned for his carriage, which pulled alongside. The gentleman handed the squirming, screaming child to a maidservant inside the carriage. Minnie heard the cries and tore loose from the overseer. She ran frantically at the two men, her arms waving. She was tackled and finally subdued by three overseers.

"Please, Massa, don't take my baby, Jeremiah. Please, pleeease, God in heaven. I pray to you, oh Lord." Minnie dropped to her knees and placed her two trembling hands together.

"Now see here, messieurs, I will not separate a child from its mother. We do not do such things on my plantation!" the Frenchman said angrily.

"Well, we do here."

"Take the child back. I don't want it."

"Very well. As you wish."

Rulam turned to the overseer and said, "Bash this little bastard's head in and dispose of him."

"Hold it, messieurs!" the gentleman said, agitated. "Will you sell me its mother as well as the buck?"

"I like Minnie where she is, sir."

Minnie was still praying.

"Very well, I'll take the child, but I can't say I approve of your tactics, messieurs!"

"Then don't say it."

Rulam stuck his hand out. The gentleman from New Orleans reluctantly took it. He was anxious to get away.

"Ship the buck with the cattle," he said.

And with that, the carriage left.

The three overseers picked Minnie up. She was still praying softly. Exhausted, she was unable to fight them any longer.

"My baby, my precious baby." Minnie had cried so much that her voice was so hoarse that only the first letter of the words were audible.

"Mama! Mama! Mama!" screamed Jeremiah. He managed to free himself from the maidservant and made it halfway through the window before being pulled back in.

Minnie watched helplessly as the carriage made the last turn and was out of sight. She watched the dust from the carriage wheels slowly eddy and dissipate into nothingness. She dropped to the ground motionless with one outstretched hand extended in the direction of the carriage.

"Minnie, why are you carrying on so? Gather her up and lock her in her cabin," Rulam ordered, standing over her with his hands on his hips.

"Please, let me pray just one mo' prayer, Massa," said Minnie in her wisp of a voice.

"I've got to hear this."

Rulam squatted down to hear Minnie's frail voice. She managed to get to her knees and back to her prayer position.

"Dear Lord, please heah me jus' dis once. If it be yo' will, Lord, watch afta my baby, Jeremiah. Please allow him to grows up strong and fine. Let him be happy and not know the sorrow and hardship I been thu … and please Lord, jus' dis once, Lord, please come down on Jessup Rulam, Lord, and make dis sorry bastard's name be a abomanation to all da peeples of da worl. Amen."

And with that, the master rose quickly. He looked around for a weapon and grabbed a three-foot-long piece of iron tube carried by overseers for discipline and protection. With one vicious and brutal blow, he bashed in the back of Minnie's skull, killing her instantly.

Tossing the tube back to the overseer, he said, "Dispose of that."

He leisurely strolled home, anxious to tell his wife of the profitable cattle sale he'd negotiated during the day and to enjoy a cool glass of tea. First he'd take a relaxing bath, wash off the splattering of blood mixed with dust, and revel in the success of his day.

*   *   *

In the carriage, little Jeremiah gave up his crying. He was sucking his thumb, snuggly cradled in the maidservant's lap.

"He is a rather cute child, don't you think, Prissy?" said the gentleman from New Orleans, looking at the sleeping child.

"Yes, sir, I do."

"What did they say his name is?"

"Jeremiah, I believe, sir."

"Well, that sounds like a good name there, young Jeremiah."

He felt pity for the orphaned child. He said, "I believe I will give you a last name, young Jeremiah. It's a good name because it's my name. From now on, you will be Jeremiah Savorié."

After a while, he said quietly, "It's a long journey home, Prissy."

"Yes, sir, it's a long way home," Prissy agreed.

CHAPTER 8

I HAD NEVER REALLY BEEN around black people before that fifth grade year in 1968, save for the occasional visit to town with my mother when we went to pick up groceries or the monthly visit to the barbershop, which happened to employ an authentic black shoeshine boy. This antiquated stereotype seemed to be stilted, but it was true.

My first conscious awareness of black people was at a yearly ritual, customary on farms in the South in those days, called hog killing. It is what the name says it is. You grew up hogs, you killed them, you ate them.

It was also customary at that time to hire people that were skilled in that fine art to carry out the deed. People earned a pretty good living traveling from farm to farm providing the aforementioned skill set. Most of the time, they were black.

I remember peering around from behind my mother, tightly holding the back of her dress. She, and I, surveyed the grizzly act from afar.

I remember vividly the black man calmly easing himself to within three feet of the doomed hog. He raised his .22-caliber rifle, took steady aim, and put the bullet perfectly between its eyes. The beast fell straight down and flopped over while all four legs convulsed and quivered. Within two seconds, one of the executioner's partners stuck his razor-shaped knife to its throat and slit it. They wanted it to *bleed out* while it was still shuddering.

My mother forgot about me temporarily. She was mesmerized by watching something die too. Suddenly, she noticed me behind her and said that I had seen enough; but of course, I hadn't.

* * *

I slipped away from the house as soon as possible; I had to make another visit to the slaughter site. I inched closer and closer to the black men while they were carving off pieces of meat. They tossed them into a huge, black boiling kettle of water, precariously balanced between two poles over a roaring fire.

I noticed one of the men stick a piece of some sort of flesh on a stick and hold it over the flames. As he squatted there, twisting the simmering meat slowly around and around in the flame, he noticed me observing him from the shed. He motioned for me to come on over. Daddy was hanging around talking to one of the men, so I felt it was safe to join the one who invited me.

"Come on and set a spell. I'm just cookin' me a kidney for lunch," he said with the absolute biggest smile I had ever seen. I didn't know anybody could show that many teeth.

"A kidney," I said casually. I didn't know exactly what that was, but I figured you weren't supposed to eat it.

"Yeah, man, that be good."

I could see some sort of juice dripping from the kidney and sizzling in the fire.

"Yeah, man, we eat every ting from the rooter to the tooter."

He meant from the hog's snout to its rectum.

"I'm gonna make me a listener sandwich. What did we do wid dat bread?" asked the other one, floundering about in the cab of their 1959 Ford pickup.

After he found the loaf, he went about fishing an ear out of the boiling kettle. He made a few scrapes with a knife to remove any lingering hair and slammed it between two slices of bread that were judiciously coated in mustard. Then he put what appeared to be half the sandwich in his mouth. The man chomped down with a twist of his head, an *um um*, and an approving smile.

"Who dis fine gentleman be?" said the one that was talking with Daddy, but now had joined us.

"My name is Matthew," I said. Now I felt completely safe being around the friendly black men.

"Well, Mr. Matthew, my name is Charlie, that be Norris, and that ovah thea, eaten on that listener, be Ralph Jr. How about joinin' us for lunch? Ralphie, bring that bread on ovah hea so we all can make us a san'wich."

I had the best time that day. They cooked different parts of the animal for me to sample. They burst into delighted laughter at the subsequent frown on my face because of the pungent taste I had never tried before. I believe they were as enthralled by me as I was by them.

"That was Benny you just killed," I said. "He was my favorite one of the bunch."

"Oh, I sho am sorry to heah dat, Mr. Matthew," said Charlie sincerely."But that's what the Good Lord done put Benny on dis worl fa. He put him hea to make you and yo folks happy. Now you git to enjoy Mr. Benny for many months to come. That was Mr. Benny's job, and he do a fine job of it. You be proud of Mr. Benny. OK there, Mr. Matthew?"

"OK," I said, smiling up at Charlie.

Mother hollered for me to come back to the house, and they told me goodbye. Their gigantic smiles made me believe they genuinely enjoyed me being with them. I know I enjoyed it. My first experience with black people was a positive one. I learned they ate strange and different food then we did, but they were nice and warmhearted. Yes, they were.

* * *

This was nothing like the description I got from my three cousins from Sand Mountain. According to them, blacks descended from gorillas; we were created by God, but they were monkeys; they would steal everything they saw; they would lie; they would rape your mother, if they got the chance; they were dumb because their brain was the size of a walnut, and they couldn't swim. If one ever got after you to cut your throat and steal your money, get into the nearest body of water. You'd be safe.

It was years afterward that I happened to see some black people swimming in a lake—a different part than the whites swam in, of course. I realized the information I had received from the cousins was rather dubious. I was, at the time, so shocked that black people could actually float on the water that I yelled it out loud from the car as we drove by. My mom reassured me that black people could swim if they knew how.

"If niggers can't swim," she said, "it's because they hadn't learned how."

"Oh," I said, learning something new. "Rex and Timmy and them told me they couldn't swim because the water wouldn't hold them up; something about a curse."

"I don't know why Dale hates niggers so much," she said, talking about her brother who was the cousins' father. "He'll let them believe anything, I reckon."

I had to realize that a lot of the things I heard about black people didn't jive with what I saw in them. It was inconsistent with my few experiences.

For instance, the taxi driver in Jess Rulam didn't fit the setting, not because he was black, but because Jess Rulam was so small, a taxi service was superfluous. Anybody could walk to every store in town in five minutes. Daddy told me he mostly drove old folks from store to store.

He also didn't fit being black either. He was invariably polite and friendly. When my dad and I walked past him on the street, he was always leaning against the taxi, reading a newspaper. Seeing us approaching, he lowered the paper, bent slightly at the waist, and greeted us with a warm smile, saying, "Good afternoon, Mr. Levy. I hope your day goes splendidly for you."

In fact, I found that most of the older black people I ever had any encounters with were also, to a fault, the most considerate and kind people I had yet to meet; much more so than the white people I knew. I came to the conclusion my cousins were full of shit. I liked black people. I couldn't wait for them to come to Jess Rulam. I knew the others in my class looked down on them, but not me. I knew that the black kids had to be the same kind of considerate and friendly people as the old ones I had the pleasure of meeting and knowing.

I was wrong.

* * *

Pete had just met up with me and John as we were heading to our new classroom. "Well, what do y'all think about these black kids?"

"I don't know." I shrugged like I had no opinion.

"I'm glad you didn't call 'em niggers," John said, whispering at me. "I'd hate to get the hell beat out of me the first day before I even make it to the classroom."

"Ah, they ain't gonna do nothing." Pete sounded overly confident. "They're scared to death of us."

Bart and Andy approached from behind and Philip, Thad, and Jude were ahead of us in a huddle, talking.

"There's not as many as I thought there'd be," said Jude.

"Most of 'em went to that big city school in Barclay," said Bart. "I'm glad of it too. I don't like niggers. Damn, I got to stop saying that word."

"Yeah, you'll get the hell beat out of me because they won't know which one of us said it," said John with a half-laugh. "They like to pick on the scrawniest," he added as a caveat.

"In that case, I'll get the hell beat out of me all day," I said. They all laughed. I didn't want to share the fact that I didn't think we had a thing to worry about because all the crap they heard about black people was bullshit.

"Where's big-ass Harold?" asked Pete.

"Big-ass Harold is standing behind you, you dumb-ass," said Harold, appearing suddenly. After a pause to look around and assess the situation, he came to a conclusion. "Oh boy, this is just what we need, more damn niggers."

"Shut up, Harold," John said in a loud whisper. "They won't do nothing to you, but they'll stomp the hell out of me and Matt."

"I swear to God, you get to be a bigger pussy every year, John," mused Harold. "Come on." Harold headed to our new room with us closely behind. Coach, who was now our fifth grade teacher, started calling roll. All the same gang was pretty much intact.

He called all Jess Rulam kids first and then he got to the black kids who had transferred from Orr:

"James Cater."

"Here." *Tall, wiry, flat face, long arms, lightning quick.*

"James Jones."

"Here." *Bigger, broader, heavily muscled, powerful, not as long arms.*

"James Anthony Jones."

"Here." *James Jones's brother—smaller, skinnier, lightning quick too.*

"James Earl Jones."

"Here." *Tall. Taller than Jesse, a beanpole, skinny neck.*

"We got three James Joneses," said Coach, startled. "Are you kin?"

"Brothers. I'm called Earl," the last James Jones said.

Brothers? I thought. *Three brothers in the same class? And they are all named James? What the hell?*

"OK," Coach chuckled, and continued calling the rest of the black kids.

"Shelia Gregory."

"Here." *Pretty black girl, well-dressed, proper looking.*

"Patricia Smalls."

"Here." *Ordinary, plain, nice smile, smart.*

"And Shirley Wells."

"Here." *Something wrong with her face; birth defect of some sort; proper, more proper than Patricia; probably smartest kid in the class; including the whites; not from this state; Michigan, I think.*

That was it—seven black kids in our class. Nothing like I imagined. I didn't see any problem. How could there be with only seven in the class, and three of them girls?

***

The recess bell rang, and Coach told us to watch ourselves. He had to go to the office and do some paperwork. I was wondering if we were going to play football, if Coach would quarterback, if the four black kids were going to play with us, and if they played, would the fact they looked five years older than us translate into them kicking the shit out of us?

Or, mainly, would there be any trouble on the playground? The three Jones brothers didn't look as nice as the *old* black people.

I was right.

"Which one of you whiteys wanna fight?" said James Cater, pushing Bart in the chest with his finger hard enough to move him backward.

When you imagine in your head that a bunch of black boys want to start a fight on the playground on the first day of school, even at the unsophisticated age of ten you don't *ever* picture it as simplistic, as in *which one of you whiteys wanna fight*, but these were not sophisticated times, and these were not sophisticated people.

"How about you?" His finger brushed across my cheek.

"Hey, leave me alone," I said, pushing his finger out of my face and backing up into the safety of the gang, which was about seven of us or so. I sure didn't want to fight him.

"You sho are a runt," he said with a snicker. "Hey, Jamo, come hea and look at dis hea little shit."

Jamo was the other James; I was the little shit.

"He done quit sucking his mama's tit too early," he said, laughing as if it were the funniest thing he ever said.

I stopped liking black people.

"What, none of you white-ass white boys will fight, will ye?" said Jamo, who strolled over to join in on the fun.

Damn! Everything they said about blacks was true. I mean niggers.

"Well, I guess we just gonna ha'f to make you our slaves looked to me like."

"Dey all lined up. Give 'em stooges slap," Jamo said, holding his hand in a slapping position. He was talking about *The Three Stooges,* where Moe would slap Curly and Larry multiple times, one after the other, in quick succession.

We were all pretty much in a straight line, shoulder to shoulder, except me. I was tucked in behind somebody, cowardly. James Cater went to the end of the line and, holding his palm at our face level, walked rapidly down the line, lightly slapping the first four faces until the arm belonging to the body on the fifth face took hold of his wrist with a powerfully tight grip.

"Keep your damn monkey hands off me, nigger," said Harold, with his teeth tightly clenched.

James Cater stood looking up at Harold, somewhat startled. He turned toward Jamo and pursed his lips mockingly. He quickly jerked his wrist away from Harold.

"Well, well, dis big-ass white boy done act like he gonna fight." Cater was walking back and forth up and down the line, shaking his head, looking down at the ground.

For a black boy that was just called a monkey and a nigger, and who had spent the previous five minutes doing everything within his power to provoke a fight, Cater was sure taking his time jumping on Harold's big white ass. I didn't blame him.

Even though they were older, and much bigger, and much more physically mature than the rest of us, Harold was as big and mean as they come and an imposing figure for anybody. To his credit, Harold didn't show any signs of fear.

Cater quickened his pace back and forth, back and forth, faster and faster. I didn't know if he was trying to work up his nerve because he was intimidated by Harold's size, or if he knew enough about white kids that he figured they wouldn't fight. I wondered if this show of Harold's courage threw off his plans, or if this was just a black thing that niggers did.

Cater suddenly stopped, turned in a millisecond, and rushed his face within two inches of Harold's chin, looking up at him and standing on his toes to do so.

"You think you a bad white boy, don't ya, white boy?!" Cater was spitting his words, and his eyes looked like a crazed psychotic madman. If that's what the pacing was for, it worked.

He stepped back and turned his head toward Jamo, mumbled something unintelligible, and clenched his right fist in a ball. I knew it was about to be on. He turned his head and was about to say something when Harold's fist landed flush on Cater's lips and blood splattered. I even noticed a drop of it on my shirt later when we returned to our classroom.

He staggered a couple of steps backward and fell back on his butt. In a flash he was back on his feet, coming straight at Harold. Harold swung wildly and landed a glancing blow as a cat-quick Cater turned his face slightly and the fist whizzed by. When Harold's momentum overextended him, Cater, like a blur, got behind him. He grabbed Harold's head, twisting it from side to side. Cater's forearm was lifting Harold's upper lip, exposing all his teeth. His mouth started to bleed. Cater, for the time being, had control of Harold.

I have said it once before, and I will say it again here—Harold Spartani was the strongest kid I had ever seen. Nobody was stronger as a child than Harold—nobody. He planted a foot just behind Cater's, took hold of both of Cater's arms, struggled into a new position, and body slammed Cater to the ground. It was so hard it sounded like a bag of fertilizer had dropped off the back of a pickup truck. Thwack!

Now Harold was on top, and in control, and I was in a quandary. I hated that bastard, Harold. Anybody else, anybody, and I would have loved to see them stomp his big, arrogant, hateful, smug ass. It would have made my year. I would have sung about it for weeks, wrote about it in class, told my kids about it for years and years, and if I could paint, do a portrait of it and hang it on my wall.

But now, for this one time, I found myself pulling for Harold. This of course means that I hated dumb-ass, stupid, nappy-headed, bully-ass jigaboos more than I hated Harold. In fact, I hoped he beat Cater's brains out, what few he had that is. But, as usual, I rarely got what I wanted in those days.

Harold was on top and started peppering Cater's face with both fists, but was missing most of the time. Cater's head was like trying to hit a sewing machine bobbin on high speed. I could see Harold tiring, and I could see that Cater had a lot of experience wrestling and fist fighting, probably with the Jones brothers.

In one explosive wrestling move, he flipped Harold over and completely swapped positions with him. Cater was now on top, flailing away. Harold was on the bottom, except Harold's head didn't move as fast as Cater's. He caught every blow flush on. When Cater tired of using both hands, he moved to the left of the dazed Harold and used his right fist over and over and over. Again and again he pounded away, even taking a second to rest, before pounding away a dozen more times.

Harold was in serious trouble. He stopped fighting back. His eyes were rolled back in his head with only the whites showing. Blood was pouring from his mouth and nose, but that didn't stop Cater. If anything, it only seemed to quicken his hatred for the white boy that almost beat his monkey-nigger ass the first day of school.

Even as big a coward as I was, I knew we had to stop this or Harold might die. Pete and Bart got the same idea and started to help, but Jamo stepped forward and roared, "Any of you white asses come any closer, and I'll plant your ass in the ground."

None of us came any closer. Jamo was a hell of lot bigger and badder than the relatively scrawny Cater. *If this smaller one is killing Harold, imagine what the big one could do to us,* I thought.

No teachers around. No one to stop this assault! This was so much worse than when Harold had beat the hell out of me that one time. All I could think of was that Harold was probably getting what he deserved, but did he need to die for it? From behind us a shadowy figure emerged and in a flash was standing over the two boys. Cater drew back his fist and a dark hand took hold of his wrist in a viselike grip. Cater struggled frantically, but couldn't move his fist even a quarter of an inch.

"Enough, brother," said Jesse calmly and quietly, never taking his eyes off Cater's.

Cater looked at Jesse with bewilderment. He tried to break the iron grip that clamped his wrist but could only move his elbow up and down. Realizing that moving his hand was futile, Cater got off Harold's chest and stood up. Jesse immediately let go.

"I ain't none your damn brother!" shouted Cater with the same baffled look on his face.

But I wouldn't be surprised if he isn't Jamo's brother. Everybody else in class is, I thought.

Jamo walked up to Jesse and bumped him with his chest. This fight didn't look like it would last long. Although Jesse was as tall as Jamo, maybe taller, he wasn't nearly as thick, and given Jesse's propensity to never defend himself, I had already resolved myself to the fact that Jesse would soon look like Harold, maybe worse.

Jesse stuck his hand in the middle of Jamo's chest, which prompted an amusing smile across Jamo's face as if Jesse had just signed his own death warrant. Jamo lifted both hands in the air, clasped his fingers together tightly, and came down like a two-handed club on Jesse's arm. The look on Jamo's face spoke volumes, for Jesse's arm did not move. Jesse's fingers wadded Jamo's shirt up into a clump and pulled him even closer to his face.

"Enough," he repeated, but a little louder and backed it with an earnest glare. Jamo looked fiercely into Jesse's eyes for an eternity—ten full seconds. He stopped his struggling.

Jesse let go of his shirt. Jamo and Cater looked at each other, turned and walked away quietly, alternating confounding glances at one another and throwing occasional shoulder shrugs.

Jesse turned and administered to the same boy, who in the same place, but at another time, had committed a similar assault on him. Harold struggled to his feet with help from Jesse's hand.

With Jesse on one side and me on the other and with Harold's arms draped over our shoulders, we helped him totter to the school's office.

CHAPTER 9

HAROLD RECOVERED FROM THE BEATING, and he also got over his inexplicable hatred of Jesse. I won't say they became close friends, but Harold was friendlier to Jesse now. Jesse wasn't hated as much by the others in the class either; just as with Harold, though, they were not friends, but friendlier. I think this was due, in no small part, to the contrast between Jesse and the three Jones brothers.

The black girls in our class, on the other hand, were rather meek and polite—a startling divergence from the boys. They all seemed to be the complete antithesis to James Cater and the Jones brothers. While the black boys were loud, illiterate, dumb-ass bullies, the girls were nice, studious, and pleasant to be around. I and everyone else in class got along with the black girls just fine.

More often than not, this is the case with girls. Nature has dealt rather generously with the fairer sex. Men have an innate predisposition to defend, to fight, to be jerks, to be impatient asses, to be slobs, and to be insufferable bores. Women, on the other hand, have an innate predisposition to be nurturing, to be loving, to be caring, to be patient, and to be the backbone. Fortunately for men, women's greatest asset of all is that God equipped them with a prefrontal cortex that irresistibly beckons them to mate with and bear a man's seed, and therefore, they are instinctively willing to tolerate the inadequacies of the stronger sex. If not for women's prefrontal cortex, we would all be extinct.

* * *

The school administration didn't take so kindly to the fight and subsequent beating. The two Jones brothers were suspended for a week. Harold didn't come back to school for two days.

When he returned, his face was as black as the faces of the ones he despised. It seemed to change him though, especially with Jesse. As I mentioned, he was friendlier to Jesse, and to me.

I can't say the same for Harold's dad or the rest of the town for that matter. The news of the beating spread like wildfire, and it didn't take long before the wildfire lit a fuse.

"And so, friends, we now have the nigred children from the Orr School attending Jess Rulam School with the white children," said Pastor Scott, peering at the back corner of Willow Creek Baptist Church, looking at no one in particular.

I couldn't get out of going again. Sometimes Mama would make me go, sometimes she wouldn't. This was one of the times she did.

"Well, what are we to do about this?" He stopped peering at the corners of the building and started making eye contact.

"Should we throw our hands up in the air and run around? 'Oh the nigreds are coming, the nigreds are coming,' " he said in a mocking kind of way, running back and forth across the dais. He was demonstrating how ignorant that would be.

"No, I don't think so. That would perpetuate your anxiety over this situation." A more serious tone replaced the jollity of his previous statement.

"Now, I know that one of the white boys in fifth grade got a good beating by some of the nigred boys and sustained some injuries. And I know they were older boys; older than the boy that got the beating," he said, bouncing his hands in front of him like he was about to make a serious point.

He continued with a chuckle, "But you have to figure that the first or second day, any bunch of kids that are being thrown in school together like this, well, it's just natural they are going to find out who's toughest. Don't you remember what it was like the first day of school? Didn't we have to find out who's toughest?"

The pastor went on, sounding very philosophical. "Now, your nigred child is no different from your white child in many respects. They learn what they are taught at home, right?" He was nodding his head for approval from the congregation.

"If they hear the stories from their mamas, daddies, aunts and uncles, granddaddies and grandmamas over and over about how bad they were treated by the white man, well, you can fill in the rest for yourself." He was almost convincing me, but only for a minute. I wondered how the rest of the congregation felt.

The young pastor was from Tennessee. He was only about thirty and well liked around our community. His impassioned sermon was an attempt to squash the rumblings ricocheting all over the countryside. He made me feel a little better, for the moment anyway.

* * *

After the service was over, Mama was talking to a gaggle of her friends, as usual. I started back to the car so I could impatiently wait the eternity—ten minutes—for her, and then we could finally go home. On my way, Gerald Watson stuck his hand out. He and six or seven other men from the church were huddled in a circle in the parking lot. Most had their arms folded.

"Well, Matt, how's school going this year?" Gerald was fifty-five or -six and was one of the deacons of the church. He was one of the most respected men in the community, and everybody looked up to him, including me.

"It's going OK, I reckon." I usually didn't have much to say around grownups.

"I heard you was in on that fight at school the other day," said one of the men, fishing for details.

"Naw, I was just watching it."

"I heard them niggers jumped on all y'all," said another man with some surprise.

"Naw, mostly just Harold."

"Dern near beat him to death, didn't they?" said yet another man looking for me to confirm.

"Well, one of 'em did."

"We heard it was three of them niggers jumped on one boy," said Gerald with a little puzzlement.

"No, it was only two, but only one of 'em really fought."

"We hear he's gonna be in the hospital for a couple of weeks. Is he gonna be all right, you reckon?" asked Gerald, genuinely concerned.

"He's back in school now." I was starting to wonder where they had heard all this.

"So, he's talking and everything?" another one of the men asked.

"His face is black and blue and bruised and stuff, but he's all right." I wanted to put some truth back into this. The men seemed surprised to hear what I said.

"Well, you keep a watch out for them nigger boys, and don't let 'em catch you off to yourself at school now, you hear?" advised Gerald with real anxiety as I started walking toward our car. I nodded at him.

Mama was carrying some kind of platter out of the church, and we walked along beside each other. Neither Daddy nor my sister came with us this morning, so it was just me and her.

"I tell you, Matt, those nigger boys have steered things up. I didn't know they was four or five of them that jumped on y'all. I tell you, we're gonna do something about this." She was clearly upset.

"Mama, I told you what happened! There was two of 'em! Two," I said vehemently, holding up two fingers.

"That's not what they told me in there." Mama was shaking her head and all the while walking faster and faster to the car. "That school's gonna do something about this. You'll be next."

I gave up and got in the car. The news was definitely out.

A bunch of damn niggers had beaten up a white boy!

I started wondering if the other churches out in the countryside preached the same messages as Pastor Scott. Surely they did, that was their job—to preach love, understanding, and forgiveness. That's what the Bible was all about. I learned that in Sunday school, and the preachers had to preach what was in the Bible. I felt better the more I thought about it. Preachers were men of God and had to do what was right.

* * *

Most preachers from the other kinds of churches in town did not walk Pastor Scott's walk. They were in a lather.

"What we have here is an abomination. You understand that, right?" Preacher Surratt told his congregation at the New Harmony Methodist Church. The congregation nodded in agreement and "yes, yes," was murmured softly.

"I truly believe that the radicals in Washington and the elitist in control of our institution are forcing the blacks to come to white schools for the sole purpose of having only one race." The pastor stopped from time to time to wipe the perspiration from his upper lip with a white handkerchief.

"They want the blacks and whites to intermarry and produce all mulatto and high-yeller children. And those children are to intermarry with more whites until they have bred the nigger out of niggers, so to speak," he said with a cocked smile and a pause to let the laughs die away.

"Now, don't get me wrong here. There are some good, decent black folks out there. All of you know some good black people. But they are all old black folks. This new generation is altogether different."

The preacher's voice started to get loud again.

"They don't have any raising whatsoever. Take those five stralloping nigger boys that jumped on and almost killed that poor little white boy at school a few days ago. This is clear evidence that whites and blacks should not be going to the same schools."

At the same time, Preacher Roy Cagle was railing at Oak Hill Baptist Church. He was an old-style Southern preacher called a "ha preacher." When in the thralls of being moved by the Holy Spirit, he'd end the last word of a sentence, or a phase, or sometimes anywhere, with "ha." "We have children that want to rebel'ha against us and authority and against God Almighty'ha. Church, we don't need any more troubles'ha, no obstacles between us and the Lord Almighty'ha.

"But we can be thankful'ha, that the Lord has protective hands over us'ha, as long as we try to live in accordance of His will and righteousness'ha. That's why I'm telling you, Church'ha, that God's mighty hand is not only going to stop protecting us'ha, but is about to smote us down'ha, if we don't do something about the blacks that the United States government has turned loose on us'ha.

"They have already ganged up and beat one of ours unconscious and near death'ha. It is up to us, the people of God'ha, to let them know that we won't stand idly by while our schools are being taken over by a bunch of savages'ha. That God has put his mark on them to show that they are not to be trusted by man'ha. All that evil needs to spread all over our country is for good men to do nothing'ha."

* * *

Folks left church pretty agitated, and gathered up later that Sunday to talk about what the preachers were sayin'.

A bunch of the men were at Dennis Morgan's house: Pete's father, Jimmy Greenwood; Bart's father, Randy Adams; Jude's father,

Dewayne Dixon; Andy's father, Harvey Lykes; and Julius Spartani, Harold's father, called Jules. They were drinking beer.

The atmosphere started out light, like it had every Sunday afternoon for the last seven years. The members changed from Sunday to Sunday, depending on how many could get away from their wives. The atmosphere today, however, was becoming increasingly thick.

"What do you reckon we ought to do about them niggers, Jules?" Harvey Lykes thought this was the appropriate question to ask the man whose son was the victim of the beating.

"Nothing."

"Nothin'?!" Randy Adams couldn't believe that. He must have consumed too many beers already, because he'd swear that Jules Spartani, who was known as the biggest hothead in Jess Rulam, had just said he didn't want anything done to those savaging niggers.

"Yeah, I don't want y'all to do nothing. I'll take care of this little problem myself." Jules was staring straight ahead at the wall with no expression on his face.

"Well, Jules, you know that we'll help you," said Randy, sensing he needed to be suddenly virtuous.

"Why, yeah, we're not going to let you take on all them bunch of damn niggers by yourself. What do you think we are?" said Dennis, disturbed by the implication that they might not be up to the task.

"I know you guys would help me, but this is something I just gotta do myself," Jules said without taking his eyes off the wall. He was tormented.

"I don't doubt you could handle the nigger boys that beat up Harold, Jules, but the rest of 'em will be a little harder to handle by yourself," said Jimmy Greenwood, garrulously.

"Jimmy's right, Jules. You beat the hell out of them boys and you'll have every nigger in Jess Rulam after you," Randy said with annoyance. He wanted to show up Jules's foolishness.

"Maybe you're right." Jules put his bottle on the floor and sat up straight in his chair. "I'll probably need some help from you and maybe the whole town," he said with appreciation.

"What should we do to get even with them and teach 'em a lesson?" asked Dewayne respectfully.

"Kill 'em," seethed Jules contemptuously.

"Kill 'em!" Dewayne said with amused dismay.

"Yeah," Jules said matter-of-factly, sliding back down in his chair. He took another sip of beer and resumed staring at the wall.

The other men in the room looked at each other, shocked, amused, and concerned. Shocked their friend had suggested the murder of children. Amused their friend had suggested the murder of *black* children, and concerned that he *meant it.*

* * *

Early evening that same day, two locals in a pickup stopped at the only red light in Jess Rulam.

"Hey, Bobby, look at them two nigger boys over here." Lucky Colbert was pointing with a fluttering finger at two black boys who were ten or eleven years old. They were walking playfully toward The Hill, where most of the black people lived, without much concern about their surroundings or the goings-on.

"Why, Robert Coker, I do believe that these hea nigger boys might be the ones that beat the hell out of that kid at school," Lucky mocked.

"What are we gonna do about them yard apes that jumped that kid at school?" Bobby had an unnerving look about him.

Bobby Coker was a big, raw-boned, mean son of a bitch with a face well scarred from acne and about ten thousand fights. He was a the-more-beer-he-had-in-him-the-meaner-he-got type. You've seen them. Every town has them. Jess Rulam was well populated with them.

Lucky was not hardly as big, nor hardly as mean, and didn't get hardly as drunk. But he figured that hanging around with Bobby gave him more stature to make up for those character defects. Lucky was more of a talker than a doer; Bobby was more of a doer than a talker.

"Follow along side of 'em. Let's see where they're going, Bobby." Lucky saw an opportunity here.

"You really think those are the niggers that beat up that boy." Bobby was starting to get interested.

"I don't know, but I do know for sure, them be niggers." Lucky laughed devilishly. He was almost giddy.

Bobby pulled his truck alongside the two boys, idling along at the same speed as the now quickening paces of the two scared youths.

Lucky rolled his window down and said kind of loud to overcome the rumble of five hundred horsepower, "Where y'all going? Maybe we can give y'all a lift." He was using the impersonation again.

The two frightened boys took off in a dead sprint for the safety of The Hill. Bobby maneuvered the massive vehicle directly behind them, two wheels on the curb, and two wheels off the curb, and began accelerating. He was within two feet of the frantically screaming black boys. They were weaving in and out to avoid being run over. Bobby was masterfully managing to match each weave, zig, and zag, and actually bumped the butt of one of the boys, who almost lost his balance. That would mean a crushing death under the massive tires.

The boys could see the entrance to The Hill. They cut across the road and sped up the long drive as fast as their adrenaline-pumped legs could carry them. This community was known to the white people of Jess Rulam as Nigger Hill. Bobby pulled the loud, rumbling truck up the steep incline into The Hill's driveway only about fifty feet or so and then stopped. He and Lucky were laughing raucously. They thought this the perfect time to pop the top on a couple of Pabst Blue Ribbons.

Within two minutes, three angry black men came storming down the roadway toward the truck. They seemed to be around thirty years old and dressed well for the area. Two of them wielded wooden baseball bats. One held his up and the other had it down to his side. The other man was unarmed.

Bobby and Lucky could see and hear the outraged black men rapidly approaching. Bobby remained perfectly calm and thought the bat-carrying men rather humorous. Lucky wasn't so mellow. "Put this thing in reverse, and let's get the hell out of here, Bobby!" screamed a hysterical Lucky. "They're going to beat the hell out of us!"

"Will you relax? They're just a bunch of niggers." Bobby was so calm, he sounded philosophical.

"A bunch of niggers with bats!" Lucky was looking behind him, contemplating making a run for it if Bobby didn't start the truck moving.

Suddenly, Bobby got out of the safety of the vehicle. He calmly walked in front of the Dodge and propped himself against the hood with his arms crossed.

"What you niggers want?" he said in a low tone, completely unafraid.

The men were shocked at the brazenness of this white hick.

"What the hell you mean trying to run down those two boys awhile ago! You crazy!" The one with the hoisted bat took a step closer.

"We were just having a little fun. What's the fuss?" Bobby stuck a cigarette in his mouth and coolly lit it. He slowly reached behind his back and pulled out a long-barreled Smith & Wesson .44 stuck under his belt. He pointed it at the man with the raised bat.

"Hey, ain't you bunch of natives supposed to be carrying spears or some shit like that?" Bobby had a cocky half-smile.

The man with the raised bat slowly lowered it. He looked at the other two men with disappointment rather than fear.

The group stood and stared at one another with hatred. No one spoke. Everyone was waiting for someone else to make the next move.

In about a minute, a police car came sliding into the drive. Seeing the man with a gun and the men with the bats, Jess Rulam Police Chief Jerry Upton blasted his siren for about ten seconds. He turned the loud, echoing noisemaker back off and calmly got out of the vehicle.

Jerry Upton was a man of about fifty; tall, muscular with an athletic build. He was known to be in great cardiovascular shape and have unshakable nerve.

It was reported that the Sheriff once got a call that a black man on The Hill caught his wife with another man and promptly sliced his skull in two with an axe. Witnesses say the Sheriff calmly walked into the house of the distraught axe wielder, gently put his hand on his shoulder, and with the other hand, took the axe. The account says he calmly walked the killer to the car and never even removed his pistol from its holster.

"They reported you were trying to run over some kids, Bobby. Is that right?" The Sheriff leaned one hand on the hood of the Dodge right beside Bobby Coker's propped backside.

"We were just playing, Sheriff. We weren't really trying to run over 'em." Bobby sounded apologetic.

"I guess you were just playing with that .44 in your hand there?" The Sheriff wore a playful smile but was not amused.

"These niggers here was going to kill us with those bats they got in their hands. I was just defending myself, Sheriff." Bobby was getting agitated.

"Imagine somebody getting upset because some idiot was trying to run over their kids in a pickup truck. You reckon they need therapy?" The Sheriff was no more than six inches from Bobby's face and getting a little agitated himself.

"Give me that gun and turn around, Bobby, NOW!" The Sheriff said the last word warningly. The blood drained out of Bobby's face. He complied with the pissed-off Sheriff's instructions. He knew the cop would shoot his ass in a second.

The Sheriff handcuffed Bobby's hands behind him and roughly put him in the backseat of the police car. He motioned for Lucky to drive Bobby's truck to the station saying, "You can keep your buddy company in jail for a few days, Lucky, since you like to hang around him so much."

Lucky did not look amused.

Sheriff Upton walked up to the black men and said apologetically, "Boys will be boys and assholes will be assholes." The men shook his hand warmly and walked away with a sense of justification.

This incident quieted the talk about the Harold Spartani beating for a while but spawned a new conversation starter: *That nigger-loving Sheriff we got.* Nevertheless, no one got beat up for a while.

CHAPTER 10

TWO WEEKS HAD PASSED SINCE the beating of Harold Spartani. James Cater and Jamo Jones were scheduled to arrive back to class from the two-week suspension that very Monday morning.

We never said anything to Harold about the beating, nor did he to us. We figured that when he wanted to talk about it, he would. Everyone knew that James Cater and Jamo were supposed to return to school that morning. The suspense left the atmosphere thick with anticipation.

The bell rang, and we all scurried to our seats and waited for roll call as usual. No James Cater or Jamo Jones. I think everyone assumed the principal or county superintendent had decided to extend the suspension indefinitely or maybe to expel the two boys all together. Neither was the case.

Ten minutes after class started, there were a couple of knocks on the door. It opened quickly. In walked James Cater and Jamo Jones, followed by Mr. Andrew Biggs, the vice principal of Jess Rulam. He was the principal of Orr school before it closed.

Principal Biggs was about sixty with mostly gray hair. He carried himself with distinction and a businesslike air. He suffered no fools, but there was always pleasantness about him. I hadn't seen him much, but what I knew of him, I liked.

He put both arms on the two boys' shoulders and addressed Coach Harrison. "Mr. Harrison, these boys would like to say something to the class, with your permission."

"Sure, go ahead," said Coach, more than a little surprised.

"Um, I would like to say, um, I'm sorry for what I did, and um, it won't be happening no mo'," said James Cater nervously. He stared down at the floor and never looked up.

"I would also like to say that I am sorry too," said Jamo, also nervous, but looking up and toward Harold. "I won't ever start any mo' troubles with anybody in here from now on."

"Very good, boys," said Mr. Biggs sharply. "Now would Harold Spartani please come up to the front for a moment?"

"Come on up here, Harold," said Coach warmly, catching on to what was happening as he moved alongside the two boys and Principal Biggs.

We could tell Harold was embarrassed. He reluctantly got up from his desk and slowly shuffled toward the front to join the others. He nervously put his hands in and out of his pockets as if he didn't know what to do with them.

"I'm sorry, Harold, for—" James Cater was cut off.

"Look up at him," said Principal Biggs warningly.

"I'm sorry for what I did to you and, ah, um—"

"Keep your head up," said the principal irritably.

"I want you to, um, forgive me for what I did too." Cater put his head back down when he was finished with his speech.

"Your turn." The principal seemed satisfied with Cater and was patiently waiting for Jamo.

Jamo walked a little closer to Harold, who was staring at the floor but looked up at Jamo when he noticed his movement.

"I'm sorry for all this stuff we did to you, Harold," said Jamo guiltily with moistening eyes. "This has been tormenting me for the longest time."

Jamo stuck his hand out, and Harold mechanically shook it. I believe that James "Jamo" Jones was genuinely sorry. I couldn't say the same for James Cater.

Everybody took their seats. Principal Biggs smiled at the class warmly as he whirled around and left the room. There was a collective sigh.

* * *

It was lunch break, and after taking our plates and utensils, we found a place where the gang could sit together, as much as possible anyway. It was a queer thing that in lunchrooms, territorial chair claims were never respected.

The fifth grade had a certain area where we could sit, but in no particular order. We had to sit in the same desk in class each day, but it was a free-for-all in the lunchroom, and the gang was periodically scattered about. There were a limited number of seats at the fifth grade table, just enough chairs for our class and no more.

As fate would have it, the empty chair beside me was taken by Jamo Jones. He was searching for an empty spot and rushed to take this one while the getting was good. Cater took a chair on the opposite side from us and down two chairs, between Bart and Lori Samples.

I felt uncomfortable, even more so than when a girl sat beside me. I tried to ignore Jamo. I started eating and saying innocuous things to Pete, who was sitting beside me when Jamo tapped me on the arm with his elbow, trying to get my attention.

"Hmm?" I acknowledged him and waited for him to speak.

"I'm sorry about the fight the other day. Your name be Matt, right?"

"Yeah, I'm Matt." I was floored by his warm sincerity. "And you're Jamo, is that right?" I was trying to show sincerity myself.

"Yeah, that be what they call me, but you fellows call me James. That's my real name. My daddy give it to me," he said, smiling.

"How many of y'all named James in your family?" Pete sensed the friendliness and decided to join in with a legitimate question. I wanted to know too.

"All of us, I mean all the boys are. My daddy's name be James, so he named us all after hisself. I'm James the fourth. They be six of us boys," he said affectionately.

"How do you know which one is which when your name is called?" Bart asked curiously.

"Well, we all got nicknames we go by. I'm Jamo, and there's Spooner, and Earl, and so forth. You see what I mean?" He was looking at Bart and me to make sure we understood.

"My granddaddy came by to see me while I was out of school for my punishment for what me and him did to y'all fellows." He nodded toward Cater.

"My grand told me that what we done hurt all black peoples around here. He say, 'Boy, what you did was an abomination to all black folks for a hundred miles around here.'

"He say, 'Now dem white peoples gonna be madder than a hornet over this. They gonna takes it out on every black folk they see out and about. You done steered them hornets up that carry big stingers with 'em.' "

Jamo, I mean James, chuckled slightly as he was finishing, shaking his head understandingly. "I never thought of it like that before. My grand could always say things that could get me to feeling sorry sometimes ... Hey!" James said excitedly. "Could I tell y'all a story about my grand at recess?"

"Sure."

"Fine."

"OK with me." The three of us shook our heads in agreement.

James went on, "I told my grand that I didn't want dem bunch of white boys to thinks they could run over us, and I especially wanted dem to knows from da first day. I told him, I say, 'I want dem to see dat it was gonna be the other way around, that we was gonna be the boss of them around hea.' We was trying to show how bad we was an' showing off, I guess," James said gloomily staring, at his food.

I was startled by his elegant apology. It was not at all what I was expecting, not after what I saw of him the first day. I was even a little anxious to hear about his grand, as he called him. I looked at Pete and Bart to see their reaction. They had the same kind of amused look that I had.

Cater, however, didn't have the same countenance as James. He heard every word that James had said at the table, but never acknowledged anything one way or the other. He just solemnly ate his lunch and occasionally looked up, irritably.

* * *

A huge thunderstorm had visited the night before. The playing field was soggy with puddles of water scattered about. Coach reluctantly allowed us to go outside at recess with the instructions that we were to stay up toward the front, close to the entrance of the school, and stay out of the wet parts. The gang gathered by the four crossties, which served as a flowerbed and our seats for when we weren't playing football.

We saw James spot us and meander over. Cater looked reluctant to follow but had nothing else to occupy himself with. What else could he do, sit with the girls?

"Well, I'm going to tell you about my grand. That's what we've always called him. His name is Reverend Elijah Smith. Does y'all want to hear about my old granddaddy? 'Cause if y'all don't, I won't tell it then." James was kind of defensive, because he didn't know white people and wondered if they cared enough to listen.

Everyone either nodded yes or shrugged indifferently. I think most of them were like me, mollifyingly interested.

"Well, my grand is eighty-something years old. He was born in the nineteen eight hundreds." I knew what he meant.

"He was the son of a slave family. He wasn't no slave or nothing hisself, but his daddy and his mama was, you see. He said when he was a boy growing up, they was under them Jim Crow's Law and something he called the Black Code, or something like that.

"He say white folks wasn't nice to black folks then as they is today. He say a bunch a mean white men get drunk from time to time and hang the nearest black man they could find fo' no good reason, just to be doing something.

"He say they sure had a hard time in dem days."

James went on to tell us the story he was told.

* * *

"You go in first, then I'll come in right behind you."

"What's wrong with you going in first?"

"You're the one with the dime and a girl with a sweet tooth."

Elijah and Benny, both black, were trying to get up the nerve to go into Walsh's Candy Shop. It was the only business in Selma, Alabama, that sold candy, it and Downey Drug store, but the drugstore was out of the question.

A black man had been accused of touching some fine imported silk cloth just put on a spool inside the drugstore. He was summarily beaten and put in jail. From then on, if blacks wanted medicine, for example, they had to find a white person to make the purchase for them.

Selma, Alabama, in 1906 was just a small, poor town. It was close to Montgomery, which was its only redeeming quality. Most of the blacks in Selma were uneducated. Most of the blacks were poor. *All* of the blacks were terrified of the Ku Klux Klan.

There were black restaurants and white restaurants, a black hotel and a white hotel, a black grocery store and a white grocery store. You name it, if it was a business, there was one for whites and one for blacks, except for drugstores and candy stores.

It was rumored, however, that Mr. Walsh sold some black women some candy because their children were pressing their little black faces against the windows and smudging them up with saliva. Walsh figured it was easier than washing the huge plate-glass window front.

The dilemma for Elijah and Benny at the present time was they couldn't remember if Walsh let the women enter the store, or if they knocked and the storekeeper came outside to sell them the prized candy.

Nevertheless, candy was sold to black people, and Benny had a new girlfriend named Beatrice, and she talked endlessly about the new candy store.

* * *

Elijah Smith and Benny Jackson were best friends. They worked at the sawmill together. Their biggest ambition in life was to save up enough money between them to purchase a brand new 1906 Ford Model N.

It was an open-air type, no enclosure, with a seat that could fit four people, not so comfortably, but it was perfect to haul two fine ladies in nonetheless. They retailed for seven hundred and sixty-seven dollars at Montgomery Ford Automobile and Tractor Company. They would be known as the only black men in Selma, Alabama, with an automobile.

Elijah had pictured himself behind the wheel of a shiny red Model N ever since he saw that fancy white dude and his fancy white woman drive down Main Street the previous year, tooting his horn and putting on all kinds of fancy airs. He had to wait until the car passed before looking directly at the white woman, of course. It was unhealthy to do otherwise. He thought to himself that this was the way to live—a fancy-schmancy white-people lifestyle.

He often let swanky white people get into his head. He hated to admit it, but he also saw himself as a fancy white dude with a fancy white girlfriend. He wasn't ashamed that he was black, it's just that he would like to have been born white. Elijah would sometimes catch a nap under the big water oak tree by the mill during lunch breaks. His heavy eyes flashed scenes of himself with his fancy white tuxedo with his fancy white woman, all beautiful with all those locks of golden-blond hair and pretty white teeth.

The maître d' bows politely as the door of the fancy white restaurant opens for him and he and his fancy white woman are ceremoniously escorted to the best table in the joint.

The waiter is acting—what's that new fancy white man's word he heard the other day, oh yeah, "obsequiously"—trying to earn himself a big tip for acting so fancy. The waiter wins, and Elijah decides to patronize him accordingly and reaches inside his fancy white tux and gently removes the bulging white man's wallet full of white man's money.

"Here you are, my good man," he says in his fancy white man's voice as he is trying to fold the bulging wallet back together.

Elijah wakes up from his dream, his eyes slowly opening.

He fixes his stare on the water oak tree's branches. He looks slowly down his body and catches sight of the back of his very brown hands. The harsh reality rushes upon him, and he realizes who he is.

That was the only thing he hated about dreaming—having to wake up.

* * *

"I think there's a white woman in there, Benny," said Elijah with a loud whisper, taking hold of Benny's hand to keep him from entering a store when a white lady was present. The consequences of looking the wrong way at white women in 1906 Alabama could be deadly.

"It's all right, 'Lij. We ain't going in till she leaves." Benny repositioned himself nonchalantly by the door, leaning against the storefront while patiently waiting for the white woman to leave.

"Why don't we just knock, Benny? Damn, I don't like this." Elijah was starting to lose his nerve.

"I done told you I wanted to see all them flavors so I can pick her out the right one just for her," Benny said irritably.

"Why don't we just leave and come back just before closing time so they won't be nobody in there?" Elijah was getting more and more nervous standing in front of an all-white people's store.

Benny looked at Elijah contemptuously. "'Cause we already standing here now, that's why."

Just then the candy store door flew open and the white woman was suddenly standing at the door, glaring at the two black men.

Again, for a black man in the 1906 South, there was a right way and a wrong way NOT to look at a white woman. The correct way was to slowly and unobtrusively turn away from whatever direction the white woman was approaching and stare down at the ground with your hands behind your back until she safely passed by. That was the respectful way to do it.

This would prevent the uncontrollable black-savage urge to snatch the white woman off to the woods and viciously rape her. This of course would render the white woman dead to society. She would be *ruined*. The exact wrong way to do it was precisely the very way they *did* do it.

They stared startled at the woman for at least three seconds and then suddenly turned their backs. When she was gone, they looked at each other worriedly, but quickly went inside the store anyway.

Inside, they were amazed at the colorful jars full of candy. There was shelf after shelf of peppermint stick candy and cherry stick candy, and grape stick candy, and cinnamon stick candy. They were awed by the soda fountain with the enormous brass handle. They had never seen anything like it in person, only in magazines.

Mr. Walsh was surprisingly courteous and let Benny pick out just what he wanted—ten cents worth of cherry stick candy, which was a bag completely full. They left before anyone else came in and were gone down the street, happy they had accomplished a successful mission. Benny's new girlfriend was going to be surprised and very impressed by this sweet present.

Elijah walked with Benny all the way to his door and then went on to his own house, sucking on a piece of cherry stick candy and thinking sweet thoughts.

* * *

"Elijah, get up! Get up, son, something terrible has happened." Elijah's mother was frantic and crying.

"What's the matter, Mama?" Elijah was drowsy.

"Somebody knocked on the door a few minutes ago and said they done lynched your friend."

"No! Them damn bastards. No!"

Elijah threw on some trousers and a shirt and tore in a dead sprint out the door.

"Don't go down there, son! They'll kill you too!" Elijah's mother was screaming and bawling at the same time.

Elijah could see the light from the torches and the fire half a mile away. He came to a sudden stop as he turned onto Buford Street. His eyes were transfixed on the charred body of his best friend, Benny, gently swinging back and forth in the cool autumn night breeze. What was once a large fire beneath him had died down to a smoldering red glow.

"I make you a promise, I make you a promise, my friend," Elijah repeated with a clenched jaw, fighting back tears.

No one had to tell him what had happened. No explanation was necessary. He knew what it was, and what it was about, and that an innocent young man had died a horrifying death for nothing. All the plans he had made were gone. All the rides through the streets in the new fancy car that they were going to buy together were gone. All he had, all he ever was going to have, and all he ever was going to be, was gone. And for what? Because he had looked at a white woman?

* * *

James wrapped things up. We sat transfixed.

"My grand say he always wonder why they didn't get him too." James's eyes were moist, and they glistened in the afternoon sun.

"He say he stay awake at night wondering if they gonna come get him and lynch him the same way. He figure that woman couldn't figure out who he be was the only reason them Ku Klux Klan didn't ever get him too." James was staring at the ground and had to wipe a tear away.

I looked around at the rest of the gang to see what they thought of James's story, but they all had their eyes hidden. I figured out what they thought.

"I would like to tell y'all at little more about my grand tomorrow, if that's OK with you fellows."

"Sure, James, we can meet right here tomorrow," I said, hiding my eyes too because they were a little moist as well.

Then I bumped right into Jesse, who was actually crying. He walked over beside James and put his arm around his shoulder and said softly, "I'd surely love to hear more 'bout your grand tomorrow, James. He sounds like quite a fellow." James looked at Jesse warmly and nodded his head.

CHAPTER 11

JAMES'S SYMPATHETIC STORY ABOUT HIS grandfather stirred the hearts of all the gang members that had listened to it. Even Harold didn't say anything bad about it, which means it pulled at his heartstrings too.

The beating had changed Harold. He definitely wasn't the same person. He was quieter, and strangely, nicer now. I could only speculate that this new Harold was born because his status in the gang was diminished. He was once the undisputed leader that everyone was afraid to challenge; now he was beaten and disgraced.

He had the same great size as before. He had the same great strength as before. He looked the same and sounded the same, but curiously, he carried himself differently. His look, not necessarily his appearance, was different. I think one would say, in literary terms anyway, that his personage had changed. He seemed to me to take shorter strides, and his arms didn't swing back and forth as much.

In other words, Harold's confidence was shot. When years of accumulated pride and confidence are wiped away in a matter of minutes, is this the end result? Do you become less all over? I often wondered what he was thinking about behind those darkened, and now blank, eyes.

Meanwhile, I was looking forward to class the next day. I was curious as to what everyone thought of the new and improved James Jones.

* * *

"What did you think about Jamo or James or whatever we're supposed to call him now?" I asked Pete as we were walking into the schoolhouse. Everybody walks *into* a school building much slower then they walk *out* of one. I would imagine the same thing could be said about prisons.

"I kinda liked his old grand or granddaddy or pawpaw or what did he call him?" Pete asked. I think he was trying to act like he didn't enjoy the story as much as he did. I knew kinda how he felt.

I mean this was the same guy that had threatened to kill us a couple of weeks ago if we tried to save Harold from Cater beating him to death. Were we supposed to forget all that because his grandfather's friend got strung up by a bunch of drunken KKK killers?

"He called him 'Grand.' You call your granddaddy 'Pawpaw.' I've heard you do it," I said teasingly.

"I do, don't I?" Pete was smiling affectionately.

"Y'all hold up a damn minute. Shit." Bart was trying to catch up with us.

"Quit damn cussing, Bart," shushed John as he joined our slow march to the dreaded classroom.

"Your damn mouth is gonna get our damn asses busted." John was serious, not realizing what he was saying.

"I told my mama and them about that story last night, and they said they heard of that Reverend Smith guy, you know, ol' Elijah, what's-his-name's granddaddy he was telling us about yesterday." Bart had some excitement in his voice.

"How come they heard of him before, Bart?" I was curious about that old black man.

"Mama said she read about him in the paper before. Something about civil rights or marching or something like that, I think." Bart was unconcerned about the why, only that somebody knew of him.

"Well, I'm sure it's still too wet to play football again, so I guess we can hear more from James," said Pete mechanically.

* * *

At recess, we all took our positions at the crossties just like the day before. And just like yesterday, here came James, with Cater following along meekly as if he still didn't know what to do. The audience was set and the orator had arrived.

"Well, like I was telling you fellers yesterday, my grand done been in a lot of scraps with some mean-ass white peoples. He say them peoples from fifty or sixty or a hundred years ago was mean. He say some of these white folks today are just as mean and hateful as they was back then, they just not as apt to kill you.

"My grand had a incidence four or five years ago. He say the days of Martin Luther King and the marches was something."

James went on to tell us about his grand and the march.

* * *

"How long do you think they'll keep putting these damn letters in your mailbox, Daddy?" Mary, Reverend Elijah Smith's daughter, asked angrily.

"Well, I guess until they get tired of writing them and get tired of spending the money to drive over here ever' night is my guess, child," said Elijah in his customary nonchalant, mollifying manner.

Over seventy-five years of battling unimaginable hatred—and that's the correct word for it, the word "racism" just adds water to weaken its proof—had softened the now frail old man. His voice never got above a whisper anymore, almost a soft murmur.

"Well, how long before they ratchet it up a notch and do more than just leave ugly notes in your mailbox? Dammit, Daddy, I wish you hadn't went to that damn stupid-ass march!" Mary was scared for her father, but over the years familiarity mitigated the surprise of it.

"They gonna do what they gonna do, and I'm gonna do what I'm gonna do, and that's just all there is to it, child. If they didn't scare me when I had a lot of life left to burn, they shore as hell ain't gonna scare me now that I don't have much wick left."

Elijah and Mary were talking about the civil rights march of March 7, 1965, when Elijah and hundreds of others had attempted to begin their walk from Selma to Montgomery.

Elijah and some friends had got involved in the Dallas County Voters League to register voters back in 1963. Dallas County was majority black, and the Klan was pissed that the voting might not go their way.

The rally on March 7 was nicknamed "Bloody Sunday." The first marchers endured the state and local police wielding billy clubs, turning loose vicious German shepherds, and even using teargas on them. Elijah received over thirty stitches from the dog bites.

Elijah and his friends wrote to Dr. Martin Luther King Jr. to assist them on their next demonstration, scheduled for March 21. They were determined to make it to Montgomery or die. The Klan was determined that they wouldn't complete the march and would die.

"I'm glad we had that march, child. And we're gonna have another one in just a little while." Elijah was as defensive as he got, which wasn't much.

"Daddy, you got torn to shreds by a bunch of police dogs. *Police!*" Mary was trying to reason with him, knowing he hadn't fully recovered from the dog attack.

Just then, a faint knock on the door interrupted Mary's plea.

"See who it is, Mary," said Elijah.

"I'm scared to."

"Aw, go on, child. The Lord protects dried-up old shells of men like me."

Mary opened the door to a rather nervous and somewhat shaky white boy of about thirteen. A black pickup truck was parked along the curb across from Elijah's house.

"I have a message for Elijah Smith," said the youngster loudly. His fear was causing him to shout. It was obvious he was more or less forced to be the messenger, perhaps from a dare or the pressure from his superiors, or simply because of a questioning of his manhood. They started them out young in the Klan in Dallas County, Alabama.

"Come in, young man, come in," said Elijah warmly as he made his way to the door. He sensed the youth was terrified and probably acting against his will. "Come in here and set with us for a spell and tell us what's on your mind. Mary, see if we have a Coke in the refrigerator. Would you like a Coca-Cola, young man?"

Elijah had his arm around the kid's shoulder, escorting him to the couch. Not expecting this reception and too scared not to accept the invitation, the young white boy reluctantly obliged.

"Set down here and relax young man. My house is your house," he said with his usual warm, quiet tone. Mary handed him an eight-ounce opened bottle of Coke.

"I'm supposed to give you this message, uh, if you march next week, you are going to get beaten up." The adolescent finally got the words out.

"Well, now, let me see," said Elijah, stroking his fingers down his chin as a person would do who was in deep thought about something puzzling. "Well, you tell them that I'm an old man of seventy-seven. I shouldn't be much trouble to beat up.

"It takes me a good five minutes just to get up out my reclining chair over there, and I don't suppose it would be any trouble for a healthy young man to beat the tar out of me. Why, I don't expect I'd be any trouble a'tall. I suspecting you could do the job yourself, young man. You certainly look capable. That way the grown men folks wouldn't have to go to so much trouble.

"You tell them, if they like, I'll come out there and stand on the curb. That way they won't have to bother nobody else, and they won't have to exert themselves too much coming in here to get me."

"OK, I'll tell them what you said." The youngster jumped up and was out the door in a flash with his Coke still clutched in his hand. He quickly made it halfway to the truck before the screen door bumped shut behind him. Elijah looked at Mary and burst into a long chuckle. Mary could only shake her head in relief.

There was another knock on the screen door. Mary looked at her father, who had his hands behind his back. He sported a huge friendly smile and motioned for her to see who it was. With the same trepidation, she did.

The same white youth was standing at the screen door, absent the Coke and absent the nervousness this time. Mary opened the door and peeped out. The same black pickup was in the same spot. The remnants of a shattered Coke bottle with the still-fizzing drink lay alongside the curb.

"Come in, young man, come on in. I'm so glad you came back to see us. You ready for another Coke? Mary, see if we have any more Cokes left in there."

"No, I don't want any more. I came to give you another message. Uh, they say if you are in that march they are going to burn your house down." The youth was standing halfway in and halfway out the doorway, looking solemnly down at the floor.

"I see, I see. Well, you go back and tell them that this house is old and dilapidated and needs to be torn down. Why, I don't know how it's still standing to tell you the truth. They be doin' me a favor if they was to burn it down for me.

"I just took out that new insurance policy here awhile back from … what's that insurance company's name, Mary? Well, never mind. I believe that policy say they have to build me a bran' new house back right here in the very same spot if it burns down.

"I was kinda wishing it would burn down, to tell you the truth. I'm tired of looking at these same old dirty walls. Why, I can't believe they want to do that for me. Would you please ask them how much they charge me to burn it down?"

As the teen turned to leave, Elijah yelled in as strong a voice as he could muster, "Now you be sure and tell them that this is just between me and them and don't go around blabbing to everybody 'cause I don't want that insurance company to catch onto us, you hear!" This time Mary joined her father in a hearty chuckle.

In a couple of minutes, a shadow reappeared at the screen door. Mary hadn't bothered to close the main door. The same young man was standing on the other side of the screen, not bothering to come in this time.

"They say if you walk in that march and don't move out of this town, they're going to burn your church down." This time the young man was looking up through the screen at Elijah. There was a remorseful look about him.

"Well, you tell them that our services is growing in such numbers here lately that we gonna have to move to a bigger church anyway. We was talking 'bout addin' on to it, but that was gonna be so expensive. It'd be cheaper if we just tore it down and started over.

"Dat ol' church be there when I was a boy. It only seat 'bout hun'red people. Unless somebody sets in somebody's lap, we gonna have to move anyhows. But since they gonna burn it down, and we got 'bout two hun'red members, well, we'll jus' builds a fine brick church house back right there this time.

"The gov'ment done said that since they's been so many churches burned down around here, they gonna help with building some of 'em back. Why, the more I think 'bout it, the more I believe that'd be the best idea they come up with yet. If you don't mind, ask 'em when they could get started, please."

The boy turned away and slowly walked back to the pickup truck, looking dejected.

After a while, the boy gloomily approached the front porch once again. He went up the steps with his hands in his pockets, dreading delivering the next message. Elijah was standing at the screen door, anticipating his return.

"They said ... ah ... well, they said they were going to kill you if you walk in the march, and if you ain't moved out of here in a week."

Elijah could tell by the way the boy never removed his hands from his pockets and the way he kicked at an imaginary object in front of him, that he hated saying those words.

"Well, you tell them ... aw, shoot, I'll tell them myself."

"Oh, no, the hell you ain't, Daddy!" Mary was screaming and moving quickly toward her father. Elijah had already moved onto the porch and the rubber point of his walking cane had made it to the second step.

"You go down there to that truck full of the Klan folks and you ain't never coming back," Mary said frantically.

"I be back. I've been handling these yahoos all my life, child. I be back. Don't worry."

Elijah had about as much concern as if he were going out to feed the chickens. Mary didn't think it would make any difference, but she was scrambling about hysterically, trying to find the police station's phone number.

Elijah reached over with his free hand and affectionately put his arm over the white boy's shoulder. The teen was slowly keeping pace with the three-legged, old black man. He pulled him in closer with a warm hug and then gently let go.

"I can tell you don't have the look of hate on you yet, boy. When this is all over, how about coming by over here ever' once in a while, and we can see if you can beat me at checkers." Elijah was smiling warmly and for a brief second, the boy was too.

As Elijah and the adolescent approached the black pickup truck, a gigantic, burly white man with huge hairy forearms glared out the rolled-down window. A dirty John Deere cap adorned his head and an enormous chew of Red Man made his left jaw bulge. The man on the passenger side was blessed with similar traits, including the glare. They both seemed surprised the old man would leave the safety of his house to face them.

The teen hopped into the bed of the truck and sat down against the back of the cab. He pulled his knees up to his chin and hoped he wouldn't have to witness the assault of a defenseless, kindly old black man who had just befriended him.

"Howdy, neighbors. How are you gentlemen this afternoon?" Elijah asked in his customary gentle voice with his customary friendly smile.

The men didn't answer. They looked at each other waiting to see if the other was going to speak.

"Well, I understand the last message you sent to me said that you was going to kill me if I participated in the march next week. Is that right?"

The man with the big hairy forearm resembling a ham hock sticking out the window nodded his head and maintained the ominous glare.

"Well, I tell you, I am a sick and feeble old man that's on his last leg now, gentlemen, and that's a fact. My legs hurt. My hips bother me. My hands got arthritis in both of 'em. I can't see so good anymore. I can't hear so well anymore. I can't get around without this here cane, hardly.

"The doctor say I won't be around here much longer if I don't start eating more. To tell you the truth, gentlemen, food just don't taste the same since my sweet Emily gone to be with the Lord. Let's see, five yea's ago. Has it been that long? It don't seem like it.

"If you gentlemen get to spend fifty-one yea's with your lovely wives and then she is taken from you, well you see food just ain't as tasty no more as it used to be. That's why I'm so skinny. I hardly cast a shadow anymore." Elijah was looking down at what was left of his frail body.

"My mind is starting to go on me too. I can't hardly 'member what happen to me yestaday." Elijah took his eyes off the men, and his smile disappeared. His eyes became fixed on images, memories in the far distance.

"I can 'member the day me and my sweet Emily got married. After the wedding, her uncle drove us to Montgomery so we could catch a train to Chattanooga. That's where we were gonna spend our honeymoon, you see. I done saved me up a hun'red dollahs, and we was gonna paint the town red, you see." He was chuckling to himself, still lost in the reverie.

"I didn't see that sign that say 'No Colored People Allowed.' I sho found it out as soon as I walk in there though. A bunch a mean white men standing in the lobby there beat me and took my hun'red dollahs. They say they had's to teach me a lesson. Yes, sir, I sho learn that day, I tell you the truth, 'cause me and Emily had to hitch us a ride all da way back home." Elijah was laughing and shaking his head. "We never did have a honeymoon.

"Then I 'member my little Elisabeth. Just thirteen days old. We buried that precious little lamb 'cause that white doctor says we have to find us a black man to do our doctoring. Imagine that, a black doctor." Elijah's eyes were moistening as he continued to stare hazily at the past.

"I took my three hun'red dollahs I was saving to put down on this house here and bought that little three-foot-long, heart-shaped coffin to lay that little lamb in. I knew it costs white folks fifty dollahs less, but I didn't care. I didn't care at all.

"I 'member when I started this church here. They'd burned it down. We'd build it back. They'd burn it. But we keep building back till we outlasted 'em I reckon, 'cause it still here. I ain't kidding, you can burn it down again. I don't care.

"I 'member ever' time I try to vote they come out with a longer and harder 'literacy test' they called it. Ever' time I read it to 'em, they ask me what it means. No matter what answer I give, they say, 'That's wrong, nigger, sorry.' I don't believe ol' Socrates hisself coulda satisfy 'em even with his answers.

"One more thing I 'member, a windy night in October when I be eighteen years old." Elijah was now speaking lower than usual and almost to himself. "I made a promise to an old friend of mine that night, yes, sir, I sho did. It was that friend of mine that was swinging in that cool night breeze and them glowing red embers. Lord the things you 'member. Yes, sir, gentlemen, I aim to keep that promise."

Elijah was back from his memories. His voice was back to normal, and he made eye contact, but the joyful smile was missing, replaced by firm determination.

"I done lived through more hell than you two young fellows know anything about if you was to live five lifetimes, and now you says you gonna kill me. Well, I'm ready to go, gentlemen.

"You know, there ain't nothing dignified 'bout getting old and crippled and helpless, having to depend on somebody else to take care of you. All you are is a burden to 'em. No, sir, there ain't a damn thing dignified 'bout any of it.

"I tell you what, men." Elijah was speaking faster than he had in years and louder too. "I'm gonna give yous the chance you come here for. If I am gonna die, I am gonna die like a man and for something."

Elijah tapped his cane on the ground harder and harder as he made his way to the front of the pickup. His quiet, soft-spoken demeanor was replaced with anger and rage.

"I've been shot at, nearly hanged, burned out, shut out, and called ever' kind of monkey, gorilla, and ape they is. I've been beat till they couldn't nobody recognize me; I've been talked to like a damn dog and called everything but a human being! I'm tired of you damn crackers' bullshit!"

Elijah was shouting so loud they could hear him for blocks around. Seventy-seven years of built-up anguish had found an outlet. He dropped his cane on the pavement and slowly—like an old man would have to do—got on his knees, sat on his butt, and then lay back prostrate on the pavement in front of the truck.

"I'm a man, damn you! Made in the image of God! Just like you! Go on, run over me! I'm making it easy for you. Do it, dammit!" The truck did not start. Elijah raised his head off the pavement and glared back at the white men.

"I knew when you sent a boy to deliver your messages for you they wouldn't much to you. I knew you wouldn't gonna rise much of a welt on my ass."

Elijah's normal voice retuned as he struggled to get back on his butt. The truck cranked up, backed up, swerved, and drove past the old man, who finally got on his feet. Elijah bent down to pick up his cane and took a final glance at the truck as it sped away, squealing its tires.

The boy who was the reluctant message carrier was standing in the middle of the bed with his hand supporting him on the back of the cab. As the truck left the scene of the uncommitted crime, Elijah caught sight of the boy's free hand raised in a wave. Elijah returned it in-kind and added a hearty smile, which the boy warmly reciprocated.

* * *

It was eight days later, March 25, 1965. Elijah had been marching off and on for five long, grueling days. It was almost over now. They had covered more than fifty miles in the famous march, which would help lead to the passage of the Voting Rights Act of 1965 and make Elijah a local hero.

All the news media covered it. You have probably seen it a hundred times on old black-and-white newsreels: Martin Luther King and the other marchers arriving at the Capitol building in Montgomery.

What you didn't see was Elijah in any of the famous photographs. As Dr. King and the others were about to turn onto the street in front of the Capitol, Elijah veered off and tapped his way to the front door of Richardson Ford and Lincoln.

He happily opened the door and found his way to one of the salesmen's offices and promptly sat in a chair. He waited patiently for the commission-hungry salesman to energetically plop down behind his desk.

"How may I help you, sir?" The salesman's energy quickly dissipated when he saw that his customer was a black man. *Another black man that can't get credit*, he thought.

"I would like to purchase a brand new 1965 Ford Galaxie 500 convertible, please." Elijah sounded excited.

"Yes, sir. That will cost you forty-four hundred dollars," the salesman said aloofly.

"That will be fine," said Elijah as he pulled a thick envelope out of his shirt pocket and started counting out hundred dollar bills.

"What color would you like, sir?" The salesman stared wildly at the money, and his voice was an awed whisper.

"Candy-apple red!" Elijah continued to count.

"We have one left," said the salesman as he picked up the money while Elijah was still counting. He started counting the money himself when he noticed the dates. The first bill was 1906, the second was 1907, then 1908, 1909, and so on.

"You've been saving this a long time, haven't you, pops?" The salesman sounded rather coy.

"Yeah, I made a promise to an old friend a long time ago," said Elijah as he finished counting.

"Well, there is a matter of sales tax, but since you're paying cash, we'll include it in the sale," said the salesman tactfully.

"Thank you kindly, sir."

"Well, let's sign a couple of papers, and I'll get you your keys."

Elijah stood up shakily, but bowed graciously.

* * *

Elijah pulled his shiny candy-apple red Ford convertible—with the top down—alongside the curb of First and Main streets in downtown Selma. Three pretty young white women in their early twenties and fancy dresses were laughing and smiling. They seemed to be enjoying themselves while they waited for the light to turn red so they could cross the street.

"Woo, look at that new convertible!" said one of them.

"That sure is a nice car you got there, Daddy'o," laughed another.

They all had beautiful white-toothed smiles. If one didn't know better, one might think they were beauty contestants from out of town, the Miss Alabama Contest held in Montgomery perhaps, and they were just sightseeing in Selma. They were.

"Would you fine ladies like to drive around in a brand new Ford convertible with this kindly old gentleman?" Elijah's smile was so big, it almost made his face disappear.

"Why not?" one girl asked, laughing to the others. "He looks harmless. Scoot over, Daddy'o, I'll do the driving."

And as Elijah and the three fancy white women pulled onto Main Street in his brand new candy-apple red Ford on their way to see the sights, he shouted at every bystander at every red light in the town of Selma, Alabama, on March 25, 1965, with a smile so big that his face disappeared.

"Ain't keeping promises grand, folks!"

* * *

Back in the playground sitting on the crossties, James finished up saying, "My grand tells me that to make sho you get to Heaven and to walk this earth wif dignity is the most you can hope fo'."

James was solemn now.

"That's why I is gonna stop fightin' wif yous fellows. I wants dignity too, just like my grand."

James turned and walked away. We wiped the tears from our eyes.

CHAPTER 12

JESSE WAS CHANGING, LITTLE BY little and day by day, not only in appearance, but in personality too. He was much cleaner now. His clothes were fresh and actually fit him; his hair was combed neatly; his teeth were straighter and whiter, and he was not nearly as shy as the trampled, timid, backward first grader I saw the first day of school years ago.

He even seemed to have lunch money now. And even though he qualified for the free lunch program, Jesse never accepted one free lunch; the lunches cost a quarter at that time. I had watched him miss most of the lunches in the previous years, but not too many now.

It wasn't until a little impromptu after-school excursion that it was revealed Jesse had a job cleaning up the lunchroom every day after school. We heard him whisper to the head cook at lunch time that he had something to do and if it would be all right with her if he missed a little work today. Jesse was not only earning his lunch but an additional two dollars a day. This explained the occasional new clothes.

But of all the new changes in Jesse, the most striking improvement was in his intelligence. He was smarter than he used to be. He was smarter than me now. He was smarter than Bart, Pete, John, all of the boys in our class, and most of the girls for that matter. Along with his growing intelligence was his growing fascination with James's grandfather too. It led Jesse to accept the invitation to see a giant snakeskin.

The Jones boys and Cater were on their way to a house to see the snakeskin the Joneses' cousin had brought back from Mississippi. The cousin was visiting relatives who lived on a farm near the town of Midnight in the Mississippi Delta. The giant rattler was killed in Panther Swamp and was boasted by the cousin to be ten feet long and large enough around to encircle his entire body.

This was simply too enticing to pass up for the Jones boys. They proudly told everybody in class who would listen about the prize their cousin possessed, and they invited all of the entire class to join them in the three-mile walk from the school to the cousin's house and see for themselves the carnival-showlike freaky reptile skin.

Only Cater and Jesse accepted the invitation.

"Hey, James," said Jesse as they walked at a swift pace along Highway 9 en route to the cousin's. "Do you think I might meet this grand of yours sometime?"

"I don't know. When he came by the udder day, my Aunt Mary had to just 'bout carry him up da steps. He's awful old and sickly now." James was looking down, shaking his head gloomily. "It's gonna have to be pretty soon if you ever get to meet 'im at all."

"I would like that," Jesse said affectionately.

"He didn't look too good. I don't know if you'll ever get your chance. I don't think he'll be here another week or two."

"Well, the Lord works in mysterious ways, James. Maybe I'll get the opportunity sooner than you think," Jesse said with a smile.

* * *

Harold's dad, Jules Spartani, was driving down to see a friend. He passed the boys very slowly to see if he recognized any of those he had just been daydreaming about. Jules had done quite a bit of daydreaming lately. Perhaps "daydreaming" is not the correct word—a better description might be "tormented obsession." Jules recognized Cater and James. He had their faces seared into his memory, *but wait a minute, is that Jesse too?* Jules hurriedly sped to his friend's house. "This is too good to be true," Jules mumbled out loud.

Jules knew the boys were headed somewhere on foot, and it was logical they would be headed back the same way. The plan was already formulating in his mind.

He was only about ten miles away from his friend and soon to be accomplice's house, or so he hoped. Actually, he was more of an acquaintance than a friend. He only met the man once at a meeting organized by another acquaintance. It wasn't actually a KKK meeting. It was more like a what-the-hell-we-gonna-do-about-all-these-niggers meeting.

* * *

Jules was born in Pennsylvania and his father, who was a supervisor at a large steel mill, asked to transfer to the company's

Birmingham facility when Jules was only ten. Jules was never quite sure why his father wanted to move to Birmingham, of all places. Something to do about the plant manager's wife, he thought.

He never imagined kids could be as cruel as they were to newly arrived Yankee kids. He also couldn't figure out why Southerners hated blacks so much. He eventually moved to Jess Rulam and blended in nicely with the community.

* * *

After several turns onto different dirt roads, he knew instantly he had arrived at the right place by the huge Confederate flag planted proudly in the front yard. The yard was also decorated with several car bodies set up on cinder blocks, fifty-five-gallon barrels cut down the middle with a game rooster staked by one leg to each barrel, and a generous supply of concrete pedestal water fountains, for some reason. The dead giveaway was a big black GMC pickup truck that he saw parked at the meeting that night. This was it, no question. The big man had indeed given him the right directions over the phone.

"Hi, Hoarse."

"Hi, Jules, come on in. I see you found it."

Hoarse's giant hand engulfed Jules's hand to mid-wrist.

"I'll be glad to talk to you about that little nigger problem you've got going."

"Well, we may be in luck," Jules said as he moved some clothes out of the way so he could sit on the couch.

"What do you mean?" asked Hoarse as he grabbed a chair from the kitchen table, placed it in front of Jules, and situated his enormous frame on it.

Jules took notice of how small the chair looked underneath Hoarse. He stuck out everywhere. One goliath hand was resting on his knee, and as Jules's eyes followed up to the thick wrist and then the massive hairy forearm, he felt confident he had the right man for the job.

"Well, you're not going to believe this, but when I was driving over here, I passed the nigger boys that beat up my son," Jules said wryly. "They was just walking along the side of the road."

"That's good, but they'll be gone by now," Hoarse said, shrugging.

"Naw, they'll have to go back the same way they came unless somebody gives them a ride back. Right?" Jules said it like he was sure of himself.

"It's possible we might catch 'em if we hurry on back and wait on 'em." Hoarse was mulling it over.

"That's my plan," said Jules with the same wry demeanor.

"What do you want to do to 'em if we get 'em?" Hoarse was glowering at Jules.

"I know you used to be in the Klan, right?" Jules asked casually.

"Yeah."

"Well, what do you think I want do to 'em, shit, bake 'em a cake?" Jules was getting twitchy.

"I *was* in the Klan when I lived in Dallas County. We tried to stop 'em from doing those damn marches. Damn, them was the stubbornness damn niggers I've ever seen. We'd catch one or two off by their selves ever' now and then and beat the hell out of 'em, but I ain't never killed a man before, not even a nigger." Hoarse was still glaring at Jules.

Jules was silent but was looking around into space, like he was trying to ponder something, anything. "OK, let's just beat the hell out of 'em then. Damn, I don't care, I'm not letting that bunch of damn niggers do that to my son and get by with it." Jules was bitterly desperate.

Hoarse looked away for a second and said, sighing, "OK, then. I need to call Snake Turley. He'll help us."

"Who's Snake Turley?" Jules was puzzled and apprehensive.

"He's a buddy of mine. He hates niggers. He's a goofy bastard, for sure. You'll like him," said Hoarse, chuckling. "He lives on the way. We'll stop and get one of his trucks. He's got two or three old junkers that'll still run. We don't need nobody identifying our vehicles."

"How do we keep them nigger boys from identifying us?" asked Jules, growing unsure about the plan.

"With these." Hoarse bent over an old trunk used as a coffee table. He reached inside, snatched out three or four white hoods and threw them at Jules. One hit Jules in the face and fell into his hands.

Jules unfolded it. He realized it was the famous Klan hood he'd only seen pictures of. He slowly and deliberately placed the hood over his head. It smelled like burlap, he thought. "Where's a mirror? I want to see myself."

"You passed one on the way in. Over there by the door." Hoarse was smiling at the fact that Jules wanted to see himself wearing a Klan hood.

Jules slowly walked to the mirror hanging on the wall in the small foyer. He peered at the image that hauntingly looked back at him. He wondered what his father would say if he could see him now.

Hoarse got off the phone and said, "Let's go cut some rope," as he passed by Jules, who was still gazing at himself in the mirror.

* * *

The dark, foggy smog dissipated enough for Jules to make out that it was an old worn-out 1950 something Chevy pickup truck that Snake Turley had just cranked as they pulled into the junkyard Snake called home. Car parts were literally lying everywhere. Jules figured the old dilapidated single-wide trailer on concrete blocks with no underpinning was Snake's living quarters and not some sort of office. The backyard had at least a hundred roosters stacked out. It was hard to hear what was said between the cacophony of crowing.

Snake was aptly named, tall, at least six foot four and wirily thin. He was moving quickly, changing positions around the truck while he adjusted the sputtering carburetor. His grease-covered mechanic's pullovers had the sleeves rolled up to his skinny, veiny biceps, exposing numerous tattoos.

"Let's go," Snake said, slamming the hood down.

"I got everything we need, I think. Jules, you get in the middle." Hoarse was in a hurry as he opened the truck door and motioned at Jules to get in.

* * *

"This is our lucky day, boys," said Hoarse as they spotted the boys on Highway 9, now on their way back to town.

"Damn, how many are there?" asked Snake, like he was expecting only one or two.

"There's five of 'em, looks like to me," said Hoarse mechanically. "I only brought three blindfolds, but we can use these grease rags that's under my ass."

"Sorry, I guess I should have told you there was five of 'em. I wouldn't thinking, dammit!" Jules was mad at himself for being so stupid about something that important.

"It's all right. We can improvise with what we got, boys," said Hoarse with a businesslike air, like he was almost enjoying himself.

"Put this on." Hoarse handed Jules and Snake each a white Klan hood.

The truck pulled over, abruptly cutting off the five unsuspecting boys. All three hooded men jumped out of the still running junker with Hoarse brandishing a .22-caliber pistol.

Snake and Jules put the blindfolds over four of the terrified children's eyes, but Cater started to back away from Snake when he saw the blindfold. Suddenly, Hoarse clubbed Cater in the back of the head with the butt of the pistol.

Cater hit the ground with his eyes rolled back and only the whites showing. His left arm stretched straight out. Hoarse reached down and grabbed the unconscious yet still stiff boy with a giant hand around the back of his shirt. He lifted him off the ground, whirled one revolution, and flung him with such force that the tip of the boy's shoe grazed Jules on the cheek as it flashed by. Cater landed in the middle of the truck bed and crumpled against the back of the bed so hard the entire truck rocked.

"Do as they say. Everything will be all right," Jesse calmly said, looking at James and then his brothers through blindfolded eyes. "Everyone will be safe." A slight reassuring smile appeared momentarily.

Jules and Snake tightened the blindfolds snuggly on each boy and shoved them into the truck bed. They were told to lie flat on their stomach and not raise their head up or try to remove the masks. If they did, they were promised by Hoarse they would look much, much worse than their friend Cater, who was making groaning sounds but with little movement. All the men removed their hoods and the truck sped away.

* * *

Arriving at Snake's trailer, they put the hoods back on and marched the four boys up the concrete block steps and into the single-wide.

"What about that one still in the truck?" asked Snake.

"I'll get him," snapped Hoarse.

He went hurriedly to the truck, reached over, and attached his meat-hook hand firmly around Cater's throat. He dragged him to the side, lifted him straight up over his head with the one hand, and slammed him to the ground. He reattached the meat-hook to the front of Cater's shirt and dragged him up the steps and tossed him in the middle of the floor like a sack of potatoes.

"Get those chairs over there at the kitchen table and line 'em up here," barked Hoarse at Snake.

Hoarse was like a shark that had just smelled blood in the water. A feeding frenzy was about to begin. He was becoming more and more agitated. The callous ease with which he flung Cater around with one hand like a rag doll was scary even to the hardest of asses. Jules was a big, powerful man, but he knew he was no match for Hoarse. Jules was scared of him now and regretted ever calling him.

"Tie 'em up." Hoarse threw the ropes he quickly removed from his pockets at Jules and Snake, being careful not to use their names. "I want to take this damn hood off. I can't breathe through the damn thing."

Snake sat each boy down in one of his dinette chairs he had aligned in the living room. Then he and Jules tied the boys' hands behind the chair, wrist over wrist, and then bound their feet together in firm double knots.

Jules tied the Jones brother called Earl, while Snake tied up his brother Anthony. Both boys were sobbing, "They gonna kill us, ain't they?" They pleaded, "Don't kill us, mister."

Ignoring the pleas and acting as if he didn't hear them, Jules moved to James and wrapped a two-foot-long piece of nylon rope around his wrist. James's bottom lip quivered, but he didn't say anything. He just obliged when Snake snarled, "Stick your black-ass hands behind you. You're not so tough now, are you, boy?"

"I'll get this last one." Snake got behind Jesse, who already had his hands behind him and in position. He looped the nylon around each wrist and pulled it taut with a grunt. Then he moved around front and did precisely the same thing to his feet. At about the same time, Jules finished with James and he and Snake joined Hoarse, who was watching without his hood on.

"You can't breathe for shit in those things," said Snake, removing his hood.

"No, I'd never make it as a Klan member," laughed Jules.

"They didn't make the damn things with comfort in mind, that's for damn sure." Hoarse was rubbing his scalp. He slammed a John Deere cap on his head.

"What are we gonna do now?" Snake asked Jules.

"I don't know. What do you think we ought to do?" Jules was looking at Hoarse, who was looking at the boys with a bit of a half-surprised and half-pissed look.

"The first thing we got to do is tie *all* the little bastards up," roared Hoarse.

When Jules and Snake turned around, they saw the rope in a small neat bundle behind Jesse's chair and in front of his feet. Jesse was leaning forward in his chair with his hands clasped together and his elbows resting on his knees. His blindfolded head turned directly toward the three befuddled men.

"Damn, I thought you tied him," boomed Hoarse.

"I thought you did too," added Jules.

"I thought I did too," laughed Snake, scratching his head.

"Well, tie him again. Damn." Hoarse was not amused. "Hey, Jules, come over here, we gotta talk," whispered Hoarse to Jules.

Meanwhile, Snake had a thought: *Tie up that slippery-damn-half-nigger-thing of a kid.*

Snake positioned himself on his knees behind Jesse's chair and carefully examined the rope. He held it firmly in both hands and wondered if he *did* forget to tie this last kid up; nothing seemed wrong with the rope. He snapped it a couple of times just to make sure.

While Snake was contemplating the mystery of the rope, James whimpered and mumbled something hardly audible.

"My granddaddy is somebody important in da worl'," muttered James, sobbing.

"What? What did you say kid?" Snake pushed James on the shoulder to get his attention. "Speak up or shut up, and it better be shut up."

"My granddaddy is somebody important in da worl'!" This time he shouted.

"Keep that damn nigger quiet over there, or I'll quiet him myself," bawled Hoarse irritably.

"Woo-wee, you got yourself an important nigger granddaddy," Snake said quietly to James. "Let me tell you something: There ain't no such thing as an important nigger, kid."

"My grand is. His name is Reverend Elijah Smith ... and he be friends with Martin Luther King heself, and he's gonna find you and ... and kill you," James shouted and sputtered and cried all at the same time.

"What did you say your old damn granddaddy's name was, boy?" Hoarse abruptly left his conversation with Jules and stomped over and put his face within inches of James's. "Say it again, dammit. I want to know if I heard what I thought you just said," hissed Hoarse, seething at James. "Say it now, damn you!"

"He is, he ... the Reverend Elijah Smith, and he know the honbrel Martin Luther King." James didn't know quite how to say "The Honorable," a term he always heard used before Dr. King's name.

"You mean he *knew* the nigger King until the *honorable* James Earl Ray put a bullet in him last year," said Hoarse with a snicker.

"I know he's dead," sighed James.

"Lord, Lord, thank you, Jesus, it's a miracle," yelled Hoarse with a clap of his hands over his head. He was trying to imitate black parishioners.

"Y'all, come here a minute." Hoarse was motioning for Snake and Jules to join him in the kitchen.

"I'll be back to tie you up right this time. You take that blindfold off and you've killed yourself and all your buddies, you got that?" Snake whispered into Jesse's ear. Jesse nodded.

"Today is my lucky day, boys," said Hoarse as if he had been blessed.

"What are you talking about?" asked Jules curiously.

"That nigger granddaddy they're talking 'bout is the one we tried to stop from having those damn marches back in '65 in Selma. Shit, this is too good to be true. I owe that nigger big time. He got my own son hanging 'round him somehow or 'nother and talked to him about all that equality nigger shit, and now my boy is at the University of Alabama leading civil rights demonstrations on campus. That old fart nigger made a hippie out of him." Hoarse was so worked up his voice was shaky, and Jules thought his eyes were even getting moist.

"What have you got in mind?" asked Jules, growing apprehensive.

"I'm gonna hang 'em," said Hoarse nonchalantly. "I'm gonna call ol' honorable Reverend Elijah Smith, or whatever the hell them niggers call each other, and tell him I'm gonna hang his grandson, just like that. I still got his number from when we used to call him years ago."

* * *

Fear pulsated in Jules. He imagined the boys all in a line, hanging from a giant oak tree limb, each one swinging in opposite directions. Then, he saw bloodhounds chasing after himself, Hoarse, and Snake over sage-grass-covered fields and small rocky brooks and ditches. And then he saw a noose placed over his own head and zipped tight to his throat, like he did to the tie that went with his suit.

And then, for some mysterious reason, that he had no way of fathoming, he saw the red glow of a once huge flame that burned itself down to a simmering ember.

He turned his head and looked solemnly at the whimpering, bound, and blindfolded boys. All were facing straight ahead, sobbing with each breath, except Jesse, who was staring with his blindfolded eyes right into Jules's own.

CHAPTER 13

"I'VE CHANGED MY MIND, HOARSE," said Jules reluctantly. "I don't want to really kill these kids. Let's just scare 'em good." Jules kept his voice down so the boys wouldn't hear.

"We ain't gonna kill 'em," Hoarse groused, not caring if his captives overheard him or not. "I told you I ain't never killed anybody, and I ain't starting now."

"That kid laying on the floor is in bad shape. I hope he don't die." Jules had concern in his voice, which Hoarse sensed.

"Aw, he ain't hurt that bad. My old man used to thumb me around worse than that before breakfast. Shit, niggers is tough."

Hoarse was somewhat jovial and turned to look at Cater, who was still moaning and rolling from side to side. Then, Hoarse caught sight of Jesse with his head pointed right at him. He was still not tied.

"One of y'all tie that kid up that's looking over here like he can see us," Hoarse grumbled.

"I got the rope right here," said Snake. He was popping the rope and moving toward Jesse.

"Well, what have you got in mind?" asked Jules curiously, relieved Hoarse wasn't going to do what he thought he was going to do a few seconds earlier.

"Listen to this, Snake," yelled Hoarse, motioning to Snake to come back to their huddle. Snake had already begun to tie Jesse's hands behind the chair.

"Let me finish with this kid's hands."

Snake was humming as he was looping the rope this way and that way with an occasional grunt to demonstrate how hard he was pulling the slack out of the nylon at just the right spots. He gave one big final overly exaggerated "UMM!" on the last tug, just to make sure. Then he hurried over to hear Hoarse's clever plan he was sure he had just come up with.

"You know where the old covered bridge is over at Horton's Gap? Where they blocked off the road that goes to it years ago? I reckon it hadn't fell completely down yet," whispered Hoarse, like he *now* didn't want the boys to hear him.

"Yeah, I've stopped to look at it before," said Jules, wonderingly.

Snake nodded his head in the affirmative.

"Well, I'm gonna call up the old nigger reverend and tell him if he can make it there in two hours, he can save his grand chitlins from being hanged." Hoarse was chuckling, finding himself rather amusing.

"We'll take a couple of cotton sacks and fill 'em up with something, ah, hay, or I don't know." Hoarse was getting ahead of himself.

"Hey, I know!" Snake said in a vehement whisper, snapping his fingers. "I got that dummy in the shed." Snake looked at Hoarse and Jules like he'd just come up with a new drug for the clap.

"That old mannequin they threw out of the dress shop?" asked Hoarse, surprised Snake still had it.

"Yeah, it'll look a lot better than a sack of hay." Snake had a good point.

"OK, I'll call the old nigger and tell him if he calls the cops I'll shoot all the boys on the first sight of 'em," Hoarse said with a big smile as if this was the most fun he'd had in years. "And he better be there in two hours, and it better be just him and whoever drives him." Hoarse was getting more amused the more he thought about it. "Y'all watch them close while I make this call."

Hoarse got a tiny piece of paper out of a compartment in his wallet and picked up the phone hanging on the kitchen wall. Snake and Jules walked back to the living room to the four bound boys and the one unbound boy, who was now staring at Snake.

"Shitfire!" gasped Snake, grabbing hold of Jules's shoulder while his saucer-sized eyes stared straight at Jesse. "I'm telling you … I tied his hands as tight as I could get 'em."

* * *

Snake was walking in slow motion behind Jesse's chair with his eyes fixated on the nylon rope. It was coiled up on the floor just exactly beneath where Jesse's hands had been expertly bound no more than two minutes ago.

"Well, shit, tie 'em up again," sighed Jules, reflecting on what Hoarse had said with regards to Snake being a goofy bastard. "I'm going outside to take a piss. I'll be back in a minute." Jules needed a moment by himself to take all this in.

Snake picked up the nylon rope, tied a slip knot in it, and carefully pulled the end tight. He looked at the rope and looked at Jesse, then looked at the rope and looked at Jesse again. He was more than perplexed. He was downright enchanted.

Snake kneeled down behind Jesse's chair. He calmly asked Jesse to put his hands behind him, if he pleased. Snake methodically and very deliberately tied the child's hands exactly as he did twice before, and he believed it sincerely.

He carefully inspected his work when he finished; he held Jesse's bound hands, turning them this way and that. He tried to pull the hands apart like he was testing the tensile strength of the ropes. He stuck his fingers in between the tight loops and was convinced it was impossible to get free, especially for an eleven-year-old kid.

He hesitated a few seconds after he let go of the masterfully tied hands. He showed a certain lack of confidence in his work. He really wasn't expecting anything to happen, but this was turning into a weird-ass day.

After a few seconds of watching, there was no movement of Jesse's hands whatsoever. Snake moved around the front of Jesse's chair. The exact same care that he took with his hands, he now put forth on Jesse's feet—the precise loop around that ankle, the careful loop around this ankle, and the slack pulled out thusly.

"A loop around and back over, pull tight. There, the knot is done perfect." Snake was saying the instructions to himself. A satisfied smile appeared on Snake's face as he sat back on the heels of his boots to admire his work. He had just put a good five minutes labor into it.

Suddenly, he caught a glimpse of something lying on the floor behind Jesse. He leaned his head over to the side to get a clear line of sight. "*Oh, my God, no!*" shouted Snake so loudly and so frightfully that Hoarse and Jules both assumed there was a tragedy.

Hoarse was standing between the kitchen and the living room when Jules burst through the front door. Both men were startled by the bloodcurdling shriek. They had completed what they were doing—Hoarse had just got off the phone with Elijah Smith, Jules had finished pissing behind a tree.

"What the hell is it, Snake?! That boy's dead, ain't he?!" Jules was approaching Cater. His glassy eyes were open, but he was still only semiconscious.

"No, that ain't it," growled Hoarse in a low guttural voice, staring at Snake.

Snake backed himself against the couch, took one more step back and fell in a sitting position with his hands over his mouth. Jules took his eyes off of Cater and looked at the wild-eyed, weeping Gene "Snake" Turley.

"What is it, buddy?" Jules bent down and put his hand on Snake's trembling shoulder in an attempt to be sympathetic. Jules knew Snake was in the midst of a breakdown.

"He can't be tied by a rope," Snake whispered shakily. As he said the word "rope," Snake broke down crying impishly into his hands.

"Is that all that's damn wrong with you, you goofy son of a bitch?!" shouted Hoarse, seething with anger. "You ain't got enough sense to tie a damn nigger kid up. Where's the damn rope?" Hoarse looked around the room for it. He hadn't noticed the cords, one coiled up behind the chair and the other in the same arrangement under Jesse's feet, but he saw them now.

"There it is!" he shouted.

Hoarse bent down and angrily snatched up the rope. Jesse leaned back in his chair and placed his hands behind his back. His blindfolded eyes were accompanied by a hint of a smile on his lips.

Hoarse quickly tied a double knot with his hands so big the nylon rope appeared like a shoelace to Jules. He could hear the rip sound that a rope makes when it's sliding against itself. Hoarse positioned his massive body in front of Jesse and blocked out Jules's view, but he could still hear the same rip sounds.

Hoarse was much too massive—six foot seven and three hundred and fifty pounds—to be getting on his knees. He just sort of bent over, resting his elbow on one knee while he tied Jesse's feet. When he finished, he straightened up with an *ump* sound. He put his hand on the small of his back and stretched a little. He then turned toward Jules to tell him to load the boys into the pickup.

But he never got to say it. He saw Jules's eyes had a startled, bewildered look in them. They were focused on something on the floor behind Jesse's chair. Hoarse quickly turned to see the rope was coiled up once again in a neat pile on the floor.

"What the hell is this shit?" said Hoarse in the same guttural voice he used when saying something softly. "Damn!" Hoarse was snorting like a bull and almost knocked over James's chair, huffing and puffing to get to the mysterious rope. This time he got on his knees and tied the rope so hard that Jesse flinched with pain when Hoarse tightened the slack.

When he completed the last loop and gave the knot a final herculean pull, he heard Snake give a haunting shriek and cried out, "Look!" He leaned his gigantic head to one side so he could get a look at Snake. His peering eyes followed the direction of Snake's eyes, which were affixed on the rope he had just tied securely around Jesse's feet.

To Hoarse's wonder, the nylon rope was once again lying on the floor, coiled up in a neat little pile, just as the rope he had finished tying around Jesse's hands had been a minute earlier. He must have thought the untieable rope was amusing, because he began to chuckle as he made eye contact with Jules.

"It's a trick rope or something. Shit, gotta be," Jules said as he examined the rope at Jesse's feet.

"The only problem with that is I don't have any damn trick rope." Hoarse's amusement shifted into bizarre puzzlement. "Me and you cut the damn things from the same rope. Remember?" Hoarse's eyes were a little wild and his voice was three octaves higher. "There is another rope in one of them trucks out there." Hoarse was waving at Jules to go get it.

"I knowed they was something. I knowed it wouldn't just me. I knowed it," muttered Snake. "You can't tie him neither, can you?" Snake appeared somewhat relieved that he wasn't going insane.

"Shut up ... we'll tie him!" Hoarse was examining Jesse's hands like a jeweler at a pawn shop examines a fake diamond. Jules returned shortly with a long lariat used for cattle wrangling.

"That ain't mine. That's a buddy of mine's. We don't need to cut a piece of that off." Snake was adamant about it.

"He'll get over it." Hoarse had already got his knife out as Jules handed him the cord. Hoarse cut a two-and-a-half-foot piece of the lariat off and handed it to Jules. Then Hoarse measured a piece the length of his arm—about three feet—and went about methodically binding Jesse's wrists, hands, and most of his arms with the stiff lariat piece.

When Hoarse finished with Jesse's feet, they both stood up and peered intently at the knots. They were the size of grapefruits. Both men had an unsure look about them though. Nothing happened. Relief.

"OK, put a blindfold on the one on the floor. He looks like he's coming around, and then tie him." Hoarse was making his way to the door. "Let's load 'em up and head for the bridge. Looks like it's getting dark." Hoarse was looking at the setting sun. "Snake, wake up! Get that dummy in the shed you been sleeping with." Hoarse had a malicious smile on his face.

"I ain't slept with no dummy," quipped Snake as he made his way past Hoarse and through the door.

"That's what they all say, Snake, ol' buddy," Hoarse mumbled mostly to himself, gazing at the red glow of a forlorn horizon, deep in thought. "Get them to stand up. Then they can hop to the truck and lay down in the bed." Hoarse was looking at Jules and leaning in the doorway.

He walked over to Cater and picked him up with one arm under his neck and one under his knees. "I'll get this one." He carried Cater out to the truck like a baby and gently—for him—laid him in the open bed.

When Hoarse returned, he found the boys struggling to stand. "Let's help 'em up right quick," said Hoarse as he put his meat-hook hand on Anthony and lifted him straight up. Jules did the same with Earl. Next, Hoarse lifted up James. Then Jules went over to Jesse and was about to put his hand on his shirt at the shoulder when suddenly, Jesse stood straight up with no assistance.

"Good job, boy," said Jules, unconsciously.

"Thank you ... Mr. Spartani," said Jesse nonchalantly.

Jules turned, shocked. He made sure Jesse still had on his blindfold. He did. Then he checked to see if his feet were still tied. They were. The same grapefruit-sized knot was still in place.

Jules's eyes made their way to his hands. They were positioned in front of his crotch, one wrist over the other and still tied tight with the same huge knot the way Hoarse had left it one minute ago. Good.

* * *

The boys were in a single file, hopping toward the door. Jules was wishing they had waited to tie their feet until after they were in the pickup. He was also wondering how Jesse knew who he was. *Maybe he recognized my voice*, he thought. This was going to be a problem he would think on later.

Jesse was the last boy to be loaded. Hoarse approached him just as with the others. He was about to place his hands under Jesse's arms. He stopped suddenly and peered at Jesse's crotch.

"How the hell did he do that?!" Hoarse looked at Jules, astonished.

"Do what?" asked Jules as he made his way around Jesse to get at what Hoarse was looking at. Jules looked at Jesse's hands, still tied with the same knot. "How did he get his damn hands in front of him?!" The stunned Hoarse cut Jules off. Snake was making little six-inch jumps off the ground with both feet, pointing with his index finger and laughing like a mad scientist.

Jules simply didn't notice it before, but playing it over again in his mind he clearly remembered Jesse's hands were in front of him when he stood up from the chair. *Hoarse tied them behind him, didn't he?* Jules was trying to picture that scene in his mind, but it wouldn't focus.

"You probably tied 'em that way."

"Like hell I did."

"I don't remember."

"You were looking right at me!"

"He probably slipped 'em under his feet when we weren't looking." Jules was desperately searching for a logical explanation.

"Well, load him up and let's go," said Jules, placating the man-mountain.

Hoarse sighed tiredly and said, "OK, let's go."

He was about to pick up the tied boy, when Jesse said, "I'll walk, Hoarse." Then Jesse stepped out of the rope around his ankles and calmly walked to the truck. He placed his hands on the tailgate, stepped on the bumper, swung a leg over, and sat down alongside his friends.

Hoarse looked at Jules, held out his palms, and said with near hysteria, "Of course, why the hell not?" Hoarse walked to the side of the pickup bed, placed his muscular hairy forearms across the top sideboard and leaned over with his head pointed down for a minute, wondering what he should do next. Jules and Snake were wondering the same thing.

"Well, let's go." Hoarse raised his head abruptly. "I got to see what part of the twilight zone we wind up in next."

The roar of the old junker pickup truck was broken occasionally by the sound of an oncoming car. The warm wind blew briskly through Hoarse's hair. Jesse swayed this way and that.

Hoarse was sitting catty-cornered on the bed with one massive long arm running down the top of the tailgate and the other along the top fender. Jules and Snake were in the cab.

"Does it seem weird to you, man?" asked Jules of Snake, who was driving.

"It's seemed weird all damn day to me. I'm losing my mind." Snake's reply was sincere.

"Don't it look weird? I mean, it's kinda green looking. Everything has a green tint to it. Do you notice it?" Jules was looking all around the scenery en route to the bridge.

"Yeah, I do. I know it can get funny looking at dusk around here sometimes, but this is weird," said Snake, agreeing.

"Man ... what am I doing here? This is sooo weird." Jules was still looking about with confusion.

"What are *you* doing here?!" Snake said. "What the hell am *I* doing here?! I tell you, Mama, wake me up, please!"

"I got a feeling ... I'm on a ride straight to hell, kid," said Hoarse uneasily toward Jesse, but not looking at him.

"You don't *have* to go to hell, Hoarse," said Jesse softly, lifting his hand and slipping the blindfold over his head.

Hoarse looked at Jesse with an emotionless face, as if he was expecting something else strange to happen. He softly said, "It's too late for me, kid. I've been doing bad things for a *long* time."

"Who told you it was too late, Hoarse?" Jesse asked.

"I don't know. The Bible, I guess." Hoarse didn't want to answer and looked away.

"I believe you'll find it says the exact opposite, my friend," said Jesse with a smile.

"How is it not too late for me, kid? Damn, when does it start not being too late for somebody like me?" asked Hoarse with a sad voice, looking away into the dusk again.

"Start by going to see your father, Hoarse."

"My father? I don't even know where that piece of shit is, kid."

"You know that's not true. You know he is in a state nursing home in Hattiesburg, Mississippi."

"That's right; I signed a form the state sent me a year ago. How did you ... well, I won't ask how. I'm afraid to know how." Hoarse looked away again. "If you could have seen what he was and what he done to me and Mama, you wouldn't sa—"

"I see him now," interrupted Jesse, slowly closing his eyes. "A dying, lonely old man who wakes every hour with tears running down his face. He calls out to an invisible wife and reaches for a son who isn't there. When a brief minute of sanity allows it, he longs to see the son for just one minute. He yearns to say, 'I'm sorry, son. Could you forgive me for what I've done? I love you, son.'

"This is his only wish before he dies and he is so frightened of death that he is scared to close his eyes. Afraid of where he will be when his eyes won't open for the last time. When his eyes do open in this world, he faintly sees his trembling hand grasping lovingly for a son. The grasp is filled with air."

Jesse watched a tear roll from Hoarse's eye and disappear into a stubbly black beard. Hoarse wiped the tear away and quickly turned his head. Jesse noticed the massive torso convulsively expand and contract in silent weeping. He leaned over and put his hand on Hoarse's quivering shoulder and whispered close to the big man's ear, "Go to your father, and cry no more."

"What then?" asked Hoarse, turning back around. "What does somebody like me do then? How do you know all these things?"

"I don't know how I know these things."

"How did you get out of those ropes?"

"I don't know how. I just ask the rope to move, and it does." Jesse was looking down, genuinely puzzled.

"In a little while, I'm either gonna wake up in my bed and out of this funky dream, or be on my way to Mississippi," laughed Hoarse.

"One more thing you have to do Hoarse."

"What's that?"

"Forgive your son, so that in forty years he doesn't have to do the same thing you are about to do."

Hoarse shook his head and understood, then smiled at Jesse warmly.

***

When the truck came to a stop at an entrance to a cow pasture off Horton Gap Road about a half-mile from the covered bridge, Hoarse lifted Cater up like one would an infant and sat him on the ground.

"Get these boys out of the truck. We're getting out of here!" Hoarse shouted loudly at Jules and Snake.

"Man, am I glad you said that," said Jules happily.

"That makes two of us," said Snake, even more overjoyed.

After they got all the boys out of the truck, Hoarse pulled Jules, Snake, and Jesse to one side and whispered, "Will you untie everybody for us after we're gone and wait for the grandfather?"

"He knows who I am, Hoarse," said Jules. "I'm going to jail. That's all right though; I'll take the blame for it. It was my doings. I won't tell 'em who helped me." Jules was stern about this.

"Go home and love your son, Mr. Spartani." Jesse was pulling his blindfold back over his eyes. "A person can't see what's in front of him with a blindfold on, can he?" Jesse smiled.

Hoarse gave Jesse a slap on the shoulder and walked over to Cater. He removed his wallet, pulled out all the money in it, and stuffed it in Cater's shirt pocket. Then Jules did the same and so did Snake.

Hoarse turned to Jesse and said, "He's better, but they still need to carry him to the hospital. I'll find out how much the hospital charges and pay for it."

"I'll pay half of it, Hoarse," said Jules, and he turned to look at Snake.

"Don't look at me. I'm broke," said Snake.

They all laughed, loaded themselves in the truck cab, and sped away. Jules stuck his hand out the window and waved at the blindfolded Jesse, who stuck his hand up in the air in response. Jules tuned to his two accomplices and said, "Been a hell of a day, hadn't it, boys?"

Hoarse quietly added, "Amen, brother."

* * *

Jesse untied the Jones brothers and had Cater sitting up when Mary and Elijah approached the covered bridge. James flagged them down and helped the decrepit old man out of the car. They were all overjoyed. Elijah embraced his grandchildren passionately.

"I am so blessed that the Lord heard my prayers, children. The Lord is a good Lord. Amen." Elijah's tears dripped down his face as he continued to hug on his grandchildren. "I thought all this nonsense was behind me. I guess it may not ever be."

"Grand, this hea be Jesse. I don't know how he done it, but he somehow or 'nother talked the giant of a white man that was mean to us into let'n us go somehow." James couldn't hold back his excitement.

Jesse walked over and offered his hand to Elijah, who shook it warmly with both of his hands. He pulled Jesse into his chest and hugged him tenderly.

"Bless you, boy, bless you," Elijah whispered in Jesse's ear.

"I've heard a lot about you. It's an honor to know you, sir," Jesse said.

The many years of struggle, hardship, and degradation showed like a road map on the old man's face. The bright light of undeterred determination that had once illuminated Elijah's eyes was now replaced with the dim twilight of life's final mile.

Elijah cast his eyes upon Jesse and said, "I prayed every mile of the way over here that Jesus would somehow come down and put his protective hands over my grandchildren. It looks like He did."

And upon that, they got into the car and drove away, safe.

CHAPTER 14

AS THE DAYS AND WEEKS passed by, Jesse's metamorphosis quickened. The start of our sixth grade year was the end of a decade—the 1960s—but it was the beginning of a new Jessup Christopher Savorié.

He was mature for his years, compared to me and the rest of the gang anyway, the same way a redwood tree is too developed for a flowerpot.

Someone or something omnipotent chose 1957 for the germination of a mystery seed, and 1969 for the magical first flower to bloom.

***

"We got Mr. Kirkwood this year. Damn he's tall," said Pete, sizing up our sixth grade teacher.

"I've heard he's a hard teacher," I said solemnly. My sister had him when she was in the sixth grade, and she told me about the research paper he assigned before the year was up. I didn't know what a research paper was, but I figured it had to be hard to do.

"Is that Jesse?" inquired Pete with an amazed stare. He knew it was Jesse. He just couldn't believe how he was changing.

Taller, five foot eight—broader, thicker, and, dare I say, handsome. His teeth were straighter, whiter, and seemed to fit his head. His nose had grown outward and even a little pointed. His thick, black, wavy hair was neatly combed straight back. Picture Michael Landon from *Bonanza* with Muhammad Ali's complexion.

But Jesse was still as poor as dirt. He worked every day after school in the lunchroom. The work kept him in food and clothes. It also kept a little change in his pocket, which he always seemed to be sharing with someone, especially kids that never seemed to buy anything at the snack break.

"Yep, that's ol' Jesse," I said, smiling. I wasn't surprised anymore.

"Let's go talk to him." Pete was already moving toward Jesse.

"Hey, Jesse, whatcha been up to this summer?" Pete asked, greeting him.

"Two of my favorite people. How have you guys been?" asked Jesse with a joyous smile.

When Pete put his hand on Jesse's shoulder for a pat of welcome, Jesse reached around Pete and embraced him. I had never seen a grammar school boy hug another grammar school boy before. Apparently, Pete hadn't either, as his arms dangled limply at his side. Not knowing exactly what to do, I awkwardly stuck my hand out in handshake mode.

Jesse took my hand firmly and jerked me into his chest, giving me the same affectionate hug he had just given Pete. I managed the courage to lightly put one of my hands on his shoulder blade. I came from a long line of non-huggers. We loved each other as much as any family, we just didn't hug.

"I've been thinking about you this summer." Jesse's smile never left his face. "Matt, you look like you grew some," he said, holding out his hand in the air to indicate how tall I was. It didn't bother me a bit—he was holding it six inches taller than I actually was. Jesse knew I was self-conscious about my height. All runts are.

"Thanks. I needed to hear that," I said, laughing a little and peering up at him.

"I thought you might. That's why I said it." Jesse's laughing eyes glanced at Pete. He gave him a wink.

"Pete, you look like a man with a headful of knowledge to me. Are you ready for the new year?" Jesse's laughing eyes and smile were ever-present.

"It don't make any difference if I'm ready or not. They're gonna make me come here every day anyhow," grumbled Pete.

Jesse chuckled and put his hand on Pete's shoulder as we started toward our desks.

"Now that's what I love about you, Pete. You can make most things seem funny. I'm glad I know you both."

Me and Pete turned away and went to our assigned seats in a good mood.

* * *

Over the summer, Pete, me, Bart, John, Andy, Jude, and Philip started what would become a tradition for the gang. We spent some of our weekends at each other's houses. I spent the weekend at Bart's, Bart spent a weekend with me, and John stayed at Pete's, Philip with Andy and so on. The plan was we'd swap around until everybody spent a weekend at everyone else's house. And then we'd just go to whoever's we wanted to after that.

You never really know somebody until you know their family. You may think you know someone—know their personality, know their favorite movie, and you may even know their innermost thoughts—but you don't really know a person until you see who made them.

And so it was that on these occasions of the weekend stayovers, each of us got to see what made our best friends tick. I always assumed that since most of the gang had similar backgrounds, came from the same place, and our parents were friends with each other, it was almost the same in everybody's household. The way my family was would be the way Pete's family was and the same with Bart and John and so on.

This is what I thought, and I was wrong ... as usual.

* * *

"Hey, Pete, how did it go at John's?" I finally got to talk to Pete at lunch.

Pete looked around on each side of him and whispered, "I don't want to say anything where John can hear me." Pete was being as secretive and confidential as an eleven-year-old boy could be, sitting at a crowded lunchroom table and about to burst if he couldn't tell somebody. "I got to talk to you about this," he whispered, careful to keep his voice down.

"About what?" I felt I needed to whisper too.

"About John's daddy."

"What about him?"

"I'll ... aw, shit, I'll just tell you at recess." Pete was shaking his head like this wasn't the appropriate time or place.

I looked at him with concern and nodded my head to let him know I understood.

I had been around John's father, Freddy Harper, several times. He was always funny even when he wasn't trying to be, just like his son. John was always comical, usually with a short, dry wisecrack.

He didn't have to put a lot of thought into them, they just came naturally. Even when he was being serious, they showed up.

But they were almost always self-deprecating and negative. Freddy was like that to a certain degree, but not as bad as his son. I always liked Freddy Harper. He was affable and seemed harmless, also just like his son. I couldn't imagine what Pete had to tell me that was so bad concerning Freddy.

Grammar school time is like prison time—slow. It took at least eight hours for the two hours to pass till recess. I just had to know the secret. I just had to know, because, you see, I was supposed to go to John's next.

We no longer had our usual football game, as was the tradition for the previous five years, because starting this year, sixth graders could go out for junior high football.

Pete and I met up after the bell and strolled around the edges of the yard. I anxiously waited for Pete to tell me what was on his troubled mind.

"I don't want this to get out, Matt, about John's daddy. I like John a lot, and I don't want to embarrass him or make him feel bad in front of the class. You understand what I'm saying here?"

"Yeah, sure, Pete, I like John too. I won't tell anybody. What is it?"

"Well, Saturday, me and John were watching cartoons and John's daddy came in the room with us with a beer in his hand. This couldn't have been much past nine o'clock. We'd just got through eating breakfast. John's mama can make good pancakes by the way.

"We were in front of the TV not really talking or saying anything. John's daddy says, 'Ain't there anything on besides this shit?' Real hateful like. You know how he's kinda quiet and funny usually. I could tell his speech wasn't right, and you could smell he'd been drinking a lot.

"I knew Friday night he'd been drinking, but he stayed off by himself and didn't talk to anybody. When we went to bed, I didn't really think much about it, except I didn't know he drank at all. John didn't say anything, so I thought nothing about it.

"The next morning, I couldn't tell if he just started drinking a lot of beer for breakfast or if he was still drunk from the night before. Anyway, John looked at him like he was scared that something was gonna happen when he said what he did about what we were watching on TV. I could tell John was embarrassed, by the way he looked at me.

"John got up and said to his daddy, 'Watch what you want to.' He motioned with his head for me to follow him outside. We were walking toward the barn, and John said, 'I hate it when he gets like this.'

"I didn't say nothin'. I didn't know what to say anyhow. John says, 'I hope he don't get any worse, but that's stupid as shit. It'll be hell the rest of the day.' John looked worried about it, you know. I could tell by looking at him.

"I said, 'I didn't know your daddy drank.' I was just trying not to make a big deal out of it so John wouldn't be put on the spot. Shit, Matt, what do you say at a time like this?

"John says, 'I didn't know he drank either till he came home sober one day.' I couldn't help but laugh, you know how John is. He's always funny. He weren't laughing though, but he don't ever laugh at himself, you know.

"Me and John hung around the creek down there in the bottoms till it got to be lunchtime. Then we went back to the house to get something to eat. We went in the kitchen, and there were some sandwiches on the table. I heard John's mama. Her name is Judy, ain't it? Anyway she hollered, 'I made y'all some sandwiches on the table.'

"She said it from the back porch. She was setting on the top step with her back turned away from us. The door was open, and I could see her through the screen. She was holding a washcloth or something to her mouth. John said, 'Grab a couple of them sandwiches, and let's get out of here.'

"About then, John's daddy come busting in the kitchen cussing and ravin' and throwing things. I was scared to death. He starts screaming, 'Dammit, Judy, where did you hide my damn keys?'

"And then he kicks the screen door open, and Judy jumps up and starts running and screaming for him to stay away from her, and he was chasing after her saying he was going to kill her.

"John threw his plate on the table and run through the door and down the steps after them. I tell you, Matt, I didn't know what in the hell to do, so I just set down in a chair at the table, hoping like shit that John's daddy wouldn't be the first one to come through that door. 'Cause if he was, I was running out of the damn house myself.

"After a few minutes, sure enough, here comes John's daddy in the door, breathing hard and cussing under his breath. He walked right past me like he didn't see me. In a little while, John and his mama came back in. I don't know what happened out there, but John's shirt was torn and so was his mama's blouse. Her lip was swelled up, and she was bleeding a little out of her mouth.

"John told me a little later that he hated his dad when he's like this and when he gets old enough he is going to move him and his mama out of there. I asked him if this happened all the time, and he said about once a week and sometimes twice a week.

"That's why he didn't ever seem to want us to come to his house on the weekend. I see why myself now. He said his daddy can go for a couple of weeks and not get this way sometimes. He was just hoping this was going be one of those times. I guess it weren't."

I never knew that about John. He never said anything about his daddy, good or bad. I only was around his daddy when he was sober and then he was a nice and likable man. You'd never suspect he was a raging alcoholic.

I'd been around alcoholics before. Everybody has. I could tell a drunk when I saw one, even when they were sober. There is nothing more annoying than a sober drunk. But Freddy Harper was not like that. He was funny and self-deprecating, and humble to a fault. I was shocked. John had been to my house, and we had a great time. Before I heard the horrible story from Pete, I couldn't wait to go to John's house. But now I had to come up with an excuse to get out of going this weekend. I was too scared to go, and John was too embarrassed to ask me not to come.

If I simply walked up to John and said I decided I didn't want to come to his house, he would figure Pete told me what had happened and it might humiliate him. I was worried about how to do this, and Pete didn't want John to think he was a blabbermouth. I was in a spot, but this was only Monday, and I had till Friday to come up with a plan.

* * *

It was Wednesday on the playground. I saw John, Jesse, and Bart talking out by the flagpole. I had concocted an excuse to get out of my dreaded visit. It sounded believable and would save face with John. I noticed John hadn't mentioned anything to me about my scheduled visit to his house all week.

I considered saying nothing at all and pretending I forgot about it, and maybe it would just dissolve away. But alas, my mother called John's mother to confirm my visit and to make sure she had some chores for me to do and to let her know if I was any trouble. I hoped Judy Harper would try to get out of it somehow, but since her son had already come to everyone else's house, she must have felt obligated.

"Hey, guys, what are y'all talking about?" I wanted to get in on the conversation so I could act casual when I got around to letting John know I couldn't make it this weekend.

"We're talking about when we have each other over on the weekends," Bart blurted out.

"That reminds me," I said, wanting to go ahead and get it over with since it was already brought up, "I can't make it to your house this weekend, John, 'cause this is the weekend my cousin from Muscle Shoals comes in to see my grandmother, and I always go and see my cousins 'cause they don't get to come that often." Which was true, except they weren't coming this weekend.

"Well, that's OK. Come some other time." John tried to sound disappointed, but I could tell he was relieved. "Well, shoot," said John, trying to sell that he had really been looking forward to me coming. "There's a big sycamore tree down at the creek with a big long limb that goes all the way to the other side but grows kinda down to the ground. You can walk out on it all the way to the other side and jump off on the other bank." That's irresistible to an eleven-year-old boy.

"I'd like to come, John," said Jesse, startling us all.

"You would?" spit John with his mouth agape.

"Yes, it sounds like it would be a lot of fun. I'd like to meet your family, if it's not too much trouble," said Jesse with earnestness.

It never really occurred to us to invite Jesse to any of our homes. The fact was that none of us felt fully comfortable around Jesse. He was a mystery to us all. Matters didn't get any better when James and his brothers returned to school after the kidnapping and told very confusing stories about Jesse not being able to be tied with a rope and something about slipping his hands from the front to the back, and how he talked a giant madman killer into letting them go, and how the madman killer cried like a giant baby. A super-nice guy, but too damned weird, we all thought. But now John was in a spot.

Since I wouldn't go, and since John's mama was expecting one of us anyway, and since Jesse asked in front of other people, John reluctantly invited Jesse to take my place. He didn't want to, but what could he do?

John was uneasy the rest of the week. He didn't know which bothered him the most: the uncomfortableness of Jesse and his mystical exploits, or if his dad was going to get belligerently drunk in front of another classmate. John didn't have a lot to say the rest of the week.

I think Jesse sensed something was wrong with John on Friday at recess, just one hour before both would load themselves onto John's bus and to what promised to be—to John anyway—a very long weekend.

"Don't worry, John, everything is going to be fine, you'll see," said Jesse with a pat on the shoulder as he met up with John and me. John didn't say nothin'. He just nodded agreeably and shrugged at me. I knew what John meant—oh, shit, long weekend.

* * *

"I like your farm here, John," said Jesse as the two climbed down the bus steps. "It seems real quiet and peaceful here. I'll bet you really like the quietness." Jesse turned and looked at John.

"Shit, Jesse, the only way it ever gets quiet on this place is for my dad to accidentally find his truck keys." John blurted it out before he realized it, but he was kind of glad he broke the ice to Jesse as a warning of the possible unpleasant things to come. John had a terrible feeling that his dad would be on a bad drunk this weekend.

"That's too bad, but it looks like to me a place that could have a lot of joy." Jesse was taking in a panoramic view of the farm with his hands on his hips, like a farmer sizing up a field before he started to plant.

* * *

John and Jesse had a dinner of salmon patties and biscuits and gravy—a kind of breakfast for dinner sort of thing that all the families of the rural South were accustomed to. Freddy was not there. Judy sat quietly, hardly speaking, with an anxious and worried look about her.

John seemed worried too, but not Jesse. He was sopping up the last of the gravy with a biscuit as if he hadn't a care in the world. John only managed a few bites. Jesse looked at John's worried face and smiled heartily.

"Dad is probably off somewhere getting drunk, Jesse." John felt it was time to make a preemptive strike. Judy looked up at her son briefly and tilted her head down, her arms folded across her lap.

Jesse looked at John with his mouth full of biscuit and said, "So?" Then he looked across the table at Judy and said heartily, "Miss Harper?" Judy looked up at Jesse. "You make the best biscuits I've ever ate." Jesse gave her the same hearty smile he gave her son.

"Thank you," she replied meekly. She rose and went to the back porch and began to cry into her hands. She sobbed gently.

Jesse watched John watch his mom as she left. He saw the pity on John's face for the mother he held in his arms so many times as she wiped blood from her lips. As John watched his mother cry, Jesse saw a light reflected in the large, glistening teardrop in the corner of John's eye. In slow motion, it gently trickled down to his cheek.

In the reflection of John's tears, Jesse saw Freddy Harper making broken promise after broken promise to quit. It would be the last blood his fearful, weeping wife would ever shed and the last time his bitter son would ever be ashamed of him.

Jesse could see John trembling while lying awake in his bed, dreading his father would choose this night once again to enter his son's room

* * *

It was about nine o'clock, and the lights were off in the living room. John, Jesse, and Judy were lazily watching an episode of *Hee Haw*. John thought that the show was so corny that it was funny, but not on purpose. The sound of Freddy's pickup truck interrupted their program.

"Let's go to my room. I'm getting sleepy," said John, nervously.

"Go ahead, John. I'll be in in a minute. We don't have TV where I come from," returned Jesse, teasingly.

Judy hurriedly went to the kitchen. John shook his head at Jesse and disappeared into the temporary serenity of his room, hoping Jesse would soon follow.

The front door flung open. A staggering Freddy Harper passed through and stood wild-eyed in front of the TV, trying to focus on who was sitting on the couch.

"Gaddammit! Every time I leave, John's brought some damn new kid home with him from school." Freddy was slurring his words so badly, you could barely make out what he was saying. He weaved a couple of times and fell backward on the couch, being careful not to spill his Wild Turkey. He clutched the bottle with both hands to his bosom as he flopped down.

He peered at Jesse, trying to focus. His head bobbed like an owl searching for just the right spot of light. Jesse sat calmly, looking rather pleasantly at Freddy and not saying a word.

"You that half-nigger kid that's in John's room, ain'tcha? I didn't mean to call you a nigger kid, it's that I've had a li'l doo much to drink." Freddy was trying to sound apologetic, though he slurred so badly he kind of tapered off in the end.

"John's been trying to tell me ... that you the fastest ... most swiftest ... most hardest to tackle nigger he's ever seen. I guess you niggers have to be pretty damn fast to keep them loins and shit from taking a bite out of that ass. I'm sorry for calling you a nigger kid, it's that I've had ... an ... li'l too ..." Freddy was bobbing and weaving his head, and his hands were unsteadily trying to find his mouth with the bottle.

Freddy tried to sit forward on the couch, but despite his best efforts, he couldn't quite manage it. He slumped back and said, "John says he's scared of ya ... 'cause ... you some kind of ... special nigger. Well, I tell ya ... why don't ya just ... try to scare me ... nigger ... I didn't mean to call you a nig ..."

Freddy's eyes slowly closed halfway. He stared through slit lids at Jesse. His eyes opened quickly and saw Jesse smiling at him wryly. Freddy sleepily closed his eyes again. They opened once more to see a hazy yet still smiling Jesse.

Jesse said, "As you wish."

John's dad's eyes closed like a curtain being drawn on the third act.

***

Bam! Bam!

Freddy's eyes jolted open. Jesse was gone. He turned his head toward the door.

Bam! Bam!

He realized it was someone pounding on the door. He struggled to his feet and tried to stand as he gathered his bearings.

"Open up. Police." He heard the loud, authoritative voice boom from behind the door.

He staggered toward the door but felt a sharp pain in his leg. One more step and he sensed the openness of his shirt, which was almost torn from his body. He felt soreness in every muscle and joint.

He stopped to investigate and looked down at the tattered pieces of what used to be his shirt. He clearly saw blood gushing from his ripped pants leg. He tasted blood in his mouth as his tongue touched the edge of his split and bleeding lip.

Did I fall off the couch? No, that wouldn't have done this much damage. Did somebody come in here and beat the hell out of me while I was passed out? Could it have been my son, or my wife, or both of them? His mind raced wildly.

"Open up in there, or we'll break it down!" He heard the same officer's voice between the loud pounding.

He put his hand on the door latch to unlock it and saw the twirling blue flashes of the lights on at least three police cars showing through the slit of the door. *What the hell is going on here!* His thoughts got muddled.

He opened the door and two police officers in dark blue uniforms stepped inside. A third officer standing a few feet behind them was holding a flashlight in his eyes.

"Do you own a 1968 burgundy and white F100 Ford pickup truck?" demanded the first officer. Looking down at Freddy's hand, he added, "I'll take that." He snatched a .22-caliber revolver out of Freddy's trembling hand. Freddy looked shocked—he thought he was still clutching his bottle. The other officer forced his way past Freddy and started looking in every room of the house, one by one.

"You didn't answer my question," said the officer sternly.

"Yes, yes. I have a Ford truck," said Freddy irritably. He thought somebody probably stole it out of the yard because he never took his keys out of it.

"Were you driving it about an hour ago?" asked the officer, getting closer to Freddy's face. He got a good whiff of his alcohol-reeking breath.

"An hour ago?" Freddy was rubbing the back of his stiff neck trying to remember. "Yeah, I guess it was an hour ago." Freddy now figured somebody reported him driving drunk, which was all he needed.

"Yo, Chief!" yelled out the policeman looking around the house. "You better get in here!"

The chief and Freddy hurried into the kitchen to find the officer down on one knee in front of a woman's body lying on the floor, face down in an enormous pool of bright-red blood.

Freddy's eyes opened wide in shock. His mouth dropped in horror. He slid down onto his knees against his wife's lifeless body. He rolled her bullet-riddled body over into his arms and cried out, "No, Judy! No, my precious wife, no, no, no ..."

The chief put the barrel of the revolver to his nose and sniffed. "This pistol has just been fired. Looks like you hit the big time, boy. Cuff him." The chief tossed a pair of handcuffs to the officer kneeling on the floor next to Freddy.

The cop took Judy's blood-soaked torso out of Freddy's hands and gently laid it on the floor. He wrenched Freddy's limp arms behind his back and snuggly cuffed his wrists. He lifted Freddy to his feet, supporting most of his weight as Freddy's knees had trouble locking into place.

"Did you check in every room, Pruitt?" asked the chief of the other officer.

"All but one I think," said the cop, pointing to a room down the hall. The chief left the handcuffed Freddy and the officer and cautiously walked in that direction. Freddy was in shock and felt faint. He wanted to throw up.

A million thoughts were running through his muddled and confused mind, but the one he kept hold of was how much he loved his wife. *How could I have done this?* He must have threatened to kill her a thousand times, but he knew he could never, ever actually do it. Could he?

* * *

Flashes flickered on the screen of Freddy's mind. He saw a vividly colored scene of a pretty young mother gently rocking in a chair her husband had bought her specifically for this occasion. She was tenderly holding an infant named John up to her breast. A proud young father named Freddy Harper knelt affectionately beside the rocker.

The young mother's soft strawberry-blond hair conspicuously covered most of her beautifully glowing face. She adoringly looked down on the infant she loved with all her heart.

When she looked up into the eyes of her husband, he could only think to himself, *My God, you are so beautiful. What a blessed life I have. Thank you, God, for blessing me.*

The father took his infant son from one pair of loving hands into another. He couldn't remove the prideful smile from his face if he tried. His eyes soaked in the miracle he held in his hands.

He thought to himself, *I made this. Me and my beautiful wife made this. No, me, my beautiful wife, and God made this. And by God I will never let anything happen to either one of them.*

Just then the month-old son smiled in his sleep the precious way infants do sometimes. The father's heart overflowed, the cup runneth over, and he felt he must hold his son in his bosom next to his heart. He lifted the infant up and held up his own chin to make room on his chest.

Suddenly the scene changed to black and white.

He sees the chief—in slow motion—coming from his son's room back toward him in the hall. His hand moves to his belt. He unhooks a radio and moves it up to his lips saying, "Yes ... we're ... going ... to ... need ... a couple ... of ambulances ... out here ... we ... have ... two ... bodies ..." then everything returns to normal.

"I'd say the boy was hit in the face and fell backward off the bed and hit his head on the edge of the nightstand. Just from looking at it," says the chief to Pruitt.

"That would explain the call we got from Miss Harper, wouldn't it?" returns Pruitt.

"Yeah, it would ... OK, I think I got this sorted out. Mr. Harper there hit the boy, and he fell against the table and died. After some kind of struggle, Miss Harper phoned the police. That's when he jumped in the truck, went about a half a mile and hit the Volkswagen head on.

"Somehow he managed to make it back here. It don't ever seem to kill the drunks, just everybody else. Don't it, Pruitt? Then he shot his wife," says the chief, trying to write it down on a pad.

"Well, you've had a busy night, haven't you?" The chief yaks sarcastically as he kneels down beside Freddy, who is on his knees, in and out of sanity.

"The only good thing for you is that since you're drunk, they probably won't fry you. You'll get to replay this night over and over again every day in prison for the rest of your life. Drag this piece of shit out of here!"

Pruitt grabs Freddy around the back of his shirt, what is left of it, and drags him on his knees toward the front door.

The only awareness Freddy has is of his screams of agony as he cries uncontrollably, "Please, God! Please, God!" He doesn't notice the drool flowing from his mouth or the static blaring from the chief's radio as he tries to report back to the office.

* * *

Freddy jolted himself awake and lunged forward with a loud "Please, God!" The TV static blared and drool dripped down the front of his shirt. A clammy sweat soaked his clothes. As he started to stand, the whiskey bottle tipped over and poured out on his lap.

Freddy stood and looked at all four walls of the dark room lit only by the television, which had quit broadcasting. Everyone at the station had gone home for the night. He moved over to the TV and pushed the "off" button. A deafening silence was accompanied by the piercing tick-tock of the wall clock.

He moved to his son's room, and for more than five minutes he stood silently and stared at the two boys fast asleep in front of him. He wiped away a steady flow of tears.

Back in the kitchen, he poured the remainder of the Wild Turkey down the kitchen sink. He did the same thing with the bottle in the cabinet.

Freddy turned to his bedroom and went to his sleeping wife. He sat by her side and played with her slightly graying but still strawberry-blond hair, gently letting its softness tickle the insides of his fingers.

"What is it, Freddy?" Judy said sleepily.

"I love you," Freddy said. He cradled her in his arms.

Judy could feel the occasional tear gently land on the side of her cheek as her husband rocked her back and forth with the same tenderness she used to rock her son.

"Tell me what's wrong," she said with concern. She had never seen her husband act like this before.

"Where did you put that phone number of that minister that you called? You know, the one that came by here that was going to help me get over my drinking problem. I ran him off, remember?"

"It's in the drawer in the kitchen, next to the coffee pot. Why?"

"Me and the Good Lord need to have us a talk. Go back to sleep. I love you."

Freddy went back to the kitchen, put on a pot of coffee, and found the number in the drawer. He sat in a chair and sipped coffee for the rest of the night. He looked restlessly at the ticking clock on the wall and wondered if six o'clock was too early to call, or should he wait until six thirty?

CHAPTER 15

IT WAS MONDAY, THE SECOND week of school, and it was also the day of our first official practice of organized football. I was scared to death!

Not only was I short, but I made up for it by being skinny. Skinny was actually being kind, more like scrawny. I was bolstered by the fact I was faster than everybody else in the class—except for maybe Jesse. I was thirty pounds lighter than everybody else also, and we were practicing against seventh, eighth, and ninth graders.

The bell rang for recess, which was now our football practice time. Mr. Kirkwood said the boys who signed up for football could go to the locker room under the old gym, which stood within sight of our school and Jess Rulam High, where both junior high and high school kids went. The rest of the class would go to the playground as usual.

All those who were going to practice were to wait in the school hall for Coach Harrison, who was in his second year as the assistant junior high football coach. He would lead us to the locker room and me to my doom. One by one we peeled off in opposite directions as we exited our classroom. The smart kids would head to the playground for gentle, peaceful play; the dumb-ass kids would head for a sunbaked football field to bash each other's brains out.

Bart appeared first and lined up next to me against the wall, then Jude, Andy, Pete, and John. Bearing right was Thad, all three Jones brothers, and then came Cater, who could only watch because of his concussion. He was followed by Pete, Harold, Philip, and Simon. Jesse came out last, but instead of following the class to the playground, he turned abruptly and took his place in the line of scared rookie football players.

"I didn't think you were playing football, Jesse," I said, surprised.

"I'm not, Matt," Jesse said, smiling at me. "I'm going to see if I can be the manager. I believe I heard it pays ten dollars a week. Besides, I'd like to see what is so important about football that it has you so frightened."

I thought that was a strange comment. How did he know I was so scared? I was afraid to look down at my feet; I might have been standing in a puddle of my own piss. But I wasn't the only one who looked concerned. The Jones boys were nervously taking glances at Jesse.

I knew this because I was nervously taking glances at the Jones boys. I could see a surprised grin cross the face of the approaching Coach Harrison as he noticed Jesse.

"All right, men, follow me." I was surprised Coach didn't ask Jesse why he was in line. We arrived at the old gym—it was called that ever since the new gym, which was across the street, was built a couple of years ago—and took the sunken entrance, which led to the basement where the football lockers were hidden from the public.

***

Before the games on Friday night, and before the games with the paper cups began, the gang had ceremoniously gathered around this mysterious enclave.

We paid strict attention to the cheerleaders for the signal that they were about to assemble in a single file, place their hands on their hips, and prance down the hill on the south end of the field and gloriously lead the team back up the hill and on to a brilliant victory—theoretically anyway.

We watched for the "signal" and followed at a safe distance.

Football had become a way of life for the community of Jess Rulam. The town was highlighted on Channel 6 News once about six years earlier for its football prowess. The varsity football coach, Conrad Peppers, had been hired a little later, after the legendary Coach Dionard Hickson retired with three State AA championships. Jess Rulam High had produced seven Parade All-Americans and over a dozen Jess Rulam alumni had played Division I College football—a truly remarkable feat for a school its size.

Every male child within fifteen miles of Jess Rulam dreamed of making the football team. The stories told at the drugstore gathering of the elders were mesmerizing for a lad of five or six. It was enough to make one race back home and pester his father to throw passes in the backyard, hard ones too. It was enough to push tiny muscles to struggle an emaciated body up a chin-up bar and do ten push-ups, boy-style.

Everybody played then. If you didn't, there was something wrong with you, or you were just a sissy. Whether you were scared to play didn't matter; it was safer to play. The ass-kicking on the field was less humiliating than the disgrace from not playing. "Fag" and "queer" were synonyms for cowardice for not playing football.

Coach Peppers had had no championships, and only one playoff game, which he lost badly. The team had won only five games the previous season. His seat was hot, and getting hotter. This was why we were about to practice football with the older kids, I presumed, so Coach Peppers could cool his seat with his forward-thinking plan. He figured if we practiced with the junior boys, we might be strong football material once we were eligible to play high school ball.

Coach Peppers needed to sell his plan to the Gridiron Club to offset the news that none of the much ballyhooed black kids from Orr were coming out to play football for Jess Rulam High this year. The news was that they didn't appreciate being called niggers by some of the white fans from the stands on the first day of practice. After that, Coach Peppers closed the practices, but it was too late. All the black football players from the school formally known as Orr High had turned in their uniforms.

* * *

On September 2, 1969, the first black high school students from Orr High had arrived at Jess Rulam. Though in the previous year the elementary students had been bused in, the high school had had to wait one year longer to close due to a football schedule contract and dispute.

Coach Peppers had been beside himself with anticipation of the arrival of the black football players. There were seven players from Orr who would be playing varsity football in the fall. Six of them were going to be starters.

Coach Peppers was a former University of Alabama football player from 1959 to 1961. He was a second string defensive cornerback for Coach Paul "Bear" Bryant's 1961 National Championship team. He had called the famous coach and informed him of his new job as head coach four years ago. Coach Bryant always wanted former players to stay in touch and let him know how they were coping with being ex-football players.

Peppers called Coach Bryant again, this time in the summer of '69, to let him know black players would be on his team for the first time.

"Coach Bryant?"

"Yes, this is Coach Bryant."

"Coach, this is Conrad Peppers."

"Conny, how are you? You still coaching that high school team up there?"

"Yes, sir, Coach. I am."

"Well, how you coming out up there?"

"It's been kinda tough."

"Well, hang in there, Conny. You knew it wouldn't gonna be a picnic when you hired on."

"No, I knew that. Coach, I have a half-dozen or so black boys coming out this year from Orr High that they're busing in here. I recruited them, actually."

"Well, that's good, Conny. I've talked to several other coaches about blacks, and they all got the same story."

"What's the story, Coach?"

"Well, they say that they'll play their ass off for you. They won't quit on you. They got nowhere else to go. Sports are a way out for them. And, most of 'em are, well, pretty damn good. And I'll tell you something else about blacks, Conny: For the most part, they're pretty damn good kids.

"Coach, that's why I'm so anxious to get started. I've got about three or four of these kids that could play for anybody in the country, including you."

"I wish to God I could recruit 'em. I would. I'm about ready to recruit one anyway. I don't give a damn what they say. We need 'em, and I'm going to have 'em. It's just a matter of time, Conny. Maybe we'll play somebody that's got some black boys on their team, and they can see how good they are."

"I'm glad to hear you say that," Coach Peppers said. "I can't wait to get started. These will be the first black players in this county. It's historic!"

"One thing I need to tell you, Conny," Bryant said.

"What's that, Coach?"

"You can coach players, you can't coach fans. Don't be surprised if this gets ugly from some of your supporters. It's hard to change people. I know what I'm talking about here."

"I think we'll be all right. I think these people want to win worse than they want to be asses, Coach."

"Don't underestimate the power of the asses of the world, Conny."

"Thanks, Coach. I'll keep that in mind."

* * *

It was August. Coach Peppers was nervously catching glimpses of the clock hanging just above the doorway of his office. The first practice would start at three. What should he tell everybody? Should he say something to the white players? Should he say something to the black players? Or should he say nothing at all? No, he would have to say something. This would be the first time that any of these players had ever dressed in front of people of different races. He had to say something, but what?

He made up his mind that he wouldn't plan what to say. It would just come to him, naturally, just like the blocking scheme on a screen pass.

One by one, the varsity football team members made their way into the locker room. Coach Bone, the line coach, informed everybody to pick a new locker. If they played last year, they could stay at their old locker cubicle. Coach led the freshmen and the black players to the equipment room and fitted them with practice uniforms.

After everyone was equipped, Coach Peppers brought a game jersey to the black players with the numbers they wore at Orr. He made arrangements with the returning white players to graciously give up their number if it clashed with the black players'. After a few grumbles and sullen looks, the whites reluctantly accepted new numbers. The explanation that it would help team unity and ease the angst of the black players was hard to argue against.

As he handed each black player a jersey, he added, "Welcome aboard." It was responded to with a, "Thank you, Coach." As he handed Markus Keys his jersey, he thought, *This guy just looks fast.* Markus Keys was from the nearby black town of Beth Anthony along with most of the other students who had attended Orr. The rest were from Jess Rulam.

The students were given a choice to either attend Jess Rulam or the city school system of Jericho, which half the students did. Coach Peppers made several visits to the school, in essence recruiting the star athletes. His efforts were rewarded when seven of the players decided to come to Jess Rulam, in effect saving his job, or so he reasoned.

Markus Keys was considered one of the top college prospects in the state of Alabama. At the state track meet held in Montgomery the previous spring, he ran a then Alabama state record of 9.35 seconds in the one-hundred-yard dash.

Markus Keys was not only fast on the track, but he was also fast off the track. He and some players from his school had decided to go to the Jess Rulam football field in the summer before the start of the school year and summer practice to do a little working out. It consisted mostly of running pass patterns and some conditioning.

It was the same time the Jess Rulam varsity cheerleaders practiced their cheers, tumbling and such. Markus was an attractive eighteen-year-old. He had distinctive features that reminded people of a very young Billy Dee Williams—"straight" wavy hair, brilliant white smile and all.

Karen Meade was the head cheerleader. She was a senior and had just broken up with her boyfriend of three years. She was simply the most stunning girl in Jess Rulam High School. She had short brown hair that curled cutely toward the front and a movie star smile, and, of course, a "cheerleader" build that passed for a swimsuit model. She was the 1968 Homecoming Queen.

She was carefree, gregarious, and somewhat daring—just daring enough to notice the rather attractive black football star giving her the eye and to not be offended by it. It was innocent enough. The football players were getting a little closer and a little closer to where the cheerleaders were tumbling, chatting, giggling and who knows what other cheerleader stuff.

Neither one had any misconceptions or illusions. A black guy thought he would break the ice and be friendly to a pretty white girl. A pretty white girl would be friendly to a future classmate, a stranger to the school and to white people. Or, maybe they thought each other attractive and wanted to acknowledge the fact. They were fully aware it would probably end at that.

The school janitor, Mr. Bordon, just happened to be cleaning the band room, which just happened to have a window, which just happened to have a great view of the football field, which just happened to have a black boy and the homecoming queen white girl giggling and laughing rather intimately, or so Mr. Bordon thought. This discovery might just happen to give a seemingly unimportant, unappreciated, overly mocked, and attention-starved janitor some important information that would make him suddenly, a very, very important person at Jess Rulam. That was his thinking anyway.

* * *

"OK, this will be our first practice together as a team," said Coach Peppers, addressing the first integrated football team in Colvin County history. "I know you're a little curious about some of the colored kids that will be playing for us this year. And, by the same token, I know that you colored players are probably just as curious about your white teammates."

Coach continued, "That's natural. But what you've got to remember, the most important thing here, is that we are a team. We will be practicing as a team, playing as a team, winning as a team, and, I hope not too many times, losing as a team.

"No one is any more important on this team than anyone else. No individual player, or players, will be praised when we win, and no player, or players, will be blamed when we lose. We win, lose, or tie as a team. Do you understand me?" Coach was looking around the room at the in-unison head nods.

"One other thing: These colored teammates here are going to be playing in some hostile environments, especially on Sand Mountain. I will be expecting you to watch their backs. They are your teammates, and I'm expecting you to act like it. Now finish getting dressed, and let's go have a good first day of practice."

Coach Peppers left the locker room feeling he had said what had to be said, and quite frankly, he thought he did a pretty good job. *More than adequate, hell it was good*, he thought. The confident smile grew unrestrained across his face as he walked out of the fieldhouse and to the practice field.

Coach Bone noticed a rather large crowd gathered outside the fieldhouse as he waited at the entrance for the players to finish dressing so he could lead them out. It was not unusual for the first practice of the year to have several fans and supporters to check out prospects and offer support.

Coach Peppers had a certain spring in his step as he made his way to the practice field. He had seen as many as fifty people come to watch the first practice before, but he must have passed at least one hundred, if not more, today.

He thought it only mildly curious that no one seemed to be asking him any questions. He thought perhaps it was because they were excited about the black players joining the team this year, and were, perhaps, a little intimidated by it.

Something in his subconscious, an eerie feeling of trepidation, told him to stop and turn around. He did just that, and saw the crowd break into two lines forming what to him was a victory line about two hundred feet long.

He thought it was a miracle the town had come to give him and his newly integrated team such a showing of support. He was actually a little worried that some of the more backward, redneck faction of the community would be hostile toward the blacks. But this showed how wrong he could be, and that he himself was, in fact, being judgmental of his still somewhat newly adopted home.

As he started back toward the fieldhouse, the thought occurred to him that this was actually a showing of support for him and that the coldness that he felt as he walked past those dreary people on the way down to practice was kind of a surprise party, and they didn't want to prematurely let the surprise out of the bag, so to speak.

Coach Peppers was within fifty yards or so of the fieldhouse when Coach Bone emerged from the entrance between the lines of white people with the team following him. The thought occurred to him to hustle to where the line ended so he could greet his new team amid the cheering crowd. This new team could mean a new beginning for his football career. Then he thought he heard something.

"Get your nigger ass back on The Hill!"
What! What was that?
"We don't want you around here!"

"Go get you a nigger girlfriend. You ain't got no business with a white girl!"

He did hear it. His heart sank for the poor black kids who were looking around in disbelief and didn't know what to do.

"Monkeys don't belong in school with white people."

Laughter came from a few that thought that was funny.

The first black player stopped and so did the rest of the team. Then, one by one, all seven of the black kids went back into the fieldhouse. Some had a look of fear. Others wore anger on their faces. The white players didn't know what to do.

Some yelled, "Shut up, you damn fools!" Others just looked at each other in incredulity. Eventually, all the players on the varsity football team returned to the fieldhouse.

Seething anger overtook Coach Peppers. He started in a dead run toward the crowd. His teeth were clenched. The veins in his neck bulged. He completely lost control.

"What the hell is the matter with you stupid-ass people? You're all crazy as hell!"

Coach was literally jumping up and down and waving his cap like a madman.

Someone in the crowd said, "Nigger lover."

"You all can go to hell!" Coach roared.

When Coach got to his office, Coach Bone was sitting in a chair looking down at nothing.

"Why don't you go out there and say something to that bunch of retards and tell them to get the hell out of here. You live around here. You know these people, Coach." Peppers was pleading with Coach Bone.

"What can I do?" asked Bone skeptically.

All seven of the black former football players from the now-closed Orr High School turned in their jerseys that said "JRH Panthers" across the front. They'd had the jerseys for approximately fifteen minutes. Coach Peppers could only watch as they placed the jerseys on the edge of his desk and quietly left the fieldhouse.

* * *

I remember the mysterious locker room being, well frankly, a letdown. What I surmised in my head as a gladiator suite for majestic warriors was in reality a musky, moldy dump that smelled like three hundred pounds of used jockstraps were being stored there for safekeeping. A combination of sweat and crotch permeated the air.

We were led to a room that had boxes of helmets, shoulder pads, pants, practice jerseys, thigh pads, knee pads, and shoes. We were told to find something that fit, put it on, and get on the field. My fingers were trembling as I tried on different helmets.

Coach Jackie Dobbs was looking at his watch and then at Coach Harrison and then at his watch again.

"How long can it take them to put on their damn pads?" Coach Dobbs was getting a little exasperated. Dobbs had been the junior high football coach for the past twenty years.

What was worrying him was not so much that the sixth grade boys were taking so long to get their practice pads on, but that theywould be on the field, period. If he had his way, they wouldn't.

Being a junior high football coach is a thankless job—hours of extra work for very little extra money in addition to being a full-time teacher. Since Coach Peppers was on the hot seat, so were Coach Harrison and Coach Dobbs. Losing football programs that are supposed to be winning football programs are trouble for everybody.

"Coach, I got to tell you something," said Coach Harrison almost apologetically. "There is a kid in the sixth grade that is, well, something special."

"Special? You mean he's retarded. If that's it, it's OK by me. I believe we should give him a chance to—"

"No, he's not retarded or handicapped," Harrison interrupted.

"Well, what's special about him?" Dobbs mumbled while still impatiently watching the locker room entrance.

"I don't know if I should even be telling you this or not." Harrison hesitated. He looked away toward Lookout Mountain, dejectedly shaking his head.

"What's the matter with you? You sound like you're about to cry or something. What did this kid do anyway?" Dobbs was laughing and a little bewildered at the "new" assistant coach.

"I saw him do things when we were playing tag football at recess some time ago. Strange things. Unbelievable things—"

"Hold it! Is this the same kid they kidnapped and shit?" Dobbs had cut Harrison off. "I heard some of the black kids talking about this shit. You don't believe any of that crap, do you?"

"I heard the Jones boys myself, and I have to tell y—"

"Come on! Those kids were in shock. You know how black boys are when they get scared. Don't you think they're exaggerating a little?"

"I know the Jones boys are scared of Jesse right now." Harrison was getting defensive. "You tell me if you think they would be the type to scare easily when they get out here. I'm telling you, I saw that kid do something strange myself."

"What strange things did he do? Huh? *Tell me.* What did he do that you're hee-hawing around about?"

"I've been keeping this to myself. I hadn't even told my wife about it. Nobody wants to tell anybody anything that sounds crazy. You know, because it could *be* crazy. I actually thought I might be losing my mind. But the other kids saw it too. I don't know."

"Tell me, what did you see?" Dobbs had to hear it now.

"We were at the end of the period. I was trying to coax the kid into doing his best, because he was out there against his will. He didn't really want to be there, you know what I mean. You see it every day.

"It was the last play. I guess he figured if he tried one play I'd leave him alone, you know. He tore out in a dead sprint and somehow he slowed down time, except for himself. I mean he suddenly appeared twenty yards downfield." Harrison was looking into Dobbs's eyes, afraid of what he might see.

"You mean the kid is fast," said Dobbs contemptuously. "You mean you have made the breakthrough discovery that black boys can run fast. Well, we'll see if we can't get you on at the *National Geographic* or something. You've obviously missed your calling, Coach Harrison."

"No, that's not what I mean. I guess I shouldn't have told you." Harrison was feeling belittled.

"I'll tell you what I'm gonna do," Dobbs said in a mocking impression of a stereotypical used car salesman. "I'll time him after practice." Dobbs got somber. "To be honest with you, I don't like these kids being out here. This is going to be a short-ass practice."

Dobbs turned his back to Harrison and walked toward the new players.

"Line 'em up," he shouted.

* * *

If I thought the mysterious locker room was a letdown, the actual practice was nothing like I pictured either. The stretching and the calisthenics were the hardest part of the entire practice. We did some form tackling drills at "half-speed," as Coach Dobbs called it.

We actually hit harder on the playground than we did out there on the real practice field. I worked up more of a sweat getting my pads on for the first time than I did on my first practice.

The Jones brothers looked the most disappointed. I think they were expecting more to happen also. They were all disappointed, except me. I was expecting a brutal beating at the hands of my much larger classmates. Instead, not a scratch. I thought the Jones brothers would be having me for a snack before the day was up. This was a piece of cake. What, me scared?! Naw, I had it all the way.

Jesse hardly had to do anything at all. He carried out a bag that had a couple of footballs in it and a few red cones. But he was being carefully observed by Coach Dobbs.

"He's a big, tall boy, that's for sure," said Dobbs to Coach Harrison as Jesse was retrieving a fumbled football during the form tackle drill. "He looks like he would make a hell of a player." Dobbs was trying to make some kind of amends for his belittlement of the new coach.

"Coach, if you could have just seen what I saw that day." Harrison could tell Dobbs was trying to placate him. "You don't understand what I'm talking about."

"It's all right, Coach Harrison. I believe you. He looks fast to me too. He sure is quick picking the balls up and setting up the cones." Dobbs looked at Harrison with a half-sincere smile. "I have an idea."

Coach Dobbs blew the whistle, and we all huddled up. "This was a good first day of practice. Tomorrow we might start to scrimmage a little and do a little live tackling, but not too much. What we want to work on out here is the fundamentals of the game. Now go on down, shower up, and catch the buses. You have twenty minutes before school is out."

Dobbs was attempting to act concerned. "Vick, go down and see they get out of here in time to catch the buses." Dobbs turned toward Jesse. "Jesse, I need to talk to you."

"Yes, sir." Jesse hurried to stand by the coach.

"You did a good job with practice today. I know you'll do a good job with the practice we are going to have in about thirty minutes. All you have to do is pretty much what you did out here," Dobbs said with sincerity.

"Thank you, Coach. I'll do my best," said Jesse with the same genuineness.

"I was wondering if you wanted to be a manager on the varsity squad with Coach Peppers. I believe he pays twenty dollars a week." Dobbs was looking Jesse in the eye, waiting for his reaction.

"That would be great, Coach. I need to work all I can." Jesse seemed excited about the good news.

"I'll put in a good word for you this afternoon. I know he was looking for another manager yesterday. I'll tell him about you." Dobbs put his arm around Jesse's shoulder as they walked toward the new varsity fieldhouse. "There is just one thing," said Coach Dobbs wryly.

"Oh? What's that, Coach?"

"Well, at the games on Friday night, one of the managers has to run onto the field to pick up the kicking tee after we kickoff and run off the field with it. And he has only a few seconds to do it in."

"Yeah," said Jesse, smiling playfully.

"Yeah," said Coach Dobbs, not as playfully. "So we're going to have to time you to see if you're fast enough for the job."

"I'm fast enough, Coach," Jesse said kiddingly.

"Why don't you hustle on up to the new fieldhouse and see if they will let you borrow a stopwatch. OK? I sure would like to tell Coach Peppers that I timed you myself. It might make a difference if he hires you or not." Dobbs was trying his best to sell this con job to Jesse.

"Well, if it makes a difference, Coach, I don't want you to tell Coach Peppers anything that you don't have proof of." Jesse had the same kidding, playful, almost patronizing air about him. "I'll hustle on up there and ask for the watch, sir."

In long mechanical strides, Jesse started jogging toward the fieldhouse, which was about three hundred yards away.

"I can tell by looking at him he's an athlete," said Dobbs, turning his gaze from Jesse to the new coach.

"Coach, I know you think I'm probably full of shit, and I don't blame you. Hell, I don't know what to believe about this kid myself anymore. But listen to me," Harrison said, looking Dobbs eye to eye, "I'm not an idiot. I know the difference between fast and what this kid is."

"Coach," sighed Dobbs, letting almost all the air out of his lungs, "I know you think this boy is something special. I know the first time I went to the state track finals and I saw these black boys run, I knew I had never seen anything like 'em. I saw Bob Hayes run about eight years ago, and I tell you, he was something. You know, they called him Bullet Bob." Dobbs laughed playfully. "You won't never show me anybody that fast again, Coach."

Dobbs was looking patronizingly in the new coach's eyes. A dark hand suddenly appeared slowly, moving toward the waistline of the two coaches, who were facing each other.

"What the hell! You scared the shit out of me, boy." Dobbs turned abruptly to see Jesse standing within three feet of him with his hand outstretched.

"Look, the fieldhouse is the big white block building on the hill up there." Dobbs was pointing with his finger at the fieldhouse building. "I thought you knew which one it was. Just go on up there and ask Coach Pep—" Jesse's hand turned over with the palm up and then opened in slow motion to show a stopwatch resting shiny-new in his palm.

"Coach Peppers said to bring it back when you are through. It's the only one he's got that works," said Jesse to Dobbs, but looked at Coach Harrison with a wry smile.

"Where did you find it?" asked Dobbs, dumbfounded.

"Coach must have dropped it out on the practice field here, or something."

Dobbs was looking off toward the fieldhouse and scratching his head. "Well, I know what you said was funny and all that, but don't be lying to me and playing tricks on me, son. I'm too old, and I'm not in a good mood." Dobbs was a little irritated.

"I never lie, Coach," said Jesse.

"I know you was kidding with me, son. That's what I meant."

"He wasn't kidding, Coach," Harrison said joyfully. Now he had a grownup witness.

"Aw, shit! No, no, no. Don't tell me you went through all this trouble just to make me look like a horse's ass," said Dobbs, shaking his head resentfully at Harrison. "You don't know me well enough to pull this bullshit on me. Why would you do that?"

"It's no joke," Harrison shouted seriously. He then looked at Jesse, who was looking back at him. "I wish it was a joke, Coach. I'd sleep better at night." His voice was drifting off along with his gaze.

"All right, so he went from here to the fieldhouse, asked Coach Peppers for the watch, and then ran back down here, right?" asked Dobbs incredulously. He looked at Jesse, who was staring at the ground, and then at Harrison, who shrugged and appeared to be as incredulous as himself but with a nervous smile.

"We were talking ... how long would you say, Coach? One minute, a minute and a half maybe? And the fieldhouse is at least three hundred yards away." Dobbs was gazing at the fieldhouse in the distance and running his finger across his chin and mentally doing some ciphering. "That's about forty-five seconds ... three hundred yards ... *no way!*" he mumbled. "Come on, we'll go to the fieldhouse."

Dobbs made a "follow me" wave with his right arm and stormed off toward the fieldhouse, mad.

* * *

"Coach Peppers," Coach Dobbs yelled as he entered the fieldhouse door.

"Yeah, what is it, Coach?" answered Peppers as he was coming up the hall toward the three visitors.

"I have a question for you," said Dobbs sternly.

"You have my attention."

"Did this boy come up here a few minutes ago and get this stopwatch?" Dobbs held the stopwatch in question in his palm so Coach Peppers could see it.

"Yeah, he said you wanted it. Why, don't it work?" Coach Peppers took the watch out of Dobbs's hand and looked it over.

"That's it! You can stick this damn job up both your asses!" Upon that, Coach Dobbs whirled and stormed out of the fieldhouse.

"What the hell is his problem, Coach?" Coach Peppers was truly perplexed.

"He can't accept Jesse," said Coach Harrison softly and matter-of-factly as they both watched the now-*former* junior high coach stomp toward the faculty parking lot and his car.

"Who the hell is Jesse?" asked Coach Peppers.

"This boy right here." Harrison put his hand on Jesse's shoulder with a proud smile. Peppers stepped back and watched Jesse a second and said, "I'm not a bit surprised. It was time that old fart retired anyway. Me and him didn't see eye to eye. People around here are intolerant assholes, Coach."

"It's not exactly like you're thinking, Coach," Harrison said uneasily.

"It don't matter much anyway. You're the new junior high football coach." Peppers stuck his hand out quickly. "Seriously, congratulations, Coach. I hope you can work with me on this."

Coach Peppers was serious and his voice conveyed it. Harrison smiled slowly, realizing he was now *really* the new coach. Coach Peppers looked at his watch and said, "You better get ready for practice, Coach. I gotta get ready myself in about an hour."

"Yes, sir," said Harrison rather proudly. "Come on, Jesse."

"Coach, could you leave me Jesse? I need a bigger boy up here to help out. I'll pay him myself."

"Well, sure, Coach, I guess," sputtered Harrison uneasily. "Jesse, you'll be OK, right?" Harrison was looking at Jesse, hoping he would understand his meaning.

"It's what I'm here for, Coach, isn't it?" Jesse gave a big reassuring smile.

Harrison wasn't as self-assured. He looked worried, but left quickly with the thoughts of a new career on his mind.

"Come on in here, Jesse." Coach Peppers motioned for Jesse to follow him into the dressing area. Coach went about instructing Jesse what he expected of him—that the other managers would show him what to do and that he would carry him home after practice if he needed him to, and so forth.

Coach was nervously looking at his watch. He sat down in front of one of the lockers. He picked up a roll of tape and began mindlessly tearing the end into little pieces.

"You don't know what this job is like, Jesse ol' boy." Coach was more or less talking to himself even though Jesse was standing beside him. Jesse had his hands behind him and was leaning slightly forward, listening.

"Everybody hates me. You don't know what it's like … for people to hate you, and for no good reason."

"I believe I do, Coach," said Jesse softly.

"I believe you probably do at that, son." Coach Peppers stood up and put his arm around Jesse's shoulder, realizing what he had just said. "I heard the most awful things you can imagine said to those colored kids that came out for the first practice. And then those same bastards want me to win a championship without those players ... or they're going to run me off."

Coach Peppers leaned in closer to Jesse.

"If anybody tries to do anything to you, you let me know about it. I'll save you, son, from all them ignorant-ass haters, if it's the last thing I do. You hear me, I'll save you. That's what I'm here for." Coach was emotional and on the verge of tears as he turned away and walked to the middle of the locker room.

Coach felt Jesse's hands on the back of his shoulders. Jesse's grip became a little more firm as he gently turned Coach around face to face, eye to eye. "You know, that's funny," said Jesse directly, softly, and a little wryly. "I was thinking the same thing about you."

Something caught Coach's peripheral vision, a shadow on the floor. His eyes followed the outline to the wall. He saw the silhouette of the two of them cast as a living shadow on the concrete. A six-foot-three-inch man was standing in the place of Jesse's shadow and a three-foot-six-inch child was standing where Coach was. The tall man had his hands on the child's shoulders.

Coach turned back and looked at Jesse. He allowed his eyes to follow the shadow all the way to the wall once again: A grown man had his hands on the shoulders of a child.

The trembling Coach stepped back about three feet and looked quickly to the shadow on the wall. He saw the two of them at their normal heights.

He stepped forward and put his hand on Jesse's shoulder. He slowly turned his head to the wall once again. And once again the shadow of a tall man and a small child reappeared. But instead of his hand on Jesse's shoulder, the shadow showed the child's hand being held by the tall man.

Coach felt faint. He stepped back, whirled, and abruptly left the fieldhouse.

CHAPTER 16

IT WAS MAY 29, 1970. We would be graduating the sixth grade. It would be the last year the school would hold an actual graduation from grammar school. After this year, a diploma would be mailed to the parents.

A tradition at Jess Rulam for as long as anybody could remember was the graduation ceremony of the sixth grade class. I think it went back to the late 1800s, when making it to the sixth grade was considered an accomplishment in and of itself. Children grew up faster then. They had to. It took all the family members to scratch out a living, so quitting school to work in the fields was commonplace.

It was also tradition for the boys and the girls to pair up—one boy, one girl—and sit with each other at the ceremony, held in the auditorium after the graduation. It was sponsored each year by some of the parents. They brought cupcakes, potato chips, cold drinks and such.

It was to show young boys how to be gentlemen and girls how to be ladies. More importantly, as far as anyone knew, they never missed a year of the graduation ceremony in the history of Jess Rulam Elementary School. The photographs that decorated every hall and corridor bore testament to this fact.

In our class that year, we had five black boys—including Jesse, of course—and only four black girls.

*　*　*

Because of the combined KKK, regular rednecks, and garden variety white people convention held outside the fieldhouse on the first day of football practice that led to the exodus of several black students from Jess Rulam High, and because a black boy was friendly to our homecoming queen, Mr. Kirkwood was concerned about the mathematical problem he had in class.

Tradition held that the boys asked the girls to accompany them to the graduation and party afterward, and it was the girl's choice to accept or not. To avoid some rather awkward situations from occurring in class, it was all worked out in advance, the week before. Boys asked the girls, the girl said OK or not, and if not, they went to the next girl and so forth. Actually it was a good life-lesson technique to brace boys for what was about to happen to them in the future.

I asked Sharon Roads, or actually she asked me to ask her, because we had been kind of sweet on each other since the first grade. One by one, everybody got paired off. The four black boys asked the four black girls and everything worked out well—except for Jesse.

Jesse was liked by everybody in class. He was polite, well-spoken, gregarious, friendly, and now, nice looking. He didn't hesitate to ask several of the girls. Even though all the girls liked Jesse, they all pretty much had the same answer, "Sorry, Jesse, I've already been asked by" *Bart, or Pete, or Andy, or Matt.*

Sherry Wright and Thad had been liking each other for at least two years, as best we could tell. Sherry was smart and pretty, and her father and mother owned one of the largest cattle farms in the area. We all thought they were rich. They weren't, of course, but in those days if you had more than one bathroom in your house, you were rich.

About two weeks before graduation, Thad and Sherry had an argument, apparently a good one. Thad told no one, and no one suspected anything. We all assumed that Thad would ask Sherry, but unbeknownst to us, Thad asked Teresa Brewer.

This left a rather inevitable and uncomfortable situation, or perhaps it was destiny. Everyone in class paired up, except Sherry—the rich, smart, pretty, and very white, white girl—and Jesse—the poor, very mysterious black boy. Jesse *did* ask Sherry, and being put on the spot, and also being a very sweet-natured girl, and somewhat liberal to race relations, she graciously accepted Jesse's invitation.

Sherry's liberal attitude in accepting the invitation to appear at such a public event with a non-white was most likely a rebellious countermeasure for having such conservative, or should I say racist, parents.

Thomas and Margery Wright had never seen Jesse. They had vaguely heard of him—rumors actually. Like most of the other residents in the Jess Rulam community, Jesse was simply a mystery. When Sherry told them that Jesse was her escort for the ceremony, the Wrights wanted to get to the bottom of the secrecy. It made matters worse that she waited until the day before the graduation to tell her mother.

* * *

"Mother, I need to tell you something," Sherry said meekly to her mom, who was busily pouring the last of the cake mix into a pan.

"What is it, dear?"

"A boy named Jesse is going to be my escort at graduation tomorrow."

"Oh, what happened to Thad?" she asked, half-paying attention.

"He chose somebody else to go with."

"Well, boys are like that sometimes."

"There's one more thing. Jesse is a little different." Sherry had anxiety in her voice and on her face. "I mean, he's real poor."

"Well, that's all right, dear," chuckled Margery. "I don't care one bit about that." Margery sounded amused that her daughter would think she was so small as to act uppity toward someone because they were poor. But she appreciated that Sherry was aware of her family's respectability.

"What are you about to bake, Marge?" asked Thomas, entering the kitchen and making his way to the sink to wash the grease off his hands.

"Pound cake," answered his wife.

"Good, my favorite. What are y'all talking about so serious?" Thomas smiled at his wife and daughter as he was drying his hands with a dish towel.

"Some boy named Jesse is going to be her escort tomorrow, that's all. He is a poor boy. That's what we were talking about." Marge was being overly dismissive.

"Wait a minute! Just one damn minute here. What did you say his name is?" Mr. Wright was growing louder with every word.

"Jesse, I think. Isn't that it, Sherry? Why? What's the matter, Tommy?" Mrs. Wright was growing anxious and concerned.

"That's one of those nigger boys that those idiots kidnapped!" Mr. Wright was screaming. "I remember that damn name! He was the one that got 'em loose somehow! Don't you remember all that damn shit, Marge?" He was now raving.

"Oh, no! Sherry, is he black?" All the color ran out of Marge's face.

"He's dark, but a super-nice boy. Everybody loves Jesse, Mama." Sherry was attempting to calm her mother down, which she thought might in turn calm her father down. "He's just going to walk me into the auditorium and walk me back to the room. That's all there is to it, really."

"No child of mine is going to be seen holding hands with a damn monkey out in public!" ranted Mr. Wright, who was now belligerent. "Everybody in town will know about this. It ain't damn happening. I'm going to take care of this in the morning. I'm so damn ashamed of you, Sherry, I could piss fire right now."

With that, Thomas Wright stormed out of the kitchen kicking the screen door open and cussing all the way to the barn.

Sherry was terrified at the prospect the embarrassment the next morning would bring. She didn't want to go to school. She didn't even want the sun to come up. It was going to be bad. *What will he say to Jesse? Will he call him a nigger right there in front of the whole class, or the whole school for that matter?*

It was going to be bad, real bad. When Sherry's head hit her pillow, she thought to herself, *Please, Lord, let tomorrow pass without ruining my life. Somehow, soften my daddy's hard heart.*

* * *

Both of the Wrights brought their daughter to school the next morning. Red, puffy eyes made it clear that Sherry had been crying. She entered the room and took her seat. Jesse entered right behind her, sporting a new look.

He now had about a four-inch Afro. I saw some of the black boys in high school wear that style before, but not in the grammar school.

"Hey," I whispered toward Pete without taking my eyes off Jesse. "I hope everybody is seeing what we're seeing for a switch—Jesse's got an Afro all of a sudden."

Mr. and Mrs. Wright nervously stood at the door and asked Mr. Kirkwood to come out in the hall for a moment, *please*.

"Don't act a fool, Tommy. I'm telling you," whispered Margery rather sternly to her husband.

"I told you I know how to handle this. Now shut up, will you?" retorted her husband, not caring if he was quiet or not.

"Mr. Wright, Mrs. Wright, how can I help you?" The teacher offered his hand to them both, which they accepted.

"We understand that our daughter agreed to go to this afternoon's graduation thing with some kid named Jesse. We just wanted to tell him it ain't happening," said Thomas rather coolly and calmly.

"I was afraid that's why you were here. I've got to tell you that it came down to them being the only ones left without a partner is the way it happened." The teacher sounded apologetic. "But let me tell you that Jesse is one of the smartest and nicest kids in this class. He is a real pleasure to be around. I wish I had a class full just like him."

"Well, that's good, but it ain't happening. Ask both of them to come out here, would you?" Mr. Wright was growing impatient and wanted to get this over with. "Don't worry, I ain't gonna call him a nigger or nothing." He actually thought he was sounding reassuring.

"I'm not sure he *is* one to be honest with you," said the teacher under his breath. "You decide for yourself." Mr. Kirkwood put his head in the door and asked Sherry and Jesse to come to the hall for a minute.

Sherry rose to her feet. With dread, she moved slowly to the hall with her head down. She knew she was about to be at the epicenter of a scene that would be talked about for years. It would become folklore.

Meanwhile, Jesse sprang to his feet so lively that his now *six-inch* long Afro actually swayed back and forth. He didn't *walk* to the door, he *sashayed*.

Mr. Kirkwood's eyes were the size of half-dollars when Jesse appeared in the hall. They were almost as large as Sherry's.

"Yes, sir. You must be Sherry's mother and father. I am pleased to know you both," said Jesse, extending his hand.

Mr. Wright was mesmerized. To him, the boy standing before him had straight, long blond hair that curled slightly at the bottom of his collar. His eyes were a sharp blue. He then took Jesse's very well-tanned hand and shook it vigorously as a man truly relieved.

When it was Mrs. Wright's turn to take Jesse's hand, she couldn't help but notice how much he looked like one of those surfer guys from California that she saw on *Wide World of Sports.* Jesse had an absolutely brilliant white smile, set off by his dark California suntan.

Mrs. Wright thought he might have walked right out of a Hollywood movie set with those Paul-Newman-blue eyes.

Mr. Wright had the same thoughts as his wife. He thought Jesse was a startlingly handsome *white* young man. He was taken aback at the length of his blond hair. In any case, his bright blond hair did contrast well with his beautiful dark tan, he thought to himself.

The thought actually occurred to him, *How could this town get a boy that could easily play a movie star? This guy ought to be on television ... Still, there's that long hair.*

"Boy, you wasn't nothing like I was expecting," said Mr. Wright, so excited and relieved that he warmly shook Jesse's hand again. "You might want to get that hair cut though. You look a little bit like those hippies on TV," he said good-naturedly while still enthusiastically shaking Jesse's hand.

Sherry and her teacher looked at each other with utter astonishment and total incredulity. This *black* boy with the bushy Afro was about to take this *white* girl, whose dad was one of the biggest racists in town, to a major ceremony, in which more than four hundred of the town's redneck citizens would be attending. Both their mouths were agape, as Jesse, who looked more *black* than ever, stood confidently smiling.

* * *

That afternoon, Mr. and Mrs. Wright sat in the sweltering auditorium, along with hundreds of other parents, aunts, uncles, friends, teachers, and anyone else who wanted to attend the one hundred and thirteenth annual Jess Rulam Elementary School Graduation. They were impatiently awaiting the arrival of the child and her handsome if not shaggy escort.

The signal was given and the piano player began her rendition of "Pomp and Circumstance." The audience all stood. Finally, the children entered side by side, boy and girl with arms intertwined. The peculiar way girls are sometimes taller than boys in the sixth grade was made more noticeable by their proximity to one another as each couple entered the huge double doors.

There was a unique, innocent cuteness to this annual ritual. The cameras flashed from various parts of the auditorium, catching the naiveté for posterity.

The Wrights weren't about to lose the memories of their only child and her handsome long-haired escort. Mrs. Wright made sure they got a seat next to the aisle by arriving thirty minutes early, despite her husband's protestations against a longer time to sit in the hot auditorium. She was poised with her camera as two by two, other sixth grade couples passed her by. Then, there they came.

Jesse was a good ten inches taller than Sherry—that was without his now *eight*-inch Afro. His hair was so bushed out it would be hard-pressed to fit it in a bushel basket. He still looked like Jesse, but with more accentuated African traits: His skin tone was shades darker, his nose flatter and lips fuller. Me, Pete, and just about everyone at the ceremony looked at each other with head-scratching stares. Jesse strutted proudly with his chin raised; his opened floral jacket and shirt with the collar turned out over the lapel punctuated his confident stride.

Mr. and Mrs. Wright, meanwhile, were still seeing the surfer-boy version of Jesse. "Ain't he handsome?" Mrs. Wright whispered to her husband, who was thinking the same thing. "Photos, let's take some photos," she said as Jesse and their daughter were within about fifteen feet. She was hunkered down so the photo angle would be in an upward direction when she first caught the handsome couple in her viewer. Sherry looked somewhat anxious, she thought, though she had no idea why, what with that strikingly attractive blond hunk by her side.

Though he would be hesitant to admit such a thing, Mr. Wright was secretly proud of his daughter's choice of an escort. Though his hair was long, Jesse was by far one of the nicer looking kids he'd seen in these parts. The gasps and murmurs from the audience were only a testament and acknowledgment that *they* were somewhat jealous of that very fact.

"That's my daughter right there," said Mr. Wright proudly to the woman next to him when he saw the astonished look in her eyes as his daughter and date went strolling by.

"I want you to look at everybody pointing, whispering to each other, Marge," said Mr. Wright to his wife. "They must think he's something!"

"They sure do. You have to admit, Tommy, he is a nice-looking boy."

"I guess," he said with false modesty, but with a proud smile.

***

After the ceremony and before the children returned to the class, Mr. and Mrs. Wright motioned for the couple that the whole auditorium was abuzz about, to come over for more pictures. They took pictures of the pair, of the mom and daughter, of the dad and daughter, and of the mom, dad and daughter—taken by Jesse. Mr. Wright got the attention of Jimmy Greenwood, Pete's father, to take a picture of all of them together.

"You want me to take a picture of him and you?" asked Mr. Greenwood in disbelief.

"Yeah, I know what you're thinking, Jimmy, but it's all right," said Mr. Wright sternly.

Mr. Greenwood snapped the picture of Mr. Wright with his arms around Jesse and Sherry. Jesse, Marge, and Tommy wore big wall-to-wall smiles. Sherry looked apprehensive and concerned, with no smile.

"Thanks, Jimmy," said Mr. Wright, taking the camera from his friend and handing it to his wife.

"What's going on here, Tommy? Everybody in the joint wants to know if you've lost your dadgum mind!" Jimmy Greenwood was trying not to cuss in public.

"I know what everybody's thinking, Jimmy," said Mr. Wright, scolding. "I know he's got long hair. But this is 1970! Damn, you guys are going to have to lighten up a little bit." He was lecturing these backward-ass people that gathered to hear his answer.

"I gotta tell you sanctimonious people something—I'll work on doing something about that hair, but I wouldn't care a bit if Sherry started dating this boy." Mr. Wright looked over at his wife for approval of his newfound liberalism. She nodded and smiled, full of pride.

"And I'll even go one step further," he said now that everybody was looking at him with shock and dismay. He was caught up in the moment and feeling their sneering looks because Jesse was poor and had long hair.

"I wouldn't care a bit in the world to have some grandchildren that look just like him. Now what do you think of that? Come on, Marge, let's go home," he said with all the pride he could muster.

And with that, the Wrights drove home with a feeling of enlightenment, set apart in stark contrast to those backward-ass hicks.

CHAPTER 17

THE YEAR 1971 HAD COME and gone. The eighth grade brought new challenges and changes. As usual, Jesse changed the most. He was growing rapidly, now standing six feet, but still rather slim with a more athletic build. The African features he temporarily donned for the graduation ceremony were largely gone. His nose was now thinner and longer, his eyes narrowed, and his hair dark and wavy. He looked more Mediterranean, even his skin tone, and he appeared more manlike than adolescent. He reminded me of a philosopher from ancient Greece—Socrates perhaps. He walked with confidence and knowledge of things. He knew what you knew, even if you didn't know it yet. Both hands holding each other in some fashion; head bowed, not down, bowed; a long stride, but deliberately slow. He stood out like a sore thumb. The rest of us walked slouched with poor posture, just like all thirteen-year-old kids are supposed to.

A new kid named Bradley had joined our eighth grade class from somewhere in Georgia. It was about this time in the early '70s that kids started wearing their hair longer. By this, I mean halfway over their ears and maybe a little turned up in the back. This new kid, however, had hair down to his shoulders, straggly.

He was the antithesis of Jesse. He walked with poor posture and uncertainty, like he wasn't real sure where to go. There was an uneasy manner about him that showed in an exaggeratedly worried looked on his face. He carried it around with him along with his poor posture. He didn't seem like he could escape either—trapped. In a word, he looked lost.

His good points were his beautiful smile, nice straight white teeth, and a pleasant, yet nervous voice that came from small but distinguished looking lips.

Despite this agreeable side to him, Bradley was incredibly shy. One might even say he was backwards, and one would be right. There was definitely something not right here. Loner is one thing; Brad was more isolated than a loner.

He also had tattoos, which were conspicuously placed on each of his hands. This by itself would not be such an oddity, but what they spelled out was:

Misery—on the right hand.

Company—on the left hand.

The peculiar fancy writing the tattoos were inscribed in was called Bradley Hand font, which was the only thing that made any sense about this kid. Yes, Brad was a peculiar person, to say the least. I guess we all are at that age in some way or another, especially when we're trying to find ourselves. Some of us just get more lost than others.

"Matt, who's that freaky-looking kid standing over there by himself, I wonder?" asked Pete.

"I don't know him. They say he's not as freaky talking as he is looking," I answered, divulging all the information I had on the person in question.

"He looks like he could play football if he got about a foot of that hair cut off. That is if he wanted to." Pete had more to say.

"Naw, people like that don't play sports. You ever notice?" I had more to say too.

"Let's talk to him," said Pete as he started toward Brad. "Coach asked us personally to recruit all the boys we could to come out for football. Remember?" Pete stopped walking and turned toward me to see if I was game.

"Let's go." *What the hell we got to lose?* I thought.

"Hey, Bradley isn't it?" asked Pete of the strange new kid.

"Oh, yeah, I'm Brad," he said, startled.

"I'm Pete and this here is Matt. We were wanting to talk to you a little bit about football," said Pete, like he was about to sell him a whole life insurance policy.

"I'm not much of a football player, guys. I'm not too good at nothing much," he said dismissively.

"Well, you look like you could play to me," said Pete, looking at me for affirmation.

I returned with an affirmative, "Damn right he does."

"Well, shit," he said with a grunting laugh. "I guess that beats being told I look like I got rickets or beriberi or I need worming or something."

We all laughed.

"Really, though, I'm not good at any sports, but thanks for asking." He turned and went on down the hall, walking against the wall and avoiding any contact.

He finally disappeared into the haze of bodies.

* * *

I felt good about the fact that we did something nice and unselfish. Well, maybe not totally unselfish. He really did look like a football player, and we needed all the football players we could find. Things were not going well in that department.

This was the fourth school in four years Brad had enrolled in. It's hard to make friends in school; it's even harder to try to make new friends every year. It's much easier not to make friends at all; at least, that's what he thought.

It's also hard to learn in a different school environment every year. He fell behind in school, way behind. In fact, he had a deadly combination working against him: one, the constant, or more appropriately, the inconsistent changing of schools, and two, trouble reading. The two things came together in an unfunny combo which made poor Brad hate school.

The anxiety that Brad felt when he was called on to read in front of the class was, to him, almost like actually being stopped by the Gestapo and asked for papers.

The nervousness, the accelerated heart rate, the dry mouth, the sweaty palms, and then words that are normally recognizable become as unfamiliar as Egyptian hieroglyphics. The deadly silence of a room filled with thirty people as you stare at a word—p-e-r-m-a-n-e-n-t perhaps—and the word appears *p-r-e-m-a-n-a-u-n-t* or *p-a-r-i-m-e-n-a-u-n-t*—the uncomfortable silence grows unbearable with each ticking second.

The teacher finally puts what would appear to be an end to the humiliation and quietly and apologetically pronounces the word. In reality, it only exacerbates the embarrassment with an exclamation point. I felt the anxiety exude from Brad like stink from a skunk. He wore the fear on his face. It was through sheer force of will that he could make himself enter the classroom every day.

Besides reading to Miss Barkley, it was only in history class that we read out loud. If the teacher had been an actual teacher instead of a coach, and gave lectures on the subject, instead of having us read the textbook like first graders, Brad's humiliation could have been avoided. Instead, Brad forced himself into class each and every day, and I vicariously felt his pain as kids snickered and rolled their eyes when he stuttered and stumbled through sentences. He sounded, well I hate to say it, retarded.

The curious thing about Brad was that five seconds into a conversation with him, you could tell that he was a super-smart kid. He actually made decent grades in some subjects. He was a whiz at math and grasped mathematical concepts much easier than me. To me, it didn't fit. Why couldn't he read well? I didn't know, but one thing was for sure, it wasn't because he was dumb.

Another curious thing about Brad was that if you mentioned the word "mother," he would shut down on the conversation or become peculiarly silent on the matter. Another curiosity: He was a great athlete, despite claiming he was not. The gym coach noticed it right away and said as much to anybody who listened. He told Coach Harrison that Brad was the fastest kid in school and not just the fastest white kid either.

The gym coach was right—Brad had all the makings of a great football player, physically. Mentally might be a different ball game. To be good at anything, one must have confidence, and if such a thing were possible to measure, Brad would have been about a one on the confidence-o-meter. He carried self-loathing around with his bushel basket of hair. Coach Harrison and Coach Peppers both asked us once again to take another stab at coaxing Brad, and anybody else, into playing football. The natives were growing restless, and the heat to have a winning season was on Coach Peppers, who was simmering in the pot.

"Hey, Brad, what's going on with you," I asked at break one day.

"Nothing much," he said quietly.

"We heard Coach Burt say what a good football player you would make and were wondering why you're not playing."

"I wish everybody would leave me alone about this," he said, exasperated. "You must be the tenth person that's asked me to play football. I wish the hell girls were as interested in how good I am at sex as y'all are in how good I am at football. Do y'all ever think about anything else?"

"No." I was just being honest.

"Look, Matt, I know football is a really big deal around here. But you have to have somebody to drive you to practice all the time, and I don't have that. My mother works all the time, and when she's not at work, well she's just busy a lot, and she wouldn't let me, and, and I … I just can't." He was getting frustrated, especially about his mother.

"What's with your mother, anyway?" I asked playfully, not expecting a real answer.

"She's a whore, that's what!" he shouted like he didn't care who heard it.

Then he put his head down, whirled around, and was gone.

* * *

It was fifth period at shop class. Everybody had to take turns sweeping up the sawdust and such after class, and today was Jesse's and Brad's turn. Brad was upset today more than usual. He was slamming the dustpan against the side of the waste barrel and hurling the scrap lumber against the wall.

"What troubles you?" asked Jesse while stacking the thrown lumber.

"Nothing."

"Something."

"God, why does everybody want to know what's going on with me?"

"Yes, well, it's our job, isn't it?" Jesse and Brad had gotten to know each other a little over the year—not much, a little. "I care about you, Brad."

"Why, why do you care? And why should I care if you care?"

"Listen, Brad." Jesse stopped for a moment to look at him. "*Thinking* that nobody cares about you is the second worst thing that can happen to you."

"OK." Brad stopped throwing lumber and looked inquisitively at Jesse, who turned away and began to stack the lumber again. "What's the worst thing that can happen?"

"*Having* nobody that cares about you." Jesse still had his back to Brad.

"Well, I got two out of two, great." A little sarcastic grin came over Brad's face.

"Two out of two, hmm? So you *think* nobody cares about you. Then nobody does." Jesse stopped his stacking again, moved closer to Brad, and waited for him to make eye contact.

"Yeah, I mean how can two people I barely know care about me? Come on, man. I'm dumb, I'm not stupid." Brad was looking at Jesse eye to eye.

"You are not dumb, nor stupid, or unloved, Brad." Jesse and Brad held each other's eyes solemnly until Brad turned away and put his hands on his hips.

"How do you know who loves me or cares about me? I mean, really."

"It's my job," Jesse said softly.

"So your job is to clean the lunchroom and help the janitor guy and care about *me*?"

"It is a tough job, as they say, but somebody has to do it." Jesse was smiling. The comment broke the tension and even made Brad smile briefly.

"Your mother loves you and cares about you, Brad," Jesse added, still smiling.

"You know my mother?" Brad asked. The smile quickly evaporated. "Have you heard about her yet?"

"Have *you* heard about her yet?" asked Jesse, catching Brad off-guard and startling him.

"I know all about her," Brad said sarcastically. "You know how some people are addicted to drugs? Well, my mother is addicted to men, Jesse."

"I see, and this bothers you?"

"No, I like getting up in the morning with some strange man I don't know coming from my mother's bedroom wanting to know what's for breakfast."

Brad was speaking louder and becoming incensed. "I like the shit out of moving around every six months to wherever her next shack-up is. Do you know how many different schools I had to start over at? I like it a helluva lot better when they move in with us; at least I don't have to move for a while anyway.

"It tickles the piss out of me when I hear that my mother has slept with high school boys, and blacks, and anybody that will have her. I didn't mean it like it sounded about blacks. I mean she's the town slut, that's all." Brad was speaking softer at the end and finally tapered off.

"No, I suppose you wouldn't like that much, Brad." Jesse was still looking Brad in the eyes, which were now tearing up. "Your mother needs love too, Brad."

"Well, I think she damn well gets it, from every damn body!"

"She's confused right now about what love from a man is," Jesse said reassuringly.

"I don't think there's any confusion about that whatsoever. She's a damn expert on the matter. She's got a different man every week."

"She's mistaking sex for love. She is under the misconception that if she gets men to love her, she will fix bad things that happened to her as a child. I will bet that something terrible happened to her as a little girl."

"I know something happened to her when she was a kid, but she never told me what it is." Brad was calmer and becoming fascinated with Jesse's insight.

"Everybody was little once, including your mom. Evil walks the earth, and the most vulnerable to evil are the little ones. Sometimes it is unavoidable what happens to the little ones. They are as innocent and helpless as infants, and the evil one robs them of their innocence. It is a theft that is difficult to overcome, and many times the thief goes unpunished in this life.

"She believes she is damaged, and she has to prove that men will want her and that will give her value. I want you to understand this, what I'm about to tell you, Brad: There is *One* who values her as much as He does any of the saints. I want to tell you something else: *You* have value as well."

Brad turned away so Jesse wouldn't see him begin to cry. "I don't know what value I have. I'm not good at nothing ... and can't even read that good, especially in class. I'm stupid, and I can't learn any damn thing."

"Not true. All you have is a disorder that makes you special." Jesse was standing especially tall as if he had an announcement to make.

"Makes me special? How am I special?" asked Brad, unconvinced.

"Have you ever heard of Alexander Graham Bell, Thomas Edison, and Albert Einstein?" asked Jesse wryly.

"Of course, everybody has," Brad answered, wiping his face and sniffling.

"They each received the gift that you have. How about Leonardo da Vinci, Thomas Jefferson, and George Washington?"

"What! Are you kidding me? They all had what I got?" Brad was in disbelief.

"Yes, so did John F. Kennedy, Woodrow Wilson, and Andrew Jackson."

"I do not believe this!" Brad was energized.

"And F. Scott Fitzgerald and Agatha Christie, and even Muhammad Ali all have or had the same gift you are blessed with."

"How is this a gift? I don't have any gifts. If I do, they are hidden from me!" Brad said, starting to see this new revelation as a ploy to temporarily make him feel better.

"Everybody has gifts, Brad, especially you."

"What gifts do I have?"

"Well, they say you're a good athlete. That's a great gift to have. You already have a powerful build. I'll bet if you worked at it, you could be a great weightlifter. Or, they also say you're really fast. You could be good at football."

"Everybody has already tried to get me to try that," Brad whispered vehemently. "I don't guess I could get the gift of girl magnet, could I?"

Jesse laughed. "See, that's another gift! You're funny. Then there is the great gift of your mind. Remember all the great people in history I just told you about? They are some of the greatest thinkers the world has ever seen. You really had to be smart in the first place to be awarded the gift."

"How is it a gift? I don't understand? I struggle trying to read and spell, and sometimes I get numbers mixed up. This is a curse, not a gift." Brad was getting a little flustered.

"Inside that mind of yours is a treasure trove of imagination. Just like in the minds of all the others with the gift, you simply have to unlock the treasure chest and show it to the world." Jesse was holding his hands apart and above his head to display the great size of this coveted gift.

"How do I accomplish all this you say I can do?"

"Do you really want to know?"

"Yes, I really do, Jesse. Tell me how." The excitement flashed in Brad's eyes. "But, I got my doubts if I really have a gift though."

"Let me see your hands. Hold them out here a minute."

Brad held his hands out with no protest because he figured like other people, Jesse wanted to see his tattoos. Jesse looked around and found a pencil lying on a table and then seized hold of Brad's right hand, the one that said *Misery*.

Jesse looked at Brad with a sardonic smile and said, "We need to change this."

Brad didn't say anything, but he was bewildered as to what Jesse meant. He thought, perhaps, Jesse was going to try to write something across the tattoo. He also knew that a lead pencil doesn't show when you write directly on skin. He should know—he had tried often enough. A felt-tipped pen was the only way he could see how Jesse could change his very clever *Misery* and *Company*.

He was also wondering why Jesse had the pencil upside down as if he were going to inscribe something with the eraser. Surely Jesse didn't think he could write something with the eraser. *What's he about to do?* Brad asked himself.

Jesse looked closely at the word *Misery*.

"Did you know that this style of writing is called Bradley?" Jesse asked.

"Yes, I saw it in a book at the tattoo parlor. That's why I used it."

"OK, we'll keep it the same then," said Jesse, like he was asking someone if they wanted fries with that.

And with that, Jesse moved the pencil's eraser up and down across the word *Misery*. It rubbed off easily, engulfed in a layer of eraser material just like on a sheet of paper. Jesse blew the eraser residue off Brad's hand, smiled joyfully, and winked at him like he was letting him in on a witty little secret.

Then Jesse turned the pencil around and wrote the word *Half- Empty* where the erased tattoo was before. It was in the same font and color. When he finished the first hand, he asked for the second.

Brad's saucer eyes were fixated on the new tattoo. He rubbed it like it was Aladdin's Lamp. He was aghast it was not rubbing off.

Jesse gently took Brad's left hand and repeated the procedure in the exact same way as the other hand, except this time he wrote

Half-Full to replace the word *Company.* Brad's lower lip trembled uncontrollably.

"How did you ...? What are you ...? Are you some kind of magician or something?" Brad was about two seconds from running out of the building hysterically screaming at the top of his lungs or hitting his knees and asking for mercy. He did neither, but rather stared blankly.

"*Half-Empty, Half-Full,* that's where you're at right now, Brad," said Jesse in a matter-of-fact manner. "That's better than *Misery* and *Company*, don't you think?"

"I used to pray that my life was different, but things never got any better, so I stopped." Brad was still mesmerized.

"You're under *Conviction* right now, Brad. You have been for a while."

"What do I do to change my life, and my mom? What do I do, Jesse? I'm just a lost kid ... I don't even—"

"Listen to me, Brad." Jesse had both of his hands on the frightened Brad's shoulders, and was staring him intently in the eyes. "Go tell your mother what happened to you today. She has been praying for a way out of her old life. There's a tent revival tonight where the old gas station used to be. They just got into town. Go tonight, you and your mom. Listen to the message Brother Barney preaches. It is just for you and her."

Jesse turned and started to walk away.

"Will you be there?" Brad quivered.

Jesse stopped, turned slowly, peered gently into the boy's face, and said softly, "Always."

CHAPTER 18

BRAD WENT HOME FRIGHTENED, CONFUSED, and yet drawn back to Jesse's words that resonated like a pinball inside his head. Different words ricocheted for a millisecond, flying away into space, only to return to the same spot for yet another millisecond of disjointed confusion.

He couldn't shake the unshakable. Jesse's words wouldn't, couldn't leave the recesses of his bewildered mind. Though he tried to think of something else, those words were there like a toothache. The more he tried not to think about it, the more he thought about it.

Just when he was beginning to think of not going to the tent revival, he'd look at the tattoos branded onto his hands. They were a constant, throbbing reminder.

He gazed at the tattoos—*Half-Empty* and *Half-Full.* Rubbing and wondering consumed the rest of his ride home on the bus while he speculated what the words meant, unsure of what he was going to say to his mother.

His mother was home from work when he got off the bus. On Fridays, she got off early from the coat factory where she had worked for the last month.

Ann was a startlingly pretty woman of thirty-two. She was petite with delicate features, which included small, pursed lips like her son's and big green eyes that actually twinkled. She had a small button nose and cute little ears, along with her sensual neck, which all beautiful women seem to have.

The most eye-catching feature she possessed was her arresting smile—the kind of smile that is indescribable. You just know it when you see it, bright and pleasant to look at the way a moth looks at a flame. She had dainty little feet and hands, yet a full, curvy, sensual figure that she strategically highlighted with a tight-fitting wardrobe. Even her work clothes were chosen to show off her sexuality.

Her nature however, was of sweetness—specifically and carefully designed to attract men. She laughed at their jokes; she was agreeable in conversation, and attentive to their needs. And yet, there was a coquettish mischievousness that made her even more attractive. Yep, it was easy to see why men would be drawn to her like a moth to a flame. Unfortunately, most of them lasted about as long as a moth *in* a flame.

It would be hard to imagine a woman as pretty as her being so promiscuous. She could have any man she wanted. Why would she want so many? There was definitely something wrong. Those two things didn't twine.

Though she was very sweet by nature, she was very defensive if Brad ever said anything about her men. She was especially emotional on this matter. She didn't want to talk about her selfishness toward the needs of her men as opposed to the needs of her son. Brad found it easier not to bring it up, though it was constantly on his mind.

He remembered one time that he got into a heated fight over some guy who lived in Georgia. Turkey Neck, he called him. Another anomaly about the pretty Miss Ann was that she seemed to be attracted to men less attractive than her looks warranted. Turkey Neck was living with them in their nice two-bedroom house, which had central heat and air.

He insisted they move with him to a two-bedroom trailer with no central heat or air and only one window unit, which was in their bedroom. And it was in another town. Brad had to share a bedroom with Turkey Neck's daughter, who was three years older than Brad.

The fight erupted after the new school he had to start at did a head lice inspection, and he was singled out in front of everyone for being infested.

* * *

"Mother," Brad said, gathering up his courage, "I have to talk to you about something."

"What is it, hon?" she answered mindlessly while she was doing the dishes.

"Something happened to me today at school."

"What's that, sweetie?" She was still only half-listening.

"Well ... this happened." Brad stuck the back of his hands over the kitchen sink and under her nose.

"What did you do to your tattoos?" She looked startled and annoyed at the same time. "Why did you change them, Brad? I gave you forty dollars to get those stupid tattoos, and now you've changed them." Then her annoyance shifted to puzzlement.

"How did you do that? I didn't give you any money," her voice tapered off. Soon she was mumbling to herself. "You didn't get the money out of my purse? I didn't have any money in my purse."

Now her pretty little lips were moving with little sound.

"How did they remove the old tattoos with no scarring? It's clean skin, like nothing was ever there. You couldn't have left the school today. They would have called me, Brad!"

She was getting a little hysterical. She grasped both his hands, saying, "Tell me, son. Tell me the truth. How did you do this?"

"A boy at school changed it," Brad said with a kind of dread, like trying to tell someone he had just seen the real Santa Claus.

"How?" she demanded. "How did he do it *at* school? How could he have removed the other one so clean?" She was sounding bewildered once again. In a softer voice, she said, "It was a real tattoo parlor we went to. I mean, I saw him do your tattoo with a real tattoo gun. I don't understand. I mean ..."

She thought about it hard.

"Mine is still there," she said as she rolled up the cuff on her jeans to expose her left ankle. There was the little tattoo: *Touch Me Babe*. It was from The Doors song and was one of her favorites. She got it the same day Brad got his. She often liked to do daring things with her son to show him that she was, indeed, a cool mom.

"It was a real tattoo, and now it's gone. How? What does this mean: *Half-Empty, Half-Full*? I don't know what's going on here."

She looked worriedly into her son's eyes, saying, "I feel so strange right now, Bradley." She slowly started meandering around the kitchen, looking around at different spots but not looking for anything in particular—more like a daze.

"Jesse told me we should be at a tent revival they're having where an old gas station used to be, and that a preacher would be waiting on us."

"Who's Jesse?" She was still in a meandering daze.

"The boy I was telling you about—the one that put the new tattoo on me."

"How ... how could he do it?" She was mumbling again.

"He erased it off and wrote it back with a pencil."

"*How in the name of God did he do it?!*" she asked him, screaming hysterically.

"I think *that's* exactly how he could do it, Mama."

Ann grabbed her son in a loving embrace, and they sobbed pathetically.

* * *

Reverend Barney closed the first of the weeklong tent revivals with a prayer, asking that all those who accepted Christ as their Savior that night would find the peace in their lives they were searching for and had not been able to find until tonight.

Ann and Brad felt these words were spoken specifically to them. The peace the preacher mentioned in the prayer enveloped both of them fully. *The funny thing about having peace of mind and spirit*, Ann thought, *it's so relieving and so easy to get. I wonder why I waited so long to receive it.*

Ann no longer felt ashamed of her past because that is exactly what it was—the past. The abuse that happened to her as a child was now hard for her to picture.

The painful memories were dissipating quickly, the same way a dream seems to fade away when we wake from one, and soon, it was impossible to remember it at all.

Brad also felt the inner peace that eluded him for so many years. He felt a love for his mother that was callused over by the scars of a painful and unhappy childhood. Just like his mother's memories, they seemed like mist now.

As they left the tent through the flap opening, Jesse appeared to greet them. He was all smiles.

"Jesse!" erupted Brad wildly, shaking his hand. "I didn't see you. Were you here tonight?"

"Yes, of course."

"I didn't look around. It doesn't matter. Do you know what happened?"

Brad was bubbling over with joy.

"I do indeed. Congratulations to both of you. It's going to be a new beginning for you," Jesse said as he gave each of them a hearty hug.

"I don't know about you, but I feel like we've met before," said Ann, finishing her hug with Jesse and putting an arm around Brad.

"I hear that all the time." Jesse was smiling warmly.

"The strangest feeling came over me when I saw the tattoos you put on Brad," she continued. "I can't explain it. It was like a sign or something. I won't ask you how you did it. I'll just thank you for doing it." Ann couldn't restrain herself from giving Jesse another hug.

"You are most welcome, ma'am."

"Tell me, though," said Ann a little inquisitively, "what do they mean?"

"I think they are self-explanatory," said Jesse as he turned and walked slowly away. "Read them again, and you will see."

And with that, Jesse disappeared into the serenity of the night air.

Brad and his mother looked at each other for a moment. Brad held his arms out and turned the back of his hands into the light streaming from inside the tent.

The left hand read: *Filled!*

The right hand read: *Fulfilled!*

Their eyes widened in amazement just like before, but without the fear this time. They both simply and warmly laughed. Suddenly, Ann stopped laughing. She had a curious look on her face, like she had just remembered something. She walked over to a five-gallon bucket, dumped the little bit of trash inside it on the ground, and turned the bucket upside down.

It was inside the same beam of light cast from the tent that had exposed the new message on her son's hands. She placed her left foot on top of the bucket and slowly rolled up her pants leg. To her amazement and delight it read:

You Have Been Touched, Babe!

* * *

Brad returned to school with a new look, a new attitude, and a new perspective on life.

He cut his hair into a crew cut no more than half an inch long. He was the first boy in years to sport this hairstyle. He was unrecognizable at first glance. Only with considerable concentration could his classmates figure out who he was.

He still managed to stand out in school, however. In the beginning, it was because of the length of his hair, and now it was still because of the length of his hair.

He and his mother paid a return visit to the tattoo parlor in Riley, where they got their original tattoos. The owner of the parlor had a display case and inside were beautiful silver crosses on chains, among other various trinkets for sale. Ann remembered how they seemed out of place among the knives with naked ladies on the handles, the swastikas, and coffee mugs decorated with a likeness of Satan and such.

She purchased two of the chains and crosses. Ann and her son made them part of their everyday wardrobe ensemble. The new cross was the second most conspicuous thing about them, after Brad's new haircut.

Brad navigated the school halls a little more confidently now. He no longer hugged the walls, and he walked with his head up. He made eye contact with passersby whenever it was appropriate.

I did a "Three Stooges" double take when he approached me after class.

"Hey, Matt, wait up a minute." Brad was hurrying up behind me. "I need to talk to you about something."

"Man! I hardly recognized you, Brad. What happened to you?" I wasn't kidding.

"Oh, I got rid of a few things that I was walking around with that made me different from everybody, but in a bad way. Things that said, *I am different from you, and hey there's something wrong me.* I got my hair cut too!" He laughed, and I laughed too.

"I want to go out for football. I know football season is over this year, but I want to start right now for next season. How do I do it?"

"That's great. I'm glad to hear it." I was in shock really. "Just meet me in front of the old gym after school, and we can go tell Coach Harrison together. He'll be jumping up and down about it. You'll be my first recruit," I said, relieved and excited for Brad.

"Good, maybe he'll give us a coupon or something; it's five points for every recruit." Brad was still funny without really trying. "I'd like to start lifting weights too. How do I do that?"

"The only way junior players get to lift weights is after school at the fieldhouse," I informed him. "There's an assistant coach, Coach Benefield. He's a real smartass, and he's in charge of the weights. None of us like him, and most of us can't get rides after school, so none of us work out much."

"I think my mom will come and pick me up after she gets in from work. I should be finished by then." Brad sounded confident for the first time since I had been around him.

"I still don't know anything about it. I mean lifting weights. Will the coach teach me how?" he inquired meekly.

"He's a real jerk about his weight room. It's like he bought everything in there himself. But I know for a fact that the Gridiron Club raised the money for all those new weight machines and barbells and stuff." I really didn't like Coach Benefield.

"Well, what do I do to get started? Do I just show up there after school and he'll show me what to do?"

"No, we have to see Coach Harrison and tell him you're going out. Then he'll give you a voucher that you give to Coach Benefield. But, you have to have somebody to work out with you. They have a rule that nobody can work out by themselves. Safety rule, I guess."

"I wonder who I can get to work out with me?" Brad was confused and getting a little apprehensive.

"I know what you can do!" I just had a great idea. "Do you know a boy named Jesse?"

Brad stared at me wryly for a second and said, "Yeah, we've met."

"Well, great," I said, a little relieved. "He cleans up the fieldhouse every day after school. If you know him, you know he takes a little getting used to."

"He's the reason I'm going out for football, and lifting weights, and everything. I owe him my life," Brad said, never taking his eyes off mine. I knew that he must have been introduced to *that* Jesse. Yeah, *that* one. I knew what he meant.

"Just take your voucher to Coach Benefield and ask Jesse to help you. He's one of the few people that can put up with that asshole."

I wasn't being cute about this. The new assistant coach was an incredible bore. He loved to hear the sound of his own voice bragging about when he played football, and how good he was, and the many scholarships he received, and how much weight he could lift. And if he hadn't gotten his knee hurt, he could have played at Alabama, and probably went pro.

Another thing that made him a bastard was that he never passed up an opportunity to belittle someone. He made fun of everybody.

He seized on any flaw and highlighted it in front of as many people as possible. *The maximum embarrassment possible* was his motto, and he wielded it like a sabre.

For example, there was the time when this ninth grader, who was physically challenged, had to do a chin-up for gym class. There was a requirement in those days that a student couldn't pass gym class if they couldn't do so many chin-ups, sit-ups, and so forth.

This kid, whose name was Jean, was hopeless. So the gym teacher had mercy on him and devised a compromise. If Jean could do one chin-up before the school year was up, he would pass him.

Hearing this, The Asshole dropped by one day when the gym teacher was gone to give Jean some *encouragement*, as he put it. Jean was faithful in his regimen of vigorously trying to pull himself up a little higher and a little higher each day. The Asshole told Jean to mount the chin-up bar, and he would show him a new technique he had learned that would help people like him do a chin-up. He told Jean the mysterious long, slender box he was carrying was a reward for the boy if he mastered it. A rose, perhaps? The Asshole wouldn't say. He told others, "It is what he deserves for the effort he's put forth thus far."

Jean set his jaw and jumped up to take a firm grip on the bar. He was swinging slightly back and forth with his feet about a foot off the floor. He turned his head to receive instructions. He didn't see The Asshole, but he heard him.

"When I was a boy, and I went to help my grandpa load his hogs up on his truck, if there was one hog that was just plain stubborn or stupid, we just gave him a little jolt to help him along."

Jean felt the sharp burning pain of the cattle prod, or hot stick as we called it. It contracted the muscles on his buttocks and expanded all over his body. Jean fell to the floor with a scream. He was in agony.

The Asshole was laughing uproariously. He said in his mean, sharp, maniacally laughing voice, "Shocking, isn't it?"

* * *

One more trait that asshole Coach Benefield possessed was that he hated black people. This was a particularly troubling trait for Coach Peppers. Ever since the black players from Orr walked off the field before that very first practice back in 1969, he had been dutifully, if not desperately, trying to persuade black kids to play on the varsity team.

Up until this year, every black student abided by an unspoken *law*: No black student would play football in front of those racist, redneck, backward, inbred, stupid, honkey-ass white people. A black kid could play junior football, but once in tenth grade, they either had to transfer to Jericho or not play. It was a *law* that was followed strictly, and without exception. This was much to the consternation of Coach Peppers and his future as a head football coach.

It had been three years however, and the black kids were growing weary of the *law.* Some of them didn't want to transfer to another school when they got to the tenth grade in order to play football. It was a long drive out of the way, and they had a perfectly good school right here where they could play. Coach Peppers argued this point passionately.

Coach Peppers was beginning to make headway on the younger black kids. The one thing he didn't need was a racist assistant coach. Unfortunately, that's exactly what he got.

At first, he just rolled his eyes at his new assistant whenever The Asshole said something outrageous. As he saw more and more of The Asshole in action though, the more he despised him. *If only the principal hadn't hired him,* he wished.

Coach Peppers knew he couldn't fire him, not after what happened with the old and now former junior high coach. He wished, no he prayed, that something would make Coach Benefield quit.

* * *

Brad was on his way to the fieldhouse when he saw Jesse on his way there too. He was glad he found him before he entered the figurative lion's den. He had heard so much about The Asshole, he had apprehensions. In a word, he was intimidated.

"Jesse, do you mind helping me get started lifting weights? I want to be really strong when football season starts next year." Brad was looking at Jesse for approval.

"Excellent choice, Brad," was all Jesse said. Brad looked ominously at the fieldhouse they were about to enter.

* * *

"Coach Benefield, this is Brad. He is going to be lifting weights after school for a while," said Jesse. The coach was reclining at his desk, reading some magazine or other. Coach Peppers let Benefield sit in the fieldhouse till six o'clock to supervise the football players that wanted to do their workouts after school.

"Fine, just don't tear up any of my new machines," he said. He sat up and grumbled, "Especially those new Olympic bars and weights. You got that?"

He reclined in his chair again with a smirk on his face and said to Jesse, "I have a question for you, Jesse. Why do the lions in Africa go around licking each other's ass?" He waited for Jesse to look at him, and then laughed. He answered his own question, "To get the taste of nigger out of their mouth."

This was his joke of the day. He had a new one for Jesse every day. All black jokes, all racist, and all deliberately pointed at Jesse. And every day, Jesse merely smiled and went about sweeping, vacuuming, and cleaning, never saying a word.

"One other thing, Jesse," said The Asshole. Jesse and Brad took a couple of steps toward the weight room.

"Yes, sir?"

"I want you to put a mark on the barbells where those dumbasses are supposed to put their hands. They don't seem to know how wide to grip the damn bar. I already put some chalk marks on them for you. Use a more permanent marker. Now, I don't want any question about where the marks go. You got me, boy?"

"How do I do that, Coach?" Jesse asked.

"Shit, do I have to tell you everything? Why don't you just surprise the hell out of me. Use your damn head and do something imaginative for a change." The coach looked back down at his magazine.

"As you wish," said Jesse almost in a whisper.

***

Jesse showed Brad how to do bench presses, and military presses, and squats. Brad was a quick learner and soaked it up like a dehydrated sponge. Then, he showed him how to do barbell curls and tricep pushdowns and crunches. Brad was a natural weightlifter and surprised himself at how strong he was.

Brad looked over at the huge chart on the wall which listed all the records: bench press, three hundred and twenty-five pounds; squat, four hundred and fifty-five; dead lift, four-sixty. He said to Jesse, "Before I graduate from here, I'm going to have all those records."

"I believe you will before then, Brad."

Just then a car horn honked and Brad said, "I'll bet that's Mom. I got to go, Jesse. Thanks for everything."

Brad gave Jesse a hug goodbye and was scurrying out the door when Jesse said, "Tell your mom to keep up the good work."

"OK!" Jesse heard Brad's voice as he disappeared out the door.

***

It was approaching six o'clock at night. All the players working out for the day had come and gone. No one was at the fieldhouse but Jesse and Coach Benefield. The crickets and frogs were playing their usual beautiful songs outside, paying reverence to the impending night.

A radio playing loud heavy metal music for most of the evening suddenly, for some bizarre reason, began playing a symphony orchestra performing Pachelbel's "Canon in D Major."Benefield thought how strange that a radio station would switch to classical music in mid-song. He could see the radio from where he was sitting, so he knew that Jesse couldn't have changed it.

What was even stranger was the sound coming from the weight room. It resembled the haunting sound that an old iron passenger ship makes at sea, like steel being tortured. It was time to go home anyway, so he made himself get up and check out what was going on back there. The music, and then that sound. *How weird*, Benefield thought.

The lilting sound of the "Canon" seemed to be growing louder as he made his way past Jesse, who was finishing up his chores by sweeping the hallway. He stopped just beyond Jesse and asked him bluntly and rather angrily, "Did you put the marks on the barbells so there's no mistaking where to put their damn hands?"

"See for yourself." Jesse put the broom down and walked out the door to go home.

The orchestra was hitting the crescendo of the ever-louder "Canon" as the coach entered the weight room. The lights were off and for some reason wouldn't come on when he flipped the light switch.

A beam of light from the hall added an eerie, shadowy solemnity to the room filled with stainless steel, exercise machines, steel cables, and foam padding. *Why is the radio playing this song over and over and louder and louder?* he wondered.

He made his way around each machine and finally to the back of the room to the free weights. He wasn't sure, but he thought for a split second one of the legs moved.

A sudden dread enveloped him. Every one of his senses suddenly and inexplicably heightened along with the now earsplitting "Canon." He could hear other sounds even above the radio. He sensed shadows moving behind him. A nervous jerk of his head caught nothing except his own trembling shadow.

He looked down at the barbell used for curling and realized it had the unmistakable zigzag bend in it of an E-Z curl bar. He realized they didn't have an E-Z curl bar. When he lifted the bar up into the beam of light coming through from the hall, he saw a ghastly sight. His already rapidly pounding heart beat harder and faster.

Where the grips had been on the curl bar, there were now indented fingerprints and thumbprints. The blood drained from his face when the light revealed that someone's hand had literally squeezed the ruts into the steel of the handgrips. The metal squirted between the fingers like playdough, even leaving uneven pieces of sharp-edged steel residue along the edges.

He dropped the bar and whirled around to make a hasty escape from the nightmare he found himself in. He saw something that made him shriek. It probably could be heard a good half-mile away.

The beam of light revealed that the brand new Olympic bar in its place at the bench press had two perfectly tied bulging knots of twisted metal in it. The end slipped through itself and pulled tight, just like the knot in his shoelaces. Instead of the soft cloth of a shoelace, this was *one-inch diameter steel*! Someone or some *thing* had tied the brand new Olympic barbell into a knot. And, the knot was *dead on* the mark he had made earlier with the chalk.

He left the fieldhouse in a dead sprint, screaming in horrified shrieks and flailing his arms just like a madman, which he had indeed now become.

Jesse turned as he heard the lunatic approaching and said, "Coach, did you like the way I used my imagination on the barbells?"

The former *Asshole and now madman* almost knocked Jesse down when he hysterically ran past him.

"I take that as a yes," Jesse said, but didn't get an answer.

Coach Timothy Benefield slung gravel and cut doughnuts out of the fieldhouse driveway that night. He didn't even return to get the things out of his desk.

The last we heard he was counseling troubled youth in a ghetto in Atlanta.

CHAPTER 19

JEAN STENCIL'S FAMILY HAD LIVED in Jess Rulam for over fifteen years. His father owned and operated an old-time country store on Main Street in town. His mother dutifully helped his father each day when she finished with the household chores. He ordered supplies and merchandise, and she kept the books. The store was the last of its kind—a mom-and-pop general merchandise store that sold sundries. I used to ask my mother what sundries meant; I don't remember her ever telling me. She would mumble something about little stuff or something. I don't think she gave me the same answer twice. I still don't know to this day what sundries are.

I can still remember the smell of the leather goods that permeated the store. I remember the brogan boots displayed on a flat table, not shelves, along with folded Levi's jeans and work shirts.

You could buy groceries, feed, seed, and clothes. Clothes were thicker in those days and made to last. This store seemed to have one, and most times only one, of everything. They even had a saddle. I used to catch my mother not looking and mount the saddle, and I was Roy Rogers, vicariously of course. If she caught me on it, I was Roy Rogers with a red ass.

Anyway, Jean was a sweet kind of child; polite, courteous to all, and helpful whenever possible. You know the type—the kind of child parents would be proud of. Jean was also well-rounded. By that, I don't mean that he was worldly and well-accomplished with desirable and varied abilities or achievements. I mean he was fat. Not just fat, but morbidly obese. He came by it honestly. His father was round as was his mom. Likewise for his brother, who had already graduated from high school and was now in college. There was his younger sister, who was still in grammar school, and she, like everyone else in the family, was round.

Yes, this entire family was born round. It was merely a consequence of two round parents producing round offspring. It happens with eye color, hair color, blood type, height, and unfortunately, weight.

One can easily accept inheriting blue eyes, or brown hair, or type B negative blood, and nobody cares. If you inherit fat, then there is a problem—people care, especially schoolkids.

I wasn't sure whether the cruel jokes really didn't bother Jean or if he merely learned to deflect the razzing in hopes that if he ignored the minions, they would eventually go away. In either case, one thing was certain—he never showed an exposed nerve.

* * *

Jean entered the old gym as he had for the last six months—determined. The old gym was where PE class was held each day; the new gym was strictly off-limits for everyone except basketball players. The oldgym was aptly named. It was built in 1913, and said so on one of the columns that introduced the steps. It hadn't been updated since.

There was a certain majesty about the old gym, however. All brick of course, with a wide set of concrete steps—not *just* concrete steps, but *white* concrete, the kind they can't seem to pour anymore—that led to the tall wooden double doors that were one of three entrances to the building.

Everything inside was wooden. Wooden floors, of course, wooden bleachers, all eight rows of them, and two sets of wooden steps that led down to the basement. There was one on each side of the wooden, double-door entrance: one for home, one for visitors.

There were sets of beautiful wooden handrails that helped escort basketball players to the basement dressing rooms for the last sixty years. It used to amaze me at how well they held up with nothing more than an occasional coat of varnish every other decade or so—the wood they made was tougher back then.

It even still had the original lights. Five-foot-long pieces of thick electrical wire—you've seen this wire before in old buildings; its coating is silver and fuzzy—hanging from exposed beams. At the end of the wire is a pie-pan-shaped collar that reflects the light from a five-hundred-watt bulb.

Nostalgia exuded from this place like the sweet smell of an overturned bottle of Old Spice. I used to try to imagine kids from 1913 playing basketball; for some reason, I just couldn't. It was like trying to imagine your grandparents as kids.

Jean didn't have nostalgia on his mind when he entered the historic, or prehistoric, building. He had a chin-up on his mind. I have often wondered why relentless determination was wasted on people like Jean. What was his goal here? "Why?" I used to ask Jean.

I knew what the PE coach had told him, but I advised, "He doesn't care if you do that damn chin-up or not, Jean. You're going to get an A for the class just like everybody else."

To which he would always reply, "I want to because *I* want to."

Upon hearing his gutsy answer, it always crossed my mind: *If you have this much determination for a damn chin-up, why can't you simply stop eating so damn much!*

Junior high football players had regular PE class in the off-season. Jean and Brad shared the fifth period gym class and became friends. I suspect Brad could sense the pain Jean had successfully suppressed all these years. Perhaps he felt a kinship of sorts, or more aptly, a brotherhood. Brad once felt uncomfortable in his own skin, and he perceived the bulbous Jean now felt the same.

"Jean," Brad said in the direction of his new friend as he casually made his way over to the chin-up bar. "Why do you put yourself through this every day?" It hurt Brad to see Jean struggle to pull himself a mere three inches, and that was on good days.

"You don't understand, Brad. You're one of those people that don't have to struggle with weight problems."

"Why are you so determined to do one stupid chin-up?"

"For the same reason the guy climbed the mountain: Because it was there." Jean's answer was determined.

"Well, maybe if you just dieted a little Jean, it would make it a lot easier." Brad thought he was being helpful.

"*Diet!*" Jean was getting incensed. "I don't eat anything but celery and cottage cheese now. Me and my mom are on the same diet."

"How come you're still big?" Brad was earnest.

"Everybody thinks that I eat a lot. They see fat, they think fat. I'll bet I don't eat as much as you do. I'll bet I don't eat half as much as you do. I don't know why I'm so fat." Jean looked temporarily dejected. The look was quickly replaced with determination as he once again took a gander at the chin-up bar.

Jean's words puzzled Brad. He didn't know quite what to make of the fact that he really didn't eat much. He thought maybe what

Jean considered very little was actually a lot. Still he wanted to help. With his newfound life, and newfound perspective on life, he felt more and more like he could help, especially with someone who was on the outside looking in. Still, he didn't know exactly how.

Jean seemed really smart and aware of what was going on around him. He struck you as a person who would have found a way to solve his weight problem by now, on his own. After thinking about it, Brad didn't feel qualified to help, but he knew someone who did.

One other question puzzled Brad as he watched Jean huffing and puffing to pull himself inches up the bar: Why was he trying to do a chin-up when it was so patently obvious that no matter how hard he worked at it, no matter how determined he was, he would never, ever be able to pull his three hundred pounds up that bar? It was figuratively and literally an exercise in futility, and everybody knew it. Why didn't he?

It was a joke around the school. The fat boy who hangs a few seconds on a bar each day and thinks he's exercising. Poor Jean was the only one who wasn't in on the joke ... or was he?

"Jean, I know someone that might be able to help. In fact, I know he can." Brad was waiting for Jean's grip to weaken so he would finally let go of the unconquerable bar and look at him.

"Yeah, who's that?" Jean was rubbing the calluses that had grown thick on his hands over the many months of hanging and struggling with a bar that never seemed to get any closer to his chin.

"A boy named Jesse. You've seen him around school."

"Yeah, I've seen him. Ain't he a little weird? I mean, he's too nice, too polite, you know. Why is he so quiet? Why does he just smile at people and stuff? Weird!"

Jean was clearly apprehensive about Jesse, as were most people. "I've heard rumors and things about him. I don't think my folks would want me talking to him, Brad."

Jean was shaking his head to let Brad know he wasn't interested in talking to the weird guru who meandered through the corridors and shadows of Jess Rulam High School.

"He's a cool guy. The coolest I've ever met. He changed my life, and my mom's." Brad was staring Jean eye to eye and Jean was staring back.

"How?"

"I can't tell you."

"Why, what does that mean? Is it a big secret? Is he funny ... you know what I mean?" Jean was more or less joking as he turned his attention back to the enemy—the stubborn chin-up bar.

"No, I told you, he's cool."

"Look, Brad, I appreciate your concern and all that, but all I need help with is beating this damn chin-up bar, man."

"That's what I mean."

"He knows how to help me do a chin-up?" Jean made a puffing sound with his lips dismissively, then said, "Come on!"

"He's the smartest kid I've ever seen! I'm telling you!" Brad was wearing Jean down.

"OK, I'll talk to him! But let up, OK?"

* * *

The next day, Jean once again, faithfully and inexplicably, reassumed the ritual that controlled one hour of his life each day. He just mounted the bar and completed one repetition, as he called it. It was a herculean pull of approximately one inch. He was about to attempt another when he heard the soft footfall of someone behind him.

"You enjoy hanging around this place?" The voice asking the contrarian question was Jesse's.

"Very funny! You must be Jesse."

"Not meant to be funny, just merely jesting, and yes, I'm Jesse."

"Well, Jesse," Jean said, dropping from the bar, "I'm trying to do a chin-up before school is out. Brad said you knew a lot about it. What do you think?" Jean thought he would get right to the point. He wasn't interested in a lot of mumbo jumbo.

"Why?" Jesse asked.

"Well, because Coach Burt told me if I could do a chin-up before the year was up, I would pass PE class."

"You know very well that you're going to pass the class whether you accomplish a chin-up or not. What I mean is, why do *you* want to do a chin-up?"

Jean paused for a minute as he gave the question some thought.

"Because of the way he said it, right here in front of everybody, and because everybody laughed at me. He said it like saying, *If I could fly to the moon by the end of the year."* Jean had a bit of poison to his tone.

"I see, so, you feel if you could do one chin-up by the end of this year, they would stop laughing."

"I don't know, man. All I know is that everybody thinks I'm a big fat pile of shit because I'm too big." Jean was getting upset.

"Not everyone. Only the weak, only the scared, only the unsure of life."

"Look at me, man! I'm weak. I'm scared. I'm unsure."

"How about life? Are you weak, scared, and unsure about life? Or just the fact that you want to do a chin-up?"

"Did you hear what I said? Look at me!"

"I'm looking. What am I supposed to see?"

"Well, if you can't see, I'm not going to tell you." Jean was exasperated and growing more so.

"I see a fine young man who loves his parents, who loves his school, and who loves his life. All he needs is some confidence."

"How do I get confidence when I can't pull myself up from the floor?"

"There is more to life than pulling one's self from the floor."

"Not in my world."

"Then you need to change your world."

"That's easy for you to say. You don't live in my world."

"Show me. Show me your world."

"I can't show you my world."

"Is it because only you live in it?"

"I guess."

"No, Jean, many people live in your world. They just don't know it."

"Are we talking about the same world?"

"Yes, the world of the weak, the scared, and the unsure of life."

Quiet engulfed the gym. No laughter, no shouts, no shrieks, no bouncing balls, only the racing thoughts in Jean's muddled mind.

"What? What do I do to get out of this world and into another?" asked Jean, meekly.

"I thought you'd never ask," said Jesse.

And with that, Jesse began to teach Jean.

"First, you're going to have to like yourself."

"How do I do that? I'm fat."

"Why? Why are you fat?"

"Because I was born that way."

"Precisely. The whole point of you not liking yourself because of the way you were born is *pointless*."

"I still want to change, though. I mean, I don't want to go around looking like this."

"Looking like what?"

"Looking like the fat piece of shit that I am."

"It bothers you *that* much?"

"Yeah. How could it not? I mean, I have to squeeze through doors, and I can't get around without getting out of breath. And then there are girls. They laugh at me and make fun of me. Nobody wants to live like this. Nobody! Do you know what I mean?"

"Yes, I do. Unfortunately all too many people think this way."

"Help me then."

"I will, but you have to promise that you will use your newfound life to help others."

"Others like me, you mean?"

"Others like everybody."

"Deal."

And with that, they shook hands.

"Do you know why you were born fat?" Jesse asked like it was a biology class.

"No, of course not. How could I?"

"Long ago, in another time, when men were few, and food was hard to come by, the cold winter produced in man a need in our bodies to adapt to the harshness of the winter cold.

"Thick layers of protective fat formed around our bodies, to insulate us and sustain us when times were bad. Things changed, though. Times got better and so did our bodies. Unfortunately for some, that trait simply shows up in our gene pool from time to time. There's nothing you can do to change it. It's hereditary, actually, just like blue eyes."

"I understand what you're saying, but I don't want to hear: *That's just the way you are, accept it, get used to it. You can't change who or what you are.* I've heard that, and I don't accept it. I won't accept it. And there is nothing you can say or do that will make me accept it." Jean was actually getting angry with Jesse's implication.

"And there is one other thing," Jean continued crossly. "I was humiliated in here, in front of everybody. Right there," he said, pointing at the chin-up bar, "by an absolute jerk bastard, with a cattle prod of all things!"

"I know, and I agree with you about him, though perhaps not in those words. Nonetheless, he's getting his punishment. There is an equalizing force in the world, and that man is experiencing it right now. That's quite enough. But don't think about him, think about you."

"I don't want to be fat, Jesse. I want to be like everybody else—the pretty people, the normal people. The ones I see every day when I walk the halls. The ones that when they pass someone in the hall don't have to think to themselves, *I wonder what kind of fat pig joke they're thinking right now,* or maybe they're thinking to themselves, *I wonder how he wipes his own ass.* Do you know what a wonderful life it would be just to walk down the hall once, just one time, and not have people think that about me?"

"I will teach you how to lose weight and change your body and your mind. But you will also have to change your heart—the way you look at people, your attitude, and your life. You will need a new way of thinking and living. I will teach you, and you will learn." Jesse was patting Jean on the shoulder.

"Deal," said Jean with a smile and a handshake.

"But there is one thing you have to do for me to get started. You have to walk the hall one more time today. OK?" said Jesse instructively.

"OK, fine, but why? I mean, I do that every day, so what's that going to do for me?"

"Ah, but you never went down the hall before wearing a pair of these." Jesse pulled a pair of sunglasses out of his back pocket and placed them in Jean's hand.

"Oh, great! Now I'll be the fat piece of shit walking the hall wearing sunglasses. This will really make me popular," Jean said sarcastically. He put them on. "Naw, nobody's gonna pick on me now that I've got these on. What's the point?"

"No point, just one of the things you have to do to get to where you want to be," Jesse said as he turned to leave.

"Where will these take me?" shouted Jean to the departing Jesse.

"To the other end of the hall probably," Jesse hollered back, not turning around.

"Why?" Jean returned.

"Because you need to see both ends of the same hall." Jesse was barely audible by now.

* * *

Jean was more than a little apprehensive about following Jesse's instructions, yet he felt something was different merely by holding the sunglasses in his hands. Still, holding them was one thing. Putting on a fancy pair of sunglasses and sashaying up and down the halls of the school building was a different matter, especially if you never wear sunglasses, period, and most especially, not at school.

And yet, there was something in the air. He'd heard the words *rarefied air* to describe this eerie ambience that suddenly filled the halls of Jess Rulam High School.

He didn't want to put the sunglasses on because he knew he'd still be aware of everyone's judgments. The snide looks would somehow telegraph to his brain, *Does this fat turd think he's suddenly become cool? He's still just a fat piece of shit trying to draw attention to his absurdly fat ass.*

What the hell? he thought as the bell rang and the avalanche of kids streamed out of the rooms and filled the halls. Jean popped the dark glasses across the bridge of his nose. Everything astonishingly appeared in high definition—this was before high definition was invented. Everything was in a greenish light. He was startled. The kids of fourteen, fifteen, and sixteen disappeared, and were replaced by thirty-five- and forty-five-year-old adults.

He was shocked, but not spooked. He kept his cool as best he could. He lifted the glasses up slowly, and the scene changed.

The wing tips and loafers on the adults became the platform shoes and sandals of the teenagers; slacks and skirts morphed into bell-bottoms and minis; dress shirts and pullovers were now T-shirts. The worn faces of middle age turned back to the pimples of youth.

Jean felt like one of Rod Serling's victims in a real-life *The Twilight Zone*. He realized these were the same people—the same people decades later. He wasn't sure of this until he saw a man of about forty-three fluttering about trying to open a locker with the worst comb-over he had ever seen. The man had a scar on the inside of his right palm.

When he flipped up the glasses to check his sanity, he saw Scott Willoughby standing at his locker, scar on the right palm and all.

Pulling his glasses back down, the handsome young Scott, the football jock, the ladies' man, who, it was rumored, had banged half the girls in Jess Rulam High from the ninth grade on up—lying about women *had been* invented by then—was now a beer-bellied, balding, glasses-wearing, nerdy-looking, insecure shell of a jock.

Jean watched with utter satisfaction as Scott, who just a couple of days earlier had told him to get his lard-ass out of the way so he could pass, nervously looked around to assure himself no one saw him fidgeting with his comb-over. He was making sure the few hairs he had left covered as much of his bald head as possible.

Jean raised his glasses again. He spotted Brittany Knight, another in a long and distinguished list of babes that totally ignored him at best, and at worst, showed disdain for him. Jean thought she was so pretty and so desirable. He imagined what it would be like if she were his wife, after he developed his male-model physique, of course.

Now, the curiosity of knowing if all the sit-ups, push-ups, and yes, the dreaded chin-ups, and the gagging on the bland cottage cheese until he could puke, were worth the effort; he had to know.

He hesitated before he pulled down the glasses slowly. To his amusement and, to a lesser degree, his disappointment, the beautiful, young teenage fantasy girl was now a middle-aged, saggy-faced, graying-rapidly unattractive woman.

Dark veins crisscrossed the once sexy legs she had once used to tantalize him and every other boy as she sashayed her luscious figure up and down the hall in her miniskirt. The round, firm butt was now flat and wide. Her once gorgeous face was a road map of deep ruts and well-defined lines leading to deep, dark circles around her eyes.

Opening her locker, Jean chuckled to himself as the forty-three-year old Brittany glanced quickly to either side and took a lightning-fast swig from the flask of brandy she hid under her books. He figured the stress of staying sexy and not succeeding had taken its toll.

Jean moved up the hall, periodically lifting and lowering Jesse's sunglasses, exposing the fact that Hank had gained one hundred pounds and was now fatter than him; Beth too had gained a lot of weight, all in her ass. Mitchell was slumped over with arthritis, complete with twisted, gnarly, swollen hands. What happened to Cindy's once beautiful smile? Why, did she forget her dentures today? *Yuck,* he thought, *what a hag.*

No one looks even close to the same. Nothing like they do now, Jean thought as he made it to the end of the hall.

Before going outside, he turned to take one last look at the befores and afters. The hall was filled with vibrant and attractive, no, downright beautiful teenagers like he so longed to be; glasses down, the hall was filled with just plain ordinary people, just like him.

When Jean handed the mysterious sunglasses back to Jesse, he did it with a new perspective. He was beginning to understand what Jesse had meant.

"I don't know if that really just happened, or if it was my imagination. I don't know who you really are, but for some reason, I'm looking forward to the lessons."

"I will teach you, and you will learn well."

"Where did you get those sunglasses?" Jean asked jokingly.

"Off a rack in your own store," Jesse answered pleasantly. And with that, Jean began a new journey down a different path.

CHAPTER 20

TED MARION WAS NOT A typical ninth grader, though he dressed, talked, and usually acted so. He had a single peculiarity: He laughed inappropriately sometimes. It was not only the timing of his laughter, but it was the sound of his laugh that caused us all to wince in embarrassment for him. It was a freaky quality that left everyone uncomfortable.

He was normal in every way, save for when someone was caught in an embarrassing spot or an injurious accident. After a slip on a piece of ice perhaps, or, if someone received tragic news, Ted's shrieking laugh was heard. He sounded sinister, like the horror movie actor Peter Lorre.

We all thought Ted laughed out of nervousness or concern when someone fell, got hurt, or had a relative pass away. Most of us wondered if he was even aware of his inappropriateness.

Ted never seemed to smile when he laughed, and he didn't seem to be able to control it. It was more of a reflex action—at least that's what his friends assumed. He also appeared to be oblivious to it as he was unapologetic for its poor timing. What was even more curious was that Ted had a different, more normal laugh for a joke or something funny.

Our friend Ted's peculiarity only appeared in the last couple of years. None of us could recall later, when interviewed by a psychologist, hearing the shrieking, mad-scientist laugh in the first few years.

***

As best we could remember, Theodore Marion had joined us sometime in the third grade. We all agreed he was completely normal. And, we also agreed he was pretty much normal through grammar school.

Things started to change somewhere in the seventh grade. He grew tall and nice looking. He fit right in with the rest of us, even after he developed the peculiar laugh. Only one of us was aware of what was going on.

Ted's father was Miles Marion ... *Miles Marion*. I remember the first time I heard the name, and I thought to myself there was something cool about it, the way it rolled off your tongue. How could anyone with a name like Miles Marion have a problem? But he did, and what a problem.

Ted's mother was Joyce Marion, nice name, not the same flow, but nice all the same. She was meek, whether born that way or whether it was drilled into her by years of lonely desperation. She had to be meek. Her husband was an overbearing asshole. He dominated her like a bridge dominates the water flowing beneath it.

She was his captive, his possession, his wife. They were all the same to him—there was no difference—and anyone who didn't believe the same was his enemy. He liked to show his dominance to those who came around. He demonstrated it so that when anyone left his residence, they left knowing that was his woman, and there was nothing anyone could do about it.

It makes you wonder, though, what this does to a woman's psyche, her dreams, and her aspirations. We didn't know about what it did to her, but we did find out what it did to his son ... the tragic things.

* * *

It all began in September of our freshman year. I stopped to talk to Jesse just outside the old gym. I liked to talk to Jesse. It was invigorating, it was informative, and he was never, ever out of things to say on any subject.

Pick a topic, any topic; something in the news, sports, Watergate, or anything that was happening at the time. He had an answer. It wasn't always the answer you were expecting, but damn, he was smart. The smartest person I'd ever seen.

He put people to shame, not in a bad way, not the way you imagine, but in a good way, a positive way, and it was something to behold. I'd witnessed him argue with the smartest teachers in our school. I thought they were smart until I heard them alongside old Jesse. They got so exasperated and literally blue in the face, totally exhausted, and they would never win.

I've seen cursing and huffing and puffing, and things being thrown. I've heard voices raised to a feverish pitch, but not from

Jesse. His voice never got much above normal, not even in a crowd. No matter how heated the argument, there he was, composed, relaxed, and in charge. No cursing, no shouting, no screaming, because he didn't have to. You see, he was always right, and he knew it, and in a strange way, you knew it too.

Everyone wants to be right, but only those that are not sure about their position like to argue loudly. And, when they are *really* not sure, it can get heated. Jesse brought that out in people. I've seen it many times.

* * *

Jesse and I were discussing something, I can't even remember what. I was arguing, and he was winning of course. Pete came by and told us that he had just seen Ted pounding his fist into the solid steel handrail leading up the library steps. Pete said he was hitting the rails hard enough to break every bone in his hand.

This wasn't the first time someone had seen him doing such a thing. Reportedly, he was seen pounding his fist into a school wall. Another time we were told it was his head.

Recently, Ted started appearing with multiple wounds on various parts of his body. I know Andy and others told anyone who would listen that they saw slashes on him, cuts that looked like they were made with a knife. Andy went on to say that he and his classmates were getting ready for PE one day when Ted removed his shirt, revealing cuts in straight rows across his hairless, young chest.

Ted apparently didn't try to hide them from anybody, but he never acknowledged them either. He didn't seem to care and never said a word about them to anyone. Andy said he was afraid to provoke Ted by bringing attention to them, particularly as he had noticed Ted's bizarre behavior lately. He assumed Ted had put them there himself.

"What do you say to a crazy person that won't set them off?" Andy asked someone he was telling about the cuts he saw on Ted's chest. "I was afraid of what he might do, so I said nothing. I mean, what do you do?" Andy was baffled, as were the rest of us.

"Ted is in great trouble. I sense it," Jesse mumbled to himself. Then he said to Pete and me, "I must help him. There is going to be trouble here today—big trouble. Go tell the teachers or anybody you can find that they may have to evacuate the school.

"This was meant to happen, and I'm afraid," Jesse continued, looking off into space, "I won't be able to stop it. It must happen. It *will* happen. A great truth will be unveiled because of it. It will be glorious, and you will be witnesses.

"So, Matt, you and Pete go fetch Andy, James, Bart, and all the others in the gang. You know who. It's time you learned a little bit about me and why I'm here. Things are going to change for you today. It will be up to you if it is for the better."

And with that, Jesse sprinted off. He left Pete and me standing and staring at each other in total confusion, as he'd often done before. However, this time it was different. We knew it and we felt it. He said he was going to reveal to us something about himself, which would be a relief. All of us constantly wondered about this mysterious boy-man we all knew and admired but didn't understand.

Who was he? *What* was he? These are the questions that mystified those of us in his circle of friends, which included me, Pete, Thad, Bart, John, Philip, Tommy, James, Simon, Jimmy, Andy, and Jude. That was it, yes, twelve of us in all.

We discussed Jesse amongst ourselves many times over the years that we knew him. He had at one time or another done something strange, something inexplicable, something magical. Usually it was to us individually and certainly to no more than three or four of us at a time. We never witnessed his supernatural powers as a group, not since the fourth grade, which was so many years ago it seemed like only a myth now.

Today had the makings of a revelation of some sort. It was something we all needed, believe me, and that's what Pete and I told the others. We told them exactly what we knew, what Jesse told us. We were eager to see, to be enlightened, and to have clarity in a situation we didn't understand.

Maybe we weren't supposed to understand, we debated, because we were too young before. But maybe today was the day—the day of reckoning, the day in which we little boys were to become men. I didn't really know if today would be *that* day of reckoning, but there was one thing for sure: Something was going to happen, and it was going to happen soon.

***

What did happen was that a beleaguered, haunted Ted Marion brought a gun to school—not just a gun, but a double barrel shotgun. He hitched a ride to school with Danny Sizemore, a friend of his and his family's who lived just up the road.

He told Danny when he first got into his car that he was bringing the shotgun with him to leave in the car till school was out so he and Danny could go bird hunting on Danny's farm. It was something he did before, so Danny thought nothing of it.

Ted reached the point where pounding his fist into steel handrails or decorating his bare chest with deep cuts from a razor-sharp knife no longer quieted the pain, which was now as constant as a toothache. He decided he would end it another way, a sure way, one way or another. This was it.

Young Ted Marion was carrying a secret—a dark, ugly secret he could share with no one. It was a family secret he and only one other family member were privy to. But that's not exactly true either. There *was* one more family member that also knew the secret. She knew it only too well. Only the sheer hideousness of it kept it from surfacing to her conscious mind. So to her it didn't exist. It didn't happen, it never happened, and she actually believed it herself.

Everyone has secrets—everyone. Ted's secret was different from ours.

Ted Marion was being sexually molested by his own father. He had been since he was five years old.

He tried oh, so hard to keep it in, but the deformity manifested itself outwardly. At first it was in little things and then in bigger things. The uncomfortable laugh was one symptom, and now, in the disastrous situation I am about to describe.

Who among us would act differently? If we were in his shoes, how could we imagine our reaction? How could we imagine being in his shoes, period? We knew nothing of these things in those days. We were still making fag jokes to our classmates. We thought *those* people—homosexuals—were perverts, the only perverts we knew about at the time.

Our little minds could not comprehend such a thing as a father having sex with his own son. Who can, really? Parents didn't talk about it to their kids. No one could blame them though—they probably didn't know of such things either. If they did, they kept it to themselves, as they probably should.

So we were completely in the dark that day as the gang all gathered. We were all assembled as one by one the police cars arrived. No sirens, just the whirling blue lights that send the unmistakable signal to your brain that something is wrong, very wrong, or else they wouldn't be here.

* * *

Jesse met us at the side of the old gym at the basement entrance to the junior high's locker room. He didn't say anything except, "Follow me. Don't say anything, don't do anything, just watch and learn." We did what he said. We entered the locker room and went up the steps that led to the basketball court.

There we saw the door that was kept locked most of the time, which led to a small landing. It was only used when they played a junior basketball game so people could exit the building more expeditiously. Just on the other side of this door was Ted, holding his loaded shotgun at Adrian Strange's head.

Adrian Strange was his real name. Despite the oddness of it, he was quite normal. He was a nice kid—polite, neat, and well-dressed. I liked him. He was just plain unfortunate this day and happened to be walking by at exactly the wrong time—I mean the timing that Ted decided to put his deadly plan into action. Unbeknownst to Adrian, he would serve just nicely as a hostage.

Ted seized Adrian as he was the first to walk by after Ted decided the exact location to carry out his plan of execution.

We had a good view of everything, despite being behind the door. There were two windows diametrically placed on each side of the door. Architects in those days liked balance. We could also hear quite plainly what was being said on the landing outside. They also didn't insulate things very well in those days either.

What was being said was nothing, except Ted's soft mumblings, which were, as best we could tell, something like, "Here it comes, boy. Here it comes."

To our chagrin, Jesse stepped up to the door and knocked on it, like he was knocking on any typical door. He full well expected to be let in.

"We're not buying anything today," said Ted in a put-on voice, like he was imitating a housewife. Then came the laugh, the mad scientist laugh, the Peter Lorre laugh, which we were all accustomed to, except this time it was louder and a tinge more pronounced. It lingered longer in the tension-filled air.

"Ted, it's Jesse. I'm coming out to talk to you." Jesse gave the doorknob a turn and found it locked. Unperturbed, he turned and looked at us wryly with a coy twinkle in his eye and an odd mischievous grin, like he was going to enjoy this. It temporarily set our minds at ease.

Jesse turned the knob again, and it unlocked this time. This did little more than cause us to glance at each other. We were accustomed to Jesse's strangeness and not surprised by much he did anymore. But then something even stranger happened.

A bright yellow light like a body-halo began to glow all around Jesse.

"What is that glowing around you?!" Pete shrieked. We all cowered but stayed put, scared but not about to miss anything.

"The truth!" Jesse answered. "I'm about to confront evil head-on. You are the only ones who will see it. *It* will have a dark glow, as does *the one* who causes it. I am the Truth as revealed by the Father. And now you know."

* * *

Jesse opened the door, stepped onto the landing, closed the door behind Him and walked toward Ted. He sat beside the shaking Adrian with Ted's double barrel pointed right between his eyes.

The police were everywhere by this time. They must have come from different towns because Jess Rulam only had four police cars, and there must have been a dozen, at least, surrounding the old gym. They all had rifles, and they had them all pointed at Ted Marion's head. He had no cover to hide behind, no protection from the police if they opened fire. It would be like shooting fish in a barrel, and he knew it.

"What are you doing out here, Jesse?" asked or more like shouted, Ted.

"I've come out here to save you, Ted," answered Jesse calmly without looking at Ted.

He simply placed his head on his folded arms that rested on his knees and stared at the concrete floor of the landing. The glow became brighter. Ted's eyes became larger. He stuck his hand and arm inside the yellow glow and wiggled his fingers.

"Save me from whom?"

"From yourself, of course." Jesse lifted his head and was now peering at Ted.

"Don't you know what this gun is for? I'm going to kill old Adrian here."

"No, you're not. You know full well that your plan is for the police to shoot you down because you lack the courage to do it yourself. Adrian is just the inducement. But, you have me now. In fact, Adrian, why don't you go on home?"

"Go on, Adrian," Ted said, not taking his even more confused eyes off Jesse, who now returned his head to the down position. The terrified Adrian bolted upright onto his feet, fled down the steps and around the corner, never looking back.

"Save me, you say. Well, then why aren't you saving me? You gonna save me by taking a nap." The hyena laugh followed.

"We have to wait for your father to get here, which will be shortly."

"What's my father got to do with this?"

Hearing this, Jesse raised his head and said sternly, "Everything."

Jesse was right.

Moments later, Miles Marion arrived at the scene along with his wife. The mass of police, students, and bystanders only added to the growing mayhem. The police told Miles that his son was holding a hostage with a loaded shotgun. They further explained that the best thing to do in a situation like this would be for the father to try to talk the son into surrendering his weapon before something bad happened—something real bad.

The police hadn't tried to talk to Ted yet. Four or five of the policemen held Ted in the crosshairs of their high-powered rifles, waiting for him to hint at pulling the trigger on Adrian at first, but now Jesse. The rest were scurrying about in a futile attempt to keep the ever-gathering crowd back out of the way of danger.

Miles reluctantly agreed to try and talk his son down. He seemed, however, to be more concerned with whether Ted had said anything to the officers or if he wrote a note explaining why he was doing this.

"He just wants attention," he told the police chief.

The police chief countered, "He's got it."

A dark glow appeared around Miles. It was gray at first, and then got darker the more he spoke.

Miles looked forlorn as he headed down a small ramp. He occasionally stopped to look back at his wife and the now silent crowd. He could see his son was not pointing the shotgun at Jesse or at him, but had the end of the barrel positioned under his own chin. His lower jaw rested on top of it like he was Rodin's *The Thinker.*

"What are you *doing* here, Ted?" asked his father, annoyed. "Are you crazy?" His aura got darker.

"I don't belong here anymore, Dad."

"Belong *where,* you fool?" The space around him got darker still.

"Here, on earth. I don't belong with the living anymore," Ted said, looking past his father and into emptiness. "I've been bad for so long. I need to be with the dead. I hear them begging me to join them. I need to go where the bad people go."

Miles turned around to see the crowd's reaction to what his son had just said. He thought his voice and Ted's sounded like they were coming from a loudspeaker.

He knew everyone there could hear every word he and his son spoke to each other, and he looked worried. He actually thought about turning around and telling the crowd and the police to go on home because he could handle it from here. But he knew they wouldn't.

"Why, Dad? Why did you do this to me?" Ted sniffled at first, and then he sobbed and cried uncontrollably. He dropped the gun down by his side. Meanwhile, Jesse stood up slowly. He was standing right beside Ted, glowing brighter yet.

Miles was thinking that all Jesse had to do was grab the gun and this would be all over. He would take his son home and that would be the end of it. But that's not what happened.

"Why did you do this to me?!" Ted screamed the words so loudly and with such force that the veins on the side of his neck distended a good half-inch and slobber and snot spewed with every syllable.

Miles turned quickly and took a nervous look at the crowd behind him. He indicated with hand gestures he didn't know what his psychotic son was talking about.

"You're the reason I'm here! This is your fault!" Ted shouted again at his father with the same verve as before.

This seemed to anger Miles. He fretfully looked back and forth at his son and the crowd. He was sure he could detect the look of understanding developing on their faces. His anger began to boil inside him like a volcano. This was his son, and the little bastard was not minding him.

"No! I'll tell you whose fault this is, dammit." Miles was shouting in the same manner as his son. "It's his." His outer glow was almost black.

Miles ran a few feet toward his son, stuck his index finger straight up like he was making a "we're number one" gesture. He slowly and deliberately extended his finger at his son.

When his accusatory arm was extended halfway toward his son, his finger began to bend backward at the knuckle joint. When Miles's arm was fully extended, his index finger was bent into a U shape and pointing straight back at his own chest.

Miles let out a horrific scream, grabbed hold of his finger, and fell to the ground in agony. He grimaced. His glow was jet black now. He contained himself for a second and slowly but cautiously removed the hand uncovering his disjointed finger. To his relief he saw that his finger was completely normal.

He looked toward his son, who was looking back at him with the same bewilderment. He extended the same finger once again in Ted's direction, and once again his finger bent into a painful U. The more he pointed it, the more it bent back toward himself. When he pulled his finger back in toward his own body, the less it bent.

Ted was close to fainting and felt weak. He was as pale as if he literally saw a ghost. To the crowd watching, it looked as though Miles simply fell to the ground in horrendous pain and was making some sort of pointing gesture toward Ted.

Ted left the landing slowly, walking down the steps dragging the shotgun behind him like a pitiful little boy drags his bat back to the dugout after striking out. His father leaped up and started toward his forlorn son. He met him at the bottom of the landing.

Ted quickly raised the gun and pointed at his own father, who stood motionless, staring wild-eyed down the barrel of the double barrel shotgun.

The police officers' fingers tightened precipitously on the trigger of their rifles. They awaited the go-ahead from the chief to fire upon the distraught boy. They looked over at the nervy chief, who had his right hand raised. When he dropped his hand, they'd open fire.

Jesse was still standing on the landing above. He said to Miles, "Mr. Marion, you, sir, have an evil spirit that found a comfortable dwelling in the recesses of your mind."

Jesse's glow was so bright, it was painful to look at.

Miles and Ted turned and looked up at Jesse, who was pointing at Miles. The chief's hand remained in the air a bit longer.

Then Jesse continued, "All you have to do is say the word. By confessing your sins to each and every one of these witnesses and asking for forgiveness, the evil spirit will leave. You and your son's torment will be gone too."

"Confess what? What the hell are you talking about? Who the hell are you to talk to me in this way? You're just some damn nigger!"

"I was afraid you were going to say that. It is never too late, even for you," said a sad-looking Jesse.

A blank stare came over Ted's face as he slowly lowered the shotgun to his waist. He calmly handed the heavy gun over to his father, who received it in the same manner. Then Ted shuffled past his father and in a trancelike walk moved toward the crowd.

The chief started moving toward Ted while his father remained still, with the shotgun resting across his forearms.

Ted stopped and spoke to the crowd. "I have something to tell you all. I have been living with an evil spirit that possesses my father. I didn't know that till a few minutes ago."

"Shut up, you damn little fool," Miles fumed at his son. He moved the shotgun into the ready position.

"The evil has been violating me since I was five years old. He made me have sex with him since I was a little kid." Ted shuffled a little closer to the crowd, then he stopped and turned toward his father.

"You crazy bastard! The only thing to do is put you out of your misery," Miles yelled.

Miles slowly raised the shotgun up to his son's chin, taking aim. His thumb pulled both hammers back. The *clicking* sound reverberated in the stillness of the air. Miles looked down the weapon's sights at his son, who showed no concern that he was about to be executed.

The end of the barrel shook. The double barrels peeled apart at the seam, like a flailing banana skin. One barrel folded in a circular motion to the right; the other barrel folded in a circular motion to the left. Both barrels ultimately formed a double U pointing directly at Miles's head. The man was trembling and his face looked forlorn, just like his son's. Miles's aura became much lighter, almost gray again.

"Son," said Miles from trembling lips.

"Don't!" shouted Jesse, extending his arm.

The explosion sounded like a cannon, literally. The billow of smoke hid what happened to Miles's head, but the pelting of both windows with blood, skull, and brain matter left no doubt.

All twelve of us flinched backward when the splattering of what was left of Miles Marion's brain hit the windows. It sounded similar to bugs hitting a windshield.

I like to think that for a brief moment, just before he pulled the trigger and committed suicide, Miles had a moment of clarity in which he saw himself for what he really was—a monster.

I believe he made the fateful decision to end his own life, rather than live the rest of it in torment, in bitter anguish for what he had done to his son for so many years.

* * *

Jesse jumped from the landing and ran to Ted. He cradled the numbed boy in his arms. He took Ted's chin in his hand and turned his dazed eyes toward his own. Then he said quietly and calmly, "Ted, listen to me. What happened here today was set into motion by a fate that I have no control over. There is nothing wrong with you that can't be repaired. You were merely the victim of a soul that was lost. That fate doesn't have to be the same for you. You can be healed and live a wonderful life. I will show you how, if you will believe in the One who sent me.

"They will put you away for a while, but I will be there with you. I will be there physically, when it is permitted, and I will also be with you in spirit, long after visiting hours are over.

"Say the word, and you can change from the relentless torments of evil to a peaceful existence, the way the One who sent me here intended for you all along."

Ted put his hand inside the glow and acted like he was splashing water on his face.

"Please help me!" cried Ted. He embraced Jesse and wept, but they were tears of relief.

* * *

The chief's final report stated that Miles Marion had attempted to murder his own son with a shotgun because the boy was confessing that his father was a child molester. It went on to say that the gun misfired and exploded in Miles Marion's face and that only the stock and a few pieces of shrapnel were left. Ted was put into a psychiatric facility for a while, and Jesse did visit him often. He was finally released once his sanity was restored.

The psychologist the County assigned to the school to help us cope didn't really help matters much. We had witnessed something the other kids hadn't. None of us twelve told the psychologist about Jesse. We were afraid to, because we didn't fully understand ourselves what we had witnessed that ugly and terrifying day.

All we were certain of was that Jesse had intended for us to witness what had happened and ponder the meaning of it all. He succeeded.

CHAPTER 21

CHARLOTTE MANDEL WAS A QUIET, bashful young lady; unassuming in many respects, except one—she was gorgeous. However, no one respected her because she lacked respect for herself in all aspects, no expectations, no predilections, or exceptions. You see, the lovely Miss Mandel was a slut, but not just any slut, but a doozy of a floozy.

Needless to say, we made fun of Charlotte for her promiscuous lifestyle choice when we weren't trying to hook up with her—when no one was looking, of course—but that goes without saying. We were horny tenth graders; she was a slut. Charlotte wouldn't strike you as that type, a slut I mean, by the way she dressed. In fact, I always thought she dressed nicely, in a rather typical manner. The way she dressed was indistinguishable from the rest of the girls at that time. All the girls wore miniskirts and platform high-heel shoes. The only thing that distinguished her from the rest was that she looked much better in them.

She had long blond hair that was either perfectly straight by nature or made that way by one of the many contraptions that most likely clutters the aptly named vanities of most every female under the age of seventy. I don't know specifically what the contraptions are called.

Charlotte seemed to wear the perfect amount of makeup to highlight her delicate features, which included beautiful blue eyes that sparkled like diamonds, highlighted with tan eyeliner. Her golden hair covered approximately half her face most of the time, which only seemed to add mystery.

The one thing that always made me notice her more than her competition was the choker necklace she always wore. I'm not exactly sure what you call it, but whatever it's called, I am sure it was there to accentuate a lovely neck. In any case, she was hot!

Charlotte wouldn't strike you as being particularly slutty by the way she talked either, not at all the way the media portrayed them at the time. The stereotypical foul-mouthed, battle-axe, hooker-type who poured lewd, sexually suggestive innuendoes from her mouth like a sailor on shore leave was not her manner, or any other slut that I actually knew, come to think of it.

In fact, she had a rather sweet manner of speaking, with a subtle simplicity that, coming from anyone beside her, would convey innocence, except we knew she wasn't innocent. She was naughty, yet nice, and some of us were glad of it, her naughtiness I mean.

I was one of them. For it was she to whom I owed the great pleasure of eliminating my name from the very unpleasurable list of the uncool guys. Yes, those guys. The ones you didn't want to associate with; the hapless ones that meander the corridors of every school and who carry upon them the very uncool stench of virginity.

This specter was unshakable on a young man in those days and no amount of cologne or stylish hairdo or even a make-believe swagger could pose as an adequate substitute for the real thing: that you had actually had sex with a girl.

The greatest benefit of that accomplishment, that once seemed unattainable, is that a certain confidence exudes outwardly in your walk and your talk. It announces to the world, or at least to the tenth grade, that *I am no longer a virgin. I am cool, and being cool is fantastic.* I was most appreciative to the lovely Miss Mandel.

My appreciation, however, ran a little deeper than the usual show of gratitude. I used to watch her when she didn't know I was watching. I watched the way she did the little things on her way to her locker. I'd find myself drifting off into romantic reveries.

I watched for her to smile at someone; how pretty she was when she did that. *How could someone from around here be that pretty?* I often wondered. A certain feeling of importance filled me as I allowed the thought to enter my head: *This beautiful girl had sex with me. Me! And I mean something to her. I had to mean something, didn't I?*

And I watched her some more, waiting for her to flip her hair to one side when she wanted to see with both eyes. I watched her golden hair that was so shiny it reflected the fluorescent light like a mirror in the sun. It seemed to radiate, instead of merely shine like it did from most girls.

And I watched her longer still, for the one thing that set her apart even further from the other girls who were just merely pretty:

her choker necklace. It accentuated her persona. It matched her, from head to toe; it belonged on her, around her luscious neck. On the other girls, the ones who wore them, they didn't seem to go, but on Charlotte the choker was in place. It made her ... *her*.

The peculiar thing about my reveries regarding Charlotte was that for a sixteen-year-old high school boy with rampant hormones, and whose object of his obsession was known for her sex appeal, I hardly thought about having sex with her. How odd, I thought, that this would happen, that I would hardly think about having sex with a slut. Then I'd have to admit something I didn't want to admit, not to myself, and certainly not to anyone else. I was in love with Charlotte Mandel, and I was sad because of it.

This was not a little thing, or it didn't seem like a little thing at the time. I was hopelessly in love. I should have shared my thoughts about these feelings with my best friends, and they would have rejoiced with me, or teased me. I wanted it, but I knew I couldn't have it with her.

It should have been a happy time, a glorious time instead of one of the worst times of my life. How could I be happy about being in love with a slut? I even began to feel anger toward Charlotte for causing me to feel this way because she had robbed me. She robbed me of the bliss I should have experienced through my first love affair.

She robbed me of the opportunity to share thoughts and feelings I had saved for years, just so I could share them with someone I loved. Mostly, she robbed me of the greatest thing about being in love—the wonderful sensation of specialness, that I was special to someone else, that she thought enough of me that I held a special place in her heart. And then the ugly but true thought entered my mind and ruined everything: *I wasn't special ... but merely next.*

That harsh reality was reinforced every time I saw her flirting with the next guy in line—the next guy who would get the privilege of knowing her pleasure to which I was privy. The next guy who would experience what I had experienced, and come to know what I knew. I was jealous of the next guy, and I was ashamed of it.

I desperately wanted to talk to someone about my predicament, but whom? I couldn't very well talk to Pete or Bart, or any of the gang. You don't talk to guys about being in love. You talk to guys about having sex, not about being in love with the slut. The teasing would have been unmerciful. There was only one person I could talk to about this, and I dreaded it like a dental appointment.

Jesse was not the easiest person for any of us in the gang of twelve to talk to. He seemed to expect us to know more than we knew. Anyone else could talk to Jesse, and he was meek and soft-spoken, and had more patience. With us on the other hand, it was different. He seemed impatient and grew weary of our ignorance almost immediately. Needless to say, we avoided him.

None of us even knew how to talk about the subject of Jesse among ourselves. We were afraid to say who we really thought he was. If four or five of us were ever together, the conversation would eventually get around to Jesse and then end abruptly, just like it always did, with each one wondering what the others were thinking and afraid to say it. So the conversations ended, with uncomfortable stares at each other.

However uncomfortable talking to Jesse seemed, there was one irrefutable fact: Jesse was always right, whether we wanted to hear it or not. I knew Jesse had the answer, but I dreaded the fact that he would wonder why I didn't. The fact that I would walk away feeling dumb didn't outweigh the pain in my heart of forbidden love for a slut that I carried around my neck like a yoke. I bit the hard bullet and found that it was softer than I had imagined.

* * *

"Jesse, I need to talk to you about something," I said rather loudly as he was about to turn a corner.

"I can tell something is bothering you, Matt," he answered without turning to look at me. "Let's sit in the library. No one is there now, and we can talk." He was right, no one was there. We sat, and I began cautiously.

"You told us to talk to you about our troubles, and I've got one. But it's hard to talk to you sometimes, Jesse. You said you'd teach us things about life and how to live it, but you kinda scold us like we're children. So it makes it hard to talk to you."

"I see. And what are you but children? You have just begun life, and life has just begun you."

"I've been around for sixteen years," I said rather defensively. "Don't that count for something?"

"Yes, it counts. It means you have sixteen years to come to the conclusion that you know nothing."

"How come you don't talk to other people this way?"

"I teach each accordingly, but for you and the other eleven, you have a different road to travel, a more difficult road. Therefore, the lessons are sterner so that you may buffer what comes against you."

I wasn't about to ask him what road, not without the others with me to hear it.

"I have a problem that's bothering me. I don't understand why people are the way they are." The frustration and concern were in my voice.

"What is *your* problem?" Jesse looked amused. "And who is it that has you so perplexed?"

"There is a girl in the tenth grade. Her name is Charlotte Mandel."

"I know who she is."

"Then you know about her?"

"I'm curious what you know about her, and the nature of your concern." Jesse peered at me closer. After a considerable pause, wondering if I should tell the truth, and coming to the inevitable conclusion that Jesse seemed to know the truth anyway, I decided to be truthful.

"She's a slut, and I'm in love with her." I just blurted it out.

"I see, and this is why you are so distant? You've been near yet far away because of the thoughts latched hold of your conscious mind?"

"Yes, because I know I shouldn't. I can never be seen actually dating the school slut. What would everybody think?" I no sooner got the words out of my mouth than I knew I had said the wrong thing to the wrong person.

"I see." Jesse had that smile on his face that meant a lesson was coming. He leaned in and began to teach.

"So, Matthew, you have taken advantage of this girl's vulnerabilities, yes?" He had me.

"Yes."

"And since then, you have a certain attraction?"

"Yes."

"You are now drawn to her loveliness, the subtleness of her manner, the sweetness in her voice."

"Yes."

"For the first time you see her as someone whom you could love, as a mate for life perhaps. If only it weren't for those blasted others whose judgment would accompany your friendship and fellowship? Do I state it correctly?"

"Yes." I was waiting for a lecture about being a whore-hopper.

"There are two great forces at work simultaneously. Both were created by the Father, so both are right. One force is the animal, which is in man, just like all the created creatures that walk the planet. There is the relentless pull at the center of his being that urges him to mate so as to perpetuate the species. This is man the animal.

"There is another force which is at the essence of mankind. You were also created with this essence from the Creator. The scriptures say that is the *image of the Creator*. They are different words for the same force.

"This essence has merely manifested itself outwardly in your conscience, and you are now bearing the fruit of what you know in your essence, in your very being, is wrong."

"Are you saying that I'm being punished? And this is why I'm depressed?"

"It's all part of the growing process, Matt. Everyone experiences this same process. It's what is *gleaned* from it that is important."

"I don't like this part of the process. Why is it in me, the process I mean? What am I gonna learn from being in love with a whore?" I was really puzzled.

"Sympathy, empathy, insight, clarity, and wisdom. Isn't it a glorious world, Matt?" Jesse was beaming; me, not so much.

"How am I going to learn all this from her? How am I going to learn why she is a slut?" I was to the point of complete frustration. I didn't quite understand what Jesse was saying. The philosophical way he talked was over my head.

"You are going to ask her."

"What?! I'm just gonna walk up and say, 'Excuse me, Charlotte, but I was just wondering, why are you a slut?' And she is going to tell me?" I was frustrated and growing more so.

After a long pause, in which Jesse stared into my eyes for what seemed an embarrassingly long time, he rose from his chair and said, "YESSSS," and with that he left me at the table to ponder my own unsure thoughts.

* * *

Charlotte was standing at her locker looking absolutely stunning as always, but today, especially so. She had on a short dress, which made her luscious legs the object of desire of any male with the slightest drop of testosterone, arousing them where they stood.

Every inch of her is adorable, I thought to myself as I approached; every inch from the top of her shiny golden hair to the tips of her hot-pink-painted toenails. I wanted her right there, right then, and for a moment I didn't care who knew it.

"Charlotte, I have to ask you a question." I got her attention. She turned in slow motion revealing the most beautiful smile I had ever seen.

"I have a question I want to ask *you,* Matt." She had a mischievous tone in her voice.

"Sure, what is it?" I was curious.

"I want to know if you would drive me home after school today." The mischievousness of her voice was even naughtier. She stood there flirtingly, seductively, hot—red hot.

"Do you know where I park my car?"

"Mmm hmm," she said sultrily as she leaned back against her locker and her miniskirt leaned with her, exposing even more of her tantalizingly sexy thighs.

"OK, I'll see you there." I had to turn and leave abruptly, for obvious reasons.

* * *

I really didn't know for sure if she would actually come to my car. With flirtatiousness comes flightiness, and I knew it. But, to my delight, she was there waiting, more alluring than ever. At the moment I didn't know if I was lucky or cursed. At that moment I didn't care. All I knew was that I wanted her, and I knew I was about to have her.

The ride over to her house was even more tormenting. She sat there in my car seat with her miniskirt pulled up so far that her exposed panties made me proud of my driving skills. I was literally driving with one eye on the road. The other was totally fixated on the luscious strumpet that I had sampled in this very car a month ago, and who was now mesmerizing me.

I didn't believe I could hold out long enough to make it the last mile to her house. I knew she wouldn't have invited me to her home unless no one was going to be there. Fantasies of pure unadulterated lust filled my consciousness. I began to imagine the very first move I was going to use, more like fantasize actually.

I was going to grab her around the waist, whirl her around and at the same time run my hands up her miniskirt and pull her panties off in one swift, well-orchestrated move that would put James Bond to shame. I wasn't thinking about anything as we walked to her front door, not about me and my problem, not about her and her sluttishness, certainly not about Jesse and any would-be reason for any of it.

She opened the front door to her home and stepped inside, turning slightly sideways. I entered at the same time. I looked hopelessly and haplessly through the prism eyes of a boy in love and in lust at the sensuous smile that captured my heart. It gave me the reassuring confidence that I was about to experience something I would never forget. I was fixated on her sparkling blue eyes when, suddenly, they disappeared before my stunned eyes. One second she was there, the next she vanished into thin air.

I looked down, and there where Charlotte had stood was a child who looked to be about a five-year-old girl wearing a grownup's clothes.

The little girl took my now trembling hand and said in her sweet little girl voice, "Come on in, Matt. What ya standing in the door with your mouth open like that for? Why ya look so funny all of a sudden for gosh sakes. Hadn't you ever seen a girl before, for crying out loud?"

The little girl pulled me by the hand, and I followed. I was in such shock, and I didn't know what else to do. Her tiny feet filled less than half the high-heeled shoes. They made a steady flopping sound with each of the little girl's steps. Her little toes slid down almost completely through the open end with each subsequent step, exposing hot-pink-painted toenails.

The miniskirt she wore dragged on the floor, and the excess fabric from her blouse draped from her tiny frame. The sleeves hung a foot beyond her hands. Then I noticed something that made the blood drain from my face—a choker necklace hung loosely around her slim little neck.

"My God," I said out loud. "It's you."

"Of course it's me. Who did you think I'd be, for crying out loud, when I invited you over here to play with me? Gosh almighty, but you sure are a dumb ol' boy."

She continued to tug me along by the hand, and I reluctantly followed in a daze of utter confusion. I looked about the house and saw no one at first, but as I was tugged into little Charlotte's room I caught a glimpse of a woman passed out on the couch with what appeared to be a three-fourths empty bottle of liquor on the floor, one hand hanging lifeless beside it.

"Sit down in that chair, and I'll make the tea," she said sassy-like. She started assembling a plastic tea set on a tin platter that had flowery pink and blue drawings of teapots on it. "How do you like your tea? I forgot to ask." She giggled in the same sassy little girl tone.

"Go on and set down for gosh sakes. You can't drink tea standing up, you big dummy."

I figured I had two choices: Go screaming out of the house like a lunatic or sit down and enjoy a nice cup of tea with a five-year-old Charlotte, who sixty seconds ago had been a fifteen-year-old Charlotte. Either way, I was going to wake up in the same place: either in my bed at home, or wearing a straitjacket at Belleview.

As I took my place in the tiny chair, she poured me out a hot cup of make-believe tea, and then she poured out her heart.

"I sure am glad you could make it this evening. I don't get to have much company. My mother doesn't allow me to have company over. She sleeps a lot, especially when she drinks her tea. She wobbles around and says mean things to me, but that's OK 'cause I can't understand her most of the time 'cause her tea makes her talk funny."

"Where is your daddy?" I asked the loquacious Charlotte with my knees uncomfortably pressed against my chest and wondering if the tiny plastic chair could support me.

"Well, I have a daddy, but I don't see him much. He came over last Christmas. That's the last time I saw him. But that's OK too, 'cause he don't like me much anyhow."

"Why doesn't he like you?" I was wondering why she would say something so odd.

"Well, he don't ever come to see me." A sad look appeared on the talkative little girl's face. "He said he don't like little girls. He wanted me to be a boy so I could do boy stuff with him. But I don't mind that though. I'm a girl, and that's just that."

She continued, "I must be ugly. Do you think I'm ugly, Matt?"

"No, I think you're pretty, Charlotte." I was caught off-guard by the strange question.

"Well, my daddy thinks I'm ugly. He told me so ... and he told me I had better learn to be a good cook if I was ever gonna get a husband someday. I tried to show him I could make good tea last Christmas, but he said it weren't worth fooling with. Why don't you try some of the tea?"

I picked up the tiny cup and made a slurping sound with my lips.

"Mmm," I said and smiled at the sad little girl.

"Do you think I make good tea, Matt?"

"I think that's about the best cup of tea I've ever had, Charlotte."

Her sad blue eyes began to tear up. She lunged forward and hugged me around my waist as hard as her tiny little arms could squeeze me.

"If I make you tea will you come back to see me some more, Matt?"

"I'll come anytime you want me to, Charlotte."

She still held on to me tightly.

"Do you promise, Matt? Oh, please, say you promise. My daddy said he would come to my birthday party this year, but I guess my bad tea made him not want to. You really like my tea, don't you, Matt?"

Her hug finally loosened.

"I really do think you are a great cook, Charlotte."

"Do you think that other people will like my tea?"

"I think everybody is going to love your ... tea." It was at that point I realized she told me what Jesse said she would.

"I have to go home, Charlotte." I got up from the miniature table and started for the door.

"Oh, don't leave me now, Matt." She wrapped herself around my leg and was crying. "Please don't go now. Please don't go now. Look what I can do."

She jumped up and ran to her little tea set. "Look, I'll make some more tea if you won't leave." She frantically reassembled the cups and the little pot.

I ran out the door and got in my car and sped off slinging gravel and making as fast a getaway as I possibly could from the crying, frantic little girl, who was desperately trying to please me with her make-believe tea.

I would never look at Charlotte again without seeing the desperate little girl offering the only thing that would bring her the attention she never received at home: a make-believe cup of *herself*.

CHAPTER 22

IT WAS AN INTERESTING YEAR, 1974, to say the least. Football was unbearable that year. It was our eleventh grade year, our junior year, our next to last year. We were slogging through it as we did the previous year. Morale sucked, not just for the football team, not just for the school, but for the whole town of Jess Rulam.

In Alabama at that time, the high school system was divided into classes, depending on the number of students enrolled. Since Orr High students were now being sent to Jess Rulam, our class rating was moved up.

All of this was significant because it meant we now scheduled and played the bigger schools in our area. With the influx of the black kids, and the fact that the black kids didn't play football for Jess Rulam, we had become a small fish in a big pond. We got the shit beat out of us almost every Friday night. It wasn't Coach Peppers's fault of course, but that didn't mean he didn't get the blame for it. His morale was understandably down and this spilt over into our morale, which in turn spilt over into the school morale, which of course spilt over into the town morale, and so on. It was generally a gloomy place to be.

However, if there was one thing that happened for us that year that made it memorable, good or bad, is that we got introduced to alcohol and drugs. Isn't it funny how those things seem to go together? It's all timing, really. Show up at just the right party, in which you meet just the right friend, who in turn introduces you to just the right new kid, who happens to have just the right drugs that everybody is doing, and have your life changed forever. Show up at a different party at a different time and have a different life. Time and circumstances change everything for everybody.

* * *

We lost our fourth straight game. It was Friday. It was the school dance held after each home football game, win or lose. It was the gang, and it was party time.

There is a built-in recklessness that comes as standard equipment in all teenage boys. Not an extra or an add-on, but standard. We didn't look at it as reckless at the time. How could we? We had no point of reference, only our own measuring stick to go by, and since we all used the same measuring stick, the sticks all contained the same lines to cross.

If one or two decided that *this* line was OK to cross, then obviously it was OK to cross *this* line since it was clearly marked on my stick the same as it was for the rest. Who would know anyway? It wasn't like we were breaking any federal laws or anything by smoking a little pot or drinking a little beer.

The school dances at Jess Rulam were the same for every school across America at that time. They consisted of little more than music played through the public address system. That was it. You danced, you went home, unless you found some buddies, who just happened to have some beer and maybe some weed, and then time and circumstances changed.

* * *

I got dressed after the game, which was a pummeling as usual, and as usual I walked across the road to the new gym and the dance, and also as usual, I passed on dancing. I didn't then and still don't today trust any male that likes to dance. As usual, I found members of the gang huddling on the bleachers. Someone mentioned beer— not unusual. Someone mentioned a joint. Then, someone mentioned someone's house and that we would meet there, and the party would actually begin.

* * *

"Where are we going?" I asked Bart as we were deciding who was going to ride with whom.

"I don't know exactly. Let's just follow the crowd. Maybe somebody knows where we're going." We both laughed. "Get in with me," he said. I did.

"You want a beer?" Bart asked as he always did. But this time I accepted. Usually, I declined drinking beer, at least till later on in the evening. Not because I thought it was immorally reprehensible, not because it was something I made the decision not to do, but for the simplest of reasons: Because I didn't like the taste of alcohol in any form, beer or liquor, it didn't matter.

I never told anyone about what happened to me at Charlotte's house that day. How exactly do you do that? We all knew that something was strange, peculiar, mystical, magical, and supernatural about Jesse. Whatever the terminology you use, it all led to an unhappy conclusion: Was he real or were we crazy?

None of us had answers. None of us wanted answers. None of us even knew how to ask the questions. It affected every aspect of our lives, like an inevitable, mysterious cloud that cast an eerie shadow over us wherever we went.

I could only catch fleeting seconds of conscious thoughts when Jesse wasn't in control of them. Ironically, the free thoughts only seemed to come when I was engaged in what I was sure—at the time I was doing them—were things he would vehemently disapprove of. Judging by the behavior of the others, I could tell they had the same feeling.

Thus, I wanted a beer that night earlier than I usually did. I had something I wanted to talk about with the others, and if it took the courage that comes from a can of Budweiser, then so be it.

We were going to talk about Jesse this night, or I was quite literally going to go insane. I wanted to know what the others were really thinking, even if their thoughts, like mine, were bolstered by the inhibition-breaking elixir know as beer. Bart and I remained silent as we followed the taillights of the car just ahead of us and finally arrived at Jimmy Lingerfelt's house. He was the school's biggest pothead. His family owned a successful car dealership, and they just happened to be out of town.

There must have been two dozen or more cars arriving when we did and more came later. Eventually, the whole football team showed up. Yep, this had all the makings of a good ol' pot smoking, beer drinking, making out with loose girls good ol' time.

A perfect time for us twelve to get together, get wasted, and hash this Jesse thing out, or get lucky with some girl, whichever came first. In either case, I was ready for something good to happen.

Unfortunately, I neither talked to any of the gang, nor did I make out with any girl. The one thing I did manage to do was get wasted, as did all the rest. We drank beer, we passed around a joint, and then we passed around another joint, and drank some more beer.

Despite the intoxicating atmosphere of the evening, it was remarkably bland. Nothing happened. As usual, Pete, John, and Andy left, then me and Bart; one by one, and then two by two they left. Whoever rode over with somebody left the party that night with their ride home, or went back to their own car, which was parked at the gym.

* * *

The news didn't reach us till the middle of Saturday morning. Pete's mother called my mother. I was watching cartoons at the time, *Scooby-Doo* I believe; I thought Daphne was hot. I heard Mama's voice above the roar of the TV, and I knew instantly something was wrong.

The car carrying my fellow football players, Marty Mayo, Robert Cash, and Harold Spartani, had left the highway on Riley Gap Road at a high speed and crashed into an oak tree ... *and all three were killed instantly.*

A memorial service was held at the school Monday morning, and then school was let out for the rest of the day. Harold was hard to get out of my mind. All I could think about was that a onetime enemy of mine had undergone a transformation and now was a good friend. At least he *was*. He had developed a close friendship with Jesse, which was the biggest cause of his transformation. Jesse wept when he heard Harold's name. Coach Peppers told the players to go home, as there would be no practice for the week. That meant he was canceling this coming Friday's game. We would meet back the following Monday and watch the game film from our last game and try to establish some semblance of a life again.

The gang's mood was lethargic and despondent. None of us left that morning, and word was put out for us twelve and the rest of the football team to meet at the fieldhouse. We met at the small set of bleachers. It took minutes before anyone could speak.

When it got uncomfortable, Pete finally said, "I don't know what to say. You all know what happened. I wish this had never happened, but it did. I think we all need to go home and think about this. Does anybody have anything to say?"

"I don't think I'm ever getting drunk again," said Larry, the tight end.

"Me neither," chimed in one and then a chorus of others.

"What makes you so sure?" came a voice from inside the fieldhouse. We turned to see that the voice belonged to Jesse. He emerged from the fieldhouse door holding a reel of game film and a rag.

"We lost three people because of drinking damn beer and getting high. How much more of a reason do you need?" said Tyler O'Shields, the quarterback.

"I see," said Jesse as he wiped off the outside of the reel. "That is as good a reason as any."

"Look, Jesse, I know you don't approve of our behavior and the things we do," continued Tyler, "but we're not like you. You don't ever seem to do anything wrong, and you are always scolding or getting on us about something we're doing that you don't approve of."

"And you find this an inconvenience? Or does it worry you because you are traveling down the wide road of the many despite the signs that are warning you to turn back."

"And that's another thing." This time Roger Duncan, one of the running backs, spoke up. "Who talks like that? You're not any older than the rest of us, but you walk around here like you know everything. No offense, man, but you're just the manager, the water boy for Christ's sake."

"Now that it's been brought up," chimed in Steve Sharks, a lineman, "none of us needs to hear you tell us that what we did was a stupid thing. I mean, we feel bad enough. But you and your goody-two-shoes attitude about everything are too much right now."

"I agree with you, Steve. I heard enough of this shit from my old man." This time it was our star wide receiver, Nolan Locklear, who rarely spoke up. "I feel bad enough about losing three of my best friends without some kind of lecture in that weird-ass talk of yours."

Everyone nodded and murmured among themselves in agreement.

"Look, Jesse." Tyler's tone had quieted. "I know you probably think that you're helping us, but I got to be honest with you—you don't play football. You're not out here busting your ass with the rest of us. You're big enough to really help this team. What are you, some kind of water-boy philosophy major?"

"Really!" said Steve. "There's nothing you're going to say to us that's going to make us listen. So why don't you go on back in there and get the film ready to watch for Monday, or sweep the locker room or something. This meeting is for football players only. All you are is talk. We want to see something from you, because there is nothing you're gonna say that's going to make us regret what happened any worse than we do now."

"As you wish." Jesse was spinning the film reel in his hand and disappeared back into the fieldhouse.

The meeting broke up, and players started for their cars. The members of the gang of twelve just looked at each other knowing that Tyler and Steve and the rest had said the wrong thing to the right person. All we could do was wonder what the repercussions would be.

* * *

It was Monday afternoon, and one week had passed since the memorial service for the three fallen Jess Rulam High School football players, who were tragically taken. The remainder of the football team met at the usual time to do the usual thing done every Monday to start the week of practice in preparation for the next opponent: that was to watch the previous game's film.

There was definitely something eerie about walking into the fieldhouse for the first time without all of our teammates. A lonely gloominess emanated from the three lockers that sat unused—no one was clamoring about them, hunting for an undershirt that didn't reek; no one was searching for a pair of socks that they were sure someone had stolen and that they would have to jokingly steal back; no one needed a sweatband or a kneepad, and no one ever would again from those three lockers.

"Come on, men. Let's watch the game film and try to put together some kind of a plan for Friday." Coach Peppers's usually upbeat tone was replaced by solemnity. We shuffled and stumbled clumsily into the film room and took our seats.

"Jesse, bring the last game's film in here, will you?" Coach yelled.

"I thought it was already in here," he mumbled to himself, looking around for a film he thought he had placed on the table earlier, but it was not there now.

Jesse brought the canister containing the two reels of game film, one for the first half, one for the second half. Then he took his place by the light switch. He wore no emotions on his face, just a plain straightaway stare.

We grew a little restless like we did every week as Coach Peppers took forever to thread the film through the projector. For someone who had done it a thousand times before, he always managed to stick the film into some place or another it didn't belong and invariably say the word "shit" at least once, which usually got a chuckle from us, but not today.

"OK, it's ready. Now listen up." Coach usually said something about the last game before he started the film. "We're going to go over this film slowly today. I want to show you what you've been doing wrong. Maybe if you see what happens when you play the game the wrong way, you can learn something. OK, Jesse, cut the lights." Coach sat down and Jesse flipped the light switch off.

The room went totally black for a moment, and the bright projector light shone powerfully against the white screen. There was always anxious anticipation for the game film to start. Just as in a group photo that you are in, the first person your eyes seek out is yourself.

It was the same with the game film, whether from the kickoff team or the return team, you nervously waited to see yourself, to see how you looked on the play that was about to burst onto the four-foot-wide screen. Would you be singled out for excellence or castigated for a poor effort? Whichever it was, I always supposed it was better than to never be mentioned at all.

Dust particles danced in the spotlight, for that brief moment of time anyway.

Boom! The black-and-white image appeared of both team captains as they headed back to their respective sidelines after the coin flip. In three years of film viewing, the coin flip itself was never actually shown, only the captain's departure afterward.

The kickoff came to me. I caught it and headed up the middle and was immediately tackled.

"We have to do a better job, *people*, of sliding over to the middle and forcing their middle people to the outside on middle returns. We just let them come right through." Coach was sounding irritated, as usual.

We broke the huddle quickly and hustled to the line and got down in our stance. The play was a handoff to Roger Duncan up the middle for three yards. Nothing said.

Next play, a five-yard out pass to Nolan Locklear, complete.

"Nice job of cutting that defensive end's legs out and keeping his hands down, Steve. Good pass, good catch." And so it went—Coach praised good plays, criticized not-so-good plays, and cussed bad plays, just like in a thousand high schools in a thousand fieldhouses on Monday afternoon during football season across America in 1974.

There was one difference about this film session. It would be the last time three of the players on the screen would be seen. My eyes soon lost interest in me and glued on our missing colleagues. I think it was the same for everyone else. How could you not? I thought Coach was handling the session well. I was impressed by the way he'd say, "That was a good job by Marty," or, "That was well done by Robert," or simply, "Nice job, Harold." He spoke softly, quietly, and proudly.

As the film played on, the strobe effect of the flickering projector, the dark room, and the solemnity of missing friends created a drowsiness among us. This was not unusual—we got sleepy every time we watched a game film. When the light was turned on to change to the second half of the film, a quick look around the room caught the drowsiness in everyone's sleepy eyes, but today even more so.

The third quarter began and so did the drowsiness. We broke the huddle and jogged to the line this time—it was the third quarter after all. We were not as chipper as when the game began.

"Now, Tyler, I want you to watch yourself on this play," said Coach Peppers as he stood up to point to the sloppy play-action fake that our quarterback was about to make.

Suddenly the screen went white ... BAM! Music played ... A loud horn section blared out a tune I recognized: It was the theme for "Coming Attractions," which was probably played before every coming attraction trailer of every movie that was to be seen in every theater in every town in the early '70s.

I jumped a half-foot at the startling blare, and I quickly turned my head for reassurance from the others. Tyler, Roger, and Steve all had the same startled, no, terrified, look as I did, and as did the rest of the twelve.

But something even more disconcerting was happening at the same time. Besides Tyler, Steve, Roger, and us twelve, none of the coaches or the rest of the players were aware that anything had changed. They all had the sleepiness in their eyes. Coach Peppers was waiting for the play to develop so he could criticize Tyler's poor ball handling.

They were completely oblivious to the music and completely oblivious to the screen that was now counting down, *THREE* ... a radar sweep ran clockwise ... *TWO* ... another radar sweep ... *ONE* ... a final radar sweep ... then, *Showtime* ...

"Now, Tyler, I want you to look at yourself," said Coach Peppers, taking his three-foot pointer and placing the end on a now full Technicolor film:

Starring: Tyler O'Shields as the Quarterback
Roger Duncan as the Runner And Steve Sharks as the Blocker.
A Jessup Christopher Savorié Film
A Heavenly Father Production © Eternity

Tyler, Roger, and Steve are lounging around Tyler's house drinking beer. No one is home except them. They are all in their late thirties now and are engaged in idle conversation among friends.

"Do y'all ever think about Marty or Robert and Harold?" asks Tyler solemnly as he is about to put the beer bottle to his lips. The film stops with a thirty-eight-year-old, gray-bearded Tyler with the bottle a couple of inches from his mouth.

"Look at you, Tyler," said Coach Peppers, pointing instructively at his quarterback, who he had just stopped in mid-pass with the start/stop clicker in his left hand. Coach pointed with his right hand at Tyler's feet, which were, as Coach noted, not set sturdily enough on the ground. "Son, you can't complete anything with a base like that."

"*Do any of you see that?! What the hell is going on here?!*" Tyler's eyes were bulging, and the madman look was the same for Roger and Steve.

Tyler stood up and pointed, looking around at the sleepy group, which was shocked that a senior quarterback would take such offense at a little criticism.

"Relax, Tyler. Take it easy, son. There's no sense of you getting upset like this. You know by now I'm just telling you this so you won't keep doing the same thing over and over again. What the shit's the matter with you?" Coach was kinda laughing on the last sentence, but was clearly annoyed by his suddenly overly sensitive quarterback. Tyler sat back down, too shocked to speak anymore. Coach clicked "start."

"I don't want to think about it," says an overweight Roger, taking a swig of Bud.

Click, the film was stopped.

"Roger, you've got to sell that this is going to be a run better than that, son. That's poor effort. We want everybody on the other team to believe we're running or else they are just going to drop back into coverage and ruin our play. A play only works if the players believe in it and think that it is going to work." Coach was looking at Roger, whose mouth was open and whose confused eyes glared back at Coach. Coach shook his head, puzzled by the reaction, and pressed start again.

"We could've stopped 'em you know." Tyler takes another sip. "We knew they were way too drunk." Tyler puts his head down.

"Stop that right there, Tyler," says Steve, with his finger pointing angrily at Tyler. "It's not our damn fault what happened to them."

Click.

"Steve, look at your body language here. You want to first show that it's a run, and then you got to get into position to block. Can't you see what we want here, son? You want to trick that defense into believing one thing and then spring the play that we really want to complete. I'm going to let it run all the way through and all of y'all see what you did wrong on this play and see what you could've done better."

Click.

"You know that it's true, Steve," shrieks Tyler in response. "Both of you damn know it," he says, subdued into a drunken whisper.

"We were all drunk that night. It could have been any of us. But it wasn't, it was them. I mean, we were just kids. We didn't know to stop ourselves. How could we have known to stop somebody else?" Steve says cautiously.

"Exactly what I mean. Why in God's name didn't we know?"

"We knew," utters Roger. "My old man told me at least once a day, every day, not to get drunk and get on the roads, and so did yours. You're right, Tyler, we should've stopped 'em. I just hadn't wanted to face it. My old man was right."

"I saw Marty's daddy the other day." Tyler's face bears the blankness of distant thoughts. "You know he still hasn't gotten over his son's death after all these years. You know what he said to me?" Tyler's blankness is replaced with wonder when he sees Roger slightly shake his head.

"He said that food lost its taste that day. He said he couldn't explain it, but every meal has a different taste to it now. It doesn't taste as good. I mean, can you imagine that—the taste getting knocked out of your mouth by grief, and that it's never going to get better." Tyler's face regains the blankness.

"You guys can wallow in this shit if you want to. I'm going home. It's supper time." Steve gets up from the couch, staggering a little, and starts toward the door.

"Hold it right there, Steve." Tyler jumps up and gets within a foot of his friend's intoxicated face. "You're a stubborn asshole sometimes, and I want to kick the shit out of you right now, but I love you, man, and you're not driving home in this condition. Get your ass back over here on the couch. We're gonna stop drinking, and start sobering up, and after that, then, I might let you drive home. Come on, buddy." Tyler wears a smile that his friend has known for thirty-three years.

"OK, dammit." Steve returns the smile. "We'll do it your way." Steve also knows when his friend is serious. And he has never seen him more serious, he thinks.

The End:

Y'all Drive Safe Now, Ya Hear.

"... and the guard blocks down and the tackle rocks around." Coach Peppers was pointing to the last play of the game. "And if we could have run, I right thirty-four trap right here on the goal line, we would have won the game, but we didn't. The time ran out, and we lost another game we should have won. We will get better, people!"

Coach Peppers had the same disappointed look on his face that he had had four other times this season as the film ran out and the white screen showed brilliant white.

"Go on home today, boys. I'll come up with a plan. We'll put it in tomorrow, and we'll get after 'em." Coach walked out of the film room, flipping the light switch on as he exited.

Tyler, Roger, and Steve were on their feet, hopelessly searching the faces of their teammates for any indication they had witnessed what the three of them had just watched in horror. But that indication never came as their mates simply passed by as if nothing had happened. It was too bad they didn't stick around to see the faces of our gang of twelve. They might have felt better.

Years later, Tyler, Roger, and Steve went on to start a program to educate kids about the dangers of drunk driving.

CHAPTER 23

KERRY "BONES" CANTRELL WAS WALKING, or perhaps bouncing, down the hall on his way to the recreation room. He was carrying himself like a man in a good mood, and for good reason. His girlfriend was none other than BB LaRue.

If BB LaRue had been my girlfriend, I would've been turning cartwheels down the hall or summersaults or something, whichever conveys that you're a fool over this girl the most—that's what I would be doing.

I had heard of BB LaRue all of my life. We were both in the same grade, but to my chagrin, never in the same class. I was in high school before I discovered that her name was in fact, BB. I always assumed that it was Bee Bee, or B. B., with the B's standing for something, Bonny Beth or something like that.

BB was one of those girls that matured ahead of schedule. She started forming little bulges on her chest and curvy hips, which began to sway when she walked, in about the fourth grade, which was unusual for then as most girls didn't develop these female attributes till later and unfortunately for some, if at all.

BB didn't stop developing until she was a full-fledged, booming bosomed, curvedly cute, vivaciously viable, sensuously sexy, hopelessly hot diva, and that was on a bad day.

She was so hot I had been afraid to speak to her until we were in the ninth grade, and then it was only to show my existence, which I don't think she ever acknowledged. I don't blame her for that though; I was pretty much invisible to all the hot girls at that time.

"Diva" is technically perhaps not the correct word for her. When you think of "diva" you associate it with someone who is a prima donna, or someone who is extremely demanding and fussy. She was neither. She just simply recognized who she was: Somebody who was born out of my league.

Bones Cantrell, you might have guessed, was skinny. He was, in fact, bony, but not because he didn't eat enough or because he was sick. He was simply born that way.

Some people are born with blue eyes, some with big ears; Bones was born bony, just like the rest of his family. He and BB LaRue were an odd couple, that's for certain. But she loved Bones. This fact was not lost on the throngs of his envious and understandably jealous rivals.

What's wrong with this picture? This is what most people who saw them together in the hallways or in the cafeteria, or just lounging together on one of the rec room couches, thought. But all was not as it might seem at first glance. You see, what Bones lacked in stature, he made up for in wit and charm.

Bones came bouncing into the rec room that afternoon as he usually did, bouncing and smiling at Pete, Bart, and me as he passed us while we reclined on the overstuffed couch that was positioned around one of the three pool tables. These pool tables were judiciously placed for maximum elbow room.

The rec room, as it was called, was the bottom half of the old gym basement that was not used as the junior high locker room. It was specifically set aside for the ninth through twelfth graders. We didn't actually play much pool, but enjoyed making fun of those that did.

We were accustomed to Bones's arrival every day; the way he confidently gestured to us on the way to his and BB's reserved couch, a place they shared for years, it seemed to us. They sat on this same couch and talked the entire period. What about? We never knew.

But something was different today, because BB entered with her head solemnly bowed. She walked past us without the slightest acknowledgment and headed straight for the couch and the now concerned-looking Bones. He sensed by her unusual approach that something was wrong.

We watched slyly. We didn't want it to seem so blatantly obvious that we were so blatantly curious. A heated argument was taking place right before us, and it seemed as though BB was losing.

She was wringing her hands and sobbing. Bones rose to his feet, pointed an authoritarian finger in her face, and stormed off in a huff. Couples have fights and break up a thousand times a day in high school, just not this couple. Their odd appearance made them unique, especially in a high school where appearance and status are held in the highest regard.

And even though I was somewhat envious, and maybe even jealous of Bones, I was also strangely proud of him and even pulling for him. I was pulling for him for the same reason that you pull for the undersized, outmanned football team that is supposed to get their butts kicked against the larger, superior favorites.

How often do the shrimps of the world win in football, or in war, or in love? If he could win, maybe I could win. Maybe it wasn't out of the question if I asked the homecoming queen out for a date— she might say yes. It could happen. It could happen as long as a creature such as Bones had a girlfriend like BB LaRue.

Perhaps that's why, in a macabre sense, I saw my chances as an underdog, and having a fighting chance with superior women, vanishing away before my eyes. My chances were somehow diminished with the weeping BB wringing her hands in anguish and Bones storming away with unfettered indignation.

Another thing was happening to me—a strange thing. I suddenly saw BB as a vulnerable human being. I believe my experience with the whole Charlotte episode changed the way I saw people. BB was no longer this superior dreamgirl that we boys had sweaty dreams over, but she was a person, just like us, with troubles thrust upon her. I suddenly felt sorry for her, and I wanted to help, and she looked like she could use it.

So, bolstered by my newfound wisdom, though slight it may be, I decided to sincerely and earnestly ask BB what was wrong and if I could help. Pete thought it was a bad idea when I told him my plan and suggested I stay out of it, which is usually a good idea, but Pete wasn't privy to my insights. So I reluctantly went to see if I could help the distraught BB anyway.

"BB, something wrong?" I asked caringly.

"Oh, Matt, yes something's wrong, but you can't help." Saying that, she burst into full-fledged sobbing.

"Listen, BB, I know Kerry a little. If you like, I could talk to him, but I got to know what the problem is. I know you guys have been going together for a long time. I hate to see you like this." I wasn't being nosy. I really wanted to help.

"I've got a problem, a big problem, and I can't tell you or anybody else about it. If it gets out, and my mother finds out, I'll have to move away. So I just can't tell." Her voice was breaking up, and she was now crying harder.

"BB, listen to me. I know what I'm talking about here." I saw an opportunity. "I know somebody that is a hell of a lot wiser than I am that can help you."

"Unless he has six hundred and eighty dollars, he can't help me at all," she blurted out suddenly, then realized what she had said and looked at me with embarrassment.

It took me a few seconds to put it together.

"BB, you're pregnant?" I asked, concerned more than shocked.

"Please don't tell anybody, Matt. If this gets out and my parents find out, they'll kill me." She was pleading more than asking.

"BB, I don't know how he does it, but Jesse Savorié can make all this a lot better." I had sincerity in my voice born from truth.

"I need money for the abortion. When I told Kerry, he said he didn't have it and that I was going to have to come up with it myself." She was starting to panic. "Can you help me raise it?"

"I can do better than that. I'll introduce you to Jesse," I said with satisfaction.

"I know who he is," she said like a deflating balloon. "Everybody knows who he is. I've seen him around. He is a little weird, isn't he? Besides, how can he help?" She sounded down on this idea.

"You've got to trust me on this one." I got very stern and very serious. "Meet him after school today, and you'll have the answers."

BB didn't say anything; she just nodded her head, sighing.

* * *

I told BB to meet Jesse behind the fieldhouse at two thirty. There were some chairs under a canopy there so the coaches could have a place to escape from football and contemplate other things, like where they were going to find a job next year.

I briefly told Jesse about BB, and this is where he suggested she meet him. He didn't ask for details, and I didn't give him any other than I thought she should meet with him. He just looked into the distance as I saw him do many times before.

"She is about to receive a wonderful blessing," he said with that same wry smile a teacher has which always precedes a lesson that the soon-to-be student will never, ever forget.

"Take it easy on her, would you, Jesse? She's been through a lot," I said, kindly. I have been on the other end of his lessons, and I know they can leave a person shaken.

"It's not up to me, I'm afraid. She will be given the blessing she needs. This is all I know. I only ask for the blessing that is necessary, and it will be glorious." Jesse was beaming.

I knew that look, and I knew two things: BB would never forget what was about to happen, and it was not going to seem glorious at the time. I didn't envy Miss BB. In fact, I was afraid for her because I had a feeling this one was going to be tough. I prayed she would be tough enough to endure it.

* * *

BB did reluctantly make her way to the canopy behind the fieldhouse and found Jesse reclined in one of the chairs. She really didn't know why she had gone up there. She was hoping Bones would have come to her before now with the money and everything would be fine. But he hadn't, and since she had no other plan, why not see if Jesse had some money she could borrow?

"Hi, Jesse. I guess I'll just sit down here and we can talk?" BB wasn't sure about anything at this point.

"If you wish." Jesse stood up and offered BB a chair, then sat beside her.

"Matt told you about my problem and what I need, I guess?" BB was hoping that Jesse already knew.

"Only that you need a blessing," Jesse answered quietly, looking into BB's stressed eyes.

"Then you don't know that I'm pregnant, and I need money for an abortion." BB was emotional and angry that she had to repeat it again to someone she didn't know well.

"Is that all? This is no problem at all, BB." Jesse reclined back in his chair and put his hands behind his head, locking his fingers as if he had heard it might rain Tuesday.

"You'll help me then?" BB was sounding much more enthusiastic. *Maybe this guy can help*, she thought.

"Of course. You will receive everything you need." Jesse turned his head toward BB and gave her a reassuring smile.

"The quicker I get it out of me, the better. I don't want it in me five seconds longer than necessary. You don't know how I've worried about this. Kerry ran off and pretty much told me to take care of it by myself. Man, you really don't know somebody till something bad happens to you." The nervousness of the moment made BB babble.

"No, once you get to know someone, you look at them totally different." Jesse peered at BB, who silently stared back at the strange way Jesse had said what he just said.

"So how do we do this, Jesse?" BB was anxious to get the money.

"Go to the park. You will meet someone there that you know. She will help you out of your problem." Jesse turned his head away but was still reclined like it was no big deal.

"The park, now? You mean right now? Somebody I know will help me? Who? I mean, I'll know her when I see her?" BB was confused over the strange instructions. "You will set this up, right?"

"It's already set up. All you have to do is go and receive everything you need." Jesse got up and left.

BB decided she had no choice but to go to the park and meet this mysterious person that she somehow knew and get from her what she needed to help her out of this dilemma. *Oh, brother!* she thought.

* * *

BB drove to the park alone. The park was always empty this time of year and especially this time of day. *Good. The less people around, the better.* It was peaceful and beautiful in the fall. She wondered, *How could anybody have problems on a day like this?*

She wandered around the park a couple of times, which didn't take long as the park in Jess Rulam was only about ten acres, tops. She saw no one. She thought that weirdo Jesse had sent her on a wild goose chase just to make fun of her. *Just what I need.*

She turned and started back for her car. Then she saw what appeared to be a four-year-old little girl sitting on one of the benches by herself. No adults were anywhere in sight. She wondered how she could not have seen her when she passed the bench just a minute earlier.

Why is the little girl sitting by herself? Where are her parents? What kind of people would leave their little girl by herself? The more she thought about these things, the angrier she became, and the more curious.

She approached the little girl, who suddenly saw her coming. The little girl grinned from ear to ear. *She's acting as if she knows me, but I have never seen her in my life.*

"Mommy!" the little girl shouted joyously.

She immediately and enthusiastically hopped from the bench and dashed as fast as her short little legs would move, even skipping a time or two. She passionately embraced BB's leg. She squeezed it so tightly, BB felt the loving little girl tremble with the strain of it.

"Mommy?" repeated BB, startled by what she had just heard.

"Listen, sweetheart." BB extricated herself from the little girl's powerful embrace and knelt down so she could look the confused little girl in the eye. Perhaps she looked somewhat like the little girl's mother. If the little one got a good look at her, she'd see that BB was not her mother at all.

"I'm not your mo …" BB stopped in mid-word, as something took hold of her senses. She *did* recognize this little girl, or at least she looked familiar anyway. She stared into the little girl's blue eyes with wonderment.

She looks like me, or at least the way I looked when I was a little girl.

"What's going on here? What's your name, sweetie?" BB held the little girl's arms firmly. She didn't want to acknowledge to herself the truth. It temporarily made her angry.

"Why, Mommy, you know that my name is DD," she giggled, surprised her mommy was such a dodo head.

"DD? How did you get a name like that?" BB was puzzled the little girl had such a peculiar name.

"You are such a dodo, Mommy." DD put her tiny finger against her mother's nose and gently tapped it.

"You said that your name was BB because your mother called you Beautiful Baby and since my name was Dory you called me DD because I'm your Dory Darling. Don't you remember, Mommy?"

BB remembered that at one time she liked the name Dory. She had not thought of Dory Darling though. A name like DD suddenly made perfect sense. A sudden chill enveloped her very soul.

My God, this is my child, my baby—the baby I have inside me right now!

A thousand thoughts and a thousand emotions bottlenecked in her mind. She simply couldn't process them all. Without warning, panic gave way to serenity, nervousness surrendered to tranquility, sadness disappeared, and simple joy permeated her every fiber. In a word, she was *happy* that she had such a beautiful little spitting-image of herself.

Her eyes suddenly saw through new lenses. The park looked different. The world looked different. And the darling little girl looked different—Dory Darling, DD to be exact. Through the new lenses, she saw her as DD, her loving little daughter. She loved her back.

"What do you want to do now, Mommy?" burst out DD, who started running this way then that way, so excited that her mommy was now with her. She didn't know what to do first.

"What do *you* want to do, DD?" asked BB, chasing little DD playfully. DD screamed and giggled and tried to make her escape from her mother's playful hands.

Little DD wasn't quick enough though. BB gathered up her snickering little angel from behind and cradled her quivery, jingly, precious little body just like her mother used to do her, she remembered.

The exposed little nape of her neck was suddenly, inexplicably, and indescribably delicious. She had to have a nibble; she playfully gobble-gobbled on it tenderly.

It occurred to her why her mother used to do the same thing to her. It was simply too irresistible not to. She had a baby girl that she loved so much that the phrase *I could just eat you up* became crystal clear now. She wondered why she had never understood that before.

Then little DD extended her little dumpy index finger and placed it on her mother's nose. She gently ran her finger down the front of it and softly across her two lips and stopped at her chin. DD's big blue eyes followed the path of her own little finger focused into her mother's eyes. Her big, moistening eyes and her two perfect little lips said, "I love you, Mommy."

For that one moment in time, BB didn't have any more problems—no tests to take, no boyfriends that disappeared at the first sign of trouble, no disapproving parents to hide things from, and most important of all, what seemed just moments ago to be a parasite sucking the very life out of her was now the most magnificent blessing ever bestowed on her. BB thought herself fortunate to be alive, and being alive was fantastic.

"Mommy, would you push me on the swing?" DD asked with her big puppy-dog eyes still peering deeply into her mother's melting soul.

"Well, of course, sweetheart ... I'll race ya."

BB pushed her daughter back and forth, back and forth. The perfect little profile of her innocent face turned to the side with exuberant anticipation of her mother placing her hands on her shrugging little shoulders; then *push,* and away she went, gliding gently through the warm Alabama autumn air.

"There's the slide, Mommy. Let's get on that. Let's race. I'll bet I beat ya this time, Mommy." And they were off.

BB was almost running in place as she let her giggling, stumbling, giddily happy little DD stay just ahead of her on the race to the slide.

"I beat ya, Mommy! I won! I won! Mommy, can we do this forever?" BB thought it the sweetest voice she had ever heard.

She scooped up her daughter and scurried up to the top step. She placed the laughing little bundle between her legs. Time slowed down as they started down the slide.

A moment captured in time, slow time, still time, when BB saw the floating blond hair, the angelic smile, the innocence of the little one. She thought to herself, *I made this out of my body; this came from me; and if I never in my life do anything again, I did something once that I'm proud of. How bad can I be, if I can do this?*

BB placed her head against her daughter's as they got to the bottom of the slide, and DD placed her hand against her mother's head and nestled it in tight. She turned quickly and hugged with both arms around her mother's neck and gently kissed her mother on the lips. Then she was off on another adventure with her mother following close behind, giggling almost as loudly as her little DD.

After thirty minutes or so, BB said to her tired bundle of love, "Let's sit down on the bench for a little while. Mommy's tired and needs to rest."

"OK, Mommy. Sometimes mommies get tired and have to rest, don't they?" said BB, all grown and prissy as she and her mom walked back to the bench.

"Yes they do, sweetie."

"But they don't ever let nothing happen to their girls, do they? 'Cause that's what mommies do, ain't it?" she asked with a little giggle at the end. "You won't ever let nothing happen to me, will you, Mommy?"

"I'll die before I let anything happen to you, angel," BB said as they arrived back at the bench. She put DD in her lap as she sat down.

A single cloud temporarily blocked the sun and a gentle, slightly cooler breeze lightly lifted DD's golden hair as BB lovingly admired the preciousness sitting on her lap.

"'Cause sometimes I have bad dreams that something bad is going to get me and I can't find you anywhere, Mommy."

"I will always be here for you, DD. Now and forever." BB, filled with motherly instincts, gave her concerned daughter a tight hug of reassurance.

The sky was a little more overcast and the breeze picked up again. BB hoped it wouldn't rain. She didn't want this day to end.

"What would you do to keep something from getting me, Mommy? I get scared when I'm by myself, but I think, *Now you ol' DD, you stop that worrying 'cause you got the best mommy in the world, and she ain't never going to let anything happen to her little girl.* Ain't that right, Mommy? That's right, ain't it?" She gave a little laugh of reassurance on the last sentence.

The quaintness of DD's tender voice as she searched for assurance from her mother that she would always be there for her struck a very tender spot in BB's heart. A stream of tears made their way down her cheeks.

The breeze turned into gusts. A plastic cup blew off one of the benches, and a paper plate whipped across the ground in front of them. BB held her daughter's little blue dress down on her lap. The sky was getting noticeably darker.

"Would you hold me like I was your little baby girl again, Mommy? The way you used to when I was little?"

"Of course I will, sweetheart." BB cradled her scared little girl into her bosom. She rocked back and forth like she was sitting in a rocking chair.

"That bad thing is trying to get me again. I can hear it. I have bad dreams about it, and it almost gets me sometimes, and I can't find you anywhere, Mommy, and I'm afraid it's going to get me someday. But you won't let it get me, will you, Mommy? No, you won't, will you? 'Cause you love your little girl, don't you, Mommy?"

DD had raised her little head to see her mother nodding yes. Her big eyes were tearing up, and she nestled her head down in the protective bosom of her mother, the place where nothing bad happens to little girls.

The breeze was now a fairly strong wind. Debris swirled in tiny little eddies here and there. The cloudy darkness was ominous, and BB thought a bad storm was coming to put an end to their frolicking. She thought she heard a roaring sound in the distance. She couldn't quite make out what it was.

"DD, this storm is coming quickly. We have to get out of here." BB had to shout to make herself heard above the wind and the ever-increasing roar.

The two-foot-tall funnels whisked about the debris, and some of it dashed by her head.

"It's the bad thing, Mommy. Do you hear it? It's coming to get me again. Hold me tight. Hold me tight. Please say you will never let go of me. Please say it." BB could feel her daughter's tiny heart racing against her own chest. Her little arms clutched so tightly around her mother's arm, it was starting to go numb.

"DD, I think it's a tornado," BB shouted. "We have to get to where it's safe!"

The debris swirled more violently now. Some of it was sucked high into the air. The roar was much louder.

"We can't get away from here, Mommy. I try and try, but I can't get through nowhere! I'm scared, Mommy! Hold me! It's going to get me, ain't it, Mommy? Promise, promise me you won't let it get me!" BB took hold of her trembling daughter's shoulders and peered deeply into her frightened eyes. They desperately searched for some kind of reassurance from her mother. She would not let the *bad thing* get her.

"DD, I will never let anything happen to you, ever. I love you with all my heart, DD. We are going to stay together forever, I promise." She embraced DD passionately and stood up with her nestled on one shoulder and said into her sweet little ear, "Let's run to my car and get out of here."

BB ran with her daughter clutched against one shoulder toward her car. She frantically wanted to get away from the quickly approaching tornado. Its roar was now almost deafening. She dodged tree limbs, trash cans, and all manner of debris. It was becoming more dangerous every second.

She saw the spot just ahead where she had entered the park, but something was wrong. She could clearly see through the swirling dust, paper, leaves, and an occasional piece of tin, that a thick piece of pinkish-colored plastic had lodged against the two concrete columns, which served as the entrance.

A piece of plastic? I'll bust through it if I have to, she thought.

As she got closer and closer to the plastic, she thought she could make out some red lines of different thicknesses traversing the plastic obstruction. She stopped and pressed her shoulder into the barrier. To her horror, she realized the barricade was not plastic but some kind of living membrane complete with blood-flowing veins. And what was even more horrifying to the now hysterical BB was that the ghoulish, vein-riddled membrane *encapsulated the entire park!*

BB turned frantically in time to see a limb ripped from a tree and be sucked straight up into the ominous black sky. The roaring sound coming from directly overhead was so deafening, that holding on to a coherent thought was as implausible as the living, veiny membrane that held them captive.

I must keep my head, BB thought. *I must keep DD safe. She is all that matters to me right now. I love her so much, I will die before I let anything happen to her!*

BB's eyes fixated on an even more horrific scene. The whirling, sucking, roaring wind was now concentrated into one superpowerful spot far in the distance. She could make out that trees were being uprooted.

The ground would finally let go of its old friend it had fed and watered for years and years. First one root, then another, then another, and finally the century-year-old stalwart of the forest was forced to give up its hold on life to the relentless, powerful life-sucking vacuum and disappear into the black sky above. It was heading straight for BB and the trembling, sobbing, bundle of love.

BB turned to the sinewy membrane and pressed her free hand into it. Her hand penetrated six inches inward. She noticed one of the veins pulsating about every second or so as if being fed blood from a giant beating heart.

BB stepped back so she could see how far the membrane extended upward. She saw no end. She lay her free hand across one of the pulsating veins and felt the unmistakable sensation of coursing blood.

Things went momentarily silent; no wind, no roar of the vacuum, no clanging debris. One thought stopped time and space in their inevitable tracks; one thought was all she could hear—*My God, I'm inside my own womb!*

BB ran along the impermeable membrane, one hand clutching her daughter, the other brushing against it hoping to find some weakness. She had to find some tiny hole to get the adorably loving DD through to save her from the *bad thing*, which she now knew as the giant life-sucking vacuum.

Though she tried, BB could no longer fight the urge to cry. She cried uncontrollably with each stride. They were not quick enough to outpace the roaring, sucking sound of the rapidly approaching *bad thing* bearing down on them.

"I've already tried, Mommy. Every day I try to find a way out of here so I can be with you, but I can't ever find you. Where do you hide every day, Mommy?" DD began to cry just like her ever-weakening mother.

A terrible dread enveloped BB. She was beginning to accept that there was no escape from this prison. She turned her head briefly to witness the inevitable life-sucking machine perform its evil, singular job, which was what it was invented to do: Take a beautiful thriving tree standing in all its glory one second and turn it into an empty hole in the ground the next.

The evil machine was inching closer and closer, step by step, only fifty yards away now. It had only one purpose, which BB now realized was *to suck the life out of her precious little daughter, DD.*

BB was running harder and harder, but moving slower and slower. Something was terribly wrong with her legs. Why was she getting so weak? She should be moving faster than this. What was wrong?

She seemed to be running in slow motion. The harder she tried, the slower she ran. As the ominous death machine closed in, she could think of nothing but her daughter. Her crying intensified with each passing thought of DD.

She peered over at DD, who undulated back and forth with each of her slowing strides. Her little head was turned first toward the bad thing, and then toward her mother. Her big blues eyes were saying, *I love you, Mommy, I'm scared*. Minutes earlier, they were as clear as a June morning and now conveyed the unholy look of terror.

"Run faster, Mommy. Run faster! The bad thing is going to get me! You promised me, you promised you wouldn't let it get me, Mommy!" The words coming from her pleading daughter should have made her move faster, but to BB's horror, she was running slower still.

BB screamed, "Stay away from her! Stay away from my daughter! Stay away from my baby! You're not going to get her, you bastards, no!"

A trash can lid came crashing at BB's feet. She tried to hurdle it but was so exhausted and weak that she tripped and fell instead, spilling DD headfirst onto the ground.

DD flipped end over end a couple of times and came to a rolling stop. She raised her head and sat up just in time for her weary mother to see her eyes become the size of silver dollars. The suction from the vacuum dragged little DD along the ground; she was sitting up and screaming at the top of her shrill voice, "The bad thing's got me, the bad thing's got me! Don't let it get me!"

BB stood up on her wobbly knees and lunged at her screaming child, but the wind moved DD an inch out of reach. BB tried crawling as fast as her weary legs and arms would pull her. She screamed with half-filled lungs, "Not my, baby! Please, God, don't let them take my baby!"

The doomed little BB stayed inches from her mother's outreached fingers.

A sudden gust sped DD away. With a thud, her crumpled tiny body slammed against a tree.

Lying on the ground, completely spent of the last drop of energy, BB looked through the haze of swirling debris and the wavy mist of half-consciousness. The giant vacuum was directly over her little DD, her feet caught in the fork of the large oak tree she had bounced off of a minute earlier. She was suspended by the wind of the giant vacuum pulling her violently upward. The ravenous wind pulled off her little blue dress and sucked it into the black sky with a *thup* sound.

BB thought if she could manage to get to her feet, she might somehow, someway, miraculously climb the tree and pull her terrified daughter to safety.

She pushed mightily against the cold, hard ground, but her energy and now her hope was gone. All she could do was witness the horror of what was to happen next in helpless anguish. It would be a scene that would never, ever leave the recesses of her weary mind.

BB rolled over onto her back and screamed until nothing came out from her spent lungs. The only sound she could hear was the relentless pleading of a little girl saying, "Don't let the bad thing get me, Mommy. I love you. Don't let it get me!"

* * *

The bright Alabama autumn sun was somewhat painful on BB's eyes as she tried to open them. She was lying on her back in the middle of Jess Rulam Park. She squinted. She sat up as the realization struck her. She looked down at her tattered clothes. One shoe was missing, her blouse was torn, and she was covered in cuts and bruises.

The distinct taste of her own blood was in her mouth, and she could feel a large bulge on her forehead. She looked around the park, and everything was the same as when she had arrived. The trees were not disturbed. There was no roaring sound. No wind whatsoever whipped around, and no eerie membrane held her captive.

She screamed, "DD!" She looked down at her half-exposed stomach and put both hands around her midsection. She remembered DD and felt her love. BB felt joy for the world.

* * *

BB entered the fieldhouse where Jesse was working after school. She walked in with her clothes tattered and wearing only one shoe. She was battered and bruised from head to toe. Jesse was standing in the hallway staring at BB as she approached. BB stopped, looked deep into Jesse's eyes, and gave him the most passionate hug she had ever given another human being. They wept with joy.

CHAPTER 24

THE FALL OF 1975 ARRIVED surprisingly fast. Though I was but seventeen, an axiom I heard all my life actually began to make sense: Time *does* speed up as you get older. It took an eternity to go from a toddler to the first grade, eons from the first to the sixth grades, a decade from the sixth to the ninth, and from the ninth to my senior year, not so long.

I didn't actually realize until recently that the process of aging is just like our tax system, *progressive*. The higher your bracket, the more you pay ... not with taxes, but with life. In 1975, I was only beginning to make my first payments.

One person who was making his payments in a timely manner was Coach Peppers. He was not only making his payments, but also his wife's, his children's, the other coaches', and the entire school's. He was making his payments on time, paying back the accrued interest that had been building for years. Payback was wearing on him.

* * *

Jesse continued to morph, now fully grown physically, standing six-three and two-hundred-thirty-five muscular pounds. Your eye was drawn to his broad shoulders and tapering waist. Not an ounce of body fat covered the bulging, rippling muscles of this seasoned bodybuilder. Though his countenance never warranted it, kids moved over a couple of extra inches out of respect when they passed him.

His emotional uniqueness for a supposed man-child still in high school was perhaps oddest of all. He never laughed, only chuckled occasionally, and only as a way to make a point. He never got mad, at anyone, for anything, only periodically disappointed, and only, seemingly, at members of the twelve.

He made us feel stupid without really trying. We learned from him the hard way.

* * *

It was our senior year, our last year of high school, our last year of football, and for Coach Peppers it seemed inevitable that it was his last year as well. He knew it. He gave his best, but like so many would-be champions of the lost causes, he had lost. The champions of lost causes are numerous on pages of fiction and are easily portrayed on the screen, but in the harshness of real life, the endings are rarely happy.

In the austerity of high school football in north Alabama in the mid-'70s, soon-to-be fired football coaches spend a lot of time on the phone during the offseason. It becomes a time when the words, "I owe you one" from longtime friends are called in. Like most words made at a jubilant moment, they are merely jests.

A winning head football coach has many friends who speak in long sentences when the subject is, *I'm moving up the ranks to a bigger, better, more prestigious school. Want to join me?*

The sentences become much shorter when the subject is, *I need an assistant coaching job. Can you help?* Coach Peppers was hearing a lot of short sentences lately.

* * *

Jesse knocked on Coach Peppers's office door, which was usually open but was shut a lot lately.

"Come in."

"Coach, is this first practice going to be done the usual way this year?"

"Yes." Coach seemed irritated at the mere question.

"OK. I'll set everything up for you, Coach."

"Jesse, wait a minute. I want to talk to you."

Coach got up from his desk and moved around to the front and leaned against one corner with his arms folded and one foot crossed in front of the other. His body language signaled he had something serious to talk about.

"I'm here anytime you want to talk, Coach. You have but to ask."

"How close are you to the other black kids in this school?"

"As close as I am to the other white kids in this school."

"Jesse, I'm in trouble. I need your help. I'm down to my last straw here." Coach Peppers's voice had a desperate tone to it. "I don't know how you do it, but kids follow you around and most of them hang on your every word. The teachers around here are afraid to talk to you.

"I saw something in here one afternoon that has been on my mind, and I can't shake it. There's something going on with you I don't understand. Some power, the shadows on the wall that day, the way Coach Dobbs quit, the way Coach Benefield left out of here without a trace.

"I don't know who you are; I'm not even sure *what* you are. But you have something. I don't know if you have something for me, or not," Coach Peppers continued, shakily.

Jesse listened, expressionless.

"But I'm scared to get fired. I'm scared to move my wife and kids one more time, and the words 'This time is the last time' are wearing thin on them. I'm running out of promises I can't keep. I'm thirty-five years old."

The desperate, shaken, and now-broken coach slowly shuffled over to the only window in the office and disappeared into a distant conversation with himself as much as with Jesse.

"I played for Coach Paul Bryant. I worked my way to starting. Me! Look at me! I'm five feet nothing. I'm a hundred and nothing. I worked my way to starting on a national championship team. Me! For Coach ... Paul ... Bryant."

"They call him Bear, do they not?" inquired a soft-spoken Jesse.

"His players call him Coach Bryant; that's how you know who's a former player and who's not. A player would never call him Bear. But I played for him. Now look at me—a hapless loser high school football coach that's about to get run out of town on a rail.

"I had all the answers. My wife believed in me. Hell I believed in me. She was so pretty the day we got married," whispered Coach to a faraway something outside the window somewhere. "I married over my head, you know."

Coach turned to Jesse and chuckled, then reassumed his stare out the window.

"You've seen her. How do you think guys like me get girls like her? It's because they think they're getting the guy that was the champion. What happened to that guy? Where did he go? I know that's what she has to be thinking. I mean, how could she not?"

Coach tapered off until his lips moved without sound, still staring out the window into nothingness.

"So," said Coach, snapping out of his reverie, "what do you think I should do?"

"I think you are the victim of misplaced priorities. You seem to be under the illusion that your importance as a man lies in the outcome of the stupid trivialities of a child's game."

"That's it! You've summed me up—I'm a stupid triviality." Coach was still looking out the window but lucidly now. Jesse continued to stare at Coach, pondering to himself.

"I think it is time for your lesson. I think it is time for this town's lesson. Don't you agree, Coach?"

"Yeah, teach us," said Coach somewhat sarcastically, still looking out the window.

"As you wish."

"I wish! I wish indeed, ol' Jesse," he said, still discouraged.

"I'm going to talk to the blacks." Jesse walked out of the office.

Coach, realizing what Jesse had just said, followed him to the door and shouted, "What about?"

"Stupid trivialities, what else?" answered Jesse without looking back.

* * *

Tim Richey, Jeffery Hope, and Eric Prater would start school as seniors this year. Jewel Hill and Wallace Moore would be juniors. They were all being entertained, more like held captive, by a couple of local hustlers and white-haters named Jerome "The Jet" Jones and Elmore Dupree. A dozen or so other black kids were scattered about.

Tim, Jeffery, Eric, Jewel, and Wallace were great athletes who did not transfer out of Jess Rulam, as had become the mandatory custom for all black athletes considering playing any kind of varsity sports. These particular students chose not to play rather than transfer. Driving distance issues were the general summation by the Jess Rulam coaches, who could look but not touch such coveted prizes.

The two neighborhood agitators were holding court at The Court, a basketball/tennis facility that was part of the park where the local kids met after school to hang out sometimes. Today it happened to be all black kids—white people didn't hang around when The Jet and Dupree showed up.

Court was in session today because a nasty rumor was floating about that the five kids in question were considering breaking with tradition and the unwritten law, ironically called the Black Code, that a black student would never play varsity sports for the *honky-asses* at Jess Rulam High School.

The Jet and Dupree were the prosecution, judge, and the enforcers of this street law. What started out as a voluntary tradition, because it was the right thing to do, became the decree of the land because these self-described white-haters and convicted criminals—armed robbery—would intimidate anyone who had second thoughts. There was no escaping their justice.

So it was this Friday afternoon the two thugs found five boys playing basketball together at The Court. These were quiet kids that caused no trouble, from good, yet poor families that couldn't afford for their children to transfer to another school. The boys were wasting their God-given talents, and they knew it.

Unfortunately this made little difference to The Jet and Dupree, who had another golden opportunity to act thuggish and to demonstrate their thuggishness in front of as many of the whites as possible. This was their main purpose, actually: not to intimidate the blacks as much as the whites who happened to be watching.

These two were not above driving their Harleys alongside white girls walking alone and offering them sex whether wanted or not. Either way the girls were labeled with the moniker of "bitches" by the thugs. It was a sport of theirs, to catch some whites at just the right locations and just the right numbers and start a fight, which they always won.

Years in prison, and on the just as harsh big city streets from which they had migrated, had hardened these two to a fine edge of precision thuggery, particularly Elmore Dupree. He was six-four and two hundred and fifty pounds of ass-stomping, tattooed muscle. He managed to put Donnie Brown, who was thought to be the roughest, toughest redneck in the area, in the hospital, in what witnesses said was a fair fight. Fair fights were, however, few and far between for The Jet and Elmore Dupree.

One of their favorite pastimes was to castigate black kids for being friendly with white kids. They berated them in front of the whites and any onlookers, using every kind of racial slur they could imagine in their rather unlimited brains on this one subject. They did it because the whites were afraid to do anything about it. Black, tattooed ex-cons with gold-capped teeth, giant Afros, sitting astride roaring Harleys, were enough to keep the most racist honky-ass white people's mouths shut.

The Jet and Dupree were feeling a little more salty today during court than usual. The white, honky-ass Jess Rulam Police had been watching the two rather closely lately. Some unsolved break-in robberies of a few of the local businesses, and the fact that The Jet and Dupree always seemed to have plenty of cash without holding down any discernible jobs, made them suspects number one—a fact that pissed off the two thugs even more at honky-ass white people.

* * *

Jesse heard The Court session long before he saw it. The words "honky-ass white people," peppered the air. Then he heard, "I will personally kick your nigger-ass myself."

A group of ten or twelve scared black kids were standing, trapped, against the chainlink fence encircling The Court. Among them were the five athletes questioning the outdated—they thought—unwritten Black Code.

One of the detainees shouted, "Jesse." This broke the obscenity-filled rant The Jet was in the process of unleashing on his unwitting captive audience.

The Jet and Dupree turned to see Jesse's imposing figure standing behind them. Their surprised expressions soon turned to a sickening dread as many others could attest who had had the misfortune of being caught in the crosshairs of the haunting glare of one Jesse Christopher Savorié.

"What in hell are you?" The Jet was uneasy at the ominous glare he was receiving.

"Funny that you and I would be thinking the same thing," returned Jesse in a low monotone, never taking his glare off the two thugs.

"Funny? There ain't nothing funny about me, or my, ah, colleague here." The Jet snickered as he patted Dupree on the shoulder.

"Nor is there anything intelligent," Jesse said in the same monotone.

"Are you calling me stupid?" The Jet looked at his colleague for reassurance when he was speaking to Jesse.

"Only when you open your mouth. I can't speak for the other five percent of the time." A lone snicker came from the kids against the fence.

Dupree spoke up. "You some kinda honky-ass mixed-up freak show. I done be gonna lay down the way it gonna be."

"Well said. Obviously you're a poet." Jesse's voice never changed, nor did his demeanor. More than one snicker came from the kids.

"You trying to act and talk like you're white. Why is that?" asked The Jet in his best mocking white-man voice. He laughed, holding his hand out for Dupree to slap.

"You act and talk as if stupidity were a virtue. *Why is that?*"

More snickers and laughs came from the kids.

"You talk funny." The Jet poked his index finger lightly into Jesse's chest four or five quick times and walked around to the other side of his colleague. "I don't know any brother that talks like that. People say you are a soul brother, ain'tcha?"

"It's humorous that you should once again hit upon *precisely* what I am. A *soul brother* indeed."

"I'm keeping it real. I talk the way a *real* black man talks. I don't know what the hell you are. Some kind of white ass-kisser sounds like to me."

The Jet stuck his lips out at Jesse, mocking him. "You afraid to talk like a brother. You afraid you'd get kicked out of the white ass-kisser club?"

"I would think that for a race of people that has been castigated, mocked, enslaved, brutalized, and oppressed for four hundred years, and all of which is caused by a hunger fed by the perception of the oppressors that you are a stupid people, well, I should think that starving the hunger would make more sense than feeding it."

"What the hell are you talking about, you honky-ass-looking fool?" Dupree was getting angry.

"Both of you bore me senseless," said Jesse, exhaling with exasperation. "Stand aside now. I have business with these students. I will not have a duel of wits against unarmed men." All the kids laughed. The Jet quickly moved behind Jesse.

"I think I'm gonna have to take this honky-ass myself." The Jet was seething.

"I don't believe a man that appears to be infested with parasites should boast of his physical prowess."

The kids made a "woo" sound.

"You're treating me like a dog in front of my black people. You talk to me like a dog and cause my own people to laugh at me, I'll treat you like the bitch you are."

The Jet drew back with an open hand and slapped at Jesse, who quickly ducked. The slap rang Dupree's jaw. Enraged, Dupree drew back and aimed a fist at a now-erect Jesse, who ducked again, and the powerful punch landed between The Jet's lips. The Jet went sliding along the grass on his back, absent three teeth which landed somewhere near the fence.

Dupree was not planning on missing again. He let loose with all his might, right between Jesse's eyes. Jesse stood perfectly still, completely unconcerned about the rapidly approaching fist. Jesse waited for the zooming knuckles to get within two inches of his face. His hand moved in a blur and snatched Dupree's wrist and held it motionless in front of him.

He dragged him with no effort toward the pole supporting the basketball goal. Dupree's feet dug ruts in the ground as he was being dragged like a stubborn donkey. It was pointless for him to resist, of course. He was as powerless as a baby lamb dragged to slaughter.

Jesse noticed one of the perplexed kids rapidly chewing gum. He cupped his hand and said, "Could you please spit your gum into my hand?" The bemused child promptly obliged.

Jesse expertly stuck the gum onto the side of the basketball pole. He put the squirming Dupree's fist against the wad of gum and let go. He walked back toward the baffled kids.

Dupree pulled and tugged with all his might against the gum, but to no avail. He was stuck. His greatest effort only managed to stretch the gum a couple of inches away from the pole before it snapped his fist back into place. Some kids snickered again.

Dupree's dismayed face peered around at the now laughing kids as if he expected them to free him. He grasped his captured fist with his free hand and, using one knee against the pole for leverage, let out a frightful groan as he used the last of his great strength to break free from the Juicy Fruit gum wad.

The mighty effort *did* manage to stretch the wad three inches this time before being snapped back into place just as before. The cowed Dupree wore a puckered expression on his panicky face just before he whimpered like a spanked three-year-old child with its hand caught in the cookie jar. All the kids roared with laughter.

The Jet had by now regained his feet and was feeling around with one finger in a mouth for teeth that were no longer there.

"Does anyone have any more gum?" Jesse asked. He was standing in front of the group like a chemistry teacher about to charm his students with his next fascinating experiment. Someone tossed him some well-chewed gum, just as the previous kid had.

"You see, class, when you are weak of mind and ignorant of the world, the mildest of circumstances can bind you. You can easily be made a mindless slave to it."

Jesse took the gum and stretched it this way and that. Soon he fashioned a gum lasso from it. He walked over to The Jet, flung the gum lasso over his head, pulled it tight around his neck, and pulled him over onto all fours like a dog on a leash.

"Come along, boy," Jesse commanded. The Jet happily complied as he wagged his hips back and forth, turned his head, and panted with his tongue rolling out like a dog trying to cool himself.

The group of hysterically laughing kids could be heard in the streets of Jess Rulam. The Jet let out a couple of barks and pranced proudly on the palms of his hands and the tips of his toes.

"Good boy." Jesse patted his new pet on the head. "Now, sit."

The Jet sat his butt on the ground.

"Now, beg."

The Jet raised his two hands, or paws now, into the familiar dog begging position, and made whining doggy sounds. He was again rewarded with another pat on the head.

Jesse led The Jet over to one of the Harleys nearby. The Jet hiked his leg and was about to mark his territory when Jesse scolded him with a slap on the rump. The Jet immediately lay on the ground and rolled over onto his back. He spread all fours, which prompted Jesse to rub his exposed belly.

The kids were doubled over in laughter. Jesse tied the end of the gum leash around the handlebars of the Harley and walked back in front of his amused class. He said, "Hear me now."

The kids stopped laughing and listened intently.

"You cannot rely on this," Jesse said as he poked the muscular shoulder of one of the five athletes.

"This is weak, for it will eventually succumb to *illness* and *wither* with age. But develop this to its maximum potential." Jesse pointed to the same kid's head.

"This will never let you down. And you will truly never be free until you learn to use the limitless boundaries of your mind to escape those that would bind you." Jesse turned and looked at the weeping Dupree and the submissive Jet still lying on his back.

"As long as you rely on your bodies you will always be at the mercy of those who have a use for it. Your usefulness to them will end when your bodies break down with age or infirmity. No one will care what you think.

"And when time comes for you to depart this world, people will notice that you are missing, but you will not be missed. For all the good you could have left behind, you might as well never have been born. You will be buried and forgotten and little more." The group of kids pondered Jesse's words.

"But there is nothing wrong with using the God-given talents as long as *this* present time on earth values such things. Sports can sometimes advance a person to a better position from which to launch.

"It is time for you five who contemplated playing football for this school to stop your contemplations and go see Coach Peppers immediately. Tell all the others as well, it is time to begin to heal this town. Tell all the black students that you are playing football this fall, and that they should join you, and also, that it will be glorious."

Jesse and the kids left The Court that day with the whimpering Dupree still stuck to the pole and The Jet licking himself. Dupree thought he heard the kids in the distance burst into song while he pleaded for some white kids passing by to please help him get free from this wad of Juicy Fruit gum. They thought him addled and left him whimpering.

CHAPTER 25

JESSE PROVED TO BE A great recruiter. He approached *this* black student and he spoke to *that* white student. All the young men of Jess Rulam High School from the ninth through twelfth grades were enthusiastically and very persuasively asked to play football that fall.

He convinced every able-bodied boy that it was his duty to help his floundering school. He would say to this black child the time has come to forgive the school for its ignorant indiscretions of the past and rejoice in a wonderful new beginning.

He would tell this white boy, who looked like a promising athlete, but for some reason had not yet played football, that it was a wonderful opportunity to test himself and help to heal his school of a festering wound.

He went from student to student, from home to home, spreading the word, and the word was football.

* * *

"Hollis, may I speak to you for a minute?" said Jesse to Hollis Reed, a six-foot-five, two-hundred-and-sixty-pound farm boy, whose family owned and operated a dairy. "I know you haven't ever played football before. Perhaps this should be the year you make proper use of your great strength," Jesse said in his familiar philosophical manner.

"Jesse, you know my dad won't let me get out of helping him around here," returned Hollis, quietly hoping his father wouldn't come over and wonder why Jesse had come to their farm and was hindering his son from his chores.

"Besides," Hollis continued, "I don't even like football. And besides that, I've already been thoroughly hounded about not playing, so everybody has left me alone, until now. It's behind me now, Jesse. Just leave me be, and let me get this feed unloaded."

Hollis picked up a sack of feed, flung it over his right shoulder, and picked up another sack and flung it over his left shoulder, then scurried up the steps to the feed storage bin.

Hollis drove the flatbed truck to the feed mill in town and picked up five tons of supplement that had to be stored upstairs in their milking barn. At fifty pounds per sack, Hollis had two hundred sacks to get up the steep steps.

His hard-driving father was agitatedly watching this strange looking mixed-breed boy hinder his son's work. He went about washing out the cow manure from the parlor, moving from stanchion to stanchion but never really taking his eyes off Jesse.

"You are a mighty man, Hollis. Why not put your gift to a mightier work?" asked Jesse after Hollis came back down the stairs ready to reload his wide shoulders for another trip.

"Playing football is a mightier work than doing my work here at the dairy?" Hollis was amused. "Don't let my dad hear you say that." Hollis placed two more bags on his shoulders.

"What's that boy want, Hollis?" hollered Mr. Reed, who could no longer restrain himself.

"Nothing, Dad! Just visiting," Hollis hollered back, trying to sound nonchalant.

Mr. Reed had to have a better look at this boy that was damn near as big as his son. He laid the water hose down and made his way toward the feed truck, all the while sizing up Jesse and speculating why a boy that looked like him would be on his farm.

It was only about two hundred feet from the parlor to the flatbed. Mr. Reed thought he would surreptitiously approach the two and find out what was so important. He was about one hundred feet away from the unsuspecting boys when he saw his son hurry up the steps with a couple of bags of feed.

Jesse was watching Hollis walk away when he casually reached with one hand and easily pulled the heavily loaded truck three feet closer to the barn without taking his eyes off of Hollis's ascending back. Mr. Reed paused, smiled, pulled off his glasses, and yanked a handkerchief from his pocket to wipe his dust and cow-crap splattered spectacles.

"Well, what are y'all talking about?" Mr. Reed glanced at Jesse, trying not to stare, but he couldn't help it.

"Jesse here is trying to talk me into playing football, is all."

Hollis didn't make eye contact with his father, but looked dejectedly at the one hundred and ninety-four remaining sacks of feed that weren't going to walk themselves up the ever-steepening steps.

"Look here, boy, Hollis has to help me with this dairy every afternoon," said Mr. Reed, tired of somebody from town trying to convince him that his son could be a prospect. "I've got two men hired on because that's all I can afford. We got a hundred twenty-five head of cows to manage and try to squeeze out a living."

"I understand, sir. This looks like it would be a satisfying way to earn a living. I wouldn't mind working here." Jesse was taking in the surroundings of the farm.

"Boy, you wouldn't like it at all. This is hard work. Up early, to bed early. Not a lot of time for sports. I know you people like sports and games. You wouldn't like this kind of work." Mr. Reed was trying not to be insulting.

"I think I would," returned Jesse. "I've been thinking about changing jobs and trying something new. It would only be part time, of course, after football practice. How about it, Mr. Reed?"

"Boy, you got them sports kind of muscles." Mr. Reed put his finger on Jesse's biceps. "You couldn't hold up to do farmwork though. It takes a different kind of muscle here."

Jesse picked up a couple of bags of feed and placed them on Hollis's shoulders. Then he placed a couple on his own shoulders. He smiled at Mr. Reed then winked at Hollis, and they both lit up the stairs. They quickly returned, but this time Hollis placed two packs on his right shoulder and one on his left. Jesse did the same.

Next trip, Hollis wanted two bags on his right and two on his left. Jesse loaded Hollis. When Hollis got back, it would be his turn to load Jesse. Mr. Reed was amused by the competition and leaned against the barn to see when Jesse was going to say "uncle."

Next trip it was three on the right side, two on the left, two hundred and fifty pounds. Hollis slowed considerably and had to stop halfway up the steps to get his breath. Jesse walked straight up the steep steps without stopping. Hollis peered at his father. Both had shocked looks on their faces. Neither knew what to make of this.

Next, three and three. Hollis glanced at his father, who had a concerned look on his face like he didn't want him to hurt himself. All the same, Hollis needed to put this annoying kid in his place.

Jesse placed six bags of feed on Hollis's shoulders—three hundred pounds. When he made the gauntlet trip, Hollis would place the bags on Jesse's shoulders. Hollis staggered and found it hard to even stand. Jesse kept his hand on Hollis's back as he took baby shuffles over to the steps.

He placed one foot on the first step then the other. So far so good, eleven more steps to go. Hollis had to lean against the wall on the fourth step, with a grimace set to his jaw. He had to make it. He placed his foot on the fifth step, and the wooden tread snapped with his full weight crashing down. His butt bounced off the edge of the step, and he fell backward toward the ground with all six bags of feed still on his shoulders.

His father gasped, "Hollis!"

Jesse took a couple of steps forward and caught Hollis in his arms. He quickly and easily set him up on his feet. The feed was still on Hollis's shoulders. Jesse snatched up the six bags, jetted up the steps, hopped over the missing steps, and returned to see how Hollis was feeling.

"Mr. Reed, why don't you get Hollis to the house and let him sit for a few minutes. I'll finish unloading this truck."

Mr. Reed was stunned and so was his son. Hollis hadn't had time to process this yet; he felt a little weak and shaken. Jesse left six minutes later, and the truck was unloaded.

The next day, Hollis was at football practice. Coach Peppers was impressed with Hollis and felt sure he was a college prospect.

Both boys went to the dairy after practice and enjoyed a good-natured three hours of work.

Mr. Reed spent a lot of time thinking and occasionally found his eyes on Jesse. He pondered the strangeness of the world and the amazing people in it.

* * *

"Who's this fool coming up here?" asked Floyd Monroe. He was relaxing in his recliner that had outlived its usefulness for inside use, so he had moved it outside under the covered porch.

"That's that peculiar boy from the high school," said Floyd's best friend, Harvey, who was relaxing in another recliner, also relegated to outside use. Once the chairs got too ratty for the porch, they would finally be thrown away. Not a bad idea, actually.

Jesse made his way about halfway up The Hill before the two men in their late fifties spotted him coming. He was on a mission: to recruit TW Monroe to play football for Jess Rulam.

TW Monroe was considered a major college prospect. He was a record-setting running back for Jericho with over two thousand yards in his junior season. He elected to travel to the city school and keep the boycott of Jess Rulam intact.

There was no rule, however, stopping a student from returning to his original school at any time and playing football. Jesse was determined to get him to change his mind, but he had a formidable foe to overcome—TW's father, Floyd. Floyd didn't particularly like white people.

"What you want, boy?" Floyd spit it out almost as one word. That's just the way he talked—fast.

"I am here to speak to TW Monroe, sir." Jesse was fixed on Floyd. He knew this would be the battle.

"What about? He ain't here now."

"Why, sure he is, sir. You are protecting him from a danger that does not exist."

"What are you wanting him for?" Floyd was peering intently at Jesse.

"I would like to ask him to consider playing football for Jess Rulam this year, sir." Jesse's answer immediately transformed Floyd's peer into a glare.

"He's playing football for Jericho City School. He ain't gonna be playing for no other school. I'm afraid you walked up here for nothing." Floyd chuckled and looked over at Harvey.

"Shouldn't TW have something to say about this, sir?"

"Why, he sure do ... Tim, Tim, come on out here." Floyd turned and shouted into the house, "Come on out here and tell Mr. Interlocutor here you ain't playing football for no damn overseers."

TW came out of the house and sat quietly on the three-foot-tall concrete retainer encircling the porch. He looked curiously at Jesse, who he had heard many stories about but had never actually talked to.

"You know what an interlocutor is, boy?" Floyd asked with an unfriendly smile, like he was about to teach a lesson to someone who he had just caught stealing his chickens.

"I am familiar with the term, sir. I am not here to speak for anyone but myself."

"Oh, Mr. Whitey, he done sent him a mouthpiece up here to see if Tim would come on down and perform for all them fine folks. Why, he'll be a hero, a star. They'll pat him on his back and tell him what a fine boy he is. Why, they'll love him ... on Friday nights. On Saturday, he'll be just another nigger," said Floyd as he rocked back and forth furiously in his recliner.

"I understand your reluctance, and I understand your apprehension. But, sir, it's not healthy for the soul to carry around hate. Soon, the weight of it becomes unbearable."

"Listen to me, boy—what you are saying is true." Floyd sat a little more erect and used a little kinder tone as he was about to clarify his point. "But you're saying it to the wrong people, boy. I don't like hating nobody, but what choice do you have when they all hate you?

"Boy, they all started hating me long before I started hating them. You boys have got it good now. You don't know what it's like growing up around people that hate you, and you can't figure out why." Floyd reclined, crossed his legs, and let his mind wander back in time.

"I remember one time I was about five, no six. My mama wanted twenty-five cents worth of nails. She was afraid to go in the hardware store 'cause she could see they was about six or seven white men sitting around a potbellied stove close to the counter. Back then, black women didn't go around a bunch of white men.

"They get a lot meaner when they is aroun' each other. So my mama decide to send me in with that quarter, and ask the clerk for them nails. She figure maybe they don't bother a little chile that ain't never done nothing to them, you know.

"So I went in there, and I couldn't find no clerk, and I didn't know who to ask. There I be standing in front of that circle of white men with a quarter in my hand. I didn't know what to do, so I just held up that quarter and said, 'I need nails.'

"All those men just stared at me. I could feel them eyes going up and down me. Them eyes of they's cut me like razorblades. I just turned 'round and 'round, and they all had the same look in they eyes. Frowning, hateful eyes stinging me like bees that just had somebody shake they nest.

"One man say, 'Look like we got ourselves a little escaped monkey here, boys.'

"They all laugh. Why wouldn't they? That's funny, ain't it? My mama can see through the little window in the door, but she can't hear what they is saying to me.

"So one of the mens decide to give me one of the bananas in his sack he got from the grocery store. I didn't know any better. Hell, I was just a kid. I thought he was being nice to me, you know. So I says, 'Thank ya, sir,' and started peeling it. I had the biggest grin that anybody's ever seen on my face. I didn't get to eat bananas much back then. Shit, that was a treat, man!

"So I'm champing down on that banana with that big stupid-ass grin on my face and wondering why in the hell them men is laughing so damn hard. Hell, I thought I must be funny or something. Shit, I didn't know. So one of the men say to me, 'Hey, boy, can you dance us a little jig? Come on, boys, let's clap a little.'

"So they start clapping they hands and tapping they feet, so I start dancing and smiling and then I take me a big bite of banana and they just roar. Man, I was putting on a show!

"Then, one of the men say, 'Look here, boy. In the big cities that's not the way they dance. Here, curl this arm up like you got to scratch under your armpit like this. And then you make this sound, 'ooh, ooh, ooh.' So he starts me to acting like a monkey and dancing with that stupid-ass grin. Then, one say, 'take another bite.' They laughing and clapping, a hooping and a hollering, and I dance a little higher and grin a little wider.

"Then one of the men say, 'Hey, Wilber, you still got that Buster Brown box camera here at the store? We need to get a picture of this boy. He's a real natural.' The men was rolling. They all gather in 'round me, and he got that big box camera and flash! It was da perfect picture of a six-year-old black boy holding a banana and acting like a monkey and surrounded by Jess Rulam's most prominent citizens.

"Hey, boy, you want to see that picture? Well, all you got to do is go in the Gray's Hardware store right down there in town. It's right there, hanging on the wall with more pictures from the 1920s. They tell me it's a damn good picture of me. And you want to know what's *funny*? That's the only picture that was ever taken of me when I was a kid. That's *funny*, ain't it?

"No, sir, no, sir," Floyd said, shaking his head, leaning back in his chair. "I don't think no son of mine is gonna play for that damn town. No, sir."

"You have endured quite a lot, sir." Jesse's voice was low, and his words were slow and respectful. "No one can blame you for how you feel. But, sir, though hatred is sometimes understood, it is never justified.

"The people you hate are not even aware that you hate them and go about their lives blissfully ignorant that they have caused you pain. You are the one who is carrying about a painful and weary countenance.

"You strike me as man with a lifetime of experiences, some good, others not so much, but nevertheless they are stored away in your mind. Why not spend a little time sorting through them, then use that part of your heart that is full of the love you have for people, all people, and like that old keg of watermelon wine you have rolled against the house, pour out a little glass of wisdom to share with those who will listen."

"You are a fancy talker, but who is going to listen to me? I don't have all that much wisdom to share with any peoples. If I did, I be setting in a different place right now instead of The Hill." Floyd was still shaking his head.

"That is a wise answer, sir. Where would you be sitting right now if you were a wise man?" asked Jesse.

"Well, I'd be in a better area and in a better house, I can tell you that much. And I'd have a lot more money than I got right now."

Harvey laughed at what his friend had just said.

"And you would still have all these memories waiting to be shared and to be learned from. You can still be a beacon of wisdom from where you sit now, just as well as the rich man sitting in the mansion you envision for yourself, if only you used your wisdom."

"People ain't gonna listen to some old fool that never made nothing much of hisself. Why would they? You talk crazy talk."

"No, they *do* want to listen to a man who has a wounded heart. Why don't you tell them how you feel about it, and maybe they will understand. If you talk about how that changed your life, would that not be of great value?"

Floyd didn't speak for a few seconds and neither did Harvey. The two men were put on the spot pondering the situation and trying to come up with a reason why Jesse was wrong. But thoughts were stubbornly forthcoming.

"I un'erstan' what you is saying, but what's that got to do with my boy playing football for a bunch of people I hate, whether they know I hate 'em or not?"

"Wise question, sir." Jesse chuckled. "The first thing we'd do is go to the hardware store and announce that Tim decided to play football for Jess Rulam this year."

"Oh, they'll like that." Floyd leaned backed amusedly, but he was still muddled as to why he would do that.

"Then, you tell the owners and anyone listening the story of how the photograph came to be there. Ask them to remove it and let you have it. I think you should have it. Or does a better idea come to mind?"

Floyd thought for a few seconds. "Tim," he said, looking at his son, "how you feel 'bout switching schools this year?"

"Well, Daddy, you know my girlfriend, Kimberly, goes to Jess Rulam. But the coaches sure are gonna be mad at me."

"Them coaches up there is jus' using you to make touchdowns jus' like the coaches down here be doing. They gonna use you no matter where." Floyd was talking and thinking at the same time. "I got an idea though. You going with me, right?"

Jesse nodded his head. "I think that's the right decision, Mr. Monroe."

"How do you know what I am thinking?" Floyd had a wry look in his eyes and half a smile.

"Like I've said, you are a wise man," answered Jesse with the same wry look and half-smile.

* * *

Jesse and Floyd entered Gray's Hardware, abruptly swinging open the eighty-year-old, three-inch-thick solid oak doors. The small window on the right side was still there. It was just large enough to permit a mother to watch her son be humiliated. They approached the counter.

Buddy Gray asked, "How may I help you, gentlemen?"

"I want to talk to you about that photo you got hanging on the wall over there." Floyd went about retelling the story behind the photograph. Buddy was stunned at what he heard.

"I have always wondered about that picture. I thought it might have been taken somewhere else. Granddaddy never mentioned anything about it nor did Dad. Nobody ever said anything. I am so sorry about this, Mr. Monroe. I thought it was just part of the store around here, like all the other old pictures hanging on the walls.

"It's always been there ever since I was a kid, and I guess I just forgot about it. You are absolutely right. There is nothing funny about it. I'll take it down immediately and throw it away."

"No, I got a better idea," Floyd interrupted. "There's been something I always wanted to do."

* * *

A man opened the heavy oak doors and he and his nine-year-old son entered Gray's Hardware. It was a beautiful, lazy Wednesday afternoon. A few customers were browsing. They'd pick up an item, turn it over, and check the price on the bottom.

There were at least a hundred vintage photographs lining the beaded, age-stained walls. Just off to one side of the counter was an authentic potbellied stove, complete with a percolating pot of Red Diamond coffee. A round oak table was just to the left of the stove.

A wooden checkerboard with a game about halfway through was close to one end. A black man, Harvey, and a white man, Hershel, were deep in strategic thought, pondering their next move. Three other white men and Floyd were relaxing with a steaming cup of Red Diamond, their lips puckering up periodically to blow cool air across the piping hot cups.

Floyd took a sip and then philosophized about what intrigued him at the moment. The others chimed in with their opinions of the saneness, or lack thereof, regarding Floyd's thoughts. Someone would say something, there'd be a pause, then all the men would laugh uproariously.

The nine-year-old boy was curious about the chatter and the laughter and the homely setting around the potbellied stove, the table, the checkers, and the rather boisterous group of philosophers. This was irresistible to the boy.

He worked his way a little closer and noticed a framed picture just behind Floyd. It had a paper sign below it that read: *Ask me about this picture.* The sign could be hung or removed whenever

Floyd was open for business, which was to say when he came to the store and took his place in his chair.

The boy said, "Mister, what does that sign mean?"

Floyd looked at the boy for a second, got up, removed the only picture of himself as a child, set the boy in the chair beside him, handed him the picture, and began, "Well, young fellow, I tell you. I must have been about five, no six years old, when me and my mama had to come to town and get some nails ...."

CHAPTER 26

IN ALL, ONE HUNDRED AND five blacks and whites and two boys of Chinese heritage showed up for fall practice. Coach Peppers was overwhelmed, figuratively and literally. There were only enough practice uniforms for about seventy-five players. The most that had ever gone out for varsity football in the school's history was forty-one, and that had happened fourteen years ago.

Coach Peppers had to cut down the numbers with tryouts. This was the first time in his career he had to tell some students that they didn't make the squad, but please try again next year.

Any student who was a senior got an automatic pass and didn't have to try out. All players that were on last year's team didn't have to try out either, thank God. There were so many great black ballplayers this year, I would have been sweating if I had had to try out against them.

Indeed, it was a sight to behold. Out of three hundred and twenty-six students in grades nine through twelve, one hundred and fifty-one were boys. Of the one hundred and fifty-one boy students in Jess Rulam High School in the fall of 1975, one hundred and seven went out for football.

No one had ever seen anything like this in these parts. The whole community was abuzz. Even the reddest of necks was amazed at the turnout and the racist of racists was anxious to see what these *black boys* were capable of. This year for the first time in the town's history, the pejorative word was "black"not "nigger."

There were over one hundred fans and supporters attending the first practice, an amazing number for a town this size. It was almost like a game-dayatmosphere. Coach Peppers never looked at the crowd. He never acknowledged them in any way. I believe he was subconsciously afraid to. He had to have the vivid, bitter memories of what happened six years ago. If he didn't think about, it wouldn't happen again.

Coach seemed to wear a permanent half-grin. He had the look of a man in coaching heaven. This was a once in a lifetime occurrence, and he was going to savor this moment in time. He moved from drill to drill, quickly, astutely, and methodically, with the half-grin never changing.

He barked out coaching instructions as usual, but with a different tone this practice—a milder tone, a gentler tone, as if these were his children. He made no distinction between the black and the white players.

"Hustle up now, son. You'll never be a winner in football or in life if you don't give it your best."

The anger, anguish, and the bitter disappointment were replaced by an ecstatic grin and milder, easier tone. I believe for the first time since Coach Peppers arrived at Jess Rulam High School, he was happy, and we were happy for him.

* * *

The season opened with a home game against Cove Springs. The air was sticky that night—after all, it was still summer in Alabama. For the first time in school history, Jess Rulam's team running out of the locker room had black players on it. We simply jogged onto the field—bursting through a large plastic banner and jumping up and down on each other's feet hadn't been invented yet—and the crowd gave a good roar and good claps, but not great.

I believe the locals were waiting to see what was going to happen. For years, Jess Rulam's resident fans were told what a difference it would make if they had black players on the team—that *they* would be the difference-makers, that *they* had something most white boys lacked: *speed*.

This black running back was one of the best in the country, they were told. For the first time in years, teams couldn't get to the outside on sweeps, they were told, because we had speed on defense for a switch.

They were also told that teams would not be able to throw the ball down the field because we had a pass rush that simply wouldn't allow enough time for such nonsense.

This Coach Peppers dude, he seemed like a nice guy, but honestly, he had only won thirty-four games in the last seven years and *if* he had not been connected to the university, he would not still be lingering about the sidelines of good ol' Jess Rulam High, no sir. He should have been run off a long time ago, they figured. After these seven disastrous years, why was he still here anyway? Get somebody else for Christ's sake, they thought.

They figured they were keeping him around because he lobbied so hard for the black players, and that the black players were going to save him and the school from further humiliation. Well, we had black players now, and this was his final chance. No one was talking much in the stands. Usually there was a constant steady roar, or at least a mild roar of people talking.

Cerebral anticipation—I think that would sum up the atmosphere that night as Jess Rulam's kickoff team lined up. They were *thinking* these thoughts, not speaking them. They were not quite sure if they were *supposed* to talk about these things at the beginning of the season or not.

They each wondered what the others were thinking. Were they supposed to show team spirit or not? Was it impolite not to? They weren't exactly sure, so they softly chitchatted a little about this or that—anything, except the game.

As the kicker got ready to approach the ball and begin what was the most anticipated, most talked about, and certainly the most thought about season in the history of the school, everybody stopped talking. Only the students were doing the old familiar *woooo* low roar before the kickoff.

Boom! The foot hit the ball and end over end it soared into the humid, heavy summer air. Out of sheer habit, or anticipation, or just plain ol' damn-football-is-finally-here excitement, everyone in the stands stood up from wooden bleacher seats and fixed their eyes on the tumbling ball.

Number 22, a small, quick white boy for Cove Springs, gathered in the end over end on about the ten-yard line, made one juke to the right, then split the oncoming home team down the middle and took it untouched for a touchdown.

As number 22 crossed the goal line, deathly silence befell the crowd. Arms crossed, eyes rolled, disgusted looks were everywhere throughout the stands. As quickly as they got to their feet, they got back on their butts, still with arms crossed. They weren't happy, and it showed.

Coach Peppers's heart sank, no, "plummeted" is more apt. This is probably the worst case of Murphy's Law and déjà vu in history. Just before he left the fieldhouse, Coach wondered what would happen if they returned the opening kickoff for a touchdown. He found out: A few boos mixed the hot air behind him.

Coach glanced at the scoreboard before he started his habitual nervous saunter up and down the sideline.

Home 0 Visitors 7 Time 11: 48 1 Quarter

This was now stuck in his frontal lobe along with the image of one thousand flying bugs sparkling in the bright lights.

I never seen so many damn bugs as tonight, he thought.

Cove Springs kicked off to Jess Rulam, and we had a nice return to the thirty-five-yard line.

"Let's start out simple," Coach said to his junior quarterback. "I right thirty-two sweep right on two." TW Monroe swept right, made one juke, and ran sixty-five yards for a touchdown.

Jess Rulam kicked off, and it was three and out. They punted. Willis McKay returned it for a touchdown. The onslaught was on. Coach glanced up at the scoreboard just after he shook hands with the Cove Springs coaches.

Home 55 Visitors 7 Time 0: 00 4 Quarter

He jogged toward the fieldhouse and put his head down and stared at the ground, but his eyes couldn't control themselves, they had to see it once more. He fixed his eyes on the scoreboard all the way at the end of the field and only took his eyes off to shake hands with the most enthusiastic and appreciative fans he had ever seen or heard tell of.

He actually checked his back in the mirror to see if there were any bruises on it from all the patting. He figured he must have been slapped at least one hundred times.

It was hard to fall asleep that night, and when he did, he didn't stay asleep very long. A bright flash woke him: Home 55 Visitors 7.

This was what he thought, what he wished, might happen tonight.

He knew he had one of the most talented football teams in the state, seriously.

Good things hadn't been happening to him lately, so good fortune was going to take some getting used to.

***

Next was an away game with a traditional rival and one of the most hostile atmospheres in the county—Gilmore High. Coach was dreading this one from the first day of practice. Gilmore was probably the most racist place in Alabama.

Though only twenty miles from Jess Rulam, Gilmore was a mountain town, and mountain towns prided themselves on the fact that no minorities were citizens of their towns. Coach remembered hearing the word "nigger" coming from the stands once, and that was before they had any blacks on the team. That word was yelled because Jess Rulam had colored citizens.

Coach had to get the Gilmore Police Department to guarantee protection for his players. The Gilmore police said they'd provide three state troopers and five patrolmen.

Just before his players got off the bus to go to the Gilmore field, Coach Peppers told the team what to expect and how to handle it. The black players were understandably nervous. After all, they had heard all the horror stories about this place all their lives.

There was talk about moving the game to Jess Rulam since this was the first year with black players on Gilmore's field, but Coach said they were going to have to get it over with sooner or later—might as well be sooner.

He told all the black players he almost guaranteed they would hear the "n" word often. He told them not to pay any attention to it. He told them that Gilmore had changed a lot recently; that they played teams that had black players in the playoffs and that no fights happened. Coach was trying to convince the players as well as himself. Coach had more anxiety over this game than his own black players did.

All the players left the bus and jogged onto the Gilmore Stadium field. The silence was eerie. Fans were still arriving and finding their seats, but still, one could hear crickets sawing on their homemade violins. That's the way it was for the entire warm-up period—*nothing*.

Coach Peppers was waiting for at least one "nigger" shouted from the stands, yet there was *nothing*. With each passing moment, his anxiety subsided little by little. As his players jogged to the locker room before kickoff, he thought, *We just might get out of here alive.*

The solemnity of the locker room had a chilling effect. No one was talking; no one was smiling; there was no noise inside; there was no noise outside, just stone-cold silence.

Coach briefly went over the game plan. He told his players to ignore anything they might hear as they ran back onto the field. He said, "And whatever you do, don't get into a fight on the field."

Jesse led the team in prayer, as usual. Then it was time to walk through the victory line. The only problem with the victory line was that anybody could get in it.

For the first time anyone could remember the team *walked* through the victory line, not ran or jogged, but walked. Perhaps it was the atmosphere, but for some unknown reason we just followed our coach. He walked out of the locker room and through the line, and so did we.

I really think that in the tension of the moment, someone simply forgot to sprint around Coach and dash to the sideline and jump up and down in a progressively larger circle like we usually did. We were just like birds on a wire: When one flies, we all fly. But no one sprinted around Coach, so none of us did.

Most of the people in the line were fans that we recognized, but some weren't. "Hey, boy, you scared?" a short, fat man with a huge potbelly, wearing overalls that tested the tensile strength of his strained galluses, whispered loudly. The potbellied man was holding one of his hands behind his back, obviously hiding something. TW Monroe stopped and looked curiously at Fat Man.

Fat Man's friend beside him was his complete opposite. He was tall and skinny, wearing a grease-covered cap and some sort of uniform; a garage mechanic, perhaps. Both men looked like they had just got off work, brushed their teeth, and came straight to the game. In any case, they were up to no good. Unfortunately for them, the next person they spoke to was Jesse.

"Woo-wee, lookee what we got here. Now there's some real nigger horse flesh, oh, excuse me, I mean some real *Negro* horse flesh," continued the fat man.

Fat Man and Skinny laughed uproariously. The tinge of alcohol was in the air.

"You sure are a big'n. Why ain'tcha playing, boy? They holding you back for hard times?" said the greasy, tall mechanic.

Jesse stopped and looked the men up and down. Then the familiar warm smile appeared on his face. Then he addressed them thusly: "Are you gentlemen addressing me?"

"Why, yawsah boss. We be addressing you," mocked Fat Man, who still had his hand behind his back. "You know what I need worse than anything?"

"A remedial reading class," quipped TW Monroe, who waited to see what they were going to say to Jesse. He said it dryly with no emotion.

"No, smartass. I need me a volunteer." Fat Man was getting angry. "You know what for?"

"To count your teeth," said TW dryly.

Jesse looked at TW and smiled. One couldn't tell if he was ashamed of TW or amused by him.

"Nope, you uppity-nigger-looking-thing, you. I need you to test this." Fat Man pulled a short piece of rope from behind him, fashioned into a hangman's noose.

"I don't believe this boy here is all nig, I mean all Negro. What are you anyway? You some kinda Chinaman?"

Skinny was studying Jesse's features closely and not quite figuring it out. "Ain't that something? You know they said they made an announcement at school not to use any racial language at the game tonight. You know it's gonna get to where you can't say the word 'nigger' anymore." They both roared.

"Well, I gather from listening to you gentleman that using *any* words at all is a challenge you worked hard to overcome," said Jesse.

"Are you making fun of the way we talk, boy?" Skinny scowled at Jesse.

"Why, yes, I believe I am."

"Do you know what this is, boy?" Fat Man held up the rope.

"Your dental floss," said TW without cracking a smile.

"Maybe we'll just show you how it's used after this game tonight, boy." Fat Man was fuming and fumbled with the rope. He was trying to tighten the noose. "Dammit. I got this damn rope tied around my hands. Get this damn thing off me." Fat Man managed to slip the noose tightly around both wrists. The more he struggled, the tighter it got.

"Hold still a damn minute, junior. You're only making it worse."

Skinny was fumbling with the out-of-control rope, which seemed to get more and more tangled the harder he tried to untangle it. Eventually, it tightened around his hands too.

"This is the stupidest damn thing I've ever seen. Where did you get this damn rope, junior?" Now Skinny's hands were inside a tight knot around both *his* wrists.

"I see you gentleman are tied up at the moment. You see, your own ignorance will bind you up if you don't open your minds. Perhaps we can continue our conversation after the game. I will show you how to throw off the shackles of a bound-up spirit," said Jesse. He winked and both boys continued to the sideline.

The victory line broke up, and all the fans made their way back to their seats except Fat Man and Skinny, who were still standing on about the thirty-yard line with both their wrists bound tight and getting more entangled by the minute.

"What the hell is happening here, dammit?"

Fat Man was facing Skinny. They heard the smattering of laughter coming from the stands. They were about three feet apart, so Skinny got the idea to step on the middle of the rope with one foot and see if he could pull it off his wrists that way.

As he pulled, it stretched. Now the rope was six feet long in the middle and tangled around one foot, and then the other. The more he kicked at the rope, the more it worked its way around his ankles.

The Gilmore fans as well as the Jess Rulam fans were rolling in the stands. People were laughing so hard, they were bent double.

Fat Man soon got his feet entangled and found himself bound wrist and ankle and completely unable to move. A police officer dashed onto the field and asked what the two numbskulls were doing on the field with a rope in the first place.

"We were just going to have a little fun with some of them black boys, officer. We weren't really gonna do nothing to them. This big Chinaman somehow or other tied us up here, and we can't get out of it." Skinny was almost in tears.

"He weren't no Chinaman, you damn fool." If Fat Man could move, he would have slapped Skinny. "Officer, could you cut us loose? Everybody is laughing us outta here."

"Hold on, don't move," said the officer, pulling out a pocket knife.

"Don't move, my ass. My gall dern feet and ankles are tied so tight, I can't move a half an inch even if I wanted to. Cut my ass free!" Skinny was hysterical.

"This damn rope won't cut. Where did you get this? It's like it's made out of steel or something." The officer looked at his knife, then at the rope. "I can't dent this shit. We got to get this game started. Shit, they're ready to kick off!" The officer looked over to the end of the field for some help.

After about ten minutes, two more police officers, a state trooper, an ambulance paramedic, and the local metal shop owner decided to get a flatbed truck with a boom winch and haul them both to the metal shop. There they could use heavier, sharper equipment to get this uncuttable rope off the two hogtied men.

As the boom lifted Fat Man up into the air, he looked down at the spot on the field where he had been lying. Just then, the clips holding up his straining overalls gave up their struggle to remain latched. They burst open.

Fat Man wished he had worn cleaner underwear. Every coach, every player, and every fan, on both sides, was in hysterical tears.

* * *

Jess Rulam won the game 65 to 13. The starters didn't play in the second half. It was the worst defeat in Gilmore High School's history. It was Coach Peppers's most satisfying win in his football career.

A massive grin emanated from his face on the bus ride back home, as it did on Jesse's, and the entire teams'.

CHAPTER 27

COACH PEPPERS ACCLIMATED TO THE feeling of winning. In fact, it became an intoxicating habit.

He came to work earlier and he left a little later, not because he needed to worry about how to come up with a way to somehow squeeze out a victory over an upcoming opponent, but because he wanted to savor the flavor. There is no finer place to be than in the fieldhouse when your team is undefeated. Not only undefeated, but all blowout wins.

This was the team Coach envisioned from the very first day he took the job at Jess Rulam. This was the team he knew he would have someday. Everything was better. His wife was better. His daughter was better. His dog was better. Heck, man, the lunches in the school cafeteria were better. He was respected now, and other coaches were afraid of his team.

Instead of trying to strategize how you might trick a team by disguising an offense or a defense, you simply lined up and said, "Here we are. Stop us if you can." He had the most talented football team in the state of Alabama; let the other coaches worry about stopping him for a switch. None of them did.

Coach had never written the scores after a game on the big white board in the locker room before. The big board had come as a free gift from GymTech Fitness Company when he had talked the school and the Gridiron Club into purchasing all the new weightlifting equipment. He actually never bothered to fill in the scores after his first season. It became increasingly more difficult to write the scores for defeats, so he stopped it altogether.

This year, however, he couldn't wait to write the scores. He wrote them big and bold. The home team was already printed on the left side of the board by the company. All you had to do was write the opponent's name on the right side and the score, of course. He made a big deal out of it.

Before anyone undressed and hit the showers after a game, he got everybody's attention, slid over the stepladder, and wrote with a black erasable Sharpie the final score. The team unanimously burst into a shout that rattled the windows.

November 8, 1975, the board looked like this:

Jess Rulam 55	Cove Springs	7
Jess Rulam 65	Gilmore	13
Jess Rulam 48	Gillespie	13
Jess Rulam 62	Wilsonville	6
Jess Rulam 52	Pike	0
Jess Rulam 38	Templeton	6
Jess Rulam 44	Woodville	3
Jess Rulam 71	Junction	22
Jess Rulam 51	Prague	7
Jess Rulam 36	Stone Bluff	0
Playoffs		
Jess Rulam 66	Spring View	21
Jess Rulam 41	Bixby	12

Only one game remained now: the State of Alabama Class 3A Championship against undefeated Madisonville, a perennial power. In fact, as of game week, the expert prognosticators considered it a tossup. The expert consensus was that this was Madisonville's finest team ever. This was a team that won the championship two out of the last three years. Coach knew he had his hands full.

* * *

Nothing brings people together quite like winning, just as nothing can drive people apart like losing. Right now, Jess Rulam was winning. Everyone was a little nicer now, a little more polite, a little more civil, and just plain happier. Unheard of things were rumored about town.

Some wild reports had the ridiculous story of white men opening doors for black women. Some people say they saw two black men help a white man reload his truck when the tailgate on his pickup failed and half the pipes loaded in back slipped onto the street in front of Gray's Hardware.

Black men and white men were seen shaking hands on the streets. It was rumored around town that Miss Fredrickson, a white woman and town elder, had for the first time in fifty years cordially invited one Mrs. Everneza Hill, a black woman, to her weekly quilting session. Actually, it was just eight or nine old women sitting around a quilting frame and gossiping, but don't tell them that.

This newfound joviality permeated the school. In fact, when Bobo Simms, one of the black members of the football team, sat beside Kala Abernathy, a white girl, at lunch, they got nothing more than a casual glance before life returned to normal. It was no big deal. There was such fervor over the success of the football team, it affected the whole school and the entire Jess Rulam community.

And with that, it was suggested a blue ribbon panel be selected and assembled from the journalism class. The purpose of the panel would be to investigate the history of the town of Jess Rulam and in particular the founder himself. Nothing much was known about Jess Rulam that wasn't in the history books. They knew only what they'd been told, primarily that he was a rich and prosperous man, that he ran for governor, and that he had donated a lot of land and money to start the school.

It was told he was a slave owner. It was a fact that slave ownership was a sticky subject for most of the black students. And therein lay the purpose of the project. The panel would consist of five black and five white students. It would be a healing process. It made sense.

The fair and balanced panel would discover, it was assumed, that ol' Jess Rulam had in fact owned slaves, but that he had also done a lot of good things for people in general, even eventually freeing his slaves and hiring them back after the Civil War. The panel would show that a person can do bad and good things at the same time. It was thought that this would unite the school even more.

This whole project was initiated and born because of an old trunk found at the depot building that had not operated for over sixty years. It was now just a historic landmark. The old trunk was found in a little dugout cellar directly under the depot. They said it was built for protection against robbers. Some say it was just a cellar.

In any case, one of the caretakers working for the state discovered the old trunk that hadn't been opened for close to one hundred years. When they did cut off the lock, they discovered it was jammed full of old ledgers, books, diaries, letters, bank drafts, articles of incorporation, and other artifacts. It was a treasure trove of historically important documents.

Many of the letters were written by ol' Jess Rulam himself. There were other letters written by members of his family and even some written by a couple of slaves. There were so many it would take a person a long, long time to sort through them all.

This was where the panel came in. They would sort them and write the story or history of Jess Rulam. It would bring unity and a sense of closure and, most importantly, enlightenment as to what the people of Jess Rulam, white and black, had to say. And it would be discovered together, the *black and white* by the *black and white*. Right? Right.

Soon, some of the panel began pouring over the voluminous trunk full of papers. Others began with the general history, which they already knew from the history books.

They were to present the history project to the entire school on Friday, the day of the championship game. The plan was for the history to be read in parts by each member of the panel. The thinking was that a healing would occur, and the town would draw closer. Then the team would go out and kick Madisonville's ass.

* * *

Another great idea put together, this time by some of the black faculty, former Orr faculty, former Orr alumni, and some black business leaders, was to have a small banquet for the black football players the day of the championship game.

The idea was for the black community to show the black players where they had come from and how proud they were of them for how they had handled themselves, particularly with the mountain schools that year. They took some insults, but showed great character by not responding. Most everyone thought it was a good idea.

It would be about a one-hour presentation for the twenty-one black players on Jess Rulam's team. They would have a couple of inspirational speakers, then go back to kick Madisonville's ass. They'd arrive back at the fieldhouse three hours before the game.

Coach was all for it and explained to the entire team what it was and what it was for. He even arranged the bus for the five-mile trip.

The white players understood and had no problem with their black teammates getting a little separate honor, because there would be one large party after the championship and they would all be celebrating.

* * *

Friday finally arrived, and so did the rarefied air of a high school Class 3A Championship Game.

It started at two, the beginning of sixth period. A band member was strolling around doing an occasional tat, tat, tat on the double set of drums strapped around his waist. A couple of rather chunky girls in the background whirled huge flags on a pole, all wanting to be perfect for the halftime show.

There were no individuals headed to the final class of the day. They were all in small little groups chitchatting and laughing and giggling and slapping and running—what we called "grab-assing"—because this is how kids relieved anxiousness.

The smell of the concession stands, which were getting an early start anticipating the record crowd, pervaded the air with the aroma of boiling hot dogs and sizzling hamburgers.

Everyone was on their way to the auditorium for the school history reading. No one cared about one hour of boring facts about a rich old man who gave some of his money away so we could have a kick-ass football team someday.

Some of the percussion section brought their drums in with them—habit, I guess. We got to our seats and noticed there was some kind of heavy discussion and maybe even an argument going on up front with the presenters and the teachers. The mayor was there also. In any case, something was wrong.

The principal seemed to be at the center of the controversy. Now the principal and vice principal seemed to be arguing over something. Finally, the principal made his way to the podium holding several papers in his hand. He had a somber look on his face like this was the last thing he wanted to do.

"May I have your attention, please? May I have your attention, please?"

It took a few minutes for the hyperactive kids to settle down and be quiet.

"As you know, we were to have the history reading of Jess Rulam town and high school put together by a handpicked panel of students from the journalism class. They were to read it to the student body at this time. However, there is a problem." The principal sounded dejected.

"Some disturbing news was uncovered by the panel when they began to read the letters from the old trunk that you all heard was recently found at the old depot. We have had several debates as to whether or not to disclose the real history of Jess Rulam.

"It was suggested by some that this information be put back in the trunk and forgotten. Others suggested the findings be read for all to hear. The news is disturbing, to put it mildly. You see, our founding father has some secrets ... some ugly secrets. A lot of founders are flawed men, but our founder was slightly more than flawed.

"So, after great consideration, it was decided to let a letter be read to you here today. It will forever change the history of our town. It can go one of two ways. I only hope that it changes it for the better. You will have to decide."

A small, smart black girl named Kimberly Alston made her way to the podium, and the principal sat down in a chair close by. There was a murmur filtering through the student body. The revelation piqued everyone's curiosity. "Disturbing" news will do that.

It was unnervingly silent as Kimberly spoke. "It was a difficult thing, what we discovered by reading hundreds of these papers. We found out who Mr. Jess Rulam really was. And I think that this letter written by his own daughter will sum it up pretty well. It will show what kind of man this town and school is named after."

Kimberly cleared her throat and began:

> "Miss Deborah Ann Rulam, April 17, 1860
>
> To Whom It May Concern,
>
> It is with a heavy heart and much trepidation that I set this matter to paper and pen for posterity. I witnessed an event this morning that has once and for all convinced me that my

father truly is an evil man possessed perhaps by the prince of all demons himself.

My father is considered a reverent man with charm and wit. He has accumulated a great fortune due to a singular acumen for matters of business. He is a generous provider of my wanton desires. My mother is frequently the recipient of the most lavish of gifts. We both feel doted upon and undeserving of such extravagances.

However, I believe my father's generosity to be nothing more than an evil attempt at restitution for a guilty conscience. He has never developed any outward display of affection for me nor my mother. It is only through what can be purchased from the finest shops in Birmingham or ordered from the fancy catalogs in town that he shows any sense of concern.

We believe the gifts are a form of primitive ransom. He showers my mother and me with grotesquely lavish presents so he can hold our tongues hostage. I never realized that I was so easily purchased until today.

I feel worthless at the moment. It must be how my mother feels every time she sees a mulatto child who bears a strong resemblance to her husband.

My father hides behind the veil of Holy Scriptures and wields them as accurately as a duelist at those who even look at him suspiciously.

He is neither pious nor holy, but evil and demented. What I am about to say should provide the proof.

God forgive me for my insolence toward my father, but what I do, I am compelled to do by the father of my soul.

I was watching from my bedroom window this morning when I witnessed my father sell an infant of no more than four years old. He literally snatched the crying child from the tender embraces of its pleading, whimpering mother.

A particular melancholy besieged my countenance when I realized it was my half-brother he was selling or trading for a horse or another stock bull to a Mister Savorié.

I wept for the mother and child, wondering what would become of them, my half-brother in particular. My heart was sad in my bosom. I wondered how a man who proudly called himself a Christian could stand facing God in such open spaces. I did not have to wonder long. The next thing I witnessed replaced all my sadness and melancholy with abominable horror.

Minnie was on her hands and knees praying for God's deliverance when my father bashed her head in with a pipe, killing her dead in the same position she was praying to God. He sauntered off for supper as if he had just swatted a horsefly.

I was told by another slave within earshot what Minnie prayed—that God would somehow curse the name of Jess Rulam for the no-good bastard he is. And the Lord would watch over her son Jeremiah.

I pray for the very same thing. That Mister Savorié will be good to my little helpless half-brother, who left this place with a broken heart.

I also pray that the name Jess Rulam be stricken from this Godforsaken place and that someday the name be replaced with a name of honor, peace, and fellowship for all of God's people.

Sincerely,

Miss Deborah Ann Rulam"

No one knew quite what to do after Kimberly finished reading the letter and took her seat. The principal didn't elaborate much. He just said the news was going to come out anyway and that the school might as well find out now. Then he said that all the students should not let this drive a wedge between us but it should rather bring us closer. He didn't exactly say how though, and then he dismissed us.

No one said a word as we left. The black students looked at the white students with the same expression that the white students wore as they looked at the black students.

Were we supposed to apologize because our town was named after a white piece of crap?

Some of the black students did look a little dismayed and somewhat shocked but didn't know exactly what to say, or who to say it to. So nobody said anything, not a word. We all simply exited the auditorium.

This was one of those things that needs to be pondered. Reflective thinking, I believe it is called; one of those things that, the more you think on it, the madder you get kind of things.

As we watched our black teammates load onto the bus for the little get-together at their former school, we were all wishing *they* didn't think on it too much—not four hours before kickoff of the biggest game of our lives.

Coach wasn't at the auditorium for the reading. He didn't know. One of us was going to have to tell him. We chose Pete, who didn't exactly thank us for the honor.

* * *

The trip to Orr was quiet for the most part. Someone whispered, "What do you think of old Jess Rulam?" Someone else whispered back, "I figured if he had slaves, he was a fink." Another person softly said, "Most slave owners were like that." They were just rumblings really. What would you expect them to say? But there was nothing above a whisper.

The small gathering at what had been the school lunchroom went without a hitch. The former school principal told the players he was proud of how they had handled themselves in what could have been a difficult year. A reverend spoke for a few minutes on being a leader for others to follow. They had a prayer, and then everyone was given a certificate of appreciation from the Fellowship Baptist Church with the players' names printed in big fancy letters across the top. Then it was time to head back to Jess Rulam High and the pregame meal.

In all, it was a nice little showing of how proud their community was of them, and the players seemed to be grateful. They loaded on the bus and were on their way to play in the biggest game of their lives. Their minds were soon refocused on that very subject.

The bus pulled down the school drive and turned on Pratt Gap for the three-mile jaunt to the main road. Then it was only two miles back to the school. Two pickup trucks were stopped in the road ahead.

Four black men wearing black hoods covering their faces were holding shotguns. The bus stopped abruptly as two of the shotgun-wielding men pointed the guns at the driver. He quickly flung open the doors.

"Everybody off the bus," one of the masked men said calmly.

It took a moment for the realization to take hold of the boys' senses. This was literally the last thing they expected to happen.

"Take the bus on back and tell the coach they decided not to play tonight," said the same masked man to the bus driver, who was obviously in on the hijacking.

"After what I just heard about that crackerhead this shithole is named after, he'll probably believe it," said the leader of the masked men.

They loaded the boys in the trucks and returned to the now abandoned Orr school basement. A garage door was raised and the trucks pulled in with the bewildered football players. They would not participate in tonight's game if these hooded black men had anything to do with it.

* * *

Coach looked at his watch and nervously tapped the end of his pencil on the itinerary for the game. He knew the boys were due back any minute.

Good things were happening to him lately. He would not let negativity enter his mind. He had six years of stinking-thinking pushing happy thoughts out of his mind. They were not about to work their way back, not now.

He knew what had happened in the auditorium would be on their minds, but he was going to get them refocused on tonight's game. That was all that mattered at the moment. He held the team together over things much worse than this. A little thing like their hometown being named after a slaveholding, murdering son of a bitch wasn't going to stop them now, no, sir.

He knew what he was going to say; he had just thought of it. *How about we announce at the victory party at the new gym tonight, after we accept our Class 3A State Championship trophy, that a petition be written to officially change the name of the town? How about it, boys?*

Yes, that would be the way to handle this. It was brilliant. But he had had a lot of brilliant ideas lately.

Yes, things were going well lately, just like he knew they would someday. *It's amazing how winning makes you smarter,* he thought. *It really does.*

CHAPTER 28

COACH PEPPERS WAS CHATTING ON the phone with his wife when the bus driver came strolling into his office.

"Bye, hon. See you in a bit." Coach hung up the phone and peered at the bus driver.

"The players all went home. They say they ain't gonna play for no town named after a slave murderer. They say they ain't no use you coming to looking for them neither, 'cause they gonna be hid. They say the town gets what it deserves. That's all they say." The driver didn't wait for Coach to say anything and abruptly left the office and drove the bus away.

In a daze, Coach looked at the spot where the driver had once stood. He had heard what he said. Was it real or was he dreaming it? A thousand thoughts drenched his mind. The one closest to a coherent thought at that split second was that he would soon awake from the doze-off he was having.

But he didn't wake up. He just kept staring at the spot where Satan had just sent one of his minions to inform him that the last few months of joy didn't come free—time to pay up. His numb jaws were about an inch apart when he realized it and shut his mouth tight.

He waited for one of the assistants to come in and confirm the season was played for nothing, or nudge him awake. Neither happened. He was left with the silent solemnity of his befuddled thoughts. He got to his feet and panic set in.

He walked as rapidly as possible without breaking into a run. The thought crossed his mind, *The kids can't see me panic. This will send the wrong message. I must remain calm no matter what. I'm the head coach, for Christ's sake.*

He couldn't find even one of the damn assistant coaches anywhere. Have they all left too? Come to think of it, where are the white players? Have they decided to boycott the GD game too? What the shit is going on?!

He got hold of himself, took a couple of breaths and realized that the rest of the team was in the lunchroom having the pregame meal. *That's right, calm down.* He was supposed to wait for the black kids to get back and walk with them to the lunchroom. He planned on finding out how the get-together went. *That's right, it's OK.* Thoughts were getting easier to hold on to.

Get ahold of yourself, he thought. It will be all right. It will be fine. The town can't hold me responsible for what happened. I'll do the best I can with what I have. Nobody can blame me for this. They will be slaughtered in the game tonight, but I will rally my remaining team, put up a good showing, and I will be forgiven. I have to be. They will forgive me, right?

He began to think of what to say to the team as he left for the lunchroom. *How will they handle this? They'll just have to suck it up and do the best they can,* he was reasoning. *What else can they do? I can't show any panic. I must remain calm and in control. I'll act like it was just one of those things that happen to teams from time to time. Bad things happen to every team. It will be all right. It will be all right*—he must keep that thought in his mind.

The rest of the team was not eating yet. They were seated in front of their hamburger steaks, baked potato, and bottle of honey. They were patiently waiting to dig in. They were being courteous by waiting for their black teammates to join them, which they thought they had when Coach came through the door.

They saw Coach amble in, but nobody was behind him. *Where is the rest of the team?* They looked around the room at the other coaches and then at each other. The way Coach was walking to the front of the lunchroom felt like something was wrong.

"I have some bad news, I'm afraid," said Coach. His voice sounded quivery though he was trying his best to sound calm. "Our black teammates have decided not to play tonight because of what happened this afternoon." The one thing Coach was hoping wouldn't happen, had happened. A collective gasp echoed loudly through the entire lunchroom.

Before he could say another word, everybody in the room was squirming and twisting their heads to look at each other and then at the other coaches. Finally, all the dismayed eyes refocused on the embattled Coach to see what he planned to do about it. The look of panic was in the eyes of the now all-white team, and Coach Peppers was fighting hard not to reciprocate in-kind.

He started to say something then stopped. He finally said, "This is going to be all right. We got a pretty good football team right here in this room. So eat up, and come on back to the fieldhouse, and we'll put in our game plan."

Coach actually sounded somewhat convincing. The only problem was the white boys weren't buying it. It was the only time since they had been serving pregame meals that the lunchroom ladies noticed nobody had finished their plates. In fact, most were only half-eaten.

* * *

"OK, we are going to use Terry as the tailback since Mitchell is hurt."

Coach was standing at the front of the film room where the biggest blackboard hung. He didn't have to ask everybody to gather closer. They did it on their own.

The problem with that was that Terry Sprayberry was a freshman and had only eighteen carries all season. Mitchell McIntire was a senior running back but had hurt his knee during practice two weeks earlier. In any case, they were fourth and fifth string respectively. The first three were black and not present.

"Next, we'll move Matt to slot, and Bart to split."

I actually started, but only on defense and so did Bart. If you guessed that our starting receivers were black and college prospects, just like our running backs, you would be right. Coach went through who would be playing where, and we were getting sicker by the minute.

Coach made all the offensive and defensive changes. He was moving this white player here and that white player there. He was actually remarkably poised, we thought. I wish we could say the same for the rest of us. I looked around at the team as Coach was diagramming plays and positions. We collectively knew we were not prepared to lose half the team *and* ninety percent of our best players. Coach knew it too, though he put up a good front for the moment.

It didn't make any difference what kind of face Coach was wearing, we could see through him. He was hiding it well, but his voice began to betray him. He would stop from time to time and look over at one of the assistant coaches as he was drawing X's and O's, something he rarely did.

"OK, men, get dressed in about one hour, and we'll meet back here. Now listen to me, we are going to be fine. Just keep your head in the game and stop worrying. You do your best out there tonight. That's all we can do."

We walked out of the gloomy room and walked into total despair. We were about to experience embarrassment on an epic scale, and we knew it.

Coach went into his office and shut the door. None of us heard a sound coming from his room. No phone conversation, no shuffling of papers, just the squeaking of his chair rocking back and forth from time to time.

The other coaches were talking to us and attempting to put on a happy face. Each one would stop from time to time and turn their head toward the shut door and the unusually quiet room.

* * *

Thirty minutes before kickoff, the door finally opened and Coach appeared from the sanctuary of his office. He was pale and looked like he might have a fever. He reminded me of an alcoholic who hadn't had a drink in about two days.

Coach made his way to the blackboard and picked up a piece of chalk. He started to write something, but gave up and feebly lay the chalk back in the tray. Coach turned to address the players like General Custer addressing his troops before the Battle of Little Bighorn, as if he knew the outcome.

Coach's voice was weak and trembling. "I'm sorry, guys. I've let you down." Coach's eyes were moist. "I got caught up in the fact we had all these great black players this year, and I've not prepared *you* to play without them."

Coach lowered his head and put his hands behind his back. All he needed was a blindfold, and he would have been ready for execution.

"I'm afraid you are going to get pounded out there tonight. I've thought a lot about it. Due to the circumstances, I'm going to forfeit the game." Coach raised his head and looked as defeated as any man on earth.

"No! No, Coach! Don't forfeit the game. We can play with them," said Pete, getting to his feet and looking for support from his teammates. No one else said a word. Pete sat back down.

"I can't ask you to go out there against one of the best football teams in this state when you're not prepared. God has forsaken me here tonight, boys. It's too late to ask for forgiveness now. There are no more miracles left for me, I'm afraid. I've used them all up. But I will not let you suffer for that." Coach was shaking his head.

Click-clack, click-clack, the sound resonated down the hall of the fieldhouse. Everyone stopped talking and listened to what they thought they heard.

Click-clack, click-clack, click-clack—the unmistakable sound of a single set of football cleats was heard by everyone. The sound grew louder and louder, and louder still.

Jesse's six-three, two-hundred-and-thirty-five-pound frame of rippling muscles filled the film room doorway. He was fully dressed in a tightly fitted JRH football uniform.

"I've often wondered why I was given this body. Let's go find out together," he said casually.

An eruption that could have been heard in the visitor's locker room—which I'm convinced it was—exploded from the film room as every player and coach jumped to their feet and followed Jesse to the victory line. The jubilation was contagious. The fans were excited because their football team looked like they couldn't wait to get on the field.

"Jesse, I just told the team I was giving up tonight. I don't want to embarrass them. You understand?" Coach was walking alongside Jesse.

"Don't worry, Coach. My family likes you. We have a plan, and you're in it." Jesse looked at the worried Coach and smiled hopefully.

Coach knew Jesse was here for a reason, though he had no idea what it was. He also knew that it was out of his hands now, and he would have to trust in the plan, whatever it was. What else could he do but see what happened?

"Who is that guy?" someone in the crowd gasped, startled.

"That looks like that manager guy," someone answered.

Another yelled, "My God, what is he? Look at him!"

The fans were seeing the most striking figure they had ever seen on a football field, starting from his feet on up: Jesse's ankles were relatively thin, and then the bulge of the calf muscles took on the shape of two muscular diamonds. From a small knee joint, a sweep in the front of his thigh was cut and distinct, with clearly separated quadriceps muscles, seen clearly, even though he had on thigh pads.

The same sweep outward in a crescent shape formed his hamstrings and every string was clearly distinguishable. His wheels were simply the most powerful ever seen in a football uniform. His cutoff style jersey displayed an eight-pack of at least one-inch-deep crevices outlining each individual rectus abdominis muscle.

Thick abdominals and all, his waist was thirty inches, if that. He had a bubble butt of thick muscles. He also seemed to have two legs hanging from his shoulders, except they were his arms. The murmur heard from the crowd was becoming more distinct from the Jess Rulam fans: *Where are all the black players? Who or what is the comic book hero with the number 3 on his jersey?*

Eyes bulged almost as much as Jesse's muscles, especially from the Madisonville side of the field. Jesse was walking around, one might say strutting around, and every player was intimidated, including his own teammates.

The ambience at the stadium changed in a matter of seconds. One player grabbed all the attention from both sides. Every player, every coach, every fan, could not take their eyes off the striking figure pacing up and down the sideline. He did, in fact, resemble something that might have just walked off the cover of a comic book drawn by Stan Lee. He looked like a god—Thor or Hercules, perhaps?

With each step, rippling muscles changed position in a tide of herculean musculature. There were thirty thousand or so eyeballs in the stadium that night, and every one of them was focused on the man-mountain pacing the sideline like a caged lion that had just spotted a tasty gazelle for dinner.

***

"Coach, we need your captains for the coin toss," informed the referee.

"Oh, I forgot to choose any." Coach was caught off-guard. "Uh, Jesse, you and Griffin go out for the coin toss."

"What are your names, son?" asked the referee, taking out a pad and very short pencil.

"Griffin and Savorié," answered Jesse.

"Savory, Savoer ... how do you spell that?"

"Call me Jesse."

Jesse and Griffin shook hands with the two captains from Madisonville, who stared at Jesse like they were shaking hands with Godzilla.

"Captain Foster, Captain Abbot, this is Captain Griffin and Captain Jesse. This is the coin."

The referee held the coin out in the palm of his hand. "This is heads, this is tails." He flipped the coin over to show both sides.

"We would like to receive the football," said Jesse with a bit of enthusiasm.

"No, son, Madisonville is the visiting team, and they will get to call it when I flip it in the air."

"We call tails," said Foster firmly.

"It's heads." The referee was looking at the coin. "I guess I know what you want to do, Captain Jesse."

The referee patted Jesse on the shoulder pad and gave the "receive" sign to the crowd. He was walking over to pat the Madisonville captain on the shoulder and give the kicking sign when he flipped the coin over and quickly stuck it in his pants pocket. He made the kicking sign to the crowd.

The captains shook hands again, and everybody returned to their respective sidelines. The referee took a couple of steps toward the north end zone then stopped, looked perplexed, stuck his hands in his pants pocket and fumbled around, taking the coin out. He looked at the coin in his open palm. Heads was face up. He slowly turned the coin over; heads was up again.

He rubbed his eyes with two fingers and quickly stuck the coin back in his pocket.

This is going to be a very weird night, he thought to himself. He had no idea how weird this night was going to get.

"I will return the kickoff, Coach," said Jesse, smiling at Coach Peppers. "Fear not, Coach. Everything will be fine."

Coach didn't say a word, just nodded, unsure. He was no longer in charge of his fate, and he knew it. He also knew something miraculous was going to happen tonight. He wondered if he was actually asleep in his own bed and dreaming. He looked around at the cheering, boisterous crowd; he smelled the concessions. *The excited player standing beside me sure seems real*, he thought.

Both teams assumed the kickoff positions as Jesse trotted out to about the ten-yard line.

"What do you want us to do, Jesse?" asked a nervous but excited Pete.

"Don't get in the way, and enjoy yourself my friend." Jesse smiled and patted Pete on the shoulder.

Jesse looked up at the towering bright lights. He looked out at the panoramic view of the throng of standing fans on his right and on his left. He was amused at all the fuss over such trifles.

CHAPTER 29

THE STANDING HOME FANS MADE the familiar "wooooo" sound as the kicker lifted the ball in a majestic arc that tumbled straight to Jesse, who settled himself directly under the end-over-end ball.

Jesse reached up with one hand, caught the pointy end of the football, tucked it under his arm, and bolted up the field. His body became wavy, like your television does when the signal gets weak. Not really blurry, just wavy. He blazed by the coverage team, which couldn't react to the wavy mist that blew by them. No one touched him or seemed to want to.

Jesse slowed down and became *unwavy* as he trotted across the goal line for a touchdown. The referee raised his arms. A collective quiet fell over the crowd. The Madisonville players jogged off the field, each one looking around at the others, just like the entire crowd and the coaches.

The scoreboard read:

Jess Rulam 7 – Madisonville 0

No one said anything to the person next to them. Each fan from both sides, all the football players from both sides, and all the coaches from both sides, were unsure of what they had just seen. They nervously looked around to see the reaction of others who were looking at them for the same reason. There must have been at least three hundred spectators simultaneously pulling off their glasses and cautiously putting them back into place.

After the extra point, both teams lined up for the kickoff in the other direction. Except for the wavy part, the same thing happened again. This time, Madisonville's return man took the kickoff eighty-eight yards untouched for a touchdown. With eleven minutes to go in the first quarter, the score was tied:

Jess Rulam 7 – Madisonville 7

"How come you're not on the kick coverage, Jesse?" Bart asked curiously.

"I'm afraid I can only play seven plays with my gifts, Bart. There are limits on me. I have to choose wisely." Jesse was smiling as he said this.

Coach Peppers heard what Jesse had said, and since he didn't understand anything that was happening on this weird night anyway, he would let Jesse choose his own time to play.

Madisonville kicked off again to a Jesse-less return team that managed to return the ball to the twenty-four-yard line. Jesse trotted onto the field and took his place in the huddle.

Bennie, the quarterback, got the play from Coach. "I right, thirty-two sweep right, on one."

"How will we block for you, Jesse?" Pete asked.

"Poorly probably, but it doesn't matter much, my friend." Jesse was amused by the question and smiled warmly at Pete. He gave him a quick pat on the shoulder pad as the huddle broke.

The ball was snapped, the quarterback pivoted and made an underhand toss to Jesse, who snatched the ball with his right hand with a fully extended arm and simply ran ... in fast motion. In six seconds, he covered the seventy-six yards. Everyone in the crowd had the same reaction as before: The crowd, the players, and the coaches were not talking to one another. A man borrowed another man's glasses. The man who gave the glasses said to the borrower, "Keep them. They didn't work anyway." The man filming the game was vigorously wiping his camera lenses. When he refocused the lens on the scoreboard it read:

Jers Rulam 14 – Madisonville 7

The Madisonville coach called time-out and berated the referee because he did not call a penalty on the play.

"There's something funny going on here. Nobody is that daggone fast," was heard above the crowd noise. "And what's with that scoreboard? *Jers?*"

After the kickoff return, it was Madisonville's ball. A play-action fake and a bomb later it was:

Jers Rulam 14 – Madisonville 14

"Our whole secondary is new," said Coach to the assistant. "They can pass on us anytime they want to." Coach was looking around and saw Jesse looking at him. "I don't think we can stop them, Jesse." Coach kinda shrugged.

This time they squib kicked away from Jesse to about the thirty-five. "Run the sweep again," Coach told his quarterback. "I don't think it matters what play you call, just as long as you give him the ball." Coach shrugged again, as if to say, "What the hey?"

The quarterback pivoted and pitched the ball to Jesse, but this time the whole Madisonville team was waiting for the sweep as they cheated to the right and cut Jesse off. Jesse planted his foot, spun counterclockwise, and reversed the field. When he ran past the Madisonville head coach, the breeze blew off his cap, which the coach bent down and picked up in disgust.

The scoreboard now showed:

Jeru Rulam 21 – Madisonville 14

It was the first play of the second quarter. Coach looked at one of the assistants. "They're going to pass on us," he said and shook his head. Jesse trotted into the defensive huddle, and one of the players came back to the sidelines. Jesse lined up in the safety position and waited for the pass that was sure to come.

The play-action fake, the split end zoomed past the cornerback and past Jesse, who simply stood still and watched the galloping wide open receiver wave his hands for the quarterback and everyone else to see.

The arcing rainbow pass was within five feet of the lonesome receiver when Jesse leaped through the air, stuck his right hand just inside the receiver's right hand, snatched the ball before he could clasp his hands, and was off down the sideline.

The breeze blew the cap off the Madisonville coach again. He didn't bother to pick it up. He just kept his hands on his hips and stared blankly. Then he looked around, found his cap, and shoved it hard back on his bald head, pulling it snug, angrily.

Jeru Sulam 28 – Madisonville 14

"I want you to look at that crazy scoreboard," said the Madisonville coach. "Everything is out of kilter tonight. They keep changing their name." Then he pulled his cap even further down on his hairless head and gave a nervous glance at the flagpole to check the wind.

Madisonville got the ball and scored in three plays. Then a squib kick ricocheted off one of Jess Rulam's up-men and Madisonville recovered. This time it took four plays to score on Jess Rulam's hapless Jesse-less defense.

Jeru Sulam 28 – Madisonville 28

Again another squib kick, another muffed returned, and another recovery for Madison. This time, however, the Madisonville coach gave orders to run as much time off the clock as possible, and that's what they did. They purposely ground out yards, actually trying not to score too quickly—anything they could do to keep the ball out of the hands of this phantom that loomed on the sidelines of this crazy school with an even crazier scoreboard. With three minutes to go in the half, the scoreboard showed:

Jeru Sulam 28 – Madisonville 35

The Madisonville kickoff man tried to squib the ball right at one of the up-men again. He did his very best, but instead the ball skipped and bounced and tumbled the crazy way only a football can and finally dribbled down to the three-yard line where a panicky Pete fell on the live ball so that it couldn't be recovered again by Madisonville. Unfortunately, he fell on the ball just before Jesse was about to pick it up.

"I'm sorry, Jesse. I didn't know you was about to get it." Pete felt ashamed—he had probably cost his team a touchdown.

"Fear not, my friend. You only delayed the inevitable by one play," answered Jesse as he put his hand on his distraught buddy's shoulder.

The coach from Madisonville called a time-out and called his baffled defense over to the sideline, instructing, "They're going to run the only play they got, that dad-burned sweep to that really fast guy. This time, by gum, we gonna be ready for him. When the ball is snapped, both ends and both outside linebackers and both corners fly to the outside as fast as you can. He's fast, but he ain't that dadgum fast." The coach sounded sure this time.

The quarterback pivoted around and tossed the ball to Jesse, who took one counterstep to the right and jetted up the middle. The safety was able to take one step toward the flying running back. Jesse turned toward the sideline and then took off. His cleats were digging up the sod in great jetting chunks.

As he blew past the Madisonville coach, three chunks of sod shot from underneath Jesse's spinning cleats, peppering the coach.

"Coach Lumen! Coach Lumen!" The coach, who was staring

down the field with his hands on his hips, motionless, was calling for his assistant.

"Yes, sir, Coach," answered Lumen. He watched as the coach took his hands off his hips and raked the caked-up sod out of his eyes and flung it to the ground.

"We got to get us one of them." The assistant shook his head in agreement. The coach got the embedded mud out of his eyes enough to focus on the scoreboard:

Jeru Salam 35 – Madisonville 35

The halftime ended tied. As both teams made their way to their respective locker rooms, the scoreboard operators made their way to the out-of-whack scoreboard with truly puzzled looks on their faces.

* * *

"It should be about halftime by now. I tell you what, y'all boys can run on back to your masters if you want to," said The Jet, looking at his watch. "Y'all go show the honky assholes you can be good niggers, massa." The Jet was trying to sound like a slave.

"I'd rather be a damn slave to a bunch of white assholes than be a hate-filled piece of shit like you." TW was face to face with The Jet. "You know, for every white asshole I've met that called me names and looked down on me, I've had three that tried to help me and were good to me.

"We're through with this bullshit. We ain't playing your hateful games, but there is one game we will play, if the Lord's willing and we get there in time. Let's go, guys! Come on, hustle!" TW started jogging away, and the rest of his once captive teammates followed. The Jet stared at the backs of the boys as they disappeared into the night, and then he pulled his black mask off and stared disgustedly some more.

* * *

Coach Peppers didn't say anything to his players at halftime. He and the rest of the coaches sat in a huddle at the chalkboard. He implied to his assistants that he didn't know what to say or do. What they did do was sit quietly and take rather quick glances at Jesse, as did the rest of the team.

I suppose we were all wondering the same thing, really. Was this real? I had a feeling the team across the field was wondering the same thing, as were about fifteen thousand other people here tonight.

Jesse sat quietly with his head down, not looking at anyone. I couldn't stand it any longer. I had to say something.

"You said something, Jesse. You said you could only play seven plays. Why?" I asked as quietly as possible.

"I don't make these rules. I just follow them," he answered softly.

"What rules, and who makes them?" I asked once more as quietly as I could, just a whisper actually. Jesse looked at me and smiled.

"If you knew, the experience would kill you," he said, smiling pleasantly.

I didn't know what he was talking about, but I believed him. I kept quiet, afraid to think too hard on what he had just said. It hurts your head if you think about Jesse too much. I learned to live with it. We would only have Jesse for two more plays; we all had better learn to live with that too.

We had to kick off to them in the second half. Their plan was simple: Score touchdowns, but as slowly as possible. It was obvious that our defense couldn't stop them, and it was also obvious that they couldn't stop Jesse. Their cagey coach had also figured out that Jesse didn't play defense except for that one play.

It was a mathematical certainty that they'd get the ball first, they'd score first, they'd win, or at least tie. All they had to do was figure out a way to stop the impossible. Thank goodness they didn't know they only had to worry about two more plays. We figured that out at halftime. Somehow, we were just going to have to stop them on our own, somehow, someway.

They returned the ball to about midfield. Our defense took the field and out trotted Jesse. Why was he wasting his two plays on defense? Madisonville lined up, saw the imposing Jesse standing at the middle linebacker position, and their coach called a time-out.

"Whatever you do, don't throw it," the coach said as his quarterback got to within a few feet of him.

In a moment, the quarterback came back to the huddle. They lined up. The ball was snapped, the quarterback rode the ball into the fullback's belly. It was the read-option play, except when the quarterback put the ball in the fullback's belly, he forgot to let go. The ball was stuck in the fullback's belly along with the quarterback's hands. The fullback dragged the quarterback with him while the quarterback was trying desperately to pry himself free from a grip the fullback wouldn't, or couldn't, let go.

Both stopped and had a tug-of-war in the middle of the play. Both were trying to let go of a ball that was glued to their hands. Hollis blasted both of them and the ball popped free. Jesse, like lightning, snatched the loose ball and dashed for a touchdown.

Now it made sense: If Jesse played on defense, and could somehow score on the play, not only would we get a stop, but we would also get a touchdown. The math made sense.

Jeru Salem 42 – Madisonville 35

We kicked off; they returned it for a touchdown. Most of the kickoff coverage team was gone, and lane assignment was vital in kick coverage.

Jeru Salem 42 – Madisonville 42

Still half of the third quarter remained, and there was only one play left for Jesse, who trotted out on the field to a collective gasp from the Madisonville stands. Their coach made a shrugging motion to his other assistant, pulled his cap back down on his head tight and put his hands on his hips.

"What do I call, Jesse?" our young quarterback, Bennie, asked meekly.

"Fake the ball to me and throw it to Matt for a touchdown, and I will still have a play left."

And that's what happened. All eleven of their defensive players were on the line of scrimmage to at least offer some resistance against Jesse, and I was virtually uncovered.

Jeru Salem 49 – Madisonville 42

"Oh, no," said a surprised Jesse, looking worriedly at the scoreboard.

"What is it, Jesse?" I asked after my touchdown. I was actually looking for some congrats, but his dismayed look supplanted my temporary jubilance.

"The scoreboard changed. I may have used all my gifts for the day. I may be on my own from now on." A relieved look came over him. "Just as well. I knew I had to experience this as part of my preparation." He looked at me and slapped me on the back. "Let's play some football."

I didn't have a clue as to what he was talking about.

* * *

"Come on, guys, we only got about three miles to go. We can make it." TW was in a good jogging pace along Highway 77 headed toward the school. The others were right behind him on the same pace.

A big black pickup truck came alongside, then pulled just ahead and stopped. A man the size of a mountain unfolded out of the truck and stood like a giant statue in their path.

If a grizzly bear came to earth as a white man, this is it, TW thought.

The group of boys stopped within a couple of feet of the man and formed a tight group. All they could do was stare at one of the most imposing figures they had ever seen or heard tell of.

"There are nineteen of us and only one of him. We may need to get some more guys," said TW, only half-kidding. The giant walked right up to TW and folded a couple of hairy forearms across a chest that was at least four feet wide. TW swallowed hard and looked up at the man-bear.

"We were kidnapped by some men, and now we need a ride back to the school. How about it, mister?" The words were a little shaky coming out of TW's mouth, but he held his ground. If a black man can turn pale, TW did.

"Yeah, some pipsqueak black dude and his buddy came in the pool hall awhile ago bragging how they stopped this honky school from winning a championship," said the man-bear with a voice that could have actually come from a bear. "I don't guess they saw me standing behind them. They were very sorry. " The man-bear was smiling. His knuckles had blood on them.

"I can believe that," said TW to the man-bear with a smile.

"Get in, boys. Some of you can ride up front with me. I want to see the last of this game myself." The man-bear stopped suddenly, grabbed TW under the armpits with his two massive paws, and lifted him into the back of his pickup like he was a two-year-old child. He looked TW in the eyes and said, "Now, you boys ain't gonna disappoint me when you get there, are you?"

"Not if their lives depended on it, sir," squeaked TW.

"Good, pile in and let's go."

The boys filled every inch of the truck; they all got in somehow. They had to ask for volunteers to ride up front with the man-bear.

* * *

Jesse's miracle cup was empty. He was just a teenage boy like the rest of us. We kicked off, this time squib-style because of our poor kick coverage. That worked better, and we managed to stop them. Jesse lined up at middle linebacker. They ran the ball up the middle to eat up as much clock as possible, as they had no idea that Jesse was merely mortal now.

For the first time I watched Jesse as a regular man. He made his first tackle and looked surprised by it. He looked at us bemusedly, like this was a whole new experience. He learned quickly and became better with each play. But Madisonville was truly a great football team, and they scored with about ten minutes to go.

Jeru Salem 49 – Madisonville 49

We had the ball and ran the sweep to the right. Jesse ran powerfully, and it took four or five of them to stop him, but he was tackled hard for the first time since he was in the fourth grade.

"I have to say that it is a very human experience to feel yourself tested."

Jesse was still becoming acclimated to what the rest of us already knew. "This body truly is a gift. I do understand the interest in this game."

The next play, Jesse broke three tackles on and gained twenty yards. I couldn't tell who was more excited—Jesse for the exceptional run, or the Madisonville players, because they could tackle him now.

They made us punt on the fourth down and returned the ball fifty yards. They would have scored if not for Jesse running the returner down with just plain speed—the speed of a big, fast, strong athlete.

They had the ball with just a few minutes to go in the game and the score tied. Everyone was on their feet.

Fans from "Jeru Salem" cheered uproariously before the first play was ever run. We all turned to see what they were looking at and cheering so loudly over.

We spotted a bunch of black boys unloading out of a black pickup truck and scampering into the locker room. They had returned.

The adulation was short-lived, as a slant pass to the split end made the scoreboard:

Jeru Salem 49 – Madisonville 56

Coach Peppers called a time-out to give our late-arriving teammates time to get dressed. The other coach was arguing with the referee and angrily wanted to know if anybody could just arrive off the street and play in the game. The general answer he got was, "As long as they are a student of this school, well, yes."

Coach Peppers hugged every black player as they came by, and so did the rest of us. TW gave a brief explanation of what happened and informed us they were loose from jogging back from their former school. The crowd on Jeru Salem'sside was hugging each other and high-fiving anybody with a palm. Black people were high-fiving white people and the other way around.

"Jeru Salem"would be receiving the kickoff with fifty-six seconds to go in the game. TW and Jesse were back deep. Not knowing exactly when the old Jesse would appear, they chose to kick the ball to TW—a big mistake since he was one of the leading kick returners in the state. TW crisscrossed the field a couple of times, eluded half a dozen tacklers, and was finally stopped on Madisonville's forty-yard line. The only problem with the dazzling return was that it took twelve precious seconds off the clock.

The offense was huddled up around Coach Peppers. He was so choked up and so close to tears and was so hoarse from all the yelling for his team, the words were hard to get out, so he simply said, "I love you guys. Go win this game. You decide as a team how. I'll leave it up to you." And then he pointed to the scoreboard and said, "There's only one thing missing. Go do it."

The players huddled, looking at one another, waiting to see who would speak first. TW did the honors.

"I know you guys have done a lot." He was looking around at the white players. "But let me and the rest of us help now. I would be honored if you'd let me have the ball."

"Give it to him," Pete told Bennie.

The ball was snapped, TW took a counterstep to the left, then bolted to the line, and the hole broke wide open. He cut to his left, the cornerback slipped, and no one touched him. TW crossed the goal line with thirty-four seconds left.

Jeru salem 55 – Madisonville 56

The players were jumping and hugging each other, just like the fans in the stands.

"Great blocking, guys," a winded TW said, patting his white lineman on the rump. The players were waiting for the extra point kicker to come onto the field, but he never arrived. Instead, another lineman came on and said, "Coach said we're not playing for overtime. He said go for it."

"I have a suggestion," Jesse said.

We all looked and listened. For the first time in my life, I saw Jesse look tired. "They will be looking at TW or me to run the ball in for the two-point conversion, right?" Everyone nodded. "So why not fake a handoff to TW while I flare off to the right? Fake a pass to me, then dump the ball to Pete from his tight end position."

"Sounds good," said TW.

The ball was snapped; a fake handoff to TW got every player on the Madisonville side to lunge forward. The quarterback pivoted and faked the swing pass to Jesse, which caused the rest of the team to shoot even more forward after him. Then, the young quarterback saw Pete standing by himself and lobbed the ball to him. The place erupted in a cacophony of jubilation.

Everyone piled on top of Pete. All the coaches were hugging. So was every player on the sidelines, as were all the fans. They say you could hear the eruption all the way to The Hill, three miles away.

Jerusalem 57 – Madisonville 56

There were still a few seconds to go in the game. There was time for one more desperation pass, which Bobo picked off and the game was over.

* * *

You have heard that from some college football stadiums on certain Saturday nights in the fall of the year, the eruptions from the fans have actually registered on the Richter scale. The town of Jerusalem would forever have its own Richter scale. Miss Betsy

Prescott reported to the police department that she heard some kind of disturbance coming from town. She was on her front porch and reckoned it was some kind of bomb. She lived seven miles from the stadium.

White people were hugging black people. Black people were kissing white babies. Children were tossed in the air—no one was reported hurt, thank God—caps and hats went in the air in all directions. There were no black people or white people that night, just people. For a brief moment in time, they were all God's people. In that moment, a panoramic view of humanity was in full bloom, and the bouquet was truly beautiful.

People would talk about it for years. How in one night, for the first time in their lives, they actually *were* colorblind, and how this kind of blindness was beautiful. The plan was in motion, and the architect was pleased with his work.

We carried Coach Peppers off the field, and he happily let us.

As we were on our way to the fieldhouse with Coach on our shoulders, we noticed him staring at the scoreboard. He was thinking back to a similar moment in 1961 when he and Pat Trammell, Lee Roy Jordan, and others carried another coach off the field after a win over Arkansas to win the National Championship.

He thought, *I need to invite Coach Bryant up here to look at some of these boys anyway.*

He could not take his eyes off the scoreboard and the new name of his school: Jerusalem High School, Alabama.

EPILOGUE

THE TOWN, LED BY COACH Peppers, petitioned the city council to officially change the name of Jess Rulam to Jerusalem. The zip code would stay the same. The County Board of Education accepted the petition, and Jerusalem Elementary and High schools were born.

An official student council was formed by the school made up of five elected black students and five elected white students to settle any racial problems between peers. When I graduated, to my knowledge, no incidents were ever brought forward.

That one huge dose of humanity known as Jessup Christopher Savorié had taught the entire school, town, and community what it was like to be a human being—to care for something other than yourself, to trouble yourself for others.

The lessons didn't come in the form they were expecting, but the message was received nonetheless.

* * *

Coach Peppers was voted Alabama High School Coach of the Year by the Sports Writers Association of High School Athletics. They sent him an impressive plaque, which he prominently displayed on the wall just behind his desk in his newly decorated office.

He wanted everything to look especially impressive for today, because Jerusalem High School was about to be visited by an authentic football legend: Coach Paul "Bear" Bryant. "The Coach" was on a recruiting trip with three University of Alabama assistants.

Coach Peppers sent copies of the entire 1975 football season to the recruiting department of his alma mater, except for the first half of the championship game, of course. Some things are better left unexplained, Coach Peppers figured. That weird first half was safely tucked away in a secret place, and only Coach Peppers knew where.

The Madisonville head coach finally stopped calling Coach Peppers after a couple of months of relentless harassing for a copy of the first-half film. He tried as best he could to view it so he could maintain his own sanity, but Coach Peppers stoutly reiterated the film was ruined. Every time he said it, a string of *dadgummits* was heard over the phone.

* * *

A car pulled into the fieldhouse parking lot one Tuesday afternoon. The license plate frame read, "The University of Alabama." The distinctive figure of Coach Bryant was the last to emerge from the vehicle. No hound's-tooth hat, no sports jacket—just a man in his sixties. He methodically meandered toward the building, carefully taking in the pretty sights.

We were all told he was coming today, of course. There were six players on the team that The Coach wanted to meet, including TW Monroe and Hollis Reed. We were as excited as kids at a merry-go-round as the coaching icon made his way into our fieldhouse.

I shook his hand and stared intently at the larger-than-life coach. He was bigger than I had pictured, with large, powerful hands. There were deep lines carved into a face that had endured the rigors of six National Championships. He looked somewhat tired from all the travel. I remember thinking he looked older than his sixty-two years.

I believe God allows men of such distinction and influence to burn brighter and harder. It makes them easier to see. Coach Bryant was easy to see. When he entered a room, one's eyes were irresistibly set upon him. He commanded your attention just by his sheer presence.

He was more soft-spoken than I had imagined also; not at all loud, and he smiled and laughed more than you would expect. He was not what I anticipated. He was very approachable, and one could see why high school football players across the country wanted to play for him. He just had *it*. *It*—that inexplicable magic ingredient that only a handful are ever blessed with. Coach Bryant seemed to have a bucketful of *it*.

Coach Bryant shook every hand in the fieldhouse, including the managers, who had to have autographs. Half the team did also, the other half were afraid to ask. He met every player, coach, manager, and cheerleader who Coach Peppers had invited in as a showing of gratitude for their hard work.

He met everybody and gladly shook their hand, except one—Jesse's. Coach Bryant seemed to be looking around as if he were looking for someone missing from the group. Where was this mysterious phenom whose tales had made it all the way to Tuscaloosa? This was one of the reasons Coach Bryant was here. He wanted to see for himself if the stories and rumors were true.

Though he had only played in one game, the news of Jesse's feat was legend and folklore. Reliable sources said they witnessed the most incredible athlete the world had ever seen. But no physical evidence existed to bolster their claim because a bizarre accident had destroyed the game film, or that was the story. Even the man that filmed the game was not sure his equipment was functioning properly.

Coach Bryant often heard wild claims about prospects over the years, but he never heard any as wild as the one about the boy who could run fifty miles per hour.

Coach Peppers just shook his head and laughed when asked about the rumors. Coach Bryant still wanted to meet him, though. He was more curious than anything—an itch that needed to be scratched. Something inexplicable told him he needed to meet this one particular boy.

"Coach Bryant, Jesse is in the weight room studying right now. I don't know why he's not been out here to meet you yet. I'll go get him," said Coach Peppers disappointedly, because Jesse seemed uninterested in meeting a living legend.

"No, Coach," answered Coach Bryant intriguingly. "Just leave him be. I'll go in there to him." Coach Bryant was getting to his feet. "I'd kinda like to talk to him alone for a minute. I like a boy who studies—I might learn something. You're never too old or too smart to learn something new." The illustrious Coach Bryant smiled at his former player wryly.

Coach Peppers was a little antsy about them meeting, especially alone. Jesse was different than anybody Coach or The Coach had ever met. Jesse always seemed unimpressed with the famous. They were like anybody else to him. He sure hoped nothing embarrassing happened to one of the most famous people on earth.

* * *

Coach Bryant walked back to the weight room cautiously, not exactly sure where it was. He stood in the doorway of what he recognized as the weight room. He had seen a thousand weight rooms in his day. He saw that the light was off and the room was rather dim. He flipped the light switch on, and the flickering fluorescent finally made contact and lit the room.

"I hope you don't mind me cutting on the light for a minute," said Coach Bryant as he made his way to the leg extension machine, where Jesse was lying on his back reading a history book. "I don't want to trip and fall over something. I don't see as good as I used to, particularly in the dark."

"When you are trying to find your way, it is always better to have a light to follow," answered Jesse, rising to his feet.

"Amen, son. As best I could, I've tried for many years to shine a little light so a few young men could see where to go. Most of them went down the right path, some didn't, but that's life."

The Coach stood eye to eye with Jesse, as they were approximately the same height. The Coach extended his hand and Jesse took it respectfully. It was as if they were trying to see what was lying inside each other's heads.

"My goodness, son, I used to snake logs back in Arkansas with draft horses that wasn't put together as good as you." Coach Bryant took a step back and looked Jesse up and down. "You look like you could pull a couple of logs by yourself."

"Thank you, sir," said Jesse quietly.

"I've heard you're as fast as a speeding bullet, as powerful as a locomotive, and if you can jump over this building in a single bound, *I* want your autograph." Coach Bryant laughed good-naturedly.

"I'm afraid I *can* do all those things, just not for a mere football game." Jesse smiled, and Coach Bryant laughed again.

"You know, after we won a few National Championships, they used to say I could walk on water. I guess you can do that too." Coach Bryant smiled inquisitively.

"Only if the boat has sailed without me," Jesse said dryly.

"Yeah, me too," The Coach said jokingly, then asked, "What did you mean son, about a *mere* football game?"

The two regarded each other eye to eye. No smiles.

"I mean that football has become some people's God."

Coach Bryant was looking seriously at Jesse, listening carefully.

"I know, Coach Bryant, that you believe the very same thing—that people place football too high on a pedestal."

"It's funny you should say that. That's exactly the conclusion I've come to lately. You say you know that. How, son? I mean, what made you say that just now?" Coach Bryant was intrigued by Jesse.

"I know a lot about you, Coach. In fact, I wrote this on the big board just for you."

Jesse walked over to the board and pointed to what he had written in large very neat letters. It looked like a machine had printed it. This is what it read:

> *This is the beginning of a new day.*
> *God has given me this day to use as I will.*
> *I can waste it or use it for good.*
> *What I do today is very important, because I am exchanging a day of my life for it.*
> *When tomorrow comes, this day will be gone forever; leaving something in its place I have traded for it.*

I want it to be gain, not loss; good, not evil; success, not failure, in order that I shall not forget the price I paid for it.

Coach Bryant looked at the printing with veneration. He fumbled to get his wallet out of his back pocket. He found a tiny compartment in the wallet and pulled out a small folded piece of paper. He unfolded it and looked at Jesse with awe and wonder. He said, "This is exactly the devotional I've had in my wallet for years. I used to read it out loud every morning. How did you know that, son?" Coach Bryant was perplexed and shocked at the same time.

"Like I said, I know a lot about you, especially what's in your heart," said Jesse softly and soothingly.

Coach Bryant never said another word to Jesse. He never took his eyes off of Jesse's eyes when he stuck out his hand and shook it firmly. His face wore the same perplexed look of awe and wonder. He turned and left the room, rejoining his group.

The Coach told the assistants it was time to go home. He congratulated Coach Peppers once more, told the players he had recruited that he would see them this summer, and abruptly left the fieldhouse for the car.

It was about a two-and-a-half-hour drive back to Tuscaloosa. They had been driving for about thirty minutes, and Coach Bryant hadn't said a word, much to the dismay of the three assistants.

"What did that boy, Jesse, say to you, Coach?" asked one of the assistants, trying to get their now strangely silent head coach to say something. Coach Bryant said nothing, just stared out the side window.

"What are you going to do, Coach?"

"Listen to you talk me to death, I reckon," Coach said quietly, never moving his gaze.

"What have you got planned for the rest of the trip, Coach?"

"Earplugs if I can find them."

"No, Coach. I mean, are we through?"

"You sure are, if you can't stop talking."

"Do you want us to swing by any other places before we get home?"

"Yeah, swing by Auburn and see if Shug has any assistant coaches that talk less than you do he'd like to trade." Nobody said another word for thirty more minutes until Coach Bryant spoke.

"Here, print this in big letters in the locker room or the weight room, or both." Coach Bryant handed the devotional to one of the assistants. Silence remained almost all the way to Tuscaloosa. Coach Bryant continued to solemnly look out the window, but with contentment on his face.

Another thirty minutes passed, and still Coach Bryant was silent. They were almost back to the campus when one of the assistants couldn't stand it any longer. He said, "Well, what do you think will become of that boy, Coach?

"I think we're going to hear about that boy again." Coach was still looking out the window.

"Do you think you will ever see him again?"

Coach Bryant turned abruptly to the assistant and stared powerfully into his eyes. He said forcefully, "I don't know about you, but I will."

* * *

The late spring wind blew comfortably warm as the bright green-leaved tree limbs succumbed to the breeze. Birds scurried about for juicy morsels for little mouths constantly demanding more. The flowerbeds around the school were never brighter or more alive. In fact, the school was never more alive, and, for that matter, never was the town of Jerusalem, Alabama.

The Class 3A State Championship trophy was proudly displayed in City Hall; not the school trophy case mind you, no, sir—City Hall. It was part of an agreement the city council had worked out with the school—you know, politics and stuff.

Behind the trophy was a photo of a group of black and white football players. Each player, me included, signed over our numbers. For a lot of us, our fifteen minutes of fame came the day of the parade in our honor and the official signing of the blown-up photo.

*　*　*

"Man, there is nothing like the smell of honeysuckles, is there?" Pete was taking in the succulent fragrance of God's perfume.

"No, there's not," I answered happily. It was true, and this happened to be our last day of school—forever, probably.

Me, Pete, Bart, Jude, John, and the rest of the gang of twelve met just outside the band room on a little grassy hill. The beautiful little school would be missed, and we knew it.

I don't think any of us knew what we were going to do with the rest of our lives, and I'm quite sure none of us cared at the moment. We were just watching the birds and taking in the scenery.

We were going to have a little farewell party at my house. We waited for everyone to get to the hill before we took off, but after they arrived, we didn't want to leave. We saw Jesse come walking by with his head bowed as usual, deep in thought.

Jesse asked us to meet here before we went home, but this time we weren't returning to the school for the fall. We wondered why he wanted to see us as a group. He'd seen us every day and could talk to us anytime he wanted. It was a little odd, but when Jesse asked you to do something, you did it, because you wanted to.

"I'm leaving you now." Jesse startled us as he appeared suddenly, like a cat.

"Where are you going, Jesse?" Pete asked as we all got to our feet.

Jesse looked at us with the same piercing eyes that seemed to be able to read our thoughts.

"I will wander about for a while. I know who I am," he said, looking up toward the sky with a soulful, majestic look. "Now, I simply must find my next destination."

"You are Jesus Christ returned, aren't you?" asked Pete, wearing a nervous smile because he had finally asked what we were all afraid to.

Jesse's lips spread with the coy smile that had grown familiar to us over the years as his peering eyes traveled over ours.

"Your minds will grow lazy without something to think about ... I love you all. I am through here, for now."

Pete blurted out as Jesse turned to leave, "But why were you here?"

Jesse returned the coy smile warmly.

"Think, Pete, think."

His eyes gazed about the school and the mountains in the background, and then he walked off, leaving us, just like he found us—wondering.

ACKNOWLEDGMENTS

First, I would like to extend my heartfelt gratitude to my daughter Shannon for her encouragement and advice. I would have never written this book without her. I also extend my deep gratitude to my mentor and remarkable friend, Brenda Bartley. It finally soaked in.

A special thanks to my publisher, John Köehler, for simply believing in me. To my editor, Joe Coccaro, for a job well done and enduring me. And to my line editor, Cheryl Ross, for her professionalism and kindness.

To my parents, Roscoe and Trilbie, who gave me life. To my brother, Larry, and my sister, Deborah, for helping me grow up. To my other daughters Jenny and Tifany and my son, Levi, I hope to make you proud of me. And to my best friend, David Malone, for putting up with me for forty-eight years.

To the English 102 Sand Rock Class of 2013, thank each and every one of you for taking the time to read and critique my book. Your words encouraged me to have my book published. Thank you Taylor Rogers, Meghan Parker, Mary Lindsey, Cameron Mackey, Hannah Oliver, Kelsey Hayes, Megan McCullough, Melanie Vandergrift, and Paula Oliver, and to their teacher, Shannon Hood.